THE WONDERS ECHO: THE ENDURANCE TRIAL

RAM RENGEL

To Ruthie, Rafael, and Bregan:

For supporting me through all my craziness and listening to my endless ideas without calling for an intervention. You are the true masters of endurance.

Series Title: The Wonders Echo

Book Title: The Endurance Trial

Publisher's Note: This is a work of fiction. Names, characters, places, and incidents are a product of the author's imagination or are used fictitiously. Any resemblance to actual persons, living or dead, business establishments, events, or locales is entirely coincidental.

ISBN: 979-8-9948856-0-4

Connect with the Author: https://linktr.ee/ramrengelauthor

Chapter 1
The Anchor Wakes

***"When the heart of the world stirs, the periphery must listen." —* Guardian Teaching, Giza Protocol.**

— Δ —

Cairo hit Quentin with a wall of heat and brightness the moment the plane door sighed open. The air carried sun-baked tarmac, jet fuel, and—beneath it all—a spice he couldn't name. He blinked, his eyes grainy with jet lag, and shuffled along with the others into the vast glass interior of the terminal, where light pooled on polished floors and voices rose in a hundred languages.

Instinct made him inventory himself the way he'd been trained to do—dry mouth, pulse, the dull ache behind his eyes. Pre-med habits were hard to kill, even on a school trip meant for wonder instead of work.

"Right," said Sophia, her voice crisp, as precise as the stapled itinerary she clutched. She was already holding a clipboard that seemed to have materialized from nowhere. "Bags first, then group check-in with Dr. Farouk. We move together."

"Together," Liam echoed, swinging his rucksack onto one shoulder and wobbling theatrically. "Like penguins. Sweaty penguins."

A few of the students laughed. Quentin managed a smile that felt glued on. He stole a glance at the girl he'd noticed on the plane—the one with the dark plait and the not-quite-smile. Aisha. She stood a little apart from the knot of chatterers, phone in hand, but her eyes weren't on the screen. They were lifted toward the terminal's high windows, watching the light pour through them with a geometry that invited reverence. Her lips moved faintly, almost like she was counting—measuring the light and the curve of the glass as if she were inspecting the integrity of the architecture itself.

"Quentin! Bags," Sophia said, corralling him with a tap to his elbow.

"Right. Sorry." He lurched for the carousel.

Suitcases clunked and squealed their way round. Raj had already staked out a prime spot, one elbow planted like a flag. "Top tip, you've got to stand at the mouth," he said to no one and everyone. "Nab it before it escapes. Standard airport physics."

"Is that how physics works?" Liam asked, eyes bright with mischief.

"Better than your jokes work," Raj said, flashing a grin.

Quentin searched for a battered navy case with a frayed red strap and found instead the uneasy thrum of his heart—too fast, not just nerves, more like his body had mistaken the terminal for a threat. The word *tachycardic* surfaced out of habit, then he swallowed it back. Too fast was enough.

He felt painfully visible, knowing any failure would confirm the one thing he always feared. *Don't fumble this,* he thought. *Don't be the kid who trips on the first step. Don't be that kid.* He reached, missed, reached again. His hand closed on the handle an inch before Raj's, and he hauled the bag off just a fraction too triumphantly; it thudded into his shin. He tried to hide the wince.

"Nice one," Liam said, slapping his shoulder. "I mean, you've injured yourself, but with dignity."

"Thanks," Quentin muttered, wishing he had something clever to say—a line sharp enough to make them laugh with him, not at him. His tongue sat like a stone. A thousand possible comebacks flickered through his mind, all too late, none worth saying.

Nia, small and quiet, perched on a metal bench with a sketchbook balanced on her knees, her pencil making quick, sure sounds. She didn't look up when the carousel shuddered to a stop; she was drawing the curve of the glass ceiling, the swoop of swallows trapped in the architecture. She had a way of seeing that made Quentin feel both exposed and oddly understood. When she did glance up, her eyes were soft, curious—then down she went again, lines flowing. Her pencil darkened a seam of glass above, shading it as if she saw a fracture invisible to everyone else.

"Exchange group, over here!" called a woman in a linen blouse the color of dusted gold. Dr. Layla Farouk's presence settled the air. She had the sort of calm that convinced you everything—even six teenagers and an airport the size of a small city—was entirely manageable. Beside her stood a man in a navy blazer whose smile tried too hard: Professor Ellis, their American program director. He was already sweating through the armpits.

"Welcome to Egypt," Dr. Farouk said, her accent a river over stones. "I hope your flight was kind."

"Kind as a brick," Liam murmured.

"We are honored to host you," Dr. Farouk continued. "You were selected because you are scholars, artists, leaders. You will learn the old stories—but also learn how to question them."

Quentin glanced at Aisha, expecting her usual look of bored indifference. Instead, she was staring at the ceiling—not at the architecture, but at the cluster of security cameras swiveled toward the entrance. Her eyes tracked the perimeter of the glass walls, lingering on the structural seams of the terminal with a clinical, predatory focus. When she caught Quentin watching, her expression didn't soften; she simply adjusted her bag and looked through him, as if he were just another obstacle in her line of sight.

Raj puffed slightly, as if 'leader' had been addressed to him personally. Sophia's clipboard twitched in approval. Aisha hovered on the edge, listening the way some people pray—alert, deliberate, almost wary.

Professor Ellis clapped his hands once. "Right-o! Luggage accounted for? Passports? No losing passports. That's rule one. Rule two is very much like rule one."

Quentin laughed—too loudly, too late. Aisha's eyes slid to him, unreadable. He burned from throat to ears. *Brilliant*, he thought bitterly. *Exactly the sort of noise a person makes when they're trying not to be noticed.*

They formed a loose circle as Dr. Farouk distributed ID lanyards and SIM cards with the practiced efficiency of someone who had shepherded many such flocks. "You'll find Cairo a city of contradictions," she said. "Ancient and new, chaotic and precise. If you stay attentive, it will speak to you."

"What does a city say?" Quentin asked before he could stop himself.

Heads turned. His stomach dropped.

Dr. Farouk smiled, unfazed. "Whatever you are ready to hear."

Sophia made a small approving note on her clipboard. Raj smirked, as if to say, *cute*. Liam waggled his eyebrows like this was a great philosophical revelation. Quentin swallowed, wishing he could pack his words back into his mouth and zip them up.

They threaded out of the terminal, the heat rose in a palpable sheet. Outside, taxis honked in musical arguments. Vendors called over pyramids of oranges and dust-colored bread. Somewhere, a radio crackled a melody that sounded older than the airport itself. The sky was an enormous white coin.

Aisha walked just ahead of him, her posture loose, gaze focused. He caught a whiff of something citrus and sharp as she passed—the scent of her hand sanitizer or perhaps her shampoo—and immediately felt foolish for noticing. She paused once to help an elderly traveler hoist a bag into a trolley, deft and unshowy. The old woman blessed her in Arabic. Aisha's lips softened. Then she was the girl with the distant eyes again. For a second, Quentin thought she glanced back over her shoulder—not at him, but at the crowds behind, scanning, as if expecting someone to follow.

"Bus is this way," Professor Ellis chirped, gesturing grandly in the wrong direction and nearly herding them into a taxi rank. Dr. Farouk gently realigned him, and the group flowed toward a white coach that smelled faintly of sun-warmed vinyl.

As they loaded cases, Raj offered to lift Aisha's suitcase. "I've got it," he said, in the tone that suggested he expected thanks.

"I've got it," she replied, and did, with a spare flick of the wrist. Something like amusement ticked in her eyes.

Quentin slid his bag into the undercarriage and wiped his palms on his jeans. He could feel the day gathering—new city, new rules, a hundred chances to say the wrong thing. He tried to stand the way people do when they belong somewhere: feet planted, shoulders easy. *It felt like wearing someone else's jacket.* He'd spent years learning to sound calm in a lab coat he didn't own yet. In crowds, the act frayed.

Nia had moved to the curb, sketchbook up, pencil whispering. She was drawing the bus, but not the way a person usually would; she was catching the glare off the windscreen, the pattern of dust on the tires, a shadow thrown by a sparrow at the precise moment it cut the light. Her lines looked ordinary to anyone else, but Quentin felt the strange certainty she was recording something more—like a record-keeper for things no one else would admit existed.

"What d'you think, Quentin?" Liam asked, appearing at his elbow. "Grand adventure? Or dramatic heatstroke then straight home?"

"Er—both?" Quentin said. He meant it as a joke. It came out like a question mark.

Raj's grin sharpened. "You know you have to keep up, right? This isn't a museum tour."

Quentin's mouth opened. Nothing elegant emerged. "I can keep up."

Aisha glanced over her shoulder then, just for a beat. Her expression didn't change, but he had the wild sense of being measured—not mocked, not exactly, but weighed. As if she were testing whether the word 'keep' would stick to him or slide away. And in her eyes—just for a flicker—was something sharper than curiosity. A kind of recognition.

Dr. Farouk raised a hand, and the group magnetized to her again. "The bus will take us directly to Giza," she said. "You'll see the Plateau from the road. It has its moods, so don't be disappointed if the first glimpse is shy. It can be like that with wonders."

Wonders. The word tickled the back of Quentin's throat. He thought of postcards and school projects and tiny replicas of pyramids on mantelpieces. He thought of how such things shrink a place so it fits on a shelf. He rubbed his fingers together and told himself he wasn't nervous; his skin tingled anyway, as if the city were a static charge building under a jumper.

They filed on. Quentin took the seat by the aisle, then, at the last second, slid to the window. He wanted to see. He wanted—he didn't know what he wanted, exactly, only that it might be written somewhere large in the sky.

As the door hissed shut and the engine coughed to life, a luggage poster on the terminal wall caught his eye, the printed photograph of the Great Pyramid slightly sun-faded. For an instant—no more than a blink—he thought he saw a darker shape at its base, a robed figure etched into the grain of the picture. His chest tightened with a hum like a plucked wire. When he blinked, it was gone.

He looked again. It was just a poster.

But the feeling remained, a whisper under the skin, and even as the bus jolted forward into the tide of Cairo, he couldn't shake the notion that something in this city had already noticed him first.

— Δ —

The bus smelled faintly of warm vinyl and dust, with a sharp undercurrent of diesel that made Quentin's head swim. He filed it under *things that trigger nausea* the way he filed everything—like he could outthink his own body if he labeled it fast enough. He pressed his forehead to the glass, the cool surface grounding him, and registered Cairo unravel in layers: tangled traffic, horns that bleated in endless argument, a motorbike weaving through impossibly narrow gaps, then shopfronts painted in colors too bright to fade, spilling fruit and fabric onto the pavement.

Liam had already claimed the aisle seat beside him, stretching long legs and grinning at the chaos outside. "If I don't come home with a camel, my sister's going to say this trip was a waste."

"Camels are not pets," Sophia said firmly from the row ahead, clipboard already balanced against her knees like a shield. "And please don't even think about it. There are rules—"

"Ah, but rules," Liam said, leaning over the seat, "are more like strongly worded suggestions, don't you think?"

Sophia turned in her seat just enough to glare. Quentin stifled a laugh, though the sound rose too high, too sharp, betraying him.

"Camels are perfectly manageable if you know what you're doing," Raj declared from the back, voice pitched to carry. "Fun fact: they can drink forty gallons in one go. I read it in National Geographic."

"They can also spit," Liam countered. "I read that in Ow, My Eye Weekly."

Nia, tucked against the window two rows behind, didn't join the debate. Her sketchbook was already open, pencil scratching, head bent in concentration. The city outside flickered through her drawings like frames in a film—one moment a minaret rising, the next a child balancing bread on his head, then the curve of a market stall. She hardly looked up, yet her hand captured everything. Now and then her pencil darkened a shadow too long, or traced a line where no building stood—as if she were sketching not just what was there, but what lingered underneath.

Quentin watched her for a moment too long, wishing he had some small skill like that to justify his place here. The exchange program had chosen students for their promise: Sophia's leadership, Raj's brash confidence, Nia's artistry, Liam's irreverent charm—but what box had he ticked? *What talent did they see in him, the boy who stumbles and speaks too late?* Back home, even his professors had called him "quiet," as if that were a role instead of a flaw. Here, he felt more like a tagalong than a chosen scholar.

The bus swerved, jolting him against the window. Words slipped out before he could catch them: "Camels have two sets of eyelashes."

Silence followed.

Raj raised a brow. "And this is relevant because…?"

"They keep sand out," Quentin muttered, cheeks heating. He'd meant it as a clever addition, but the words had dropped flat as sandbags.

"Handy," Liam said cheerfully, rescuing him with a lopsided grin. "If I had two sets of eyelashes, maybe I'd finally look mysterious." He fluttered his lashes, which were in fact rather short.

Laughter rippled through the seats. Quentin smiled weakly, though the knot in his stomach tightened. When he risked a glance forward, he caught Aisha's reflection in the glass: her gaze flicking briefly toward him, then away. Not mockery. Not amusement. Just… acknowledgment.

He turned back to the window, where the city had thinned into the desert's edge. Cairo's sprawl fell away into low buildings and half-finished roads, and then the landscape stretched golden and endless.

The air shimmered above dunes, and far off, the sky itself seemed to lean down to meet the earth. The chatter of his classmates dulled in Quentin's ears. That low vibration in his chest stirred again—not random, not engine noise, but something syncing to the horizon itself. The vibration almost echoed against his ribs, steady and insistent, like a message he wasn't yet able to translate—a language older than history, etched with the single word: *Endurance.*

Aisha sat near the front, head resting against the glass, her eyes locked on that horizon. She hadn't spoken since boarding, hadn't reacted to Liam's antics or Raj's boasting. Her silence felt chosen, as if it carried more weight than speech. The sunlight caught in her dark hair, turning the strands almost bronze. She blinked slowly, like someone reading a language written in the air. For the briefest moment, her fingers tightened on the strap of her bag—as if she felt the same vibration too, and didn't want anyone to notice.

Quentin looked away quickly, embarrassed by the intensity of his own noticing. He pressed his palm flat against the window instead, and the glass buzzed faintly beneath his skin. He told himself it was the rumble of the engine, but the hum in his chest insisted otherwise.

At the front of the bus, Professor Ellis rose on tiptoe, microphone in hand. "Now, students, if you look to your right—well, no, my right, your left—we'll be, ah, approaching something very large. Very old. The main attraction, you might say."

The group leaned toward the windows, chatter sparking. Quentin followed their gaze. In the haze of distance, a sharp point of stone pierced the horizon. Just a hint, like a tooth emerging from sand. The Great Pyramid.

His heart kicked against his ribs. It didn't feel romantic. It felt mechanical—like a reflex arc had been hijacked by a thing made of stone.

Dr. Farouk spoke softly over Ellis's stammering commentary: "Remember, it is not simply a monument. It is a voice of the past. Listen carefully, and you may hear what it still whispers."

Quentin swallowed hard, because something—though he couldn't have said what—was already whispering to him. The sound wasn't in his ears, but under his skin, layered into the hum: a rhythm older than language, one that seemed to pulse with the single word he didn't yet understand—*Echo.*

— Δ —

The bus lurched to a stop, brakes heaving like a drawn-out sigh. The students spilled out into air that was hotter, drier, and somehow older than the city's. Quentin stumbled after them, rucksack thumping awkwardly against his side.

And there it was.

The Great Pyramid didn't simply stand; it seemed to lean out of the horizon and tower, carved against the sky in impossible geometry. No photograph had ever prepared him for its scale. The blocks weren't neat bricks but giants, weathered and pitted, each one a weight of centuries. Heat trembled in sheets off the stone so that the edges seemed to ripple. It wasn't just large—it was present, the way a mountain is present, or the ocean.

Quentin's breath caught. His skin prickled as if the air itself bent around him. The sympathetic echo in his chest spiked, sharp and resonant, as if answering something vast. For the first time he had the unwelcome thought that the Pyramid wasn't just tracking—it was listening.

"Selfie time!" Liam announced, already angling his phone, pulling Sophia into frame before she could protest.

"Stop it, Liam," she hissed, flattening her hair and trying to look respectable despite the sweat dampening her blouse.

Raj strode forward, gesturing expansively. "Did you know each block weighs up to two tons? Two tons! Imagine the manpower. If I were in charge of the workforce—"

"No one would've finished it," Liam cut in.

The group chuckled. Quentin smiled faintly but didn't look away from the Pyramid. The stone imposed a rhythm he couldn't escape, an inhale too slow to belong to anything human.

Nia had settled cross-legged on the sand, already sketchbook open. Her pencil moved in quick strokes, capturing the slant of shadow and the jagged line of erosion. She didn't draw people—not yet—only the Pyramid, her gaze fixed and reverent. Still, Quentin noticed her hand hovering longer than it should over the page, as if sketching an outline she couldn't quite admit—a faint glow around the stone, a suggestion of movement. He shivered, because he'd felt the same thing.

Quentin thought of asking to see, to say something about her art, but the words crowded and tangled in his throat.

"Remarkable, isn't it?" Dr. Farouk stood a few steps away, her linen blouse stirring faintly in the dry wind. She didn't raise her voice, but everyone heard. "Four and a half thousand years. Stones laid by hands that believed they were building eternity."

Professor Ellis mopped his forehead with a crumpled handkerchief. "And very fine stones they are. Right, students? Very fine. Now, please stay hydrated. Sunstroke is not an authentic Egyptian experience."

Quentin managed a laugh, but the sound felt distant to him. His eyes kept tracing the Pyramid's lines, how the structure seemed at once impossibly solid and strangely fragile against the desert sky. *He imagined a thousand mornings breaking across these faces; he imagined darkness locked inside; he imagined the stone remembering.*

Beside him, Aisha stood with arms folded, gaze locked on the summit. Unlike the others, she didn't chatter or pose or even draw. She simply observed. Her lips parted slightly, as if catching a sound carried on the wind. For a heartbeat Quentin thought her shoulders stiffened, like she too felt the resonance. Then her expression smoothed, unreadable again.

He swallowed, rubbed his palms on his jeans. *Say something*, he told himself. *Anything*. But when he opened his mouth, the carrier signal in his chest grew stronger, stealing the breath he'd meant to shape into words.

Sophia snapped her clipboard shut. "All right, everyone. Stay with the group. The interior tour begins in five minutes."

"Interior?" Liam whispered dramatically. "Bet it's haunted."

Raj rolled his eyes. "It's a tomb, not a haunted house."

"Same difference," Liam muttered.

Quentin followed the group as they tramped across sand that gave way beneath his trainers. With each step closer, the Pyramid seemed less a monument and more a living thing. He pressed his tongue against the roof of his mouth to steady himself, but the vibration only deepened, like a second heartbeat. His own heartbeat tried to match it and lost the rhythm.

At the base, tourists milled and vendors called, selling postcards, scarabs, cold drinks. The noise clattered against Quentin's ears, but underneath it, the stones themselves seemed to murmur. The syllables were nothing he recognized—more pressure than sound—yet his ribs knew where to place them. He touched his chest. No one else noticed. Not even Liam, who was busy haggling for a bottle of water in the worst Arabic Quentin had ever heard.

Aisha's eyes flicked sideways, and for the briefest moment, Quentin wondered—*had she felt it too?* Her gaze lingered on his chest instead of his face, just for a second, before darting back to the stone. It was the kind of look that said: *He knew.* The thought sent a nervous thrill racing up his spine.

Then Sophia barked an order, the guide beckoned them toward the narrow entrance, and the moment snapped.

Quentin dragged his feet, glancing one last time at the Pyramid's vast face. The sun caught a single block just so, and for an instant it seemed to glow.

He blinked. The glow vanished.

But the hum in his chest remained, measured and patient, steady as breath, waiting.

— Δ —

The air changed the moment they stepped inside. Gone was the burning glare of the Plateau; the passage swallowed them in cool darkness, the scent of dust and stone heavy as ground bone. The ceiling pressed low, and the walls leaned in, blocks so massive Quentin wondered how humans had ever lifted them. His trainers scuffed on smooth limestone worn by centuries of footsteps.

"Keep up, please," Sophia said crisply from the front, her clipboard now clutched like a shield.

The guide, a thin man with a badge that read Hassan, led them with a flashlight beam that bobbed against the walls. "You will see the Grand Gallery and the King's Chamber. Please remain with the group. The passages are narrow." His voice echoed oddly, as if the stone itself carried it.

Liam whispered behind Quentin, "Perfect for mummies, isn't it?" He shivered, though the tunnels were stifling, then let out a theatrical moan.

"Grow up," Sophia hissed.

Quentin smiled weakly, though his palms were slick. The deeper they went, the louder the resonance became—no longer a background vibration but a rhythm, like footsteps walking just ahead of his own.

Raj marched a pace ahead, recounting loudly: "Did you know there are over two million blocks in this pyramid? Each one carefully cut and aligned. The precision's within a fraction of an inch."

"You've read the guidebook cover to cover, haven't you?" Liam said.

"I absorbed it," Raj corrected.

Nia had her sketchbook open even here, a tiny beam of a pocket torch clipped to her page. Her pencil whisked lines of shadow, the slant of passageways. She paused once, her pencil hovering mid-air, as though her hand sensed shapes before her eyes did—curves and sigils that Quentin hadn't yet noticed.

Quentin lingered at the back, the heat from so many bodies pressing close. He dragged his fingers along the stone wall, its surface cool, faintly gritty. The instant his skin touched the stone, the sympathetic feedback surged into his bones, a shock of resonance that wasn't just felt but seen—flashes of images slamming into his mind.

He froze.

In the darkness behind his eyelids, images surged. A blur of shapes—men, shadows, chanting. Priests chanting low, hands lifted over a shard of golden crystal that did not shine—yet still imposed itself on his vision as pressure, a sterile density that flattened depth and stole contrast. The word Endurance registered not as sound but as instruction, a compression behind his sternum, before collapsing into silence. But the silence left behind a sickening hollow, as if the vision had not filled him with knowledge but stolen his own strength in trade.

Sound dampened, as if the world had slipped half a beat out of sync. A bone-deep chill replaced the warmth of the tunnel—his blood pressure dropping fast, the pre-faint slide that came with heat, stress, or something stranger.

Vasovagal, his brain offered automatically. Then, plainer: he was about to pass out.

"Quentin?" Liam's voice was distant, warped, as though underwater.

The vision swelled. The stone beneath his hand densified—cold, absolute—until sensation misfired and the chamber tilted. He gasped and the world snapped back.

He collapsed against the wall, the stone hard and merciless against his shoulder.

"Honestly," Sophia said sharply, "you're holding up the entire group."

Liam crouched beside him, face caught between worry and amusement. "You all right, mate? Egypt's not exactly faint-proof."

"Maybe he just can't handle history," Raj added with a smirk. "Two million blocks too many for his brain."

Quentin's face burned. "I—I'm fine." His voice cracked, thin and papery.

"Then stand," Sophia ordered.

Nia's pencil scratched, the sound strange in the silence. Quentin glanced at her—she was sketching him as he slumped, head bowed, palm still pressed to the stone. Her lines weren't just of him, though—behind his outline, faint curves hinted at waves or ripples spreading outward, as if she could see the vibration itself radiating through the stone. Her eyes flicked up, meeting his, then back to the page, as if the vision itself deserved to be recorded.

Only Aisha didn't mock. She hadn't moved, hadn't spoken, but her gaze fixed on him with startling intensity. Her breathing pattern shifted—shorter, more deliberate—as if sampling the space for variables, for something no one else noticed. And in her eyes, for a heartbeat, he caught not disdain but recognition—sharp and wary.

Dr. Farouk's voice cut through, calm as ever. "Give him space." She crouched beside Quentin, her linen sleeves brushing against the dust. "Jet lag is merciless. Breathe slowly. In through the nose."

Quentin obeyed, chest still thrumming. He forced himself upright, leaning against the wall for support. His vision steadied, though the thrum lingered, low and insistent. His hands were cold and clammy—his body misfiring its own alarms.

Professor Ellis fluttered forward, face damp. "Yes, yes, just fatigue. Perfectly normal. Happens to me every time I tour one of these ancient marvels. Once I fainted at Stonehenge—well, nearly."

The group laughed uneasily. The tension cracked.

"Come," Hassan urged. "The King's Chamber waits."

The students shuffled forward again, their voices rising in chatter once more. Only Aisha lingered a beat, her gaze still locked on Quentin. For a heartbeat, the world narrowed to her eyes—dark, steady, unflinching. It wasn't curiosity in her stare. It was assessment, like she was cataloguing a truth she already suspected.

Then she turned, walking on, braid swinging.

Quentin touched his right palm where it still tingled. The mark wasn't visible, not yet—but beneath his skin the resonance coiled like a brand waiting to surface. He had no explanation, no words, only the certainty that something in these stones had reached for him—and that Aisha had seen it.

The hum did not fade. It deepened, threading through his bones, a sensation he would one day learn to describe not as magic, but as a symptom—an ancient mechanism teaching the human body new ways to fail.

Chapter 2
The Measure of Worth

"The value of a component is judged not by its shine, but by its placement in the larger machine." — **Fragment of the Architect's Scroll, I.**

— Δ —

By the time they returned to the hostel, Cairo's dusk had folded into night, and the city outside buzzed like a restless hive. Neon signs flickered over cafés, the scent of grilled meat drifted through open shutters, and the honking of horns never truly stopped. Inside, though, the common room was dim and oddly homely: battered leather sofas sagged into the carpet, a ceiling fan creaked above, and the glow from an old television flickered against the wall in colors more shadow than light.

The students scattered to claim corners. Quentin lingered near the doorway, still shaken by the Pyramid, the hum in his chest stubborn as a second heartbeat rather than fading like jet lag. He wondered if anyone else had felt it, or if he alone carried the echo.

The others seemed perfectly at ease. Liam sprawled sideways across the largest sofa, shoes kicked off, one arm thrown dramatically over his eyes. "I swear," he groaned, "if I eat one more falafel ball, I'll turn into one. I'll roll all the way back to Heathrow."

Sophia perched primly at the edge of a wooden chair with her clipboard balanced on her knees, as if the battered hostel furniture were beneath her dignity. "We're not here to gorge ourselves. Tomorrow we're scheduled for the Museum of Egyptian Antiquities at nine sharp. I expect everyone downstairs by eight-fifteen." Her tone was clipped, but when she glanced up her expression softened briefly—almost concern—as though she wanted order not for herself, but to keep them safe.

She set the stack of itineraries aside and stood, her movements as efficient as her scheduling. Without a word, she began a series of sharp, rhythmic lunges in the narrow space between the sofa and the television. Her arm was extended, fingers curled as if gripping an invisible foil, her lead foot striking the threadbare carpet with a muffled *thud*.

"Still at it, Soph?" Liam asked, not even bothering to look up from the sofa. "The Junior Nationals were two years ago. Pretty sure the Egyptian mummies aren't going to challenge you to a duel."

"Form is a habit, Liam," Sophia replied, her voice steady even as she transitioned into a precise parry-and-riposte motion. "And habits are what keep you alive when things become… unmanageable." She moved with a controlled, calibrated grace that made the cramped hostel room feel like a fencing salle. To her, the world was a series of angles to be mastered and distances to be measured. She didn't just walk through a room; she controlled the space within it.

Raj, lounging nearby with one ankle crossed over his knee, puffed up like a cat. "Honestly, today was nothing new for me. I'd already studied the pyramid's design in detail. Our guide hardly covered half of what I know."

"You knew two million blocks," Liam muttered, peeking from under his arm. "Congratulations, you're Wikipedia with legs."

Raj ignored him. "For instance, did you know the pyramid was once covered in polished limestone casing stones? They reflected the sun, dazzling anyone who approached. It was called the 'Horizon of Khufu.'"

Sophia looked impressed in spite of herself. Quentin's mouth opened, a dozen words straining to get out—he wanted to mention the vision, the light that had seemed to burn inside the stone, the whisper of "Endurance" still vibrating in his ribs—but he shut it quickly. *Better to stay quiet than stumble again.*

— Δ —

Liam sat up, a mischievous grin cutting across his face. He wasn't ready to let the silence last. "Right," he said, propping himself on one elbow. "I've solved it. The pyramids? Not built by people at all. Aliens. Little green ones with chisels and very patient attitudes."

Raj groaned. "For heaven's sake."

"I'm serious!" Liam insisted. "Think about it. Perfect alignment to the stars, blocks too heavy to lift—humans couldn't possibly manage. Unless, of course, ancient Egyptians had cranes and forklifts we've conveniently lost."

"Or," Sophia said crisply, "they had mathematics, engineering, and centuries of accumulated skill. Which they did. This isn't mystery, Liam. It's history." She tapped her bound notes with a pointed finger, the sound sharp in the quiet common room.

Raj leaned forward, warming to the argument. For all his arrogance, Quentin caught a flicker of genuine excitement in Raj's eyes, like he really did love the subject more than the performance. "She's right. The pyramids' sides align almost perfectly with the cardinal directions. That level of precision wasn't luck. It was the brilliance of their architects. Something you'd understand if you read beyond conspiracy blogs."

Liam smirked. "But you can't deny it's fun to imagine a UFO hovering and dropping blocks like Lego."

Sophia groaned audibly.

Aisha sat on the far sofa, legs folded, phone in hand. But Quentin noticed the screen hadn't changed in minutes, her thumb hovering but never scrolling. She wasn't reading messages; she was listening. Professor Ellis had introduced her as a late addition to the exchange—some last-minute scholarship arrangement that seemed to arrive wrapped in bureaucratic silence. *Maybe that explained her distance,* he thought, *the way she seemed half here and half elsewhere—or perhaps it explained the subtle, wary way her eyes scanned the group, as if taking inventory.*

Aisha rolled her eyes. Raj's posture stiffened immediately, his eyes flashing with irritation—a look far too personal for casual student rivalry. "You're all missing the point. It doesn't matter how they were built. What matters is why. Monuments aren't just piles of stone. They're power. Symbols. Warnings, even." She spoke without raising her head, but her voice carried the finality of a blade slicing through the air.

The group fell into a hush, the weight of her words settling.

Quentin felt the silence like a rope tightening around his throat, but a stronger force was the hum in his chest, which suddenly intensified. It was no longer a low pulse but a crushing, non-cardiac pressure—as if his pleural space were being occupied by something denser than air. He instinctively pressed his hands to his ribs, trying to keep the words in. *He had to stay quiet. Do not speak.*

His diaphragm spasmed, breath stolen from him in a sharp, involuntary exhale.

"They don't just align with the cardinal directions," his mouth moved. The voice wasn't his. It was deeper, steady, echoing the resonant frequency of the stone, and it was far too loud in the quiet room. "They're aligned almost perfectly with Orion's Belt. Within a fraction of a degree.

And the shafts in the King's Chamber—they're not random. They line up with specific stars at the time of construction. Like... like the whole structure was breathing with the sky. And this isn't the only place like this. I read... I think there are others. An architecture of nodes, aligned to form a kind of global anchor."

The knowledge felt foreign, ancient, yet utterly true. As the words left his mouth, the single syllable he'd heard inside the Pyramid—*Endurance*—slammed against his consciousness, an intruder's mark. He stumbled back on the sofa, clutching his chest, horrified that his own body had betrayed him.

The words hung.

Sophia blinked, thrown off-balance. "That wasn't in our guide's lecture."

Raj narrowed his eyes. "Where'd you read that? Because if you're making things up to sound clever—"

Quentin shook his head, his face hot with sheer panic. The hum receded slightly, leaving him breathless. "I didn't. I don't know where I got it. I must've read it somewhere. Ages ago." The stammer was back, a welcome sign of his own personality returning.

Liam tilted his head. "Mate, you don't exactly strike me as a secret Egyptology buff."

Heat flamed Quentin's neck. He wished desperately he could reel the words back in, swallow them whole. Everyone was staring, even Nia—her pencil stilled mid-line, eyes fixed on him with quiet intensity. There was no mockery in her gaze, only unblinking confirmation, as if she too had heard something under the debate's noise.

Raj snorted. "Convenient. Suddenly the silent kid's an expert. Next you'll tell us you've cracked hieroglyphics in your spare time."

Sophia tried to recover, adjusting her clipboard. "Well, regardless, we'll hear more from the museum guides tomorrow. Please refrain from spreading unverified theories, Quentin."

Her words were polite, but they landed like a slap.

Quentin nodded mutely, heart hammering. The vibration inside his chest didn't recede; it pulsed harder, as if the Pyramid itself had borrowed his voice for a moment and refused to give it back.

Across the room, Aisha's lips twitched into something not quite a smile. Not amusement, not kindness—recognition. The kind of look that said: "Yes, you've touched the current too." Then she looked away, leaving Quentin more unsettled than comforted.

— Δ —

The argument drifted back into half-hearted squabbles—Sophia citing textbooks, Raj tossing out half-remembered trivia, Liam stubbornly defending his aliens. Quentin sat hunched on the sofa, his ears buzzing with the aftershock of what he'd blurted. *If he stayed very still,* he told himself, *maybe they'd forget he'd spoken at all.*

That was when he noticed Nia.

She sat near the window, knees tucked up, her sketchbook balanced against them. The lamplight caught the graphite sheen of her pencil lines. Unlike the others, she wasn't speaking—wasn't even pretending to listen. Her hand moved in quick, sure strokes, as though she were tracing something that already existed, not inventing it.

Quentin drifted closer, unsure why. *Maybe because she was quiet too,* he thought. *Maybe because her silence didn't weigh on him the way everyone else's did.*

"What are you drawing?" he asked, voice low.

Nia didn't startle. She tilted the page slightly toward him. The lines were unmistakable: a figure—*him*—standing before the Great Pyramid, shoulders slumped but head tilted up. Around him, Nia had drawn shading that almost looked like light—though it could've been shadow.

Quentin's stomach lurched. "That's… me."

Nia nodded, calm as a cat. "Yes."

"Why—why would you draw that?" His voice cracked, sharper than he meant.

"I don't choose," she said simply, pencil poised above the page. "I just draw what I see."

The glow around his figure seemed to shimmer under the bulb's glare, though Quentin knew it was only graphite catching the light. Still, he couldn't tear his eyes from it. The indistinct shadows behind him seemed to shift if he looked too long—menacing, watching.

His skin prickled. "It's just imagination, right? A bit of artistic license." But the resonance in his chest pulsed in answer, as if disagreeing.

Nia shrugged one shoulder. "Maybe. But my drawings usually mean something. Even if I don't know what."

Her tone wasn't mystical, just matter-of-fact—like describing weather she happened to notice, whether or not others felt the rain.

Quentin stepped back, trying to laugh, though it came out thin. "Well, it's… creative."

Raj's voice sliced across the room. "What's this then?" He sauntered over, plucking at the edge of the sketchbook before Nia could pull it away. "Oh look. Our resident silent artist doodling fairy tales again."

"It's not a fairy tale," Quentin muttered before he could stop himself.

Raj grinned, pouncing. "Oh, I see. She's drawn you. Glowing like a hero, no less. How poetic. Except in real life you fainted like a tourist with sunstroke."

A couple of students snickered. Quentin felt heat crawl up his neck.

Nia didn't rise to it. She simply closed her book with quiet finality. "You'll laugh until you don't," she said, her tone flat as stone.

Raj blinked, thrown, then forced a laugh to recover. "Creepy, the both of you." He swaggered back to his seat, though his smirk was tighter than usual.

Quentin sank onto the arm of a chair, heart pounding. His eyes darted to the closed sketchbook, then to Nia's calm profile, then away again. He wanted to dismiss it, to tell himself it was only art, nothing more. But the sketch's glow seemed to hum in his memory, perfectly in time with the pulse in his chest.

Quentin noticed a detail he had missed before. On the edge of the page, Nia had sketched a glass of water sitting on the coffee table. In the drawing, the water was mid-splash, frozen as if someone had just knocked it over. He looked at the actual table; the glass was perfectly still. But a second later, Liam shifted his weight, his knee clipped the wood, and the water splashed over the rim close enough to make his stomach drop. She didn't even look up; she just began shading the next frame.

— Δ —

The common room had thinned. Sophia had retired with her clipboard tucked under her arm like a holy relic; Raj had swaggered off to bed after one last remark about "wannabe mystics." Even Liam had drifted upstairs, leaving only the echo of his jokes behind.

Quentin remained in the lounge, hunched on a sofa whose cushions swallowed him whole. The television muttered low in Arabic, images flickering across the screen—soap operas, maybe, or the news—but he couldn't follow. His mind circled like a moth around a flame: Nia's sketch, the contrast around his figure, the whispers in the Pyramid. His chest still hummed faintly, like a secret that refused to be buried.

He pressed his palms together, knuckles white. *Why had he said it? About Orion of all things.*

A faint scuff of footsteps drew his eyes up. Aisha emerged from the hallway, her phone in one hand, a dark braid falling over her shoulder.

She looked utterly composed, though her trainers were dust-stained like everyone else's. She paused when she saw him alone. For a moment, Quentin thought she'd glide past without a word.

Instead, she stopped.

Her lips tightened into the faintest smirk. "Maybe you're not as clueless as you look."

The words cut sharper than Raj's jabs, not because they were cruel, but because they were curious—like a probe, a test.

Quentin blinked. "I—I don't—what do you mean?" The stammer betrayed him.

She tilted her head, eyes glinting under the weak lamp. "The thing about the stars. Orion. Most tourists wouldn't even know where to look."

He swallowed. "I just... read it somewhere, maybe. Ages ago."

Her smirk deepened, though her eyes didn't match—it was curiosity, not mockery, that gleamed there. "Maybe. Or maybe you felt it—what the stones were saying."

Quentin's throat dried. He wanted to ask, "Do you feel it too? The hum? The pull of the stones?" But the words stuck.

Instead, he managed, "Do you believe it? That the Pyramids... mean more than history?"

Aisha studied him in silence, then gave a small shrug. "Belief isn't the same as knowing." Her gaze flicked over him, weighing, measuring, as if deciding whether he was worth another word. Then she slid her phone into her pocket.

Quentin scrambled for something clever, something to keep her there. "I—maybe I'm not as clueless as I look." The line came out strangled, half-joke, half-plea.

Her laugh was soft, quick, gone almost before it arrived. "Maybe."

She turned, footsteps light against the threadbare carpet, and walked toward the stairwell. Quentin watched the swing of her braid until the shadows swallowed her.

Only then did he realize his heart was racing—not from humiliation this time, but from something sharper, stranger. Being mocked had always made him shrink. But being noticed—even in a mocking tone—left him oddly alight.

The television flickered, showing a desert night sky scattered with stars. For a dizzy heartbeat, Orion's Belt seemed to shimmer brighter than the rest. He blinked hard. *Just static, just a programme.*

And yet, Aisha's voice lingered in his ears: "Maybe you felt it."

He leaned back, staring at the ceiling fan as it turned in its slow, endless circle. The hostel was quiet now, but inside him, the residual resonance pressed stronger than ever. And he couldn't shake the feeling that Aisha's smirk had not been dismissal at all.

It had been recognition.

CHAPTER 3
ECHOES AND APPRENTICES

"The Shadow does not sleep. It waits for the light to falter." — **Axiom of the Shadow Order, Vigil I.**

— Δ —

The hostel bedroom was a narrow shoebox of heat and shadows. Ceiling fan blades whirred like lazy propellers, hardly troubling the thick air. It was a tight fit. Liam, Raj, and Quentin had claimed the bunks on one side, while Sophia and Nia had partitioned off their corner of the small suite with a hanging travel towel for a sliver of privacy. The arrangement felt like a fortification, which only made Aisha's absence more glaring. Because she had been a late addition to the program, the hostel's group suite had been at capacity, leaving her relegated to a single bed in the restricted girls' annex across the courtyard.

Cairo murmured through the open window—car horns in distant arguments, footsteps, a radio crooning something old and lilting. The city did not sleep; it only pretended, closing one eye while the other kept watch.

Quentin lay flat on a lumpy mattress, sheet twisted round his calves. The room smelled of laundry powder and dust, with a thread of street spice sneaking in on the draught. Every time he closed his eyes, the Pyramid rose behind them, a megalithic weight pressing down until his chest vibrated with a frequency he couldn't tune out. He'd laughed at himself earlier, laughed along when Liam joked, swallowed Raj's sneers whole—but here in the dark the truth pressed back: *something had happened to him inside those walls.*

On the bed across, Liam snored cheerfully, as if asleep were a sport he'd trained for. Raj had claimed most of the double, sprawled at imperial angles, one foot dangling over the edge like he'd claimed it by ordinance. Sophia, tucked under a small reading lamp, had propped herself against the wall with a book and a neat column of sticky notes; she turned pages with the precise finality of a judge. Nia sat cross-legged on the floor by the window, sketchbook open, her pencil whispering steady lines—*shh, shh, shh*—like tide on sand.

Don't be weird, Quentin told himself. *Be normal. Sleep.*

His heart refused to cooperate. The hum had settled low in his chest like a second pulse, not loud, not painful, just insistent—as if a voice were being held behind a door and wanted out. It was quieter here, but no less real, a reminder that the Pyramid hadn't finished with him.

He rolled onto his side and stared at the rectangle of moonlight on the wall. It carried thin slashes of the fan's shadow, a stuttering clock. He could almost measure the night by those turning blades, as if time itself had slowed to their cut and swish. *Absurd*, he thought. He pressed knuckles to his eyelids until stars burst behind them. When he lowered his hands, the room swam back: Liam's leg twitching; Sophia's lamp casting its neat, stubborn pool of diligence; Nia's pencil drawing quiet thunder.

Quentin slipped a hand under his pillow and found his notebook. It was small and battered, corners softened by years of being carried and not used. He eased it open, careful not to rattle the spiral. The first pages were filled with untidy school notes, a shopping list from months ago, then blankness. He steeled himself and drew: the slope of the Pyramid—too steep; the block edges—too neat; the narrow passageway where his hand had found the cold stone and the world had tipped. He tried to catch the angle of the light, the way the darkness seemed to hold its breath. His lines stumbled; his hand shook.

From the floor, Nia said without looking up, "You're drawing."

Quentin froze. "Sorry. I didn't mean to—"

"It's all right." She tilted her sketchbook a fraction, and for an instant he saw the curve of a corridor, the suggestion of men hauling ropes, a flicker of contrast hidden in the stone itself—like the graphite had pressed too hard in one place. The corridor on her page looked *flattened*, depth stolen, as if the air inside it had been compressed. Nia's eyes rose to meet his, solemn and faraway. "Sometimes it's easier to see when everyone else is asleep."

He didn't trust his voice to answer. He bent over his notebook and, almost without thinking, added three small dots to the sky above the Pyramid's point—*just three*—then drew the lines between them. A belt, a hunter, a shape the world had agreed upon. A prickle ran up his arms.

Sophia's lamp snapped off. "Lights," she ordered to the darkness, as if dusk obeyed her. "Museum at nine. Sleep, all of you."

Liam mumbled, "Aliens," and rolled over, hugging his pillow.

Nia's pencil stilled. The fan resumed its hypnotic sermon. Quentin stared at the three dots he had drawn and heard, beneath the hostel's soft noises, the remembered cadence of chanting and stone. He thought of Aisha's smirk, the unreadable flicker in her eyes. "Maybe you see more than you realize," he thought, remembering Aisha's words.

If he stayed here, he would go mad. The hum would drive him into the mattress and pin him there, listening to a voice he couldn't translate. He needed air. Space. A glimpse of the Pyramid under the actual sky, not the cartoon of it on his page.

His stomach tightened. *Sneaking out meant being that person,* he realized, *the one who broke rules, who came back with sand in his shoes and lies in his mouth. Sophia would pin him to the noticeboard with tacks of disapproval. Raj would feast.* And yet the thought of staying—of pretending he hadn't felt the world tilt—was worse.

He slid from the bed with the care of a thief. His bare feet found cool tile. The moon turned the window bars into silver ladders. He pulled on his trainers, wincing at the squeak of rubber. Liam snorted, then resumed his joyous rumble. Quentin held his breath until the room settled.

Nia, in the window's pale glow, watched him without surprise. She lifted her pencil and traced a small arc in the air between them. It was a simple gesture, but it felt like she was acknowledging a pattern, not inventing one—as if she saw what he carried more clearly than he did.

Quentin tucked the notebook into his pocket, shrugged into his hoodie, and glanced once at the sleeping, snoring, quietly breathing lives around him. Then he eased the door, and the corridor's cool darkness reached for him, as if the hall had lost a degree of depth.

The city beyond was awake. So was whatever had woken in him, an echo that no longer felt accidental. *And if he listened*, he thought, *properly listen—perhaps tonight it would finally say his name.*

— Δ —

The streets embraced Quentin with a rush of sound and scent. Midnight Cairo wasn't sleeping—it was pulsing, restless, alive. Neon signs buzzed over shopfronts, painting the cracked pavement in pinks and greens. Street vendors still called out, voices bouncing off concrete walls, hawking skewers of sizzling meat, sweet tea poured from brass kettles, and dates stacked in pyramids as neat as the one he had left behind. The air carried spice and smoke, sweat and petrol, woven into a perfume that was both overwhelming and electric.

He pulled his hood up, not because the night was cold—it wasn't—but because he felt small and out of place. Groups of men laughed around hookah pipes, families herded yawning children across intersections where horns blared and brakes squealed, and stray cats darted between crates with eyes like sparks. No one paid him the slightest attention. *That anonymity both comforted and stung,* he reflected.

Quentin clutched his notebook, the spiral digging into his palm. He slowed near a corner shop whose radio sang a tune older than the city, lilting and minor. For a moment, he scribbled lines—the crooked awnings, the motorbike leaning against a lamppost, the reflection of neon in a puddle. *He wasn't Nia*, he thought, *but the act steadied him.*

Then he turned down a narrower street. The city thinned here, sound sinking into cobbles. The air grew cooler, shadows stretching longer. Between buildings, he caught a glimpse of the desert edge, silvered under the moon. And there—far off, but unmistakable—the Great Pyramid rose, black against a navy sky, its silhouette slicing clean through the constellations.

His chest thrummed. He pulled the notebook back out and sketched the jagged line of its base, the sharp point straining toward Orion. He added the three dots again, careful this time, as if the stars themselves demanded precision. *Each mark felt less like drawing and more like remembering*, he thought.

"Just stone," he whispered to himself. "Just old, heavy stone."

But the word rang hollow. His chest pulsed against the denial, disagreeing.

Somewhere ahead, voices murmured. He stiffened, glancing over his shoulder. The street behind him was empty, just the shuffle of cats and the city traffic further off. The voices came again—closer now, threaded with something unfamiliar. Not Arabic, at least not as he'd heard it. The syllables were lower, stretched, rolled into a cadence that prickled against his skin.

Quentin ducked into the shadow of an arched doorway. His pulse quickened. He told himself to turn back, to head for the hostel before Sophia noticed his absence, before Raj could sneer at him for sneaking off. But his feet rooted in place.

The murmur rose, a rhythm beneath the words—cadenced, deliberate. He caught fragments as the speakers moved nearer, though the meaning was impossible to grasp. Still, the tone carried weight, authority, the kind of gravity that didn't need translation.

The hum in his chest resonated in eerie harmony with the cadence, as though the voices had been waiting for him.

Quentin pressed the cardboard cover shut and held it to his ribs, as if paper could shield him. *Go back. Don't follow*, his heart banged a warning.

But another voice, softer, insistent, whispered back: *Listen.*

The narrow street ended at a crumbling wall. Beyond it stretched sand, pale under the moon, and the dark, hulking outline of the Pyramid closer than he expected. The voices were there, just out of sight. He edged forward, breath shallow, drawn as surely as if the stone itself had looped a thread through his ribs.

Something moved in the corner of his eye—hoods, cloth shifting. Quentin dropped behind a pile of rubble, heart clawing its way into his throat.

The murmuring did not stop. It grew.

— Δ —

The desert night spread wide and hushed, broken only by the shuffle of feet and the low murmur of voices. Quentin pressed himself into the rubble, grit biting into his palms. The air was colder here, emptier than the bustling streets behind him. The Pyramid loomed ahead, a black mountain that seemed to draw breath with the sky itself.

Figures emerged from the darkness—half a dozen, maybe more. They moved with purpose, long robes trailing, hoods shadowing their faces. Their words weren't loud, but the cadence carried, low and strange, as though the desert itself leaned in to listen. Quentin couldn't understand the language, but something in it curled beneath his skin, tugging at that thrum in his chest.

He ducked lower, heart hammering. *He shouldn't be here*, he thought. *He knew it with every beat.* Yet he couldn't drag himself away.

One of the figures raised a hand. The others stilled. Quentin squinted. The man's presence pressed against the night like weight. He didn't shout; he didn't need to. His authority was a tide. Cloak heavier, darker than the rest, hood shadowing his face—yet Quentin felt his gaze sweep the desert, a gaze that seemed to strip away the dark itself.

The murmurs softened into silence. The leader—the Archon—spoke, his voice deliberate, rolling like stone grinding against stone. Quentin didn't know the words, but two of them he registered—two that lodged sharp in his mind.

A child... watching.

The words hooked into Quentin like claws. He was no child—not here, not now—but the phrase felt aimed straight at him.

The others shifted, nodding. Another voice followed, higher-pitched, insistent. Quentin leaned forward, straining to hear. The words spilled around him, strange syllables salted with recognizable ones.

"...awakened... the resonance." Quentin's pulse felt narrow and fast—thready—like his pulse went thin and fast. *He didn't know the word, but the sound behind it was the same as the one inside him*, he realized.

Quentin's skin went cold.

The Echo. He didn't know what it meant, he thought, *but he knew. His bones recognized it.* The word lit every nerve as if it belonged to him already.

He clutched his notebook tighter, wishing absurdly he could shut himself into its pages and vanish.

The leader turned toward the Pyramid, lifting both hands. The hood fell back enough for moonlight to catch the edges of his face: sharp, austere, lips curved in something that was not quite a smile. Calm radiated from him, but it was the calm of deep water—steady, fathomless, dangerous.

The robed figures bowed. The chant began again, louder this time, gathering in rhythm. Quentin felt it echo through the sand, through his knees, through the marrow of him. His heart thudded in time, unwilling, as though the sound were trying to claim him.

Something inside him surged in answer—defiant, desperate—not simply absorbing the chant but pushing against it, like two notes clashing.

He pressed his right palm against his chest to fight it back.

A stone shifted under his foot. The sound cracked the air. Quentin froze, blood draining.

The chanting stopped.

Several hoods turned sharply toward the rubble where he crouched. Moonlight caught a glint of eyes.

Quentin flattened himself against the rock, breath locked in his throat. *Run. Run now*, his mind screamed.

But before he could move, the Archon lifted a hand. The others halted instantly, as if strings held them. His gaze swept the rubble once more, sharp as a blade, pausing just long enough to scrape against Quentin's hiding place.

The Archon's voice slid across the silence, low and calm. "The boy is near. But not yet ours."

Then, with a flick of his fingers, the figures turned, melting back toward the Pyramid's shadow. Their robes whispered like wings in retreat, their voices fading into the desert wind.

Quentin sagged against the rubble, lungs aching as air rushed back. His hands shook so violently his notebook nearly slipped free.

They hadn't seen him, he thought. *Not fully. But they spoke of the boy.* And whatever the Echo was, whatever it meant, the word had landed on him like a brand.

For the first time, Quentin understood: *the hum inside him wasn't his secret alone. Others knew. Others were waiting.*

He pressed his forehead to his knees. The desert stretched silent again, but the calm was a lie. Somewhere beyond the Pyramid, the chant still echoed, threading itself into his bones like a promise he hadn't agreed to keep.

The night hadn't finished with him yet, Quentin knew.

— Δ —

Quentin eased backward from the rubble, legs trembling as if the sand itself had turned liquid. His notebook was slick in his grip, damp from sweat. *He had to get away*, he thought, *before they circle back.*

He staggered a few steps, eyes fixed on the faint glow of Cairo's lights in the distance. The resonance in his chest still pulsed, insistent, as though it wanted to drag him straight into the Pyramid. He clutched his hoodie tighter, trying to cage the feeling, when a voice cut clean through the night.

"You shouldn't be here."

Quentin spun so fast he nearly tripped over his own feet.

Aisha stepped out of the shadows. The moon silvered the edges of her braid and glinted in her eyes, dark and sharp. She wasn't out of breath. She wasn't surprised. She simply stood there, arms folded, as though she had been waiting for him all along.

Quentin's throat dried. "I—I was just walking. Couldn't sleep."

"Walking," she repeated, her tone flat. "At midnight. Through Cairo. Straight toward the Pyramid."

He tried to laugh, but the sound cracked. "Coincidence."

"Don't insult me. You heard it too, didn't you? The way the stone… answers." Her gaze was steady, harder than Raj's smirks, sharper than Sophia's scolding. There was no mockery in it—only certainty. "You felt it, didn't you? Inside the Pyramid. The hum."

The words hit like a stone against glass. Quentin's mouth opened, closed. He wanted to deny it, to push her words away the way he'd shoved down his vision. But his chest thrummed, betraying him.

"I don't know what you're talking about," he said, too quickly.

Aisha stepped closer, the sand whispering under her trainers. "You touched the stone. You saw something. That's why you're here."

Quentin swallowed hard. "And what about you? Why are you here?"

For the first time, her composure wavered. A shadow crossed her face—anger, maybe, or fear. "I know more than you. Enough to tell you this: if you keep wandering toward things you don't understand, you won't come back."

Her words should have frightened him. They did. But beneath the warning was something else. Her voice had dropped, softening not with pity but with urgency. It was the same tone she'd used in the common room, when she cut through their debate with a blade of truth. Only now it was aimed at him.

Quentin felt his jaw tighten. "Why should I listen? You've done nothing but look down on me since we landed."

Aisha's lips curved into a faint, humorless smile. "Maybe I was wrong about you."

The wind shifted, carrying the distant murmur of voices—those robed figures fading into the night. Quentin flinched. Aisha noticed.

"You saw them." Not a question.

"I—I don't know who they are."

"They're dangerous." Her eyes pinned him. "Stay away. You have no idea what you've stumbled into."

Something in him rebelled at the command. *Why does she get to decide?* he wondered. "But you do, don't you? You know more than you're saying."

Aisha didn't answer. Instead, she looked back at the Pyramid, its massive silhouette drinking the moonlight. Her face was unreadable, carved in shadow. When she turned back to him, her voice was low. "Just remember this: some doors don't close once you've opened them."

The hum in Quentin's chest flared as if in reply. He hugged his notebook tighter, unable to find words.

Aisha gave one last glance, sharp enough to cut, then turned away. Her braid swung once, a dark pendulum, before she vanished back into the shadows from which she'd come.

Quentin stood frozen, the desert wind clawing at his sleeves. *Her warning echoed louder than the chants*, he realized, *because it wasn't just a threat. It was recognition.*

— Δ —

Quentin half-ran, half-stumbled back toward the city, every shadow a threat. The voices of the robed figures still coiled in his ears, twined now with Aisha's warning. His trainers slapped softly against sand, then cobblestone, then pavement. Cairo's noise returned—cars honking, dogs barking, laughter spilling from a café—but it felt thinner, unreal, like scenery hastily painted to hide what he had just glimpsed behind the curtain.

By the time he reached the hostel, his lungs burned and his pulse thundered a rapid, thready rhythm against his carotids. He waited by the door, forcing his breathing to slow, terrified he'd faint again in the hallway where Sophia would find him. He slipped through the creaking door, heart banging, and padded up the narrow staircase two steps at a time. The common room was dark, the smell of extinguished tea lingering. Upstairs, the bedroom door groaned as he pushed it open.

Inside, the others slept. Liam sprawled like a starfish, mouth wide and snoring cheerfully. Raj muttered in his sleep, rolling over with a self-satisfied grunt. Sophia's book rested closed on her chest, her lamp extinguished with neat finality. Only Nia stirred faintly, sketchbook still balanced on her lap, pencil fallen across the page like it had drawn itself to sleep.

Quentin closed the door with care, his chest still thudding. He crossed to his bed, slid his notebook out of his hoodie pocket, and sat with it open on his knees.

His hand trembled as he wrote, "Who are they? What is the Echo?"

The words looked absurd in his own handwriting—like a line copied from someone else's diary. He underlined it twice, pressed so hard the pen nearly tore the page.

He drew, too: the slope of the Pyramid in moonlight, the robed figures with faces hidden, the taller one with hands raised. His lines wavered, shaky, but the memory was too strong to ignore. He sketched the shadows curling at their feet. And finally, reluctantly, he drew Aisha—just her eyes, dark and sharp, staring at him as if she already knew what he was.

Quentin snapped the notebook shut, pulse still racing. He rubbed his face with both hands and leaned back against the wall. The hum in his chest had quieted, but it hadn't gone. *It was waiting*, he realized, *patient as breath, like an unfinished sentence.*

He turned toward the window, drawn by instinct. The blinds were half open, the night pouring through in thin silver lines. Beyond the city glow, the desert stretched pale under the moon, and there—still visible, impossibly vast—the Pyramid rose. Its edges caught the faintest light. For a second the Pyramid looked over-defined, edges too clean against the sky. His sternum tightened with that sterile, subcutaneous pressure again.

He shivered.

And then he saw her.

Across the courtyard, on the balcony of the girls' wing, a figure stood in silhouette. A braid glinted faintly in the moonlight. Aisha. She leaned on the rail, perfectly still, eyes turned toward the same Pyramid.

He couldn't tell if she looked back, but the air tightened anyway. Neither spoke, neither moved, but Quentin felt the air tighten, the same charged thread he'd felt in the desert. The hum stirred in recognition, as though it acknowledged her presence too.

She turned first, slipping back into shadow. Quentin remained, staring at the Pyramid until his eyes ached.

At last, he dropped onto his pillow, notebook clutched to his chest. Sleep hovered near but never quite claimed him. Outside, Cairo murmured on. The Pyramid waited. *He wasn't just keeping secrets anymore,* Quentin thought. *He was becoming one. The Echo had marked him, and it didn't feel like something that could be shrugged off.*

Chapter 4
The Mark of Endurance

"Time, when captured, becomes a weapon. Its price is the mortal coil." — **Guardian Teaching, Scroll of Chronology.**

— Δ —

Morning came thin and pale, the sort of light that looked as if it had been sifted through flour. The bus coughed them onto the Giza Plateau, where the air already shimmered, and the Pyramid loomed like a thought too heavy to set down. Quentin's eyelids felt gritty. Sleep had skittered around him all night, never landing; he'd watched the darkness lighten as if the city were breathing him into another day against his will.

Sophia was brisk and bladed as ever, clipboard in hand, ticking boxes that seemed to multiply. "Water? Hats? Sunscreen? Liam, shoes tied, please. Raj, no wandering—"

"I don't wander," Raj declared, puffed with self-importance. "I survey." He adjusted his sunglasses—mirrored, unforgivable—and added, loud enough for two other tour groups to hear, "You know the original casing stones reflected the sun so brilliantly the Pyramid looked like a fallen star? Its name was the Horizon of Khufu."

"Tragic that your humility didn't survive the centuries," Liam murmured, tripping his shoelace into an obedient knot. He flashed Quentin a grin. "Ready to be dazzled, mate? Or faint artistically again? I can catch you—very gallant—though do try to faint on my good side."

Quentin managed a smile that might have convinced an optimist. The low-frequency thrum in his chest—stronger now, louder for what had woken it inside the Pyramid—flexed, slow and deliberate. Now that he stood at the base again, it pressed against his ribs like a warning drum. *It was just nerves*, he told himself. *Just tired. Just heat. Just—anything but this.*

Dr. Layla Farouk gathered them in with a lift of her hand. Calm, steady, linen blouse catching the early breeze, she had a way of making even the Pyramid feel like part of her lesson plan. "Today, we pay attention to the ordinary," she said. "How stone was cut. How ramps were raised. How people—real, tired, clever people—solved impossible problems with patience. Wonder hides there, not only in miracles."

Professor Ellis dabbed at his forehead with a handkerchief the color of surrender. "And we drink water," he added, "because passing out on four-thousand-year-old limestone is considered rude."

A ripple of laughter. Quentin swallowed; the joke skimmed past him. The sun lifted another finger over the horizon. Shadows shortened, heat unrolled. Tourists flowed around them in bright shirts and brighter voices. Vendors called out: cold drinks, tiny pyramids, mystery in plastic wrap. A camel burbled a complaint like an old man clearing his throat.

Nia had already found a patch of shade cast by a block the size of a small car. She sat with her knees up and her sketchbook balanced, pencil skating quicksilver lines. Quentin glimpsed her page—shadows coiling at the base of the Pyramid, darker than the sun should allow. From where he stood he saw the suggestion of steps within shadow, the pale cut of sky in a notch of stone. *Her drawings didn't copy—they listen.*

Aisha stood apart, near the guide rope. She had a cap pulled low, braid tucked, stance easy as if her body trusted the ground more than most. She didn't look at Quentin, not once. But her attention hooked again and again to the Pyramid's face—the way the joints met, the hairline shifts where heat and time had worked their fingers. Watching her watch it made his skin prickle. Her warning from the desert throbbed fresh in his mind: "If you keep wandering toward things you don't understand, you won't come back."

Sophia clapped to get them moving. "We'll begin at the northern face. Stay together." She pinned Quentin with a look that said especially you without wasting breath. He nodded, cheeks warming. *Keep up appearances*, he reminded himself. *Don't be strange. Don't be the boy who slinks off after moonlit whispers.*

They walked, trainers scuffing over stone and sand. The Pyramid's flank rose beside them, close enough now that the blocks towered above eye-line, close enough that the wind changed when it struck the surface and came away cooler, carrying a skein of dust and ancient dryness. A fly bumbled in Quentin's ear; he flinched. Liam reached over and flicked it away with mock-heroic flourish.

"Brave," Quentin managed.

"Decorated for services to ears everywhere," Liam said solemnly.

The guide—Hassan again, with his bobbing torch now replaced by a neat cap and patient smile—paused by a seam in the blocks and spoke about joints so tight a blade of grass would balk, about quarry marks and mason's graffiti. Raj nodded as if confirming Hassan's existence. Sophia wrote until her pen scratched outrageously. Nia drew the shadow of Hassan's hand more than the hand itself.

Quentin drifted to the edge of the group, not quite out of bounds. The northern face breathed cool on his skin. He let his right hand hover—a respectable inch from the surface—fingers spread as if the air itself had weight. *Don't touch it,* he told himself. *Don't.* The vibration surged. It felt like standing too close to a train as it thundered past: invisible, irresistible.

He brushed the stone with his right fingertips.

It was only an instant. Cool grit. Then—there—a faint tremor under his fingertips, as if something far within had stirred and turned over in sleep. The sensation shot deeper than touch—like the stone had noticed him back. *It was the same cadence from the vision inside the Pyramid,* he thought, his breath hitching. He blinked, swallowed, pressed again.

"Quentin," Sophia called sharply. "With the group, please."

He snatched his hand back, heart jogging into an unconvincing whistle. "Coming."

But as he stepped away, the tremor seemed to travel up his arm and nest in his shoulder, as if the stone had slipped him a secret to carry. He rubbed the spot, uselessly. At his periphery, Aisha's cap tilted a fraction, the briefest acknowledgement that she'd seen. Then her face was unreadable again.

They moved on. Hassan pointed, explained. Liam muttered an aside about Pharaohs needing better architects than influencers. Raj corrected a year that hadn't been wrong. Dr. Farouk smiled in a way that made you want to become the person she believed you could be.

Quentin kept pace. He nodded at the right moments. He laughed once, even. The residual resonance did not quiet. If anything, it grew more insistent—no longer a call from the whole Pyramid, but a thread tugging toward a particular fissure, a darker line where two blocks met like lips about to speak.

He glanced back at it. The joint waited, ordinary as a crack in a pavement. The vibration rippled. The thread tugged again, sharper.

It was not just stone calling, he realized with a jolt. *It was the Echo.*

Curiosity reared, dangerous and dense.

— Δ —

The tour pressed on, a tide of voices and snapping cameras. Quentin trailed at the back, the heat making his shirt cling and his mind fog. The hum in his chest had sharpened into a single tug—an invisible thread leading him not forward with the group, but sideways, toward a seam in the Pyramid's flank.

Tour ropes kept the crowd a few meters out; from the wrong angle, the place where he stood vanished into ordinary stone.

At first glance it was nothing more than a shadow, a deeper crease between two massive blocks. But as he passed, Quentin felt a faint vibration against his arm, as though the air itself shivered. He slowed and looked over his shoulder. Hassan was gesturing at the foundation stones, Liam cracking a joke about "ancient Egyptian contractors," Sophia writing furiously, Raj muttering dates with smug precision. No one was watching him.

The seam seemed to breathe.

Quentin hesitated, heart hammering. *He should stay*, he thought. *He should absolutely stay.* But his feet betrayed him. One step, then another, until he stood with his shoulder against the stone. The shade here was cooler, the air faintly damp. His hand lifted without permission. He pressed his palm to the blocks.

The vibration leapt into him, a pulse that wasn't stone or wind or tourist footsteps. Before he could think better of it, Quentin slid sideways, pressing himself into the gap. It was narrow, shoulders scraping rough limestone, dust sifting into his hair. His trainers crunched on grit. The light from the plateau shrank behind him, replaced by stale coolness that smelled of old air and forgotten time.

"Hello?" His whisper cracked the silence. No reply.

He shuffled deeper. The shaft angled slightly downward, the ceiling so low he had to hunch. His breath echoed in the stone, loud as a drum. His fingers brushed the wall for balance. Lines were carved there—faint, worn—but as his skin skimmed them, contrast snapped into place—lines that had been dust-flat resolving as if the air itself had been pressed thinner. When he pulled away, the carvings dulled back into ordinary stone. When he touched again, the pattern returned—cleaner, sharper—like the wall was remembering how to be read.

Hieroglyphs. Shapes of birds and eyes and stars.

Quentin's heart lurched. He snatched his hand back, and the lines went dull—dust-flat again. He touched once more, tentative. The pattern returned with a clean snap of definition, like the wall had decided to hold still long enough to be read.

"This is mad," he whispered. "Completely mad."

He pressed on, steps slow, shoulders aching from the squeeze. Dust rose with every move, dry and choking. The shaft seemed endless, and yet something pulled him forward, the hum in his chest syncing with the wall's snapped-into-place clarity. Each time his fingers brushed stone, the glyphs seemed to breathe with him, as though recognising him.

Sweat prickled at his temples. His notebook dug into his pocket. He thought of Aisha's words—and the way her eyes had sharpened when he spoke of Orion's Belt. She already knew more than she let on. But the warning felt distant now, drowned by curiosity.

The light from the entry had vanished completely now. Darkness pressed against his eyes, broken only by the faint shimmer of the carvings. He hunched lower, knees brushing stone. His breath rasped louder. He thought of Liam's snores, Sophia's clipboard, Raj's smirk—all distant, safe, ordinary. *He was far from them now*, he realized, *farther still from sense.*

A fresh gust of cold met his face. The shaft opened slightly, enough for him to straighten, enough for the air to thin and taste of minerals and ages. The glow was stronger here, not just in single glyphs but whole sequences, spilling across the walls like schematics stitched in light. His fingertips tingled as he traced them, one after another.

The resonant throb surged. Something lay ahead. Something waiting.

Quentin wiped grit from his eyes, coughed into his sleeve, and pressed forward until the shaft widened into a small chamber.

He froze.

The walls were carved deeper, more deliberate. Symbols of circles and towers, figures holding objects that glowed brighter beneath his touch. Dust blanketed the floor, undisturbed. A prickling certainty struck him—*Nia could have drawn this place exactly, though she had never stepped foot here.*

No tourist had been here—not for years.

Quentin's chest rose and fell fast, every nerve screaming at him to retreat. And yet—

He stepped inside.

The chamber seemed to exhale, welcoming him like a lung drawing its first breath.

— Δ —

The chamber was no bigger than a classroom cloakroom, its ceiling low, its walls crowded with carvings that shimmered faintly as if lit from within. Dust coated everything in a soft, grey veil, and Quentin's footprints were the first to disturb it in what felt like forever. The air pressed close, dry and metallic, thick with the smell of stone that had never seen sunlight.

He raised his hand to the wall, hesitant, then brushed the surface.

The carvings stirred.

They weren't random glyphs now, but pictures—whole scenes etched in painstaking relief. The Seven Wonders, or what they must have been before time chewed them down: the Hanging Gardens lush with curling vines; the statue of Zeus glowering from a throne; the Lighthouse of Alexandria blazing like a captured star. Each one connected by fine etched lines, like constellations strung across the heavens. At the center of it all stood the Great Pyramid, unbroken, crowned with a jewel of light.

Quentin's throat tightened. His fingers traced the line from the Pyramid to the Gardens, and the chamber seemed to tremble.

Then the world dropped away.

A roar filled his ears, not sound but presence. Dust, stone, air—all dissolved into a wash of heat. He blinked—and found himself not alone.

Men moved around him, half-seen through veils of smoke and fire. Priests, robed in linen, their heads shaved, their hands raised. Their chanting pounded like a heartbeat, words ancient and jagged, vibrating through his chest until he thought his ribs might split.

Quentin stumbled back, but the chamber had vanished. He stood in a vast hall, torchlight guttering against stone pillars. At the center, a block of limestone glowed from within, and on it rested something—something burning with power. A shard, crystalline, golden, pulsing like the sun captured in glass.

The priests circled it, their chants rising in a crescendo. Sweat ran down Quentin's spine though the body he wore in this wasn't his own. The leader raised a staff and struck the block. The shard sank into it, vanishing, but its glow bled outward, seeping into the walls, into the very bones of the Pyramid, until the entire structure answered.

Quentin's knees buckled. He clutched at nothing, vision blurring. The chanting swelled until it was no longer sound but force, pressing against his lungs. Words pushed into his skull, not spoken but imprinted:

"Endurance. Time preserved. The Echo shall remain."

He gasped, struggling for air. The priests blurred, their mouths open in endless invocation. His chest burned. The static had become a roar, shaking his bones, rattling his teeth. He tried to scream but only dust filled his mouth, choking him.

The weight of centuries pressed down. He saw sandstorms devour, floods rage, armies march and crumble—all while the Pyramid stood immovable, its shard hidden, its endurance unbroken. *Time itself was collapsing into him*, he thought in terror.

Quentin dropped to the floor. The dust was hot beneath his palms. He clawed for breath, every inhale rasping like knives, his body suddenly too small—too mortal—for what was pressing in. *Stop. Please stop.* The words branded themselves into him, not just heard but engraved, as if the chant mistook him for stone.

The vision didn't listen.

The priests' faces swam close, their eyes hollow, their chants drilling straight into his marrow. The shard burned behind his eyes, pulsing faster, faster, as though syncing with his frantic heartbeat.

"Endurance," the voices whispered. "Time. Preserved."

Something seized him—his muscles locked as the Echo overwrote his neural pathways. His notebook spilled from his pocket, pages fanning in the dust. His vision tunneled to a single point of light—the Pyramid crowned, eternal—and then snapped.

Darkness.

He lay sprawled on the chamber floor, lungs dragging air in ragged, desperate gulps. The carvings above him glowed faintly, then dimmed back into the ordinary dullness of stone. Sweat plastered his shirt to his skin. Post-ictal tremor hit in ugly waves—aftershocks through his forearms and thighs, fine then violent—in a panic it couldn't turn off.

The hum inside him hadn't faded. It had converted—no longer a sound he could pretend was imagination, but a persistent, subcutaneous pressure behind his sternum, like something occupying space that anatomy insisted was empty.

He pressed a trembling hand to his chest. His skin was cold, but the pulse beneath beat steady, stubbornly normal—almost insulting in its normality—while everything around it insisted the opposite.

The whisper lingered, a ghost in his ear. Not just endurance, but warning. He had been claimed.

Quentin shuddered. "Is this a gift," he wondered, "or a curse?"

— Δ —

The chamber still quivered with echoes when Quentin forced himself upright, his breath ragged, his hair plastered to his forehead. His notebook lay splayed in the dust, pages crumpled and streaked grey. He reached for it with shaking fingers—

—and another hand darted from the shadows and snatched it up.

Quentin flinched.

Aisha stood in the narrow shaft's mouth, braid hanging loose now, cap gone, her face lit by the faint glow of the wall carvings. Dust streaked her clothes, but her posture was as unshaken as if she had been carved from the same stone. She held his notebook like evidence.

"You shouldn't be here," she said, voice low but sharp enough to cut.

Quentin's pulse stumbled. "Neither should you."

She stepped further inside, the glow painting her cheekbones in molten gold. "That's different."

"Different how?" His voice cracked. "You followed me."

"I found you. I know the old gaps." She shook the notebook once, punctuation sharp. "Do you even know what you touched? What you just invited into yourself?"

Quentin clenched his fists. His body still trembled from the vision, but frustration burned hotter than fear. "Then tell me. You keep acting like you know everything—so say it. What's happening to me?"

Her eyes flicked to the wall, where the faint carvings of the Seven Wonders still glimmered. For a heartbeat, the hard edge of her expression faltered. *She was afraid,* he realized with a start. *Or she was seeing something she recognized.* But it vanished almost instantly, her controlled veneer snapping back in place.

"You're a liability," she said flatly. "Clumsy, reckless, loud. You'll get yourself—and maybe the rest of us—killed."

Quentin staggered to his feet, fury knotting into his exhaustion. "Then why are you here? Why do you keep following me, warning me, saving me? If I'm such a liability, why not just let me fall on my face and be done with it?"

Aisha's jaw tightened. Dust swirled between them, carried by a faint draft from the shaft. For a moment, silence stretched too long, the resonance in Quentin's chest filling it like a drumbeat.

"I'm here," she said finally, softer now but edged with urgency, "because what you touched matters. More than you realize. And because I'm after the same thing."

Quentin blinked. "The same—?"

"The Echo." The word dropped like stone into water, resonant, undeniable. Her tone carried recognition—as if she had been chasing it long before he ever set foot in Cairo. "That shard you saw, the Endurance bound in the Pyramid—it's real. And if it's in you now, then you're standing in my way."

He gaped. "In your way?"

"I came here to claim it," she snapped. "What you just woke. Not you. You—" Her eyes raked him up and down, taking in the dust-caked hoodie, trembling hands, the wild confusion still clouding his face. "You're not supposed to be anything but ordinary. And yet…" Her gaze snagged on his chest, as if she could see the hemodynamic struggle beneath his ribs. "Here you are."

Quentin's throat tightened. His anger wavered into confusion, into something more dangerous: *fascination.* Her words stung, but her eyes betrayed something else—*envy*, perhaps. Or *recognition.*

"You want it," he said slowly. "The Echo. You were meant to get it."

Aisha's smirk returned, though brittle at the edges. "At least you're not as clueless as you look."

Their eyes locked. The air between them seemed to stretch taut, filled with dust and the faint whisper of centuries. He hated her arrogance, hated the way she made him feel small. *But there was something between them*, he sensed, *something inevitable.*

Quentin took a step forward. "Then we're in this together. Whether you like it or not."

For the briefest instant, her face softened, eyes flashing with something too quick to catch. Then her pulse seemed to settle, her expression flattening into that opaque, practiced stillness she used like armor.

"Don't flatter yourself," she said coldly, thrusting the notebook into his chest. "The Echo doesn't belong to you. Next time, it might not let you crawl away."

She brushed past him toward the shaft, the faint glow dimming as she moved. Quentin clutched the notebook to his ribs, his heart pounding against it. *She was wrong*, he hoped—*or maybe she was right, and that's what terrified her.*

— Δ —

A sound cracked through the chamber: a footstep, muffled but near. Quentin's head jerked toward the shaft. Not Aisha's light tread this time—heavier, deliberate. Voices followed, low and clipped, too controlled to belong to tourists.

Aisha's face snapped toward the entrance, her features tightening. "They're here."

"Who—?" Quentin began, but Aisha silenced him with a sharp glance.

"Shadow Order." The words hissed like a fuse. "Move."

She grabbed his wrist and yanked him toward the shaft. The walls scraped his shoulders as they squeezed into the narrow passage. Dust rained into his hair, clinging to sweat. The voices behind them grew clearer, speaking that same guttural cadence Quentin had overheard in the desert.

"They'll find the chamber," he panted. "They'll see—"

"Not if we're gone," Aisha snapped. Her grip tightened on his wrist, pulling him forward. "Keep low."

The shaft seemed longer now, the darkness thicker. Quentin stumbled, barked his shin against stone, barely held in a curse. A torchlight flared behind them, orange and alive, shadows jerking against the walls.

A voice echoed—harsh syllables, but the meaning landed anyway: *the boy… the Echo… near.*

Quentin's heart lurched into his throat. *It was the same phrase from the desert—like prophecy catching up to him.*

He faltered, panic freezing his legs, but Aisha hauled him up without breaking stride. "Quiet," she hissed. "They'll hear you."

The shaft twisted, angled upward. Faint daylight seeped ahead, a pale promise. Quentin clawed toward it, lungs burning, legs shaking. Aisha moved like she belonged here, swift and certain even in the dark. *He hated how sure she was*, he thought, *but he couldn't let go of her hand.*

The torchlight surged closer, voices barking commands. A hand brushed Quentin's shoulder. Panic tore through him like fire. He lunged forward, crawling, and burst into sunlight with Aisha close behind.

They tumbled out onto the sandy edge of the Pyramid's base, coughing, coated in dust. The air hit his lungs with a searing, open-air shock. Aisha shoved him upright, brushing grit from her own clothes with infuriating composure.

"Smile," she muttered.

"What—?"

Too late. The rest of the student group spotted them. They hadn't gone far—Hassan's rope line still looped the northern face. Sophia's sharp gasp cut through the clatter of tourist chatter.

"Where have you been?" she demanded, marching forward with clipboard clutched like a weapon. "You were gone nearly an hour! Do you have any idea—"

Quentin opened his mouth, but no excuse arrived. His tongue was a dry rag.

Liam saved him—or half saved him—with a grin. "See? Told you he'd faint dramatically again. This time he dragged Aisha with him. Dusty pair of romantics."

Raj smirked, pushing sunglasses up his nose. "Or maybe they got lost because someone doesn't know how to follow instructions."

Heat flared in Quentin's face. He brushed at his hoodie, but the dust only smeared darker, evidence of everything he couldn't explain.

Nia, sitting on a low block with her sketchbook, didn't laugh or scold. She tilted her page instead. Quentin caught the briefest glimpse—two figures scrambling from a shaft, chased by shadows shaped wrong for human forms. *She was always two steps ahead*, he shivered.

Sophia's pen scribbled furiously. "Unacceptable. Absolutely unacceptable." She turned her glare on Aisha, who only met it coolly, as if Sophia were a child scolding a cat.

Professor Ellis dabbed at his forehead, too weary for wrath. "Just…don't make a habit of it."

Dr. Farouk's eyes lingered longer. She said nothing, but the weight of her gaze suggested she saw more than dust.

As the group shuffled on, Raj muttering trivia about "hidden shafts" and Liam narrating Quentin's supposed faint in florid detail, Quentin trudged in silence, his notebook clutched like a shield. The residual resonance inside his chest still reverberated, as though the Shadow Order's chant had followed him into the sunlight.

Aisha drifted close enough for only him to hear. "Next time," she murmured, her voice sliding into his ear like a blade sheathed in velvet, "I won't save you."

Her words left him colder than the shadows in the chamber. *But she had already begun*, Quentin realized.

Chapter 5

THE SCAFFOLDS OF SUSPICION

"A fracture in the foundation of trust is more dangerous than any blade."
— Axiom of the Shadow Order, Control III.

— Δ —

The hostel breakfast hall smelled of coffee and frying oil, with a veil of cumin and something sweet drifting through from the kitchen. Light slanted in dusty stripes through the shuttered windows, painting the long wooden tables in bars of sun and shadow. Cutlery rattled, chairs scraped, a kettle hissed like an irritated cat. Cairo, even indoors, refused to be quiet.

Quentin hovered at the end of the buffet where a tray of flatbread steamed under a cracked plastic lid. He felt volume-depleted, the kind of systemic fatigue that made the simple act of holding a plate feel like a feat of endurance. Every time he blinked he saw the chamber—carvings flaring, priests chanting, Aisha's eyes hard as flint. *He wondered if he dreamt it in a fever.* Then he flexed the hand he'd braced on the wall and felt a ghost of that answering tremor. *Not a dream, then. Something worse: a memory.*

Liam materialized at his shoulder with a stack of eggs balanced dangerously on flatbread. “Behold,” he announced, “the Breakfast Pyramid. A marvel of engineering, except mine’s edible and will definitely collapse in a tragic yolk disaster.”

“Please don’t,” Sophia said, appearing with clipboard somehow still in play at breakfast, her hair tamed into a merciless bun. “We have a full day—back to Giza in the morning, Coptic Cairo after lunch, and museum for sunset. I will not have anyone fainting, wandering off, or building structurally unsound omelets.”

Liam saluted with his fork. “Aye, captain.”

Raj set his tray down with a thump, sunglasses pushed up into his hair like a crown. “Frankly, yesterday was unremarkable,” he announced. “I’d read about hidden passages ages ago. It was only a matter of time before somebody stumbled into one.”

Quentin’s stomach clenched. He kept his gaze on the flatbread, tearing it into obedient strips. *Echo*. The word still pulsed in his mind, impossible to peel away.

“Somebody?” Liam said. “You mean Quentin and Aisha crawling out of a wall like very dusty beetles? Iconic, that.”

Sophia’s eyes cut to Quentin with surgical precision. “Next time, inform me before you go exploring. Or better—don’t.”

Quentin nodded, throat too tight for words. Across the room, Aisha stood at the tea urn, steam ghosting up around her face. She lifted the handle, poured in a steady stream, and never once looked his way. If she felt anything of yesterday’s panic in that shaft—if she remembered dragging him toward daylight while voices hunted them—her face didn’t show it. Her hair was wound into a neat plait again. The controlled stillness was back. *Only he had seen the tactical veneer crack*, Quentin realized. *Only he knew she'd chosen not to leave him.* That debt sat like grit under his tongue.

How did she do it? Frustration and awe tangled in his chest. *How was she so calm?* He remembered seeing her earlier that morning, before the sun was fully up, leaning against a battered black motorbike in the alleyway behind the kitchen. The motorbike was a black, debadged Kawasaki—built for speed and anonymity, not for a student's budget. She'd been talking to a local man in a grease-stained jumpsuit, handing him a small envelope. He'd assumed she was just haggling for a private tour, but the way her hands rested on the handlebars—familiar, possessive—said she wasn't just a passenger. In Cairo, a bike like that was a skeleton key—and Aisha already held it.

Nia had tucked herself into a corner bench beneath the window, sketchbook open beside a bowl of yoghurt and honey she'd hardly touched. Her pencil travelled with unhurried certainty, drawing not people but the light itself—the way it pooled on the tables and caught in the steam, the way it boxed Aisha in stripes as she poured her tea. Aisha's outline was already on the page, split subtly between shadow and brightness, as if Nia saw what Quentin couldn't admit aloud.

He carried his plate to the table and sat, trying to fold himself small. Liam launched into a monologue about the museum gift shop, "If I don't return with a miniature sarcophagus, my gran will disown me." Raj explained—incorrectly—the function of canopic jars until Sophia corrected him without looking up, and Professor Ellis wafted through with a napkin tucked into his collar, dispensing reminders about hydration like party favors. Dr. Farouk came last, moving with that steady grace of hers, pausing to ask a vendor through the hatch about more bread in swift Arabic. Her presence smoothed the air.

"Eat," she said mildly as she passed their table. "Learning is heavy and hunger makes fools of the clever."

Liam widened his eyes. "Then I'd best have thirds."

Quentin chewed obediently, though the bread sat in his mouth like paper. Every clink of cup and scrape of chair scraped his nerves raw. He could feel Aisha's absence like a shape pressed into the room—she had taken her tea to the far end, back to a wall, view on the door. *Not hiding, exactly*, he thought. *Guarding a border he couldn't see.*

He caught himself staring. Forced his eyes down. *The sensible thing would be to pretend*, he told himself. *To tuck the memory of her grip on his wrist and the word Echo into a mental drawer and nail it shut. He could become the tourist he was meant to be: listen, take notes, don't touch the stones. He could even apologize to Sophia properly. He could.*

The hum in his chest answered softly, like a held breath. Patient, certain, as if waiting for his denial to run out.

"Oi," Liam said, nudging him under the table. "You with us, stargazer?"

Quentin startled. "Yeah. Sorry. Didn't sleep."

Raj smirked. "Maybe if you stopped sneaking off to play Indiana Jones—"

"Enough," Sophia said, almost kindly for her. "We've all had a long couple of days."

Quentin risked another glance toward the far end. Aisha lifted her cup, and for a heartbeat her gaze cut across the room and met his. Nothing in her face changed. Not a flinch, not a smirk. But something sharpened behind her eyes—the same hard intelligence that had weighed him in the shaft. *He felt like he was taking a test he hadn't prepared for.*

Dr. Farouk tapped her watch lightly. "Five minutes, everyone. Buses don't wait for fate."

Chairs scraped, plates clattered; the room loosened into motion. Quentin stood too quickly, triggering a sharp orthostatic drop; white bloomed at the edges of his vision as his blood pressure struggled to catch up with his heart. He steadied himself on the back of the chair, willing the light to recede. When it did, the residual resonance remained, steady as a drumbeat under everything else. *It sounded like a summons*, he thought suspiciously.

He told himself, again, to ignore it.

The summons didn't care. It had followed him out of the chamber, out of the shaft, out of sleep itself—and now it followed him into daylight.

— Δ —

By mid-morning, the Plateau was a riot of noise. Tourists swarmed like ants around the base of the Pyramid, selfie sticks stabbing at the sky, guides calling in multiple languages. The sun hammered down, baking the limestone into a glare so bright Quentin had to squint. The air shimmered with heat and voices, a restless tide that pressed in on every side.

Hassan, their guide, raised his voice above the din. "Here you see the restoration scaffolding on the lower tiers—temporary, don't worry, perfectly safe." His tone was breezy, but the smile looked stretched, the kind a person wore when rehearsing reassurance rather than feeling it.

Quentin dragged himself along with the group, notebook tucked under his arm. His head still buzzed with sleeplessness, but the hum inside him sharpened, alert. *It was like the Pyramid itself had pricked up its ears*, he thought. Something in the air prickled, not quite sound, not quite touch.

The first accident happened suddenly.

A clatter, then a groan of metal. Everyone turned as a section of scaffolding near the Pyramid's north face wobbled, then folded like a drunk collapsing into a chair. Poles clanged, dust billowed. A pair of workers shouted and scrambled clear just in time. The crowd gasped. Phones shot into the air, recording.

"Coincidence," Hassan said quickly, clapping his hands as though that could sweep it away. "These things happen on sites. Very minor. Nobody hurt."

Sophia scribbled furiously on her clipboard. *This would go into my report*, Quentin imagined her thinking, *lips pressed thin.* Raj seized the moment: "I read an article about shoddy restoration practices. They say half the equipment here is out of date."

"Half your facts are out of date," Liam muttered, though his grin looked brittle.

Quentin's gaze snagged beyond the crowd. On the ridge of sand just past the roped boundary, a pair of figures stood. Robes, dark against the light, hoods low. Still as posts. Their faces stayed shaded in a way the sun shouldn't allow. Watching him—waiting for him to notice. His chest jolted. He blinked, and they were still there—motionless, silent, wrong against the tourist crush.

He opened his mouth, but before he could speak another commotion rippled. A worker's tool bag tumbled from a ledge, spilling chisels and hammers. The strap looked sliced, not snapped. One clattered dangerously close to a tourist's sandal. The woman shrieked; her husband swore. Hassan flustered, ushering them away.

Not a coincidence, Quentin's heart thudded. *Two accidents in minutes. It felt like intention. The Plateau itself bending to the will of unseen hands.*

The group shuffled along the rope line, Sophia flanking them like a sheepdog, Raj continuing his lecture about "occupational hazards" until even Liam rolled his eyes. Quentin tried to keep his focus forward, but the figures remained at the edge of sight. One lifted a hand briefly—no wave, just a gesture—and the vibration in Quentin's chest answered, low and sharp.

He stumbled. His scribbles slipped, pages flapping.

"You all right?" Liam asked, steadying him.

"Yeah," Quentin lied, snatching the spiral-bound evidence back. His eyes flicked again to the ridge. The figures were gone.

The third accident nearly turned deadly. The pulse in Quentin's chest tightened—one sharp beat like a warning knock. A scaffold worker hauling a plank faltered; the wood slipped, spinning end over end—straight at Quentin, then skidding toward the tourists beside him. Screams cut through the heat.

Quentin's legs moved before his brain did. He shoved Sophia sideways, the plank slamming onto the sand where she'd stood. A puff of grit rose. Sophia stared at him, pale, clipboard askew.

"Are you mad?" she snapped, breathless. "Charging about like—like—" She stopped, shaken, then finished more quietly. "You could've been hit yourself." Her words bit, but behind them her eyes still flicked once to where the plank had landed. *Fear had cracked her composure*, Quentin saw, *if only for a breath.*

The tourists clapped nervously, muttering relief, drifting back into their photo poses as though near-miss were entertainment. Hassan flustered louder: "All fine! Very safe! Please, this way!"

Quentin's heart pounded. He turned toward Aisha, searching for some reaction. She stood at the far edge of their group, hands clenched at her sides, eyes fixed on the ridge of sand where the figures had been. Her jaw was tight, lips pressed thin. *She knew*, he thought. *She had seen.* But like always, she gave nothing away.

Their eyes met for half a second. Then she looked away.

"Honestly, Quentin," Raj drawled, "if you want to play hero, at least pick a moment that isn't clearly your imagination. Equipment fails. That's all."

He wanted to shout at Raj—to point to the ridge, to demand they all see what he'd seen. But the words lodged like sand in his throat.

Instead he followed the group, dust clinging to his clothes, the pulse in his chest thrumming so violently it nearly drowned the tour guide's voice. *The Order wasn't just watching anymore*, he realized, *they were reaching.*

— Δ —

The bus rattled away from the Plateau, its fans humming against the desert heat. Inside, the air smelled of sweat, suncream, and the faint tang of dust shaken from clothes. Quentin slumped in his seat, his fingers still twitching with the urge to write what he'd seen—the robed watchers on the ridge.

He barely had time to catch his breath before Sophia turned on him.

"That was reckless," she snapped, leaning over the aisle with her clipboard clutched tight. "Charging into scaffolding chaos like some action hero! You could have been hurt. You could have gotten me hurt!"

"I saved you," Quentin blurted before he could stop himself. The words came out thin, swallowed by the whirr of the bus fans.

Sophia's eyes narrowed. "No, you caused panic." Her voice shook despite the anger. "Crowds surge. People get hurt when they surge. If you hadn't made a scene, no one would even remember that plank. You're distracting the group from the purpose of this trip."

Quentin's chest burned. "I saw them," he said, the words rushing out. "There were men—two of them—on the ridge. Watching. They're the ones behind it, I know they are."

Liam twisted around in his seat, grinning. "Mysterious robed men plotting to drop planks? Bit dramatic, mate. Sounds like the start of a dodgy film."

Raj barked a laugh. "Exactly. You're inventing conspiracies now. Next you'll say the camels are spies."

The bus rippled with uneasy amusement. Even Professor Ellis chuckled weakly, wiping his forehead with a napkin as if heat alone explained Quentin's imagination.

Quentin's ears flamed. "I'm not making it up!" He turned to the window, pointing. "They were right there—dark robes, hoods, just watching. And when the scaffolding fell, they—"

"Enough," Sophia cut in, her tone sharper than the squeal of the brakes as the bus slowed at a junction. "This trip is about cultural exchange, education, respect. Not your… ghost stories."

Her words landed like a gavel. The bus fell silent for a moment, only the hum of the fans filling the space. Quentin stared at his reflection in the glass—tired eyes, dust streaks, a boy who looked every inch the fool Raj painted him to be.

In the back row, Nia's pencil whispered. *Shh, shh, shh.* She tilted her sketchbook just enough for Quentin to glimpse it: scaffolding crumpling, dust rising, a figure standing below with his arms flung wide as a plank crashed near him. Her lines caught the chaos in eerie detail. But there was more—at the top corner, faint and deliberate, two shadowed figures on the ridge. *She saw it too*, Quentin's breath caught. But before he could speak, Raj leaned over the seat and snorted. "Sketches of drama queens. Perfect. She should draw you fainting next."

Nia didn't answer. She just closed the book softly and tucked it against her knees. Her silence was sharper than Raj's mockery.

Quentin turned, searching for support. Aisha sat two rows ahead, arms crossed, her profile sharp against the sunlight. She didn't join Sophia's scolding or Raj's sneering. She didn't look at him at all. *But her stillness felt deliberate*, he thought, *like a choice. A refusal to expose herself—or perhaps a confirmation without words.*

Sophia clicked her pen shut with finality. "We'll have no more distractions. Understood?"

Quentin sank back into his seat, his fists balled tight in his lap. *Nobody believed him*, he realized bitterly. Not Sophia, not Raj, not even Liam, whose jokes usually carried a flicker of loyalty. Only Nia's sketchbook seemed to whisper the truth, and she offered no explanation, no comfort.

The bus jolted forward. Outside, Cairo's sprawl swallowed the horizon, colorful signs and tangled alleys rushing past. Inside, Quentin's heart thudded with the hum of the Echo. *If the Order was already here, Sophia's rules and Raj's laughter wouldn't protect anyone*, he thought.

If the others refused to believe him, he decided, then he would have to find proof—proof that the danger wasn't in his imagination, but already walking in their shadow.

— Δ —

The hostel courtyard was hushed that night, a pocket of stillness cradled between pale stone walls. A single lantern buzzed above the archway, haloed with moths. The air carried the faint smell of jasmine and exhaust, Cairo's restless pulse softened but never silenced.

Quentin leaned against the cool wall, notebook on his knees, pretending to sketch the outlines of the fountain at the center. His pencil barely scratched the page—lines without shape, gestures without meaning. He wasn't drawing; he was only breathing, trying to ease the ache of being dismissed. *The bus ride's sting clung like grit in his mouth.* Nobody believed him. Nobody wanted to.

He drew a line, then another, and let them fade into scribbles. The residual resonance in his chest hadn't left. It kept time with the trickle of water, low and insistent. *It felt more insistent now*, he thought, *as though the Pyramid itself had followed him into the courtyard.*

The gate creaked. Quentin looked up sharply.

Aisha slipped through, quiet as breath, her braid tucked under a scarf. She moved with purpose, steps light but certain, heading straight for the shadows where the low growl of a kick-started engine soon muffled her footsteps. She didn't see him—or pretended not to. Her stride said she wasn't heading for the lounge or the kitchen. She was leaving.

Quentin's stomach tightened. *He should stay put. He didn't. Secrets were dangerous now, and his name was written inside them.* He thought of the robed figures on the ridge, of scaffolding splintering in the dust. He thought of the way her jaw had clenched when she'd seen them too.

Before his brain could catch up, his legs were moving. He left the notebook on the bench, shoved his hands into his hoodie pocket, and followed her through the gate.

Cairo at night was alive again—alleys strung with glowing bulbs, vendors packing up their stalls, the smell of frying dough still clinging to the air. Aisha slipped through the maze like she belonged to it. Quentin trailed at a distance, heart thudding, careful to keep in the shifting shadows.

She turned down a narrower street, lanterns thinning, voices dropping away. At the far end, under the husk of an abandoned wall, a man waited. Cloaked. Hood pulled low. Quentin froze, pressing himself into a doorway.

The two of them spoke in hushed tones. Quentin strained to hear, the words broken by the rustle of night wind. Still, fragments carried: "…the Echo awakened…" "…the boy… marked already…"

The words locked around him like shackles. His stomach lurched.

Aisha's voice, sharper than he'd ever heard it: "He doesn't understand yet. He doesn't matter yet. Leave him to me."

The hooded man tilted his head. His reply was lower, but Quentin caught the edge of it: "The Archon doesn't forgive mistakes," the man said.

A silence followed, heavy as stone. Quentin's breath snagged. He dared lean forward, just enough to glimpse Aisha's face in the spill of moonlight. Her expression was cold—calculated. *Relief curdled into betrayal,* he felt, something in him splitting at the sight. Not the mocking smirk. Not the reluctant savior. Something else entirely.

The hooded man melted back into the alley's shadow, vanishing as if he'd never been. Aisha lingered, staring at the ground, her fists clenched tight at her sides. For a moment Quentin thought she might crumple, that the mask might slip. *Her throat worked once, like she'd swallowed something sharp.* But then she straightened, armor sliding back into place. She tugged the scarf tighter and strode back toward the hostel.

Quentin pressed himself flat against the wall as she passed. She didn't see him—or chose not to.

His chest hammered. His palms burned with sweat. Every word replayed in his head: *the boy marked already. Leave him to me.* The Echo inside him pulsed, answering the words like they had been meant for it.

When she disappeared through the gate, Quentin sagged against the wall, weak with the force of it. He should confront her. He should demand answers.

But the memory of her eyes—flashing between concern and cruelty, warning and command—held him silent.

He slipped back through the streets, every sound suddenly sinister, every shadow a watcher. The vibration in his chest throbbed louder, as if mocking his foolishness.

Aisha wasn't just hiding something, he realized. *She was holding the key to it—and somehow, that key was already turning inside him.*

— Δ —

The hostel was still when Quentin returned, the kind of quiet that felt rehearsed rather than natural, like a stage frozen mid-play, props waiting, actors just offstage. He slipped through the gate, snatched his notebook from the bench, and padded inside. The courtyard lantern still buzzed with moths. No one stirred.

Upstairs, the dormitory was a tangle of breathing and shadows. Liam sprawled diagonally across his bed, one arm flung out as though fending off dreams, snores rattling steady. Raj lay stiff on his side, muttering occasionally, his blanket drawn with military neatness. Sophia had left her lamp on, a pale cone of light illuminating her clipboard and pen still in hand, as if she had fallen asleep mid-report.

Quentin shut the door with care and slid toward his bed. The hum in his chest hadn't quieted. It thudded harder, echoing every word from the alley, twisting them until they looped endlessly: *He doesn't understand yet. He's nothing. Leave him to me.*

He sat on the edge of the mattress, palms pressed against his knees, forcing himself to breathe evenly. The image of her speaking with that hooded figure replayed in a cruel loop. Her voice—calm, clipped, dangerous. Her veneer of arrogance and coolness had cracked enough to reveal something colder beneath. And yet, hadn't she saved him twice? Dragged him from the shaft? Warned him in the desert?

Quentin pressed his hands to his eyes. *Protector or traitor?* he asked himself. *Which mask was real? Or were they both?*

The scrape of pencil made him lower his hands.

In the far corner, near the window, Nia sat cross-legged with her sketchbook propped against her knees. The light from Sophia's lamp caught her profile, the tip of her tongue resting against her lip as she worked. She didn't look up as Quentin watched. The only sound was the whisper of graphite: *shh, shh, shh.*

Curiosity tugged him. He rose quietly, padding across the room, and crouched near her shoulder. Nia angled the book before he could ask.

The drawing made his breath stutter.

It was a figure—no, two figures, but one body. Half of the face shone in clean lines, light radiating outward in long strokes. The other half was swallowed in black, features obscured, the edges fraying into shadow. The two halves strained against one another but were bound by the same frame.

Quentin's throat tightened. He didn't need to ask who it was. The braid in the sketch, the sharp cheekbone, the tilt of the head—it was unmistakable. Aisha.

"She's both," Nia said softly, still drawing, as if reading his thoughts. "Light and shadow in the same outline."

If Nia could see it, then he wasn't losing his mind. The truth was just refusing to speak.

Quentin swallowed hard. "You don't know that."

"I don't choose." Her pencil traced another shadow-line across the page. "I just draw what I see."

The words slid into him colder than the night air through the cracked window. He wanted to argue, to tell her she was wrong, that people weren't drawings, weren't fixed. But the vision in the shaft came back to him—the priests chanting, the shard blazing, whispers of endurance. *The Echo had chosen him,* he thought. *Perhaps it had chosen Aisha too. Perhaps it had split her down the middle.*

He stepped back, shaking his head. "It doesn't prove anything."

Nia didn't answer. She closed the book gently, slid it beneath her pillow, and lay down without another glance.

Quentin crawled back to his own bed, his body heavy with dust and doubt. He lay staring at the ceiling, listening to Liam's snores, Sophia's steady breath, Raj's faint mutters. The ordinary world wrapped itself around him, but he could no longer wear it. Not after the alley, not after Nia's sketch.

He rolled to his side. Through the window, the Pyramid's silhouette cut the sky, dark and eternal, stars scattered above like watchful eyes.

The Order was moving, Quentin knew, *and Aisha was tied to them. They were bound now—whether as allies, enemies, or something worse.*

The uncertainty pressed on him heavier than stone, and it hit him then—the Echo inside him wasn't only marking him. It was binding him to her.

Chapter 6
The Architect's Blueprint

"A design that endures requires the removal of variables. The hinge must commit." — **Fragment of the Architect's Scroll, VI.**

— Δ —

The hostel room was thick with sleep. Liam snored in a long, uneven rhythm, occasionally muttering nonsense about camels. Raj shifted now and then with self-important sighs, as if even in dreams he needed to be right. Sophia's lamp had finally gone dark, though her clipboard rested beside her bed like a sentinel. Nia breathed quietly in the corner, a shadow hunched over her sketchbook even in sleep, pencil still in hand.

Quentin lay flat on his mattress, staring at the cracked ceiling. The hum in his chest refused to quiet. Every time he closed his eyes, the visions returned: the priests chanting, the shard sealed into stone, the hiss of Aisha's voice in the shaft. And then the alley—her words to the hooded man. *Leave him to me.*

He squeezed his eyes shut. Sleep would not come. Not tonight.

The sensible thing would be to tell someone, he thought. Sophia, perhaps. *She'd dismiss him, of course, but at least she'd have to write it down, catalogue it as a problem.* Liam might laugh it off, slap him on the back, tell him he was overthinking. Raj would mock him, turn it into another story where Quentin was the fool. And Nia… *Nia would only draw what she already saw, which might terrify him more than reassure him.*

He remembered the last sketch she had shown him—Aisha's face split into light and shadow. *If he asked now, Nia would only hand him another truth he was not ready for.*

No. None of them could carry this—not the visions, not the hum, not the mark. *It was his alone.*

He turned on his side, clutching his notebook to his chest. The word Echo burned on the page where he had written it over and over, as if repetition could make it real, or less real. His palm still tingled faintly from the wall he'd touched. *His whole body felt balanced on the edge of something*, he realized. *Destiny, or disaster.*

Fear gnawed at him. Every instinct told him to stay put, bury his head under the pillow, let the world turn without him. But the baseline vibration argued otherwise, steady as a drumbeat, a summons too patient to ignore, a voice that promised both ruin and revelation. It wasn't going to stop. Not tonight, not ever.

Quentin sat up, heart pounding. "I have to know," he whispered into the dark.

He slid from the bed, careful as a thief, pulling his hoodie over his head. The floor was cool under his bare feet until he slipped into trainers. He cast one last look around the room: Liam's open mouth, Raj's smug silhouette, Sophia's clipboard, Nia's quiet figure curled against the window. Ordinary shapes, ordinary breaths. *And then him*, he thought. *Marked, haunted, chosen by something he didn't understand.*

The ordinary and the extraordinary lived in the same room, but only one of them would walk out tonight.

He tucked his notebook into his pocket and eased the door open. The hinges creaked softly, but no one stirred.

The corridor stretched dim and silent. He padded down the stairs, the wooden steps groaning under his weight. In the courtyard, the lantern still buzzed with moths. The air was cooler now, scented faintly with jasmine and dust. The city hummed beyond the gate, alive even at this hour—car horns sharp, dogs barking, music leaking from somewhere distant. Cairo never slept.

Quentin pressed a hand to his chest, feeling the steady thrum beneath. *He could turn back*, he told himself. *Slip into bed, pretend he'd never seen the robed figures or felt the stone answer his touch. He could.*

But the thought of retreat sickened him more than the fear of what lay ahead.

He shoved the gate open and stepped into the Cairo night, the Pyramid a dark tooth on the horizon. Whatever lay waiting inside, whatever truth or danger or madness, he would face it.

For the first time since arriving, he was not being pulled, Quentin realized. *He was walking forward. Choosing.*

Choice was its own kind of load.

And far above, hidden in starlight, the Pyramid seemed to shimmer—*like it had been waiting for him to finally decide*, he thought.

— Δ —

The night guard at the Pyramid looked half-asleep, his chair tilted precariously against the wall of the ticket booth. A transistor radio muttered beside him, the melody faint under the desert wind. Quentin's palms sweated as he approached. He had no plan, no clever excuse. Only a crumpled wad of Egyptian pounds he'd stashed for souvenirs.

The guard's eyes narrowed when Quentin drifted close. "Closed," he said in accented English, voice heavy with boredom.

Quentin swallowed hard. "Just… just a quick look. For a project." His fingers shook as he offered the bills.

The guard considered him, then the money. A pause, a sigh. He plucked the notes with thick fingers, stuffed them into his pocket, and jerked his chin toward the rope. "Half an hour. No tunnels."

Quentin's heart leapt into his throat. He ducked under the rope before he could lose his nerve.

The Plateau was different at night. No tourists, no chatter, no clatter of scaffolding—only silence broken by wind curling over stone. The Pyramid loomed above him, darker than the sky, a weight so immense it seemed alive. *Every block looked sharper, more deliberate in the moonlight. As though the monument revealed a truer face when no one else was watching.* Its presence pressed into him, like it registered him now.

He found the half-sealed passage. It was the same seam from yesterday—the one his chest kept tugging toward.

The gap was narrow. Stones jutted inward like teeth. Quentin hesitated, palms slick. He'd be an idiot to try. *What if he got stuck? What if the stones shifted?*

The resonance inside him pulsed once, sharp and certain.

He pushed himself into the crack.

The limestone scraped his shoulders, tore at his sleeves. Dust filled his nose and mouth, bitter as chalk. His notebook dug into his ribs as he squeezed sideways, inch by inch. At one point the stone pressed so close he couldn't breathe properly. Panic clawed at him—images of being entombed alive, of his body never found.

"Keep going," he whispered to himself, voice muffled by stone. "Don't stop."

He shoved forward. A slab scraped his back, another caught his wrist, skin splitting shallowly. His hands stung, but he wriggled deeper, ignoring the way the passage seemed to close behind him, swallowing the faint glow of moonlight.

The silence inside was heavier than the desert outside—thick, suffocating, as though the air itself resented being disturbed.

The air thickened, hot and stale. Each breath was an effort. The hum grew louder, vibrating in his teeth now, rattling through his bones.

Finally, with a desperate shove, he spilled into a wider space. The passage dropped him to his knees on rough stone. He coughed, wiping grit from his mouth, and looked around.

The corridor was low, its ceiling jagged with unfinished stone. The walls bore faint carvings—so faint he might have missed them if his skin hadn't tingled when he brushed close. At first they looked like scratches from ancient tools, but when his eyes adjusted, he saw patterns: constellations, flowing rivers, the outline of something like an eye watching from every angle. The longer he stared, the more the lines seemed to move, bending like they were alive.

Quentin leaned against the wall, chest heaving. He was scraped raw, hands bleeding lightly, lungs aching from the crawl. Yet exhilaration coiled in him too—tight, reckless, dense. He had crossed a threshold. No tour guide, no Sophia with her clipboard, no Raj with his smug trivia—no one in his group—maybe no one in decades—had stepped into this place in centuries.

And the Pyramid was watching. He could feel it.

Quentin pushed himself upright, wiped his hands against his hoodie, and pressed deeper into the passage.

The cadence in his chest steadied into a rhythm—no longer chaotic, but purposeful. Like a drumbeat leading him somewhere—or someone.

There was no turning back now.

— Δ —

The passage narrowed until Quentin had to stoop, his shoulders brushing the rough walls. The air was hotter here, suffocating, as though he'd stepped into the lungs of the earth itself—air exhaled and never replaced. Dust swirled with each breath, clinging to his tongue.

At the end of the passage, a block loomed. Larger than the others, darker too, as though it had been cut from a deeper layer of earth. Its surface seemed smooth at first, but as Quentin stepped closer, faint lines rippled beneath the stone like veins under skin. The resonant frequency in his chest surged, a static load increasing with every heartbeat until his whole body vibrated.

He lifted his right hand. Hesitated. His mouth was dry, throat tight. *Don't touch it,* he warned himself. *Don't.*

His palm pressed flat against the stone before he realized he'd moved.

Cold hit first—sub-zero pressure snapping through his palm like a vice closing. Not burning. Loaded. Dense. It drove from his hand to his arm, straight into his chest, as if gravity itself had been dialed up inside his bones. Quentin cried out, tried to wrench his hand away, but his hand locked in place, forearm flexors firing hard, useless against the stone as if his own tendons had been clamped by an unseen mechanism. His knees buckled.

The chamber around him blurred. Darkness shattered into blinding gold.

He was standing—or thought he was—in another place, another time. A hall vast enough to swallow cathedrals, its ceiling lost in smoke. Men moved around him: the priests again, linen robes soaked with sweat, chanting in a rhythm that thudded through his bones. Their voices echoed endlessly, carrying the weight of centuries.

At the center of the hall stood the shard. Larger now, brighter—no longer a mere fragment but a blazing jewel of light, golden and molten, pulsing with impossible energy. Its radiance lit the priests' faces from below, carving their features into hollows and ridges of bone.

Quentin staggered toward it, drawn against his will.

The priests raised their arms. Their voices thundered. The shard lifted from its pedestal, floating into the air, and invisible stress-lines rippled outward, mapping themselves through walls, pillars, into the very bones of the Pyramid. Quentin's skin screamed as the stress-lines passed through him, forcing intolerable constraints into him—limits, thresholds, tolerances his body was never meant to carry.

Words branded themselves into his mind, deep and inescapable: *Endurance preserves under load. Time survives because structure does.*

He gasped. The shard flared, and suddenly centuries collapsed into him all at once. He saw desert winds tear across ages, saw dynasties rise and crumble, saw soldiers march, conquer, die, their bones buried beneath the same sand. He felt the weight of years pressing on his chest, endless time coiling around him, crushing and preserving all at once.

He screamed—or thought he did. The sound was swallowed by the chant.

The shard flared again.

A cryogenic clamp cinched through his right palm—sterile, bloodless—compressing sensation that drove through his metacarpals, packing his nerves in ice until the world felt distant. The stone floor beneath him shuddered, real again, gritty against his skin. The priests, the hall, the shard—all gone. Only the block before him remained, faintly pulsing, retreating back into silence.

Quentin dragged in ragged gulps of air, chest heaving. His right palm throbbed with a fierce density. When he dared to look, a mark burned there: faint but unmistakable, a sigil of interlocking lines pressed into his skin like a bruise made of old gold—burnished, dense, not luminous—before settling into the shape of a scar.

It was not just a wound, he realized. *It was a brand. For a fleeting instant, the lines tightened—half in gold, half in shadow—like Nia's drawing came alive beneath his skin.*

He clenched his fist. The mark tightened once in reply, a brief clamp of pressure under the skin.

The hum in his chest had changed—no longer a vibration, but a steady mechanical cycle, indifferent and exact, like a system stepping through phases.

The Echo had not merely touched him—it had claimed him.

Quentin crumpled forward onto his knees, gasping. "No… no, no, no…" His voice broke against the stone.

But the Pyramid didn't care.

The Echo of Endurance had bound itself to him, and nothing would unbind it now.

— Δ —

The chamber still rang with echoes of chanting in Quentin's head when a sharp voice cut through the fog.

"What have you done?"

Quentin flinched and spun, his scarred palm instinctively shoved behind him. Aisha stood in the passage's shadow, breath steady, dust on her sandals like she'd been behind him the whole time—her braid dark against her shoulder, her eyes wide, not with scorn this time, but with alarm that cracked through her composure.

"I—" His throat rasped raw. "I didn't—"

"You touched it," she hissed, stepping closer, her sandals scraping against stone. "Of all the foolish—" She broke off, grabbing his wrist before he could pull away. Her fingers were cool, firm, insistent. "Show me."

"No." He jerked back, but she tightened her grip with surprising strength.

"Quentin, show me!"

Her command cracked through the chamber like a whip. Against his better sense, he opened his hand.

The sigil tightened faintly in his right palm, golden lines shifting like a subcutaneous clamp. For a heartbeat, silence fell. Then Aisha inhaled sharply.

"They'll come for you now."

Her words hit harder than the vision itself. Quentin staggered back, shoving his hand against his hoodie as though hiding it could undo what had happened. "Who? Who are they?"

"The ones you saw," she said, voice clipped, as if naming them might summon them here. "The Order. The Shadow that waits. You've turned yourself into a signal, Quentin. A beacon."

Quentin's chest burned with an adrenergic flush. "You knew. You've always known. That's why you're here, isn't it?"

Her eyes flashed. "I know enough to survive. Which you clearly don't."

"Then tell me!" His voice cracked against the stone, echoing back at them both. "Tell me what this Echo is, why it's… why it's in me, why it chose me!"

Aisha froze, just for a moment. Her lips pressed tight. When she finally spoke, her voice was softer, but no less fierce. "You think it chose you? No. It doesn't work like that. The Echo isn't a gift. It's a chain. It binds. It marks. And the Order will never stop until it's theirs."

Quentin's breath hitched. *She's afraid*, he realized, seeing the weight in her eyes.

He stepped closer, trembling. "Then why warn me at all, if I'm just… if I'm just a liability to you?"

For a flicker, her tactical veneer slipped. Concern—or something too close to it—lit her eyes. Then she turned, shoulders taut, her braid snapping as she shook her head. "Because if you fall, so do the rest of us."

They stood in silence, breath loud in the still air, the weight of the Pyramid pressing down. The pressure in Quentin's palm pulsed again, faint but undeniable, like a second heartbeat tethering him to her words.

Their rivalry had sharpened into something stranger—an unwilling bond, two threads knotted by fate.

Finally, Aisha released his wrist, stepping back toward the shadows. "Get up. We need to move. You've drawn enough attention already."

Her tone was cutting, but Quentin no longer heard just disdain in it. Beneath the blade, something trembled—recognition, maybe even kinship.

Quentin pushed himself to his feet, chest still heaving. The mark in his right palm throbbed once more.

He wasn't sure what terrified him more: the thought of the Order coming for him, or the knowledge that Aisha—his fiercest critic, his strangest ally—was bound to this secret as tightly as he was.

— Δ —

The passage spat them out into the open night, both coated in dust, their breathing ragged. Cool desert air rushed over Quentin's skin, but it did little to ease the dense pressure still clamped through his palm. He flexed his hand once, quickly stuffing it into his hoodie pocket before Aisha could notice the tension crawling under his skin.

Aisha glanced back at the yawning crack in the stone, her jaw set. "That's the last time you step into a shaft without me."

Quentin bristled. "I didn't exactly invite company."

She cut him a look sharp enough to slice stone, then turned toward the plateau without answering.

They trudged down the slope in silence, the Pyramid behind them pale in the moonlight. The tourist ropes were abandoned at this hour, only the night wind sighing against the desert sands. It should have been empty. Safe.

But Quentin felt eyes on him.

At the edge of the plateau, near the scatter of rubble that once belonged to lesser tombs, a shadow shifted. Not wind, not trick of light. A man in robes, motionless save for the slow turn of his hood.

Quentin froze, heart hammering. “Aisha…”

“I see him,” she muttered, her hand brushing his sleeve as if ready to drag him back into cover.

The figure did not move closer. He merely stood, watching. Then he knelt, pressing his forehead to the sand in a gesture that felt ritualistic, reverent. Quentin’s skin crawled. He couldn’t hear the words, but he knew a message was being carried.

Far across the plateau, beyond the broken ridge, another presence stirred. The robed agent’s whisper carried on the wind, low but clear enough to scrape into Quentin’s bones:

“Marked.”

A heavier shadow emerged. Taller. Cloaked in black so deep it seemed to devour the moonlight. The man did not approach, yet his presence pressed across the sand like a stormfront. Even at this distance, Quentin could feel it—the authority, the patience, the menace.

And with a jolt, Quentin knew the name that belonged to him—*Archon Thales*. The knowledge was not learned but placed in him, as though whispered by the stone itself. The Echo didn’t show him faces—it gave him labels.

The kneeling agent lowered himself further. “He touched the stone. The freeze has taken him.”

For a moment, silence. Then Thales lifted his head. Though Quentin could not see his face beneath the hood, he felt the weight of the gaze. His chest tightened as though invisible fingers had closed around it.

Finally, a voice, smooth and quiet, cut through the night.

"Then the hunt begins." The words didn't just threaten him—they settled in his bones like a sentence already passed.

He stumbled back, bumping against Aisha's arm. She hissed, tugging him toward the shadows, urgency sparking in her eyes. They moved quickly, quietly, not daring to run lest their footsteps betray them.

By the time they slipped back through the rope and toward the faint lights of Cairo, Quentin's legs felt like water. His palm compressed steadily in his pocket, the mark awake and merciless.

He wanted to ask Aisha what the Archon's words meant, what the "hunt" entailed—but the look on her face stopped him. Her expression was too taut, too certain—like someone who had seen this before.

She already knew.

And whatever the truth was, it was worse than anything Quentin could imagine.

Chapter 7
Time Slips the Leash

"To command the current, you must first learn the direction of its collapse." — **Guardian Teaching, Scroll of the River.**

— Δ —

Morning came brassy and loud. The hostel's breakfast room thrummed with spoons against chipped bowls and the hiss of a temperamental kettle. Sunlight barged through the shutters in bold stripes, laying gold ladders across the long table. The toast was burned; the air smelled of coffee, cumin, and regret.

Quentin slid into the room late, his sleeve tugged low over his right hand, hiding the phantom cold still radiating there. The skin beneath his sleeve had indurated, the scar tissue hardening into a mechanical geometry that felt like a subcutaneous clamp. He kept his right hand tucked against his stomach and tried to look ordinary. Walk ordinary. Breathe ordinary. Every movement felt like a lie.

"Ah! Our fainting pharaoh," Liam announced from halfway down the table, where he'd engineered a leaning tower of flatbread and scrambled eggs. "No dramatic collapses planned for today, I hope. I forgot to bring my swooning couch."

"Don't start," Sophia said, twisting a lid off a jar of jam like it had personally offended her. Her clipboard sat beside her plate. "We are on a tight schedule—museum, then Coptic Cairo, then the Plateau for comparative shadows at four. Everyone will remain with the group. No detours. No heroics. No… improvisations."

Her eyes clipped to Quentin, as crisp as a stapled notice. He nodded, swallowing against a dry throat. "Right."

Raj arrived in swagger and sunglasses, hair slicked back as if cameras were hidden in the curtains. "I've arranged something special," he announced. "Local contacts. We might get access to an off-limits gallery—if you all behave."

"Local contacts," Liam echoed, deadpan. "Did you bribe a museum cat?"

"Jealousy is unbecoming," Raj said, spearing a date. His gaze snagged on Quentin's sleeve. "Sunburn?" he asked, voice oily. "Or hiding a secret handshake with the stones?"

Quentin's stomach knotted. "Sunburn," he lied. "Should've used more sunscreen."

Liam muttered, grin brittle, "Or maybe he's just allergic to being unremarkable."

Nia had claimed the end seat by the window. Her sketchbook lay open; she ate mechanically between lines, spoon hovering mid-air while her pencil moved. Quentin risked a glance. She was catching the way the steam from the kettle looped the morning light into ribbons. No people yet. Only traces of them—the curl of a sleeve, the shadow of Sophia's clipboard bisecting a plate. Quiet as ever, she seemed to draw what everyone else was too busy to see. The sight pricked him with unease; last night's sketch of him wrong—outlined in that faint metallic shimmer—still haunted his memory.

Aisha stood by the tea urn, braid pulled tight, expression unreadable. She poured without hurry. And didn't look at him. Not once. The deliberate omission stung more than a glare. Quentin's gaze flicked to her hands—steady, precise—and then away. Her silence weighed heavier than words, pressing against his ribs like a verdict. He remembered her warning that he couldn't go back—and the distance now cut sharper than any argument.

Dr. Farouk drifted through like a breeze the room respected. "Eat, all of you," she said gently. "The brain burns sugar when it is thinking hard, and we have much to think about." She squeezed Quentin's shoulder as she passed—light pressure, no questions, a small mercy.

Professor Ellis followed with his napkin already tucked, cheerfully oblivious. "Hydration, team! The desert is famously dry. That is its whole personality. Drink, drink."

Sophia cleared her throat. "Attendance," she said. "Say 'here' when I call—"

"We're not eight," Liam protested. "I can spell my own name."

"Attendance," Sophia repeated.

Laughter skittered around the table, thin but serviceable. Quentin murmured "here" when prompted and chased dry bread with water. The pressure in his palm synced with the second hand on the wall clock—*tap, tap, tap*—until he couldn't tell whether the noise came from the clock or from himself.

"Right," Sophia said, snapping her pen cap shut. "Bags. Hats. Sunscreen. Liam, that includes you, even if you believe you're immune due to 'Irish charm.'"

"Alas," Liam said, standing with a theatrical groan, "my freckles say otherwise."

Raj slung his bag with a flourish. "Let's not embarrass ourselves today."

Quentin rose too quickly; the room swayed, sunlight tilting on its ladders. He steadied himself on the table. The mark pulsed—once, twice—like a name being called. He forced a smile, pretending not to notice the careful space the others left around him, a moat dug by their caution.

Aisha brushed past, tea in hand. For a heartbeat, the steam curled between them. She kept her gaze ahead, but her voice, so soft he almost missed it, threaded the gap: "Keep your sleeve down."

Quentin's breath snagged. He didn't turn. "I know."

"Good," she said, and moved on, leaving a sterile chill in her wake.

Normal, he told himself, *shouldering his bag. Just be normal.*

But the mark disagreed, ticking like a hidden clock as the group filed toward the door—and beyond it, into the waiting day.

— Δ —

The bus groaned as it pulled away from the hostel, its windows rattling with every bump in the road. Inside, the group slumped into their usual places: Liam sprawled at the back, Sophia stationed near the front with her clipboard already in hand, Raj holding court two rows behind her, and Nia tucked by the window with pencil poised. The smell of petrol and warm vinyl filled the air, overlaid by the faint sweetness of the pastries Dr. Farouk had pressed into their hands as they boarded. Aisha sat in the aisle seat near the middle, back straight, gaze on the door each time it hissed shut, as if counting exits.

Quentin sat in the middle row, forehead pressed against the cool glass. He told himself to focus on the ordinary—the blur of Cairo's streets, the vendors hawking fruit, the sharp scent of spices drifting through open doorways. But the mundane no longer belonged to him. The world came at him in edges—too bright, too sharp, too slow. His right sleeve stayed tugged low over his palm; the skin beneath throbbed in a small, stubborn rhythm, the bus carrying an extra heartbeat only he could hear.

As the bus swayed around a corner, a boy in the street dropped a paper cup. Quentin's perception stuttered—an ugly frame-skip—like his visual cortex had missed a beat. The cup seemed to hang, not because the world slowed, but because his processing lagged just enough to make motion look segmented: drop, drift, tilt—too crisp, too countable.

Then his system caught up. The cup smacked the pavement. Water splattered the bus window. No one else reacted.

Quentin dragged his sleeve over his mouth, his mind racing through a differential diagnosis for the sensory lag: post-ictal dissociation or a hemodynamic glitch in his visual cortex. *What was happening to him?*

"Mate, you look like you've seen a ghost," Liam said, peering over the seat with a grin. "Don't worry, we'll keep the fainting couches handy."

Quentin forced a laugh, but his hands trembled against his knees. He clenched them into fists, feeling the pressure of the mark pulsing beneath his skin. The pulse synced for a beat with the windshield wipers, then with the indicator's tick, as if the Echo were testing instruments for a band only he could hear.

Raj, oblivious, was regaling Sophia with a monologue. "I told you, the alignment of the Pyramid isn't accidental. I have sources, serious ones. Locals. They say there's an underground passage no tourist has ever seen."

Sophia rolled her eyes. "Raj, if your 'sources' are YouTube conspiracy videos, then—"

"Jealous, because I'm ahead of the game," he said smugly.

Quentin sank deeper into his seat, the vibration in his chest building like static. He dared a glance toward the back of the bus. Nia's sketchbook was open, her pencil moving in slow, deliberate strokes. She tilted the page, and Quentin's stomach dropped.

It was him.

Not just him sitting quietly, but him haloed in a faint shimmer, thin metallic lines curling around his outline like he was charged from within. She had drawn his eyes too, wide and startled, capturing the exact stuttered instant when his perception skipped a frame.

His throat went dry. He mouthed, "Why?"

Nia didn't answer. She just met his gaze, then tapped her pencil once against the shimmering outline—*you, this*. Her expression didn't gloat or pity; it assessed, as if she'd been expecting the shimmer to arrive and had simply been waiting to catch it on paper.

Quentin jerked his eyes away, heart racing. He pressed his marked hand harder into his hoodie pocket, as though he could smother whatever force had chosen him. But the more he tried to ignore it, the sharper the world became—the ticking of the dashboard clock too loud, the whine of the bus engine almost musical in its precision, the colors outside burning too bright. Every sense was stretched taut, as if reality itself had tuned to the rhythm inside his chest.

"Correction, team," Sophia called, glancing from her phone to the aisle. "Permit window changed—Plateau first, museum after lunch, then Coptic Cairo if time allows. Stay with the group." Dr. Farouk nodded once, unbothered, as if the new order were merely a different path to the same lesson.

"Back to Giza first, then museum," Professor Ellis called from the front, cheerful as ever. "Plenty of stones to admire, plenty of sun to burn your necks, and remember—hydration, team!"

The students groaned in unison, but Quentin hardly heard them. His heartbeat didn't feel like his anymore—more like a cadence borrowed from the Pyramid, paced by the Echo. Across the aisle, Aisha's gaze skimmed his sleeve and away; under the noise, her voice cut soft and flat: "Keep it covered." Quentin gave the smallest nod.

The bus rattled on, but Quentin felt as though he was already out of step with time itself. Outside, a street mirror flashed their reflection; for an instant Quentin thought he saw a hooded shape in the rear seats where there was no one—just glare on glass. He shut his eyes until the afterimage faded. When he opened them, the city kept streaming past like a film he wasn't quite in anymore.

— Δ —

The bus hissed to a stop at the edge of the Giza Plateau. Students spilled out, squinting in the glare, adjusting hats and sunglasses, rummaging for sunscreen. The air was thick with heat already, the sand glaring like shards of glass beneath the morning sun.

Quentin lagged behind, his sleeve still tugged low, trying to quiet the restless internal cycle beneath his skin. He wanted to disappear into the group, to be just another student fumbling with his water bottle. But he couldn't shake the sense that laughter bent away from him, that chatter skipped over him, as if the group itself had decided he didn't quite belong. Even the space around him seemed deliberate, as though the others were unconsciously giving him a wider berth.

Raj leaned close to Sophia as they walked ahead. Quentin wasn't meant to hear, but the desert carried sound, thin and clear.

"You've noticed it too, haven't you?" Raj murmured, smugness curling his words. "He keeps wandering off. Collapsing, sneaking about. He's not reliable."

Sophia pressed her lips thin. "He's… a distraction," she admitted reluctantly. "And this programme doesn't need distractions. We have a schedule, Raj. A reputation."

Raj smirked, triumphant. "Exactly. Someone has to keep the group on track. Someone dependable." He straightened, puffing his chest, as if rehearsing for leadership no one had asked him to claim.

Quentin's stomach dropped. He stumbled on a loose stone, the world tilting for a moment. Their words stung more than the mark in his palm. He wanted to shout at them, to demand they see what he had seen—visions of priests, shadows in the sand, the Order watching. Instead he bit his tongue until he tasted iron. *What proof did he have, besides dreams and dread?*

Liam bounded between them, cheerfully oblivious. "Right then, shall we get our pharaoh selfies in early, before Raj declares himself king of Cairo? I'd pay good money to see him wrapped in toilet paper as a mummy."

Sophia rolled her eyes but bit back a smile. "We're here for education, not spectacle."

Raj sniffed. "I'd make a very dignified pharaoh."

"Yeah," Liam said, "if pharaohs were known for snoring through lectures."

A ripple of chuckling moved through the group, but it broke quickly, fading under the weight of the sun and Sophia's sharp glance at Quentin, lingering just long enough to sting. Even Liam's grin faltered for a second before he masked it with another joke.

Nia trailed behind them all, sketchbook hugged to her chest. Quentin caught her eye, desperate for something steady. She didn't smile, but she didn't look away either. Her quiet gaze was unreadable, yet it steadied him more than any laugh or kind word could. Her fingers tapped once against the spine of the sketchbook, as though telling him she still saw what the others refused to.

Aisha, however, was the hardest to read. She stood near the base of the Pyramid, her arms crossed, gaze fixed not on the students but on the horizon. Her profile was sharp, carved against the blazing sky, and for a moment Quentin thought she was deliberately ignoring the whispers, the shifting loyalties. But then she glanced back at him—briefly, just long enough for their eyes to lock.

Her expression was unreadable. Not mockery, not sympathy. Something else. A calculation. A silent question: "Is he ready to carry this, or will he crumble?"

Quentin dropped his gaze first. The heat pressed heavier against his shoulders.

Professor Ellis clapped his hands together, oblivious to the tension. "Right, students! Time to marvel at human achievement—one stone at a time!" His grin was bright, his shirt already damp with sweat. Dr. Farouk adjusted her hat, her gaze sweeping the group more keenly, pausing a fraction too long on Quentin before moving on. Unlike Ellis, she seemed to notice the way the group's strained giggles had thinned, but she said nothing.

The chatter resumed, shallow and uneven, but Quentin's ears rang with Raj's words, Sophia's reluctant agreement. *A distraction. Unreliable.*

He tightened his fist in his pocket, the mark pulsing with a numbing density. The world around him wavered again—the movement of the crowd stretching, sound dragging, a bird overhead seeming to stall mid-flap for half a heartbeat—an after-image his brain couldn't reconcile fast enough—before it snapped forward again.

Quentin blinked hard, heart hammering. No one else noticed.

He wanted to scream. But instead, he walked in silence, the Pyramid looming larger ahead.

And in the spaces between footsteps, he wondered if Aisha's gaze had been warning—or promise.

— Δ —

The Plateau buzzed with tourists, their chatter a dozen languages weaving into the dry wind. Vendors hawked postcards and bottled water, children darted between groups with trinkets. The air smelled of sweat, dust, and the faint tang of baked limestone.

Quentin drifted a little apart, shielding his eyes against the blaze. He tried to focus on Professor Ellis, who was waxing lyrical about "ancient engineering marvels," but his attention kept sliding away, tugged by that low cadence in his chest. It wasn't pain—not exactly—but a pressure, like the world was holding its breath. Something was wrong.

He scanned the crowd.

At first, nothing: a cluster of Germans in floppy hats, a family corralling children with melting ice creams, a tour guide waving a flag. Baseline. Harmless.

And then he saw them.

Two men at the far edge of the throng, standing too still, too quiet. Their robes were the color of sand, blending neatly with the landscape. Faces shadowed by hoods. They weren't taking photos, weren't fanning themselves, weren't moving at all. Just watching. Watching him.

The residual resonance in his chest surged, a pathological alarm he couldn't silence.

"Do you see them?" Quentin hissed to Liam, who was snapping selfies with the Pyramid at impossible angles.

"See what?"

"There—by the wall." Quentin pointed, hand trembling despite himself.

Liam squinted, then snorted. "Ah yes, the secret ninja squad. Blending in perfectly, except they forgot their invisibility cloaks." He clapped Quentin on the shoulder. "Relax, mate. Cairo's full of oddballs. No need to invent a cult following."

A few students nearby chuckled, the tension dissolving into casual mockery. Quentin's face burned. He opened his mouth to protest, but the robed men had already slipped back, swallowed by the milling crowd. As if they'd never been there.

"See?" Liam grinned. "Paranoid. You need more sleep."

Raj overheard and added with a smirk, "Or fewer conspiracy theories."

Sophia frowned, clearly annoyed by the disruption. "Stay focused, Quentin. This isn't the time." She flipped a page on her clipboard as if to punctuate her point, already moving on.

Quentin clenched his fists, nails biting his palms. The mark pulsed once in reply, dense against his skin. *Not the time? If not now—when they're right there—then when? When they're standing over them?*

But no one else believed.

No one except—

Aisha.

She lingered at the edge of the group, gaze tilted not at the Pyramid, not at Professor Ellis, but at the same patch of shadow where the robed figures had stood. For a heartbeat, her practiced stillness slipped—her lips pressed thin, her shoulders taut. She had seen them too. He knew it.

Their eyes met.

She looked away at once, folding her arms across her chest, her face composed again. Her braid shifted with the movement, hiding her expression, but Quentin had already caught the truth.

Quentin's stomach twisted. She wouldn't admit it. Not to him. Not to anyone. But silence, he realized, could be its own confession.

The group shuffled on, Dr. Farouk shepherding them toward the next marker, Professor Ellis droning happily. The tourists blurred back into harmless color and sound.

But Quentin's chest thrummed, relentless. The Order was here, walking among them, and he was the only one who could feel their gaze.

The others laughed at shadows. Aisha looked at them in silence.

And Quentin wondered how long it would be before shadows stopped watching—and started moving.

— Δ —

The hostel rooftop caught the day's last light like a shallow bowl. The city sprawled below, restless and unending, its calls to prayer rising and folding into the whirr of traffic. The air smelled faintly of smoke and bread baking, a sweetness buried beneath the grit of dust.

Quentin sat cross-legged near the low wall, notebook open on his lap. He wasn't writing, not really—just dragging his pencil over the page, sketching the same shape again and again: the Pyramid, jagged under a setting sun. Each sketch came out darker, its angles harder, until it looked less like stone and more like a wound on the horizon. His marked right palm rested against his knee, pulsing faintly. Every throb felt like a reminder, a clock ticking toward something inevitable. The sound of tittering drifted faintly from the hostel windows below, usual life buzzing on, while he sat apart.

The roof door creaked open. Footsteps soft, deliberate. He didn't look up.

Aisha crossed the roof with unhurried grace, her braid glinting with strands of copper in the sunset. She leaned against the railing, arms folded, eyes fixed on the horizon. For a long moment, silence stretched between them. Only the city spoke.

"You can't go back," she said at last. Her voice was low, almost swallowed by the evening wind.

Quentin's pencil stilled. He turned his head, but she still hadn't looked at him. "What do you mean?"

"You know what I mean." Her gaze flicked, just once, to his sleeve-covered hand. "Not after what happened in there. Not after it marked you."

Quentin swallowed, throat dry. He wanted to ask her why she was here, why she hadn't told the others what she knew, why her eyes sometimes flashed with recognition when he caught her off guard. Instead, the words tumbled out rough: "Then tell me what I am."

Aisha's lips pressed into a thin line. For a heartbeat, something raw flickered in her expression—fear, maybe, or pity—but it vanished as quickly as it came. She shook her head. "If you're asking me to name it, I can't. Not yet. But I know this: you don't get to be mundane anymore."

The words struck like a verdict, heavier than any warning she'd given before.

Frustration rose tight in Quentin's chest. "You always say that. Cryptic warnings, half-truths, acting like you're two steps ahead. Why won't you just tell me?"

Her eyes finally met his, sharp as a blade. "Because knowing too soon might kill you."

The words chilled him more than the night air. He opened his mouth to press further, but she pushed off the railing, straightening, her silhouette bisecting the amber light with surgical precision.

"Get some sleep," she said. "Tomorrow, it'll pull when you least expect it."

She turned and walked toward the door, each step quiet, measured. For a moment, Quentin thought she might glance back—some signal, some sign. She didn't. The door clicked shut behind her, leaving the roof suddenly vast and empty.

Quentin sat frozen, pencil still against the page. The city below carried on—vendors shouting, horns blaring, children laughing. The world hadn't changed, not for them. But for him, it had tilted, the ground beneath his feet angled toward something he couldn't yet see.

He looked down at his notebook. His last sketch of the Pyramid seemed different now—its edges sharper, its shadow longer. He pressed his palm against it, and a dull sub-zero pressure bled through the paper. It lingered a second longer than before, a faint branching tension spidering across the page—creases that weren't there, only felt—before the paper relaxed. Quentin yanked his hand back as if a cryogenic clamp had cinched again, his palpitations climbing into his throat.

Aisha was right. He couldn't go back. Not after this.

The sun slipped below the horizon, and Cairo lit up like a river of stars. Quentin stared into the darkening sky, the pressure rhythm in his chest steady—indifferent.

Whatever he was becoming, it was already too late to stop. Aisha had left him with a verdict she wouldn't say out loud, and that choice now welded their paths together.

Chapter 8

A Choice on the Dunes

"Two masters stand before every soul: the purpose of the structure, or the freedom of the fracture." — **Fragment of the Architect's Scroll, IX.**

— Δ —

The camels knelt like ships in dry dock, chewing with lordly boredom while the morning blew across the flats. The caravan guide—broad-shouldered, sun-browned, moustache like a brushstroke—introduced them to their mounts with the patience of someone who'd stopped being surprised by tourists. "He is Mahmoud," he told Liam, patting a camel who regarded the world with ancient disdain. "Very calm. Very good." Mahmoud chose that moment to burble a wet complaint.

"Very good," Liam echoed, eyeing the saddle as if it might bite. "Yes, I can tell. Friendly eyes. Full of murder."

Sophia adjusted her helmet with the grim righteousness of someone who'd brought her own. "Helmets are optional," she announced to no one in particular, "but sensible. Hands on the horn when mounting, feet flat, do not attempt tricks."

"Perish the thought," Liam said, attempting to swing his leg over and accidentally kneeing Mahmoud in the hump. The camel groaned like a wronged patriarch.

Raj mounted with theatrical ease, swaying into the saddle as if born to it. "Balance," he called back, smug as a lighthouse. "All in the hips. Don't fight the motion; become one with it."

"Truly," Liam muttered, "your wisdom is a gift to mankind."

Quentin gripped the wooden pommel and breathed through the strange heave of the camel beneath him. The smell was warm hay and sun-baked wool; the saddle creaked a dry complaint. Beyond the last heaps of tourist buses, the desert opened like a blank page—no city noise, just wind combing the sand and the slow grunt of animals standing. The Pyramid shouldered the horizon behind them, a black wedge against a rinsed sky.

Aisha rode near the front, straight-backed, braid tucked beneath a scarf. She didn't look back. Her camel carried her with an unsettling calm, as if the two shared a secret cadence. Even here, where the others joked and flailed, she seemed untouched by awkwardness, as though the desert itself steadied her. Dr. Farouk rode not far behind, speaking easily with the caravan guide in Arabic, her laughter snipping the wind into smaller, softer pieces. Professor Ellis had somehow arranged his scarf into a heroic, if lopsided, drape, and was already sweating through it.

The caravan bell jingled, and they set off, a slow sway-sway that settled into Quentin's hips like a lullaby. He tried to let the motion soothe him. Tried to be ordinary. But the world felt too exposed. Every grain of sand snapped into focus, too sharp to look at for long. The internal cycle in his chest didn't quiet out here; it spread, as if the desert itself were tuned to the same note.

"Tell me again why we're doing this?" Liam called, voice riding the wind. "Because I'd like to nominate the air-conditioned museum for all future excursions."

"Because," Sophia replied, "context matters. Landscape shapes history. And we have a schedule."

"Ah, the true wonder of the ancient world: Sophia's schedule."

They rode between low ruins crumbled to their knees—broken walls like old teeth, a scatter of blocks skirted by wind. The caravan guide pointed out faint lines where ancient paths had scored the earth, half-swallowed and still refusing to vanish.

Nia held her sketchbook one-handed, pencil dancing while her other hand smoothed the page against the breeze. Her strokes captured emptiness itself—the horizon pressing down, the way ruins dissolved into sand. She seemed intent on drawing what others ignored.

"Eyes up," Sophia called. "Don't drift. Keep the formation… Raj, that does not mean ride ahead."

Raj, of course, rode ahead. "Just scouting," he said, and lifted his chin toward Aisha's lead as if it were a flag only he could follow.

Quentin glanced back. The city had shrunk to a smudge, its noises swallowed. The wind ran fingers through the dunes in long strokes. For a moment, a strange calm unspooled inside him. Then the hair on his arms prickled.

He twisted in the saddle. Far behind, near the last toothy outcrop of stone, something moved. Not the commonly deceitful dance of distance; this was deliberate. A pair of figures on foot, robes tugged by the wind, cresting a low ridge and then vanishing. The hum inside him tightened to a wire.

"Liam," he said, throat suddenly dry. "Do you—" He swallowed. "Never mind."

"Do I what?" Liam nudged Mahmoud, who protested with a gargle.

"Nothing." Quentin faced forward, shame flaring, only to be quenched by a sudden, sterile chill from his palm. *Every time he pointed, the shadows would slip away, leaving him the fool.* Yet the feeling remained: the sense of being measured from afar, of footfalls placed in their wake like punctuation.

Aisha's silhouette tilted. *She had seen something too*, he felt rather than observed. The slight half-turn of her head, the cadence of her camel's breathing faltering for a beat. But she didn't call out. She kept pace. She simply adjusted her scarf as if warding off the wind and rode on. *Her silence was confirmation*, he thought, *and it chilled him more than denial would have.*

They crested a rise and the desert let them see a little farther: a scatter of low stones, a hint of collapsed doorway, the suggestion of a square ground-plan etched by time. The caravan guide lifted an arm. "Small temple," he called back. "Old. No danger. We stop for shade."

Shade meant a sliver of wall that pretended to shelter. The camels sank with grateful groans, legs folding like complicated furniture. Students slid down with varying degrees of grace—Liam dismounting as if leaping from a burning building, Sophia like a soldier following a manual, Raj with a flourish that invited applause and received precisely none.

Quentin's feet hit sand and the earth's quiet returned like a held breath. He wiped his palms on his jeans, sleeve still tugged over the indurated scar that had altered everything. The ruins squatted, patient, half-buried stories leaking from their stones.

Aisha didn't join the others as they crowded around Professor Ellis for water. She drifted toward the far side of the ruin, her eyes scanning the broken lintels with a wary, focused intensity. She disappeared behind a high, crumbling wall before Quentin could even look away.

The desert was vast—and sound carried cleanly. Somewhere behind them, footsteps still matched their pauses.

— Δ —

The ruin was little more than a scatter of walls, their stones cracked and pitted, corners leaning as though they had been tired for centuries. Wind teased sand through gaps, carrying the faint smell of dust and something metallic, old as bone.

The students fanned out with the usual bustle. Sophia unpacked her checklist, dutiful as ever, reminding everyone not to climb. Liam immediately climbed anyway. Raj strode about with sweeping gestures. Nia crouched near the base of a wall, sketchbook balanced against her knees. She looked as though she was uncovering underlying load-bearing schematics hidden inside the ruin rather than inventing them.

Quentin hung back. His pulse hadn't slowed since the caravan ride. The mark in his right palm corded, the scar tissue hardening into a dense, sub-zero knot that matched the ruin's low-frequency hum, waiting for him. He wandered along the shadowed side of the stones, fingertips brushing pitted limestone, his nerves registering the structural decay.

He wasn't alone.

At first, he thought the man was part of the tour—a guide left behind, perhaps. But the figure who stood in the shadow of a collapsed doorway looked too old, too worn, too still. His robe was the color of sand, his beard silver and tangled. His eyes caught the light strangely, holding it like cold slag—not reflecting, just densely absorbing the light.

"You shouldn't be here," Quentin said automatically, his voice too small in the desert silence.

The man smiled faintly, lines deepening around his mouth. "And yet, here we both are." His voice was rough, like stone dragged across stone. He tilted his head. "You've touched it, haven't you? The Echo."

Quentin's pulse jumped into a narrow, fast run. "What did you just say?"

The old man stepped closer, slow as drifting sand. "The Seven Wonders hold what was scattered. The Shards were split and hidden in places the world would never forget. The Echoes are how the Wonder talks back—how it rewrites a body to bear what stone was built to hold. And Guardians... we are assigned to the load, to watch the seams."

The word Echoes rang in Quentin's ears like a bell strike. He took a step back, but his heel found only sand. "I—I don't know what you're talking about."

"You do," the man said gently. His eyes flicked to Quentin's covered hand. "It presses, doesn't it? Endurance. The first Echo. Load-buffering. Threshold rewrite. Now bound into your blood."

Quentin's throat tightened. He tugged his sleeve lower. "How do you know this?"

"Because I was set to wait," the man said. "To speak when the time came. To remind the marked that the Wonders are not trophies. They are chains as much as they are shields." His gaze darkened, heavy as stone-set shade. "If shadow unites them, the world bends to its will. That cannot be allowed."

The desert pressed closer, the wind dying into stillness. Quentin's chest rattled with each breath. He whispered, "Why me?"

"I can't tell you why," the Guardian said softly. "Only what follows."

The Guardian's smile was sad. "Because the system found you, boy. Not I. Not the Order. The structure did."

For a heartbeat, Quentin felt the desert tilt, the ruin sway around him. He saw again the vision of priests chanting, the shard freezing into his palm, a cryogenic weight that nulled the desert entirely, the weight of centuries pressing down. He stumbled back, clutching his scarred hand to his chest, shaking his head. *He had to fling these words away.*

The old man didn't follow. He only raised a hand in a gesture halfway between blessing and farewell. "Guard your heart. Trust your endurance. And remember—shadows do not sleep. They are already moving."

Then the Guardian turned, robe catching the wind, and slipped behind the ruin's broken stones. Quentin realized he'd never had a clean line of sight through the ruin—just corridors of shadow and broken lintels, angles that let a man appear and disappear without ever crossing open sand.

Quentin stared after him, chest heaving, the sigil in his palm pressing steady as a brand. *Seven Wonders. Scattered power. Chains, not gifts.*

The others' voices drifted faintly around the corner—normal, ordinary sounds. *But his sense of normal had cracked open*, Quentin realized. *And through the crack, something engineered whispered.*

— Δ —

Quentin staggered out from the shadow of the collapsed doorway, his pulse still rattling in a tachycardic burst. The Guardian's words clung to him: *Seven Wonders. Scattered shards. Endurance. Load-buffering. Threshold rewrite.* His palm still pressed beneath the sleeve, the mark answering some ancient rhythm he hadn't asked for.

He leaned against a wall, trying to slow his breath. "This is madness," he whispered. "I'm losing it."

A voice slid into the silence. "What did he tell you?"

Quentin whipped around. Aisha stood a few feet away, framed by broken stone and sky. Her arms were crossed, her shadow long across the sand. Her eyes weren't mocking; they were tactically clinical, scanning him for signs of structural failure.

"You—how long have you been there?" Quentin's words stumbled over themselves.

"Long enough." She stepped forward, her braid shifting against her shoulder. "Don't waste time pretending. The old man. What did he say to you?"

Quentin's stomach knotted. "You mean… the Guardian?"

At that, something flickered across her face. Recognition. And unease. She smothered it quickly, but Quentin saw it.

"He said things," Quentin blurted, frustration boiling. "Things about… the Wonders. About what's inside the Pyramid. The Echo of Endurance." He jerked his sleeve lower. "He knew about this."

Aisha's gaze snapped to his hand. For a second, she looked almost… afraid. Then she suppressed the reflex with a sharp, tactical scoff. "Of course he did. That's their purpose. Guardians exist to wait—for fools who wake what should've stayed buried."

"What do you mean, Guardians?" Quentin demanded. "How do you know about him? About any of this?"

Her jaw tightened. She looked past him, toward the horizon, refusing to answer.

From somewhere behind the collapsed wall, the Guardian's voice carried—gravel and stone: "Two paths stand before you, child. Only one carries light."

Aisha froze. Quentin twisted around. The old man stood again in the ruin's shadow, watching them both. His gaze softened on Quentin, then settled on Aisha with the tired sorrow of someone watching a pattern repeat. "Your choices will shape more than yourself," he said. "But some paths end only in shadow."

Aisha's lips pressed into a hard line. Her shoulders squared as though bracing against a blow. Her reply cut sharper than before. "Save your riddles. I know exactly where I'm walking."

The Guardian dipped his head, sadness deepening the lines of his face. "Then may you have the endurance to bear it."

Wind swept the sand between them. When Quentin blinked, the old man was no longer in the opening—only broken stone and wind, as if he'd simply stepped back into a corridor Quentin couldn't see.

He turned back to Aisha, pulse hammering. "What was that? Why did he talk to you like that? What aren't you telling me?"

Her expression shuttered. "It doesn't matter."

"It matters to me," Quentin shot back. "I deserve to know what I'm tangled in."

She stepped closer, eyes flashing. "Deserve?" Her voice was flint. "You stumbled into this—you, with your nerves—and now the Echo has you under load. If you're not careful, you'll drag the rest of us into the dark with you."

Her words cut deep. Quentin wanted to argue, to demand answers, to tear away whatever walls she kept around her. But the fire in her eyes warned him off.

With a sharp turn, Aisha strode away, her figure slicing through the ruin's shadows until she disappeared into the sunlight.

Quentin stood alone. He pressed his hand against his chest, feeling the crushing, static load of the Echo. *Was Aisha warning him out of fear—or shielding him with silence?* he asked himself. *Was she already standing on the side of shadow?* The question gnawed at him, heavier than the Guardian's riddles, heavier even than the weight of the sigil itself.

By the time he rounded the corner of the temple to rejoin the group, Aisha was already there, standing by Dr. Farouk, calmly sipping from a canteen as if she hadn't just been speaking to a man who knew how to use the ruin's blind angles. She didn't look at him, but the stiff set of her shoulders told him the conversation wasn't over.

— Δ —

The ride back toward Cairo jolted in time with the camels' swaying gait, hooves thudding against the hard-packed sand. The sun sagged low, smearing orange and violet across the horizon, while the Plateau behind them shrank into a jagged silhouette.

Quentin kept to himself. The Guardian's words still rang in his skull, each phrase sharp as chiseled stone: *Seven Wonders. Echoes scattered. Endurance bound into load. If shadow unites them…* He tugged his sleeve lower, hiding the faint shimmer that pulsed in his right palm, but concealment did nothing to quiet the truth pressing beneath.

Aisha rode at the very back of the line, a shadow trailing the group. She didn't join the chatter or lean in to hear Raj's posturing. She simply sat straight in her saddle, eyes scanning the dunes they had already passed, as if watching for the very footsteps Quentin feared.

Up ahead, Sophia rode with her usual posture of precision, back rigid, reins neatly gathered in both hands. Her clipboard was finally stowed, but her air of command hadn't loosened with the straps. Raj angled his camel closer, leaning toward her with the careful tilt of someone confiding.

"Don't you think Quentin's baseline has shifted?" His voice was pitched low, meant for her and no one else. "Always slipping away, wandering where he shouldn't. First the fainting, then the scaffolding. And today—he disappeared at the ruin without explanation."

Sophia's brow creased. She shifted her grip on the saddle horn, gaze flicking back along the line. "He is unpredictable," she admitted reluctantly. "And it disrupts the group dynamic."

Raj nodded gravely, as though confirming her thought rather than planting it. "Exactly. A liability. If the programme looks sloppy, we look sloppy. We're here to represent our universities. Not to chase after his little dramas."

Sophia's mouth tightened. She didn't agree, not fully—not yet—but the idea lodged. "He's not… bad. Just distracted."

"Distracted," Raj echoed smoothly, lips curving. "Or something else. Either way, it reflects on all of us."

Behind them, Liam groaned theatrically, shifting in his saddle as though fighting an invisible tide. "If this camel sways any more, I'll be seasick. Horses are saints compared to these lurching monsters."

The complaint cracked the moment. A ripple of laughter drifted down the caravan, even tugging a reluctant smile from Sophia. Professor Ellis launched into a cheerful tangent about "the natural rhythm of the desert beast," while Dr. Farouk soothed her camel with a pat and a murmur of Arabic.

But Raj leaned back in his saddle, satisfaction glittering in his eyes. His seed had been planted. And seeds, if tended, would sprout into suspicion.

Quentin rode near the rear, far enough not to catch the words but close enough to feel their weight. Sophia's gaze flicked toward him now and then—measuring, uncertain. Each glance landed between his shoulder blades like a knife tip. He didn't need to hear what Raj had whispered to know it wasn't in his favor.

The desert stretched endlessly on, dunes burning under the last of the sun, the city still distant smudge on the horizon. The camels trudged in rhythm with the thrum in Quentin's chest, that strange pulse that no one else could hear.

Raj straightened in his saddle, a picture of balance and ease, his scarf tugged neatly against the wind. He looked every bit the dependable student, the natural leader he imagined himself to be. A smile ghosted across his lips. *He was weaving a story*, Quentin realized.

Quentin clenched his jaw, fingers tightening on the reins. He didn't know the details of Raj's game, but he knew the truth of it: *whatever narrative was being spun, he was at the center.*

The sigil in his right palm pressed denser. *The desert was not the only place turning against him*, Quentin felt with a sinking heart.

— Δ —

That night, Cairo hummed below the hostel like a restless hive—horns bleating, voices rising, the smell of spice and smoke drifting upward on the night air. On the balcony, Quentin sat hunched over his notebook, the pages blotched with smudges of graphite and sweat. The mark in his right palm tightened when he pressed it to the paper. *His sketches were being claimed by whatever had bound itself to him*, he thought.

He wrote the words again, scrawled until the lines blurred: *Seven Wonders. Scattered Echoes. If shadow unites them, the world bends to its will.*

The Guardian's voice haunted each syllable. Every time Quentin replayed it, he swore the man's eyes held more detail in his memory—sharper, colder—as though the Echo itself was sharpening what he saw. He slammed the book shut, chest heaving.

He leaned over the railing, Cairo sprawling like a sea of lights. From here, the city seemed endless, alive in ways he couldn't touch. And yet, above it all, black against the stars, the Pyramid crouched. *Watching. Waiting.*

"Why me?" Quentin whispered into the night. "Why not anyone else?"

The wind offered no answer.

He rubbed his face with both hands, his sleeve slipping back. The interface pressed again, unyielding and exact. He clenched his fist, as if he could bury it into his palm, but it pressed harder in defiance.

A rustle of movement caught his eye.

Down in the courtyard, a figure slipped through the gate with practiced quiet. Aisha. Her braid gleamed faintly in the lamplight as she pulled her scarf tighter and melted into the shadows of the street.

Quentin's breath snagged. *She was leaving again. Off to meet… who?* The Guardian's warning about her echoed in his head: "Your choices will shape more than yourself."

His body twitched to move. He should follow her, confront her, demand the truth she kept dangling like a knife above him. He pictured himself cornering her in some alley, words like pressure spilling out, her mask finally breaking. He should—but his feet stayed rooted. Fear pinned him, cold and sharp. Not just fear of her—fear of what he might learn. Fear of confirming the worst: *that she wasn't just tangled in the prophecy, but bound to the Shadow Order itself.*

A motorbike roared past the street below, its headlamp catching the edge of her scarf before she vanished completely. The image stamped itself into Quentin's mind—her slipping into the dark while he stood motionless above, powerless.

He backed away from the railing, pressing his notebook to his chest. The night stretched taut around him, every sound sharpened—the hum of a motorbike below, the cry of a stray dog, the faint scrape of Aisha's sandals fading into the city's labyrinth.

Quentin closed his eyes. He wanted answers more than anything, but tonight the weight of the unknown pressed heavier than his courage. Even the Echo inside him seemed to mock him now, thrumming not like a guide but like a clock counting down. He sank onto the balcony floor, knees to his chest, notebook clutched like a shield.

Far above, stars drifted indifferent. The Pyramid loomed dark against them, eternal. And somewhere in the city's veins, Aisha was moving, her path hidden from him.

The Guardian's riddle wouldn't leave him: *If shadow united them, the world would bend not just to its will—but against all others.*

Quentin stared into the night until his eyes blurred, one thought gnawing harder than the rest—*what if the only person who truly understood what was happening to him was also the one leading him to ruin?*

He wondered, with a marrow-level numbness, whether Aisha was walking toward the light—or if she was the one calibrating the shadow.

CHAPTER 9

THE MARKET OF BROKEN TIME

"Disruption is the greatest enemy of order. Eliminate the noise before it becomes song." — **Axiom of the Shadow Order, Pacing II.**

— Δ —

Cairo's Khan el-Khalili bazaar spilled around them in a chaos of color and sound. Narrow alleys bloomed with hanging lamps in every shade of glass—amber, sapphire, ruby—catching the sun like bottled fire. Stalls overflowed with brass trays, piles of saffron and cumin glowing like powdered sunsets, racks of scarves that danced whenever the wind stirred. The smell was overwhelming—grilled lamb skewers charring on open flames, the sweet cloy of honey pastries, smoke curling from pipes where old men leaned and watched.

"Souvenir camels!" Liam announced, holding up a carved wooden figurine with a missing leg. "A bargain, only slightly maimed." He shook it for emphasis; the leg rattled loose.

Sophia swooped in, clipboard clutched even here, her forehead already creased. "Stay together. This place is a maze, and pickpockets thrive in crowds. Do not wander. Especially you, Liam."

"Who, me?" Liam grinned, slipping the camel into his pocket, flipping a coin onto the tray before the vendor could protest. "I'd never."

Raj, meanwhile, was locked in battle with a spice merchant. "Two hundred pounds? Absurd. I could get this in London for half the price."

The merchant, unimpressed, muttered, "Then go to London."

Raj puffed his chest. "I'll give you fifty."

"You'll give me two hundred."

"Sixty."

Their haggling grew louder than the brass instruments clanging from a nearby wedding parade, drawing smirks from passing locals who recognized the universal theatre of bargaining.

The exchange went on, a performance as loud as the cymbals clashing in the street where a troupe of musicians played for a circle of clapping children. Drums thudded, flutes wailed, and laughter spilled like water down the stones. Nia had tucked herself near them, sketchbook balanced against a wall, pencil flying. She ignored Raj's theatrics and instead captured the line of a drummer's hand, the tilt of the boy's head as he laughed, the way the afternoon light fell in slats across the crowd.

Quentin tried to join in the mood, to let the colors and smells drown the steady pressure in his palm. He even bought a small glass pendant from a jeweler, its blue surface cracked like frozen lightning. The vendor tied it onto a cord for him with a smile, and for a moment Quentin felt ordinary again. *Almost.*

But the cycle wouldn't stop.

It pressed through his ribs, louder with every step deeper into the market. Every shout from a vendor, every clang of metal against stone seemed to strike the same hidden chord vibrating in his chest. It reached the soles of his feet, as though the ground itself whispered under the stall mats and rugs. The deeper they went, the more the noise of the market felt like camouflage—cover for something sharper, waiting underneath.

Sophia barked at Liam for trying on a fez, Raj bellowed triumphantly when he shaved ten pounds off a bag of dates, Professor Ellis wandered distractedly into a rug shop and had to be herded back by Dr. Farouk. It was hustle and bustle, laughter, irritation—the whole scene alive with the ordinary. And yet…

Aisha walked ahead of the group like a shadow cutting through color. She didn't laugh at Liam's antics, didn't glance at Raj's negotiations, didn't even roll her eyes at Sophia's instructions. Her braid swung with each step, her shoulders taut. She scanned the crowd with a hunter's gaze, not a tourist's.

She melted through clusters of people, the crowd parting for her. For a heartbeat, she vanished entirely, swallowed by a press of vendors waving scarves and bangles. Quentin's chest lurched. He shoved forward, nearly knocking over a tray of dates, but then—she reappeared further down the corridor, her eyes darting, measuring the exits.

A chill slid down Quentin's spine. *She wasn't browsing. She was watching. Waiting.*

The pressure in his chest deepened, his palm twitching inside his sleeve. He slowed, letting the noise of bargaining and music blur around him. His stomach knotted.

The marketplace suddenly felt less like a marketplace and more like a labyrinth—a place where predators could move unseen, where bright stalls were only distractions from the darker corners.

Somewhere beyond the perfumes and spices, eyes fixed on him—intent and patient. The same presence that had stalked him at the Plateau was here, threading between the stalls.

Something was coming. He could feel it, like a sandstorm on the horizon long before the dust cloud rose.

And Aisha—Aisha was already moving toward it.

— Δ —

Aisha slipped sideways between two textile stalls where silks hung like waterfalls, and in the next blink she was gone. Quentin's pulse spiked. He hesitated only a breath—Sophia's voice floating somewhere behind him, Liam laughing with a vendor—then ducked under a string of lamps and pushed after her.

The passageway he entered was cooler, the sun cut into strips by wooden lattices overhead. The smell changed too: less spice, more damp stone, old water seeping from a cracked pipe. Noise from the shoppers thinned to a muffled roar, as if a door had been closed on the world.

"Aisha?" he called, too softly to be useful.

Silk brushed his cheek. The lamps tinkled in a faint breeze. He took another step, then another, sleeve tugged tight over his palm. Aisha's shadow flickered ahead—he saw the quick turn of her head, two fingers cutting down—stay.

Figures unpeeled from the alley walls.

Three at first. Then five. Robes the color of baked sand, hoods low, faces in shadow. They moved with the economy of people who wasted nothing—not gesture, not breath. A ring closed around Quentin and Aisha so quietly he didn't register it until his way back to the market was simply gone.

Cold threaded his spine. The cycle in his chest surged, filling his ears. Aisha shifted her stance with predatory ease—one foot angled back, shoulders loose, weight low and ready. It was the stance of someone trained to fight, not survive a tour.

Quentin's mouth went dry. "Can I help you?" he said, the words ridiculous as soon as they left him.

One of the robed figures inclined his head a fraction. When he spoke, the voice was mild and precise, a blade wrapped in silk. “Marked. Take him.”

The world tightened around that word. *Marked.* Quentin’s fingers tingled beneath the fabric, the sigil in his skin answering like a struck chord.

Aisha stepped between him and the closest hood. “No.”

The refusal hung in the passage like dust motes in a shaft of light. The Order did not step back. Their formation didn’t waver. Only a slight turn of several heads—to her, then to Quentin again—as if recalculating.

“You knew them,” Quentin whispered, throat scraping. “You know them.”

She didn’t look at him. “Stay behind me.”

“That won’t be necessary,” the leader said, almost courteous. “Come quickly. Don’t make this loud.”

From the market, a burst of laughter and cymbals drifted across the roofs, oddly far away. Quentin’s knees wanted to fold. He could run—except there was nowhere to run to. He could scream—except the lane swallowed sound. A dagger flashed free, its blade curved like a crescent moon, catching slivers of broken light.

His perception sheared—inputs separating, motion turning countable.

His perception kinked under load.

The blade’s glint slowed midair. Dust hung motionless, a held breath. The lamps’ tiny glass tongues stopped their shiver. Quentin felt his heartbeat as separate thuds, great slow hammers striking the world.

And then the current snapped, everything rushing forward.

Aisha moved first. She knocked the blade aside with the heel of her hand, the strike sharp and efficient, then pivoted and drove her elbow into the attacker’s ribs. He folded without a sound. Another agent lunged; she slid under his reach as if skating on oiled stone, kicked his knee sideways, turned the stumble into a throw that smacked him against the wall. It was not pretty. Not cinematic. It was practiced.

Quentin stood useless, shock locking his joints. The leader watched like he was timing a machine, then flicked two fingers. The ring tightened.

"Take him," the leader said.

Another robed figure grabbed for Quentin's sleeve. Instinct dragged his marked hand away; fabric tore. The man's fingers brushed bare skin.

The sigil in Quentin's right palm indurated—the tissue hardening into a sub-zero knot that cabled his tendons tight. A soundless shockwave rippled outward, rattling the lamps and splitting the air with invisible force. The agent jerked back, hissing, as if stung.

Aisha's head snapped toward Quentin. For the first time he saw something like fear in her eyes—not of the Order, but of him. "Move," she barked. "Now."

He moved. Or rather, his body lurched into motion, half panic, half command obeyed. Aisha seized his forearm and yanked him down a side slit barely wider than a doorway. Wood grated his shoulder as they squeezed through; behind them a hand clutched at air a fraction too late.

"Split them," the leader's voice glided after them, still maddeningly calm. "Drive them to the roofs."

The alley kinked left, right, spilling them into a web of passages that smelled of frying oil and old copper. The bazaar's roar swelled, then dipped again as they cut behind stalls, ducked under a beaded curtain, skidded past a stack of crates that toppled in their wake with a clatter of dates.

Aisha didn't slow. "Keep up," she snapped.

"I'm trying," Quentin gasped, lungs burning.

"Try faster."

They burst into another narrow lane that split the market like a seam. Ahead, a wooden ladder leaned against a plaster wall, leading to a flat roof quilted with satellite dishes and laundry lines.

Aisha vaulted the bottom rungs and was halfway up before Quentin's hands found purchase. Behind them, the first of the Order rounded the corner at an unhurried lope, as if confident time belonged to them.

"They won't stop," Aisha said between breath and grit, already pulling herself onto the roof. She reached down, eyes flinty, hand open. "Quentin—now."

He grabbed for her, the thrum in his chest rising toward a new, sharper pitch, and the market's carnival below sharpened into a battlefield he hadn't chosen.

— Δ —

Quentin's feet barely touched the rungs before Aisha yanked him upward, hauling him onto the rooftop with startling strength for someone so slight. The bazaar stretched below like a painted tapestry ripped apart by chaos—Order agents wove through the passages, their hoods bobbing like dark buoys in a flood of color. Vendors shouted in protest as stalls splintered, tourists shrieked and flattened themselves against walls.

"Run!" Aisha didn't wait for an answer. She darted across the roof and leapt down onto a balcony awning, the canvas sagging under her weight before springing back. Quentin stumbled after her, clumsy, his stomach lurching with every shift of height. His pendant—the cracked blue glass—thudded against his chest, and for the first time it wasn't just cold, it pulsed in rhythm with the mark in his right palm.

They hit the ground again in a narrow passage thick with the smell of cumin and roasting lamb. Quentin's lungs scraped raw as they bolted between stalls, the world collapsing into jagged fragments: a pyramid of oranges toppling in a bright cascade, a child shrieking as dates scattered across the dirt, a copper tray spinning away like a gong under his heel.

The low-frequency vibration in his chest roared. And then, mid-stride, time slipped.

A blade swept toward him, flashing silver from an Order agent cutting through the crowd. The world didn't slow—his perception densified. Sound compressed into a dull band of pressure; motion lost continuity. The knife filled his vision an inch from his ribs, every detail over-resolved—the nick in its edge, the threadbare cuff of the attacker's robe, the bead of sweat mid-slide on his cheek.

Quentin lurched sideways, more stumble than skill, and the blade carved only air. It didn't feel like moving faster. It felt like the world refusing to fall apart until he was done with it. His perception snapped back with a violent jolt, noise slamming in—the stallholder's angry shout, chickens exploding into feathers, the hiss of the agent twisting to strike again.

"Quentin!" Aisha's hand clamped his wrist. She spun, her heel snapping against the attacker's temple with surgical precision. He crumpled like dropped cloth.

"You buffered it," she panted, dragging him onward. "Did you feel it?"

"I don't know what I felt!" Quentin gasped, half-tripping as they vaulted over baskets of pomegranates. "I thought I was—going mad—"

"No. Worse." Her grip tightened. Her voice dropped low, ragged. "You're marked."

They burst into another thoroughfare, wider, boiling with tourists and indignant vendors. Stalls collapsed in their wake: bolts of fabric unraveled into streaming banners, spices burst into clouds of crimson and gold, the air sharp with pepper. Shouts rose in Arabic, French, English—a storm of sound beating against Quentin's ears.

From both ends of the lane, hoods appeared. Order agents pressing in. Quentin's chest seized.

"Up!" Aisha pointed.

A crate of melons leaned against a wall. She vaulted it, kicked off the plaster, and caught the lip of a balcony with catlike ease. Quentin scrambled after her, far less graceful, propelled by panic. Melons burst under his shoes, slicking the wood with pulp. His hands clawed for plaster—slipping—until his perception stuttered again—an acute compression—just long enough for panic to resolve into coordination. His fingers hooked the edge.

He dangled, breath ragged, feet thrashing above the chaos. Aisha's face appeared above him, eyes narrowed with annoyance more than fear. "Pull yourself up!"

"I'm—trying," his arms trembled, the mark in his palm pressed flat to stone. Pressure deepened—not lifting him, not saving him, but compressing everything inward. Noise collapsed. Panic narrowed into a single motor imperative. He hauled himself over with a desperate grunt, shoulders screaming.

Aisha didn't wait. She darted across the roof tiles, each stride precise, balanced. Quentin stumbled after her, lungs burning, thoughts fragmenting under load. This wasn't panic anymore. It was a system misfiring under stress—and something inside him compensating just enough to keep him upright.

Below, vendors bellowed in outrage. Tourists raised phones, half-convinced they were watching theatre. But the Order didn't break stride. They moved through overturned stalls and panicked crowds with coordinated efficiency—silent, relentless, inevitable.

Quentin's heart iced over. This wasn't a chase anymore. This was a hunt, and he was the prey the Echo had marked.

— Δ —

The rooftops of the labyrinth were a jigsaw of sun-bleached plaster, satellite dishes, and crooked laundry lines snapping in the evening breeze. From up here, Cairo stretched wild and endless, the glow of dusk painting the city in fire and shadow.

Quentin scrambled after Aisha, his trainers slipping on loose gravel. His lungs burned; his arms ached from the balcony climb. Each leap between roofs felt like stepping off the edge of the world. He wasn't built for this—he was the boy who tripped on school stairs, not someone sprinting rooftops above Cairo like he belonged in a chase scene.

"Keep your weight forward!" Aisha barked, already vaulting over a sagging clothesline. A red sheet whipped across her face; she swatted it aside without breaking stride. Her voice was steel. "If you hesitate, you fall."

"Comforting advice!" Quentin wheezed, nearly gagging on dust.

Behind them, the first of the Order scaled the walls with terrifying ease. Hoods streamed back as they leapt, their movements precise, fluid—unnatural, as though the rooftops themselves bent to guide their steps. The rooftops filled with pursuit: sandals slapping, fabric snapping, stone scraping underfoot.

Quentin's foot slid on a patch of crumbled plaster. For a heartbeat, his body pitched into empty air, the market yawning below—stalls glowing like lanterns, vendors scattering, motion collapsing into a blur of color and noise. His stomach dropped into the void.

Then his perception compressed.

Sound narrowed. Depth sharpened. The chaos below flattened into vectors and edges—plaster breaking under his heel, the angle of the ledge, Aisha's braid snapping as she lunged for him. Panic condensed into a single directive.

Quentin gasped, driving his other foot down hard against the stone. The ledge bit. Impact slammed through his knees as the world rushed back at full force. He crashed onto the rooftop, lungs tearing at the air. The mark in his right palm constricted into a numbing, sub-zero density.

"You're not slowing time," Aisha spun toward him, eyes sharp, fury flashing. "The world didn't change. You did."

"I don't know what I just did!" Quentin shouted, voice ragged with panic.

"No one does, the first time," she snapped. For the first time, her command cracked with something else—urgency edged with fear. "But whatever that was, it won't save you twice. Move."

From the street below came an unexpected commotion. Liam.

He had darted into the corridor, waving his arms like a man possessed. "Oi! You lot!" he bellowed in his thickest London accent, voice cracking with reckless bravado. "Looking for a fight, are we?"

In each hand, he clutched skewers of half-eaten meat. He hurled them like lances at the nearest Order agent. They bounced harmlessly off the robes, but Liam didn't stop. He snatched up a tray of flatbreads, flinging them like frisbees, hollering, "Death by carbs!" Vendors shrieked in fury, chasing him with spoons and ladles.

The Order faltered—just for a moment. One agent slipped on a flying pita, skidding sideways into a fruit cart. A melon burst open, juice streaking the sand. *Even the relentless seemed human for a heartbeat.*

Aisha seized the opening. She clamped Quentin's arm, yanking him toward a ladder bolted into the far wall. "Move. Before they regroup."

They scrambled up, breaths harsh, rooftops now drowned in twilight. The muezzin's call rippled across Cairo, solemn and steady, its echo strangely at odds with the chaos of pounding feet and terror.

Quentin risked a glance back. The Order was climbing again, undeterred. One agent vaulted across a gap with eerie grace, landing where Quentin had nearly fallen minutes before. His hood slipped slightly, and Quentin glimpsed eyes pale as glass—cold, fixed on him with an intensity that hollowed him out. For an instant Quentin swore the world itself strained around that gaze—but darker, hungrier.

He stumbled forward, dread clenching in his chest. *They weren't chasing Aisha. They weren't chasing the group. They were hunting him.*

Aisha's voice cut through his panic, sharp as a whip crack. "Focus! Don't let the fear own you."

But Quentin's fear was all he had left—and with every pulse of the Echo, it felt less like fear and more like fate dragging him toward an edge he couldn't name.

— Δ —

From below, the market had turned into a theatre of chaos. Vendors shouted in outrage, tourists screamed and scrambled for cover, and Order agents darted like predators through the crush of people. But among the turmoil, one figure remained still—Nia, crouched against a sun-warmed wall, her sketchbook braced on her knees as if it were the only steady thing left in the world.

Her pencil flew, her gaze darting between the rooftops and the page, as though she were tracing something only she could see. Around her, children cried, a stallholder wept over shattered pottery, merchants cursed the chase that had destroyed their wares—but Nia's world had narrowed to the whisper of graphite: *shh, shh, shh.*

Above, Quentin staggered across a rooftop's crumbling edge, Aisha dragging him forward. He barely registered the figure below. But then his eyes caught a glimpse of Nia's sketch, and his breath snagged.

It was him.

Not as he was now—sweaty, clumsy, panic blurring his focus—but as though she had caught a moment a heartbeat ahead of reality. The lines were too sharp, too inevitable, as if the world itself had been forced onto the page. In her drawing, an Order agent toppled backward from a roof, arms flung wide, blade tumbling from his hand, mouth open in a cry that had not yet happened.

Quentin looked up in horror—just in time to see the real figure vault after them, blade flashing like lightning.

Aisha shoved Quentin aside. "Down!" she barked.

The agent lunged. His blade cut the air where Quentin's ribs had been an instant before. Then—just as Nia's sketch had promised—his foot skidded on a loose tile. His momentum betrayed him.

For one long second, Quentin saw the fall in unbearable clarity: robes whipping in the wind, eyes blown wide, the blade spinning like a silver coin. The Echo pressed louder, syncing with the inevitability of it. Then came the crash, a sickening smack against the striped awning below, followed by the vendor's shriek as fruit scattered in a wet explosion across the cobbles.

Quentin froze, chest hammering, his stomach lurching. He glanced down again. Nia had already flipped the page, sketching something new with the same calm precision, though her hands shook as if every line cost her. Her eyes glistened, but she never looked up—never dared to meet the moment she had drawn.

He dropped to his knees beside Aisha, voice ragged. "She drew it. She drew it before it happened."

Aisha's gaze flicked to Nia. For a moment, something rare broke through her tactical stillness—a flash of recognition, quickly smothered by calculation. It was the look of someone who already knew what Nia was—and had hoped not to see it confirmed. She said nothing.

The surviving Order agents shouted across the rooftops, signaling to regroup. One pointed directly at Quentin, his voice low and carrying even above the market din: "The boy. Marked."

Quentin flinched, clutching his sleeve as the mark compressed, denser. He wanted to call down to Nia, demand how she knew, but she didn't lift her head. She only drew, faster and faster, as if the pencil itself was a fuse burning toward something inevitable.

Aisha yanked him upright. "Forget the her. Move."

"No," Quentin panted, eyes locked on Nia's bowed head. "She saw it. She—she knows what's coming."

For a breath, Aisha's expression cracked. Her eyes softened—not with pity, not with kindness, but with the weight of someone who had once carried a burden too heavy for her years. It was gone in an instant, replaced with steel. She shoved Quentin forward.

"We can't save anyone if you're dead."

The rooftops shuddered under pursuit. The muezzin's call still rippled across the city, solemn and steady, but the world beneath was nothing but frenzy: overturned stalls, the metallic hiss of drawn blades, the roar of frightened voices.

Quentin stumbled onward, lungs scraping raw, Nia's sketch seared into his mind. It wasn't imagination. It wasn't coincidence either.

It was signal—and she was receiving it. And for the first time, Quentin understood: *the Echo wasn't the only power shaping their fates.*

— Δ —

The rooftops finally broke into a wider ledge that sloped toward a warren of alleys. Aisha yanked Quentin after her, their boots skidding on plaster before they dropped into the twisting lanes below. The bazaar's roar dulled behind them, replaced by the hollow echo of their footsteps ricocheting between walls stained with centuries of dust and smoke.

They darted left, then right, plunging deeper into the maze. Every turn looked the same—arched doorways leaning like tired shoulders, shuttered windows with cracked paint, strings of washing swaying overhead like ghostly banners. Quentin's lungs clawed for air, his chest clamped in a sterile, freezing pressure.

For long, frantic minutes the noise of pursuit clung to their heels—slapping sandals, faint shouts, the rasp of robes brushing stone. But gradually, it thinned. The sounds dulled, then vanished, swallowed by the labyrinth's silence. Only the residual resonance in Quentin's chest remained, as if reminding him the danger hadn't ended—merely shifted.

Quentin staggered against a wall, sliding down until his knees buckled. Sweat slicked his face, his shirt clung to his back. He pressed his sleeve against his palm as though he could smother the pressure building there.

Aisha stood opposite, arms folded, braid mussed, face shining with sweat that she refused to acknowledge. She wasn't gasping, wasn't trembling. Her calm was unnatural, a stillness that felt like another kind of weapon. Only her eyes betrayed anything—narrowed, calculating, scanning the shadows as if expecting them to peel away and reveal more enemies.

Quentin lifted his head. His voice came out raw, cracked. "You knew them."

Her silence was sharper than denial.

"You knew them," he pressed, anger slicing through his exhaustion. "Back in the alley—you didn't even flinch. You called them by what they are. The Order." He dragged himself upright, fists trembling at his sides. "Who are you really, Aisha? Because you're not just another student on this trip."

For the first time, her bureaucratic veneer slipped—not into guilt, but into something like conflict. Her shoulders stiffened, her jaw flexed as though she were weighing words against consequences. She stepped closer, her voice low and sharp. "The Echo makes you a target. That's all you need to know."

"That's not an answer."

"It's the only one you'll get." Her tone cut final, but her eyes flickered once—hesitation, quickly buried. She spun away, tugging her scarf tighter around her shoulders as though armoring herself. "Stay alive, Quentin. That's your job now."

She started down the passageway, each step measured, steady, as if chaos had never brushed her.

Quentin stared after her, pulse hammering in his ears. "You could have let them take me," he said, the words slipping out half-plea, half-accusation.

She paused. Just for a moment. Her head turned, enough for him to glimpse her profile limned in the thin lamplight. "Yes," she said softly. "I could have. But I didn't." Her voice carried no triumph, only the weary weight of a choice that cost more than she would admit.

And then she was gone, swallowed by Cairo's night.

Quentin sagged back against the wall, his body shaking from more than exhaustion. His sleeve slipped, and the mark pressed faintly in the dark, lines crawling like molten threads beneath his skin.

He clenched his fist, chest heaving. The questions multiplied faster than the answers. *Who was Aisha? What path had she already chosen? And why had she saved him when every glance suggested she might yet betray him?*

Above him, the rooftops jagged into the sky, sharp teeth gnawing at the rising moon. Somewhere beyond, the Order still hunted, patient as the desert itself.

And in the silence of the narrow slit, Quentin realized with brutal clarity: *he could no longer pretend this was someone else's story.*

The Echo hadn't just chosen him. It had put him under load.

CHAPTER 10

THE GEOMETRY OF FEAR

"Fear is merely a structural weakness awaiting the proper brace." — **Fragment of the Architect's Scroll, X.**

— Δ —

They tumbled into the hostel lounge like shipwreck survivors staggering onto a beach. The room smelled of lemon cleaner and old tea, the lamplight yellow and tired. A fan turned lazily overhead as if nothing in the world had ever hurried. Cairo's noise pressed against the windows and stayed politely outside.

Liam got there first with a flourish, hands braced on his knees, grinning too wide. "Well," he said, breath still ragged, "I, for one, enjoyed our relaxing cultural excursion. Five stars. Would be chased by homicidal monks again."

"Not funny," Sophia snapped, cheeks blotched, hair escaping its bun in furious wisps. She slammed her clipboard onto the table like a warrant.

“That—whatever that was—was reckless. Completely unacceptable. We could have been hurt. We were nearly hurt.”

Raj sank into an armchair as if he’d orchestrated the entire day and deserved applause. “If certain people hadn’t run off,” he drawled, “none of this would have happened. Some of us are here to learn, not to star in… whatever that was.”

Quentin stood just inside the doorway, lightheaded, the world still shimmering too bright at the edges. His sleeve was tugged down so hard his knuckles whitened. The mark in his right palm pressed—quiet, defiant—as if it didn’t care about schedules or lectures or the way his chest kept stumbling over its next breath.

The cracked blue pendant from the bazaar thudded against his sternum with every breath, cold as a reprimand. *He wanted to sit. He wanted to disappear into the wallpaper. He wanted to stop seeing the blade’s glint, the agent’s pale eyes.*

Dr. Farouk ushered Professor Ellis to a chair, murmuring to him in low Arabic until his color returned. She scanned the students, her gaze landing on Quentin for a heartbeat that felt like a question she didn’t ask. Her eyes were kind, assessing, and—unlike Sophia’s—held on him a fraction too long, as if measuring damage she couldn’t yet name.

“Everyone drink,” she said evenly. “Water first. Then we talk.”

Liam seized on the order with relief, grabbing bottles and tossing them around with exaggerated competence. “Hydration, team,” he mimicked Ellis, voice wobbling only slightly. He lobbed one to Quentin, who caught it on the second try.

Aisha stood at the window with her back to the room, arms folded tightly. The glass held the city in faint reflection—lanterns, scooters, the soft drift of night. She didn’t speak. She didn’t look at anyone. But Quentin could feel her attention tethered to him, taut as wire. In the window's ghost-image her gaze slid to his sleeve and away again, a warning she wouldn't voice in front of the others.

Sophia rounded on him at last. "Explain," she said, and the word had edges.

Quentin opened his mouth—and closed it again. The words he had didn't fit: the cycle in his ribs, men in robes watching him like he was an open door.

"I saw Aisha go," he heard himself say, the truth clipped of its impossible parts. "I followed. Then—men came." He swallowed. "They wanted me."

"Don't flatter yourself," Raj said. "You sprinted into an alley and panicked. You always panic. You made a scene—again—and got everyone dragged into it."

Liam bristled. "He saved my life twice today by being a scene, thanks ever so." He shot Quentin a quick, sheepish thumbs-up; his hand still shook.

Sophia's glare flicked between them. "Enough. This isn't about sides; it's about safety." Her voice trembled, then steadied. "We stick together. We follow the plan. We do not run into danger."

Quentin stared at the floorboards. The grain swam. "I didn't mean to," he said softly, hating the way the words sounded like an apology.

"Intention doesn't matter," Sophia returned, though there was a thread of worry woven through the strictness. "Outcome does." She softened—barely. "You scared us."

Nia had folded herself onto the low sofa near the bookcase, sketchbook already open. She drew without looking up, graphite whispering steady as breath. Quentin caught the curve of a rooftop ledge, a blur of robes mid-fall, Aisha's hand extended like a dark arc through blank space. The pencil paused once, then moved on. She shaded a haloed smear around Quentin's outline—subtle, like heat above tarmac—as if she were capturing a distortion, not a glow.

"Look," Liam said, dropping onto the coffee table, knees out, elbows on thighs, "can we all agree that hooded weirdos with knives weren't on the itinerary? So maybe, just maybe, we cut Quentin some slack and have a nice group meltdown later?"

"Tomorrow," Sophia said crisply, seizing control of the future like luggage. "We return to the museum. No bazaar. No detours. I'll speak to the programme coordinator." She shot Quentin a warning look that tasted like worry more than scorn. "We will present as composed and responsible." She underlined composed with the edge of her water bottle against the table, a private vow as much as an order.

Raj snorted, but held his tongue. For once. His phone buzzed; he silenced it without looking and slid it face-down beneath his thigh.

Quentin sank into a chair at the edge of the pool of light, water bottle sweating in his hands. His palm pressed to the rhythm of the fan. He saw, just for an instant, the cuff lift—and the pressure in his right palm spiked—dense and cold—as if the mark wanted air. He pinned his hand under the table's rim, pressing his palm to his thigh to smother the weight, and angled his body, a habit already forming: *hide first, breathe second. No one saw*. He couldn't be sure.

At the window, Aisha's reflection shifted. He looked up. She was watching him in the glass, not meeting his eyes directly, but there all the same. A moment, two. Then she turned away again, the set of her shoulders iron. Whatever she'd decided about him hadn't settled into mercy. Not yet.

Dr. Farouk handed Quentin a second bottle. "You're shaking," she said gently. It wasn't a question.

"I'm fine," he lied.

"Mm." She squeezed his shoulder the way she had at breakfast, a quiet weight. "When the body says otherwise, listen." Under her breath, in Arabic, barely above the fan's sigh: "Slowly, habibi. Breathe."

The room settled into a brittle quiet: the fan's slow sigh, the tick of the wall clock, the scratch of Nia's pencil. Liam made one more joke and let it die on his tongue. Raj checked his phone like a man with better places to be. Sophia wrote a list titled Plan and underlined it twice.

Quentin stared at his knuckles, white under the skin. *The lounge felt smaller than it had ever been, the air thin, all the ordinary furniture suddenly at the wrong angles. He had never felt more watched, more alone.* The Echo thrummed on, indifferent to minutes and meltdowns, keeping its own count inside his bones.

Outside, Cairo breathed. Inside, the Echo beat on, patient as time.

— ∆ —

Raj wasn't sitting. He paced the length of the iron gate, his fingers trailing along the latch. He paused, testing the weight of the deadbolt with a sharp, metallic click that echoed off the tiles. When he saw Quentin looking, he puffed out his chest and offered a patronizing smirk. "Just making sure we're locked in, Quentin. You know how Cairo is after dark—full of people looking for things they didn't lose. Someone has to keep an eye on the perimeter while the rest of you are daydreaming."

He checked his phone, the screen casting a cold blue glow over his sharp features, and stepped back into the shadows near the wall.

The hostel's lounge had thinned of its earlier uproar. Liam had slumped sideways in an armchair, a blanket tossed over him like a flag of surrender. Nia perched cross-legged on the sofa, her pencil scratching faintly in rhythm with the ceiling fan. Raj scrolled through his phone with exaggerated boredom, the blue glow lighting his smirk like a mask.

Sophia, however, was indefatigable. She gathered everyone who hadn't outright fallen asleep around the long oak table near the lounge's back wall, stacking textbooks, worksheets, and pamphlets from the programme. The dim light of a single lamp made the table look like a battlefield, its spread of pages and pens like weapons she alone commanded. She tugged an elastic from her wrist and snapped her hair into a tighter bun, as if discipline could be worn like armor.

"Since today was... chaotic," she said firmly, glaring at Liam though he was too unconscious to notice, "we will salvage the evening with productivity. A study review on Egyptian history. We're behind already, and the coordinators will expect proper notes."

Raj smirked. "Yes, let's pretend this is school and not a holiday."

Sophia ignored him. "Quentin. Sit."

Quentin hesitated in the doorway. His hand throbbed in his pocket, the subdermal pressure refusing to ease. The cracked blue pendant from the bazaar tapped lightly against his sternum, cold and accusatory. *The last thing he wanted was to sit under a lamp and for everyone to notice the mark in his right palm.* But Sophia's stare brooked no argument. He slid into a chair opposite her, slouching low so the table's shadow cloaked his lap like a secret.

On the corner of the table sat a decorative brass khopesh—a heavy, sickle-shaped blade the hostel used as a bookend. As she settled in, Sophia reached out and picked it up. She didn't look at the ornate engravings like a tourist; instead, she balanced the spine of the blade across her index finger, her thumb tracing the balance point near the hilt. She gave the air a short, clinical snap of a parry, her feet shifting instinctively into a narrow fencing stance beneath the table.

"The center of gravity is off," she muttered, her eyes narrowing with technical disapproval. "Too much weight in the belly, not enough in the tang. It's a wall-hanger, not a weapon."

Quentin watched, startled by the sudden, lethal familiarity in her grip. For a second, the studious girl with the clipboard vanished, replaced by someone who understood exactly how a piece of steel was meant to move. She caught his gaze and immediately set the blade down, her face returning to its usual facade of rigid boredom. "If you're going to study history, Quentin—tools matter," she said.

She launched into dates and dynasties, lecturing with professorial zeal. Quentin tried to follow, but his pen wandered of its own accord. His notebook filled not with notes about Khufu or chronology, but with jagged sketches: the impressed glyphs from the shaft, the priests chanting, the shard sealed in stone. He traced the looping hieroglyph again and again, the lines vibrating under his hand. The mark in his palm answered—faint load-shifts, like moth-wings against glass.

"You're not listening." Sophia's voice cracked like a whip.

Quentin hunched his shoulders. *He was. Just... in his own way.*

A shadow fell across his page. Aisha slid into the chair beside him, folding her arms on the table. She didn't look at Sophia. She didn't look at Raj. Only at the marks Quentin had drawn.

"You've got half of that wrong," she said quietly.

Quentin's pen stilled. "What?"

Her finger tapped the page, landing on the crooked symbol he'd sketched over and over. "That isn't a bird. It's a feather. Ma'at's feather. You angled it wrong." She drew the correction in quick, confident strokes. Her handwriting was spare and exacting, the kind that belonged to someone taught to copy things perfectly or not at all.

He stared. "You can read this?"

"Not perfectly." Her voice stayed low, just for him. "But better than you, apparently."

Heat rose in Quentin's cheeks. He leaned closer, lowering his voice. "Then tell me what they mean. All of them. You know more than you're saying."

Aisha's lips pressed into a flat line. "Knowledge is dangerous. You'll find that out soon enough."

"That's not an answer," Quentin hissed, more sharply than he meant.

Her eyes flicked up at him, dark and steady. "It's the only one you'll get." But instead of pulling away, she reached for his notebook, turning it toward herself.

Aisha began to annotate his scrawls in the margin, correcting a line here, drawing a clearer symbol there. "That one is endurance. That's time. And that—" her voice dropped to nearly a whisper "—is the Echo."

The word made the cold pressure bit deeper, as if agreeing. Quentin swallowed hard, unable to tear his eyes from the page. *So it was real. He didn't just hallucinate all of it.*

Aisha's gaze flickered, guarded. "It's real enough." Her jaw tightened at the word, as if "real" cost something to admit.

Across the table, Raj leaned back in his chair, clearly uninterested in study but smirking at their bent heads. His phone buzzed once against the wood; he silenced it without checking, eyes half-lidded in practiced innocence. Sophia scribbled notes furiously, oblivious.

Only Nia, from her perch on the sofa, lifted her eyes from her sketchbook to watch them with a calm, unreadable expression. Her pencil hovered mid-air. In the margin of her page, a faint outline of Quentin's hand bloomed darker in graphite—a shadow-map with no source. Her pencil didn't just trace his hand; it drew a series of faint lean in the scene, like the room's geometry favored the door. They were lines of intention, tracking paths that hadn't been walked yet.

Quentin kept his voice low. "How do you know this?"

Aisha's pencil paused above the page. "Because I had to." She pushed the notebook back toward him, the corrections sharp and neat. "And because mistakes here don't erase themselves," she added, so soft he almost missed it.

For the first time all day, the tension between them shifted—still sharp, still barbed, but threaded with something else. A fragile collaboration.

Quentin traced the corrected symbol with his finger. The cycle in his bones thrummed like a taut string. He angled his body a fraction, a learned habit now: *Keep the loaded wrist in shadow; keep breathing.*

Sophia looked up at last, the edge in her voice blunted by fatigue. "Quentin, if you're confused, say so. I can make a glossary for everyone." Her gaze flicked to Aisha's neat annotations, and—briefly—respect tempered her irritation. "We'll add these."

Raj yawned theatrically. "Yes, let's all add drawings to our homework."

"Or," Liam mumbled from the armchair without opening his eyes, "we could admit that Aisha is terrifying and right about everything." His blanket slipped; he dragged it back up with a groan. "Also that I'm asleep."

Nia's pencil resumed its whisper. She sketched the feather Aisha had corrected, weighing it against a tiny heart on a scale. The heart was heavier. She shaded in the difference, then quietly tore the page free and tucked it behind another.

Quentin almost said thank you. *But gratitude felt dangerous*, he thought, *like admitting he needed her.* The words stuck.

And Aisha, expression unreadable, leaned back in her chair as though the moment hadn't mattered at all. Only her hand lingered near the notebook a heartbeat longer than necessary, a pause that looked like regret and vanished like steam.

— Δ —

The study session unraveled slowly, like a fire dwindling to embers. Sophia's voice, crisp and insistent at first, thinned as one by one the others drifted. Liam, sprawled in his armchair, began to snore loudly, punctuating his breaths with half-muttered nonsense that made no sense to anyone but him. Raj feigned interest in his phone until even that slipped from his hand, his head lolling back with theatrical exhaustion. Nia still sat curled on the sofa, sketching in the lamplight, but her pencil strokes had grown drowsy, wavering into softer, uncertain lines.

Only Quentin and Aisha remained at the table, the notebook between them marked with a patchwork of his messy doodles and her precise corrections. The lamplight haloed her hair, throwing shadows across her cheekbones. She leaned back now, arms folded, but Quentin felt the gravity of her presence—too near, too sharp, density pooling.

He fiddled with his pen, the silence heavy. Finally, the question broke out of him. "Why are you helping me now?" His voice was low, almost swallowed by Liam's snoring.

Aisha didn't move for a moment. Then she tilted her head, dark eyes narrowing. "Helping you? Don't flatter yourself. You'd misread half the glyphs without me."

Quentin winced, though her tone wasn't cruel—just matter-of-fact. "Still. You didn't have to."

Her gaze flicked to him, steady, unreadable. Then, for the briefest heartbeat, something softened. "Maybe I didn't want to watch you drown in your own ignorance."

The words were sharp, but they carried a thread of something else, something not quite disdain. Quentin's pulse skipped. *He wanted to push, to ask again what she really knew, why she kept circling him like this—warning him, scolding him, saving him.* But the words tangled in his throat.

"Thanks," he said finally, awkward and earnest. The syllables felt too small for the weight they carried.

A pause. Then the corner of her mouth curved—barely, fleeting. Not a full smile, but close enough that it startled him more than any glare.

For a moment, the tension shifted. The heat between them wasn't just fire—it was warmth too, faint and precarious.

Before Quentin could process it, a voice slurred from the armchair: "Blimey, you two sound like a married couple already." Liam cracked one eye, grinning sleepily. "Bickering over homework like it's your honeymoon." He snorted at his own joke and collapsed back into snores.

The blanket slid half off his shoulder, dragging across the floor like an afterthought.

Heat flooded Quentin's ears. He looked down at the notebook, wishing he could sink into the page.

Aisha's chair scraped back. She stood swiftly, the almost-smile gone, her face shuttered once more. "Don't mistake this for friendship," she said softly, too low for anyone but him to hear. Her voice was a blade wrapped in cloth—quiet, but cutting.

Then she turned and strode from the lounge, her braid swinging like a blade behind her.

Quentin sat frozen, the notebook still warm where her hand had rested. His chest ached with something complicated—frustration, curiosity, and a spark he couldn't quite name. He traced the corrected glyph again, her neat strokes glowing in the lamplight.

She helped me. And she walked away.

He closed the notebook slowly, the weight of her absence heavier than the silence she left behind. The thrum in his chest lingered, low and insistent, as if even the Echo itself refused to let go of her presence.

— Δ —

The hostel courtyard lay hushed under the weight of midnight. A stray cat slinked along the garden wall, its eyes catching the lamplight like twin coins. The fountain in the center gurgled softly, water spilling over cracked tiles, its sound blurring with the faint thrum of Cairo's night traffic beyond the gate.

Raj slipped through the lounge door, careful to let it close without a sound. He paused, listening—only the faint buzz of the street, the whisper of leaves in the fig tree. Satisfied, he padded across the courtyard, phone already in his hand.

He stopped beneath the tree, where the shadows pooled deepest. The glow of his screen lit his face, sharp and foxlike. His thumb hovered for a moment, then pressed. He lifted the phone to his ear.

The call connected without a ring. Silence on the other end, thick and expectant. Raj licked his lips.

"It's me," he whispered. His voice was tight, but steady. "Yes. I've seen it."

A pause. The faintest crackle of breath came down the line, and Raj's smirk twitched wider.

"The mark," he whispered. "On his right hand. He keeps it covered—like he's afraid someone will recognize the pattern. But I saw the lines when his sleeve rode up. And when he panics, it's like the air around him tightens."

The silence pressed deeper, weighted, almost alive.

Raj's grin sharpened. "He doesn't even know what he's carrying. Not really. He panics, stumbles, makes himself the fool. Everyone blames him, which makes it easier for me. I'll stay close. Gain his trust. And when the time comes…" His voice dipped, pleased with itself. "You'll have him."

The murmur on the line this time was different—longer, lower, words he couldn't quite catch. Whatever was said made his shoulders stiffen. His smirk faltered, then returned, thinner, more careful. "Yes. I understand. No mistakes. I won't fail."

He tapped the screen. Darkness swallowed his face again. For a moment he stood motionless, the drip of the fountain counting the silence, the cat pausing in its prowl to watch him with golden eyes.

Then he slipped the phone into his pocket and exhaled. Slowly, deliberately, a smile crept across his features—one he never wore in daylight, never among the others. *Everything was moving exactly as it should be. The board was his.*

Raj turned back toward the hostel. The glow of lamplight painted his profile in gold as he stepped inside, quiet as a thief.

Upstairs, a curtain stirred. Just for a heartbeat, the faintest movement—a watcher retreating from the window.

Raj didn't notice.

— Δ —

The rooftop was quiet, far above the bustle of Cairo's midnight streets. The air smelled of dust and jasmine, cool at last after the day's furnace heat. A lone laundry sheet snapped like a flag in the breeze, its sound sharp against the hush.

Quentin sat cross-legged near the low wall, notebook open in his lap, pencil smudges dark across his fingertips. His sketches sprawled across the page—crooked repetitions of the glyphs he couldn't stop seeing: the looping feather, the jagged star, the circle cut by a line. Aisha's neat corrections glared back at him, sharp and sure, her precise strokes cutting through his fumbling ones. He traced them with his thumb, wishing—against his better judgment—that her voice were still beside him. *He wished she was here. Curt, maybe scathing, but certain. Always certain.*

But she wasn't here. She had walked away, as she always did, leaving him with more questions than answers.

Quentin leaned back against the wall, tilting his head to the sky. The stars scattered overhead like cold embers, glittering through Cairo's haze. Still, his gaze kept dragging to the horizon, to the Pyramid's silhouette. Even from here its outline was unmistakable, vast and patient, leaning into the night like a sentinel that had been waiting centuries for him alone. *It felt less like stone than a presence. It was watching, weighing, waiting.*

They would not come here, he realized, watching the crowded street below and the flickering lights of the neighboring apartments. *The Order moved in quiet. In seams. Cairo had no seams—only noise stacked on noise.* The thought offered a thin layer of protection, a momentary brace against the cold certainty that the hunt had not ended; it was merely waiting for him to step back into the quiet.

He lifted his hand. The sleeve fell back, and the mark answered his pulse. The lines didn't shine; they sat under his skin like cold wire, felt more than seen—a mapped pressure, a design that didn't belong to him.

"What are you?" His whisper cracked in his throat. He swallowed hard. "Why me?"

The Echo gave no answer. Only the insistent thrum, like a clock he couldn't wind down, like time itself had chosen him for reasons it refused to share.

He pressed his palm flat to the page. The paper didn't brighten—it warmed, faintly, and the pressure in his hand deepened, as if the symbols wanted to push back through ink and fiber. *The sight rattled him.* He snapped the book shut with a harsh clap. His pulse stumbled.

Below, movement stirred.

He froze. In the courtyard, a figure stood in the lamplight—Aisha. Her braid glinted faint copper as she tilted her face upward, toward the rooftop, toward him.

For a moment, everything stilled.

Their eyes caught across the gulf of distance. She didn't call up, didn't sneer or mock or toss another cutting remark. She only looked—steady, unreadable, a shadow balanced between lamplight and dark.

Quentin's breath snagged. *Why did she help him with the glyphs?* he asked himself. *Why did she warn him in the shaft? Why does she look at him sometimes as though she hated him, and sometimes as though she feared for him? Ally, enemy, or something in between?* He wanted to demand answers, but the words never formed.

The mark shifted again, pressure pooling beneath the cuff. Panic flared—*had she seen it?* He yanked the fabric down, hiding it against his chest.

Aisha looked away first. Her shoulders turned, her figure melting back into the courtyard shadows until only the faint trickle of the fountain remained.

The silence that followed felt heavier than any words she could have thrown at him, Quentin realized.

Quentin clutched the notebook tighter. The pressure still printed through the paper, stubborn as a bruise behind glass. He folded his arms around it, knees drawn to his chest. He rested his forehead against them, fighting the ache that pressed behind his eyes.

He was not sure anymore if Aisha was the reason he felt less alone—or the reason he had never felt lonelier.

Above him, the stars wheeled in their endless, indifferent arcs. The Pyramid crouched at the horizon, black and eternal, its weight pressing against the night like judgment. And in the hollow stillness, Quentin understood one thing with a clarity that chilled him.

The Echo wasn't waiting.

It had already marked him.

And whether Aisha walked toward him or away—his path was no longer only his own.

Chapter 11
ETERNITY PARTITIONED

"The Wonders are not monuments; they are segmented gears of the Universal Clock." — **Guardian Teaching, The Sevenfold Path.**

— Δ —

The dormitory had gone soft with fatigue, the day's chaos leaking into silence. The extra cot they'd dragged in for Aisha—a temporary fix after Sophia insisted on 'group proximity' following the bazaar—narrowed the walkway, making the room feel even more crowded than before. The windows were open to the Cairo night, curtains stirring with warm breezes that carried the faint smell of exhaust, bread, and jasmine. The ceiling fan creaked as it spun, each wobble marking a slow heartbeat in the dark.

Liam snored first, of course. He'd flopped onto his bunk without even removing his trainers, arms flung wide like a fallen knight, muttering half-dreamt nonsense between rattling breaths. Every so often, he snorted himself awake, rolled over, and immediately resumed.

Sophia, neat even in exhaustion, propped a lamp on her bedside table and read from her notes, pencil scratching brisk annotations in the margins. Her lips moved silently with every line she underlined, face taut with determination even as her eyelids sagged. At last, she set the pencil aside, fingers twitching faintly in sleep as if still writing lists in her dreams.

Nia sat cross-legged on her mattress, sketchbook balanced on her knees. Her pencil traced with half-closed eyes, moving slower and slower, as though at the cusp of sleep she could not keep from drawing. The faint lamp light brushed her face—serene, untethered, a girl already half in dreams. Her final lines curved into a half-finished circle, a glyph left incomplete before the pencil slipped from her hand.

Raj lay on his side, turned away from the others, his phone screen lit faintly under the blanket. He whispered into it, voice soft and calculated. Quentin couldn't make out the words, only the rise and fall of tone, the sly curl of syllables shaping secrets. Then the light blinked off, and the whispering stopped. Raj shifted under the blanket—too deliberate to be sleep, but Quentin had heard enough to know he wasn't the only one awake.

Quentin lay on his back, staring at the cracked plaster ceiling, arms folded tight across his chest. His body begged for rest, but his mind was a spinning wheel, sparking with everything that had happened: the chase through the market, the rooftop fall, Aisha's hand pulling him up, Nia's prophetic sketch, Raj's sly glances, the mark in his right palm loaded cold, a dense pressure sinking into bone—like a joint asked to carry too much mass.

He rolled onto his side, then onto his back again. The sheets tangled around his legs. Every time he closed his eyes, the images pressed sharper: the hooded agents whispering *the boy marked*, the priests sealing the shard, Aisha's face caught between fury and fear in the shaft.

And always, the mark—its subdermal bruise-gold shifting under the skin, edges sharpening into a hinge-geometry he couldn't quite focus on. He pressed his fist into the mattress to hide it, but the pressure remained—an anchor-weight that wouldn't let go.

He thought of home, of the ordinary quiet of his room, the posters above his desk, the sound of his mother washing dishes downstairs. That world felt impossibly far away now, like a dream already slipping. Here, everything was different—too loud, too sharp, too real.

Why him? he thought, the words heavy as stone. *What made him different? Why not Liam, or Sophia, or anyone else?*

The ceiling offered no answer. Only the faint spin of the fan, the rustle of paper as Sophia finally set her notes aside, the pencil sliding from Nia's fingers as she drifted fully into sleep.

Aisha shifted in her bunk across the room. Quentin glanced at her through the dimness. She sat upright still, back against the wall, knees drawn up, her face half-shadowed. Her eyes were open, fixed on the ceiling as if she could see through the plaster into the night sky. Her gaze flicked once toward him—sharp, unreadable. Then she closed her eyes and leaned her head back, but Quentin doubted she was asleep.

He rolled onto his side, heart thudding in the slow rhythm of exhaustion. The weight in his palm nested into the hum in his chest. His eyelids sagged despite him, every blink heavier than the last.

The dormitory sank into the hush of breathing bodies, Liam's snores rattling like broken machinery, the faint wheeze of the fan, the distant bark of a dog outside.

The last thing Quentin saw before sleep took him was a faint old-gold discoloration under the cuff—not bright, not flashing, just there, like dense metal under skin.

Quentin's eyes slid closed at last.

And the darkness took him.

— Δ —

Silence arrived first—so complete it felt like a substance, pressed hard against Quentin's ears. Then the dark thinned, not into dawn but into a sky with no stars at all, a smooth slate dome that swallowed light rather than offered it. He stood on a plain that couldn't decide between stone and sand; under his trainers, grit rasped over bedrock, as if the desert had been peeled back to its bones.

Ahead, a shape grew from the earth—a pyramid, but unfinished, its lower tiers crisp as cut sugar while its higher courses dissolved into scaffolds of shadow. Ramps spiraled up and up, then shivered into nothing, and the edges of the structure breathed faintly, as if stone were trying to remember it was alive.

Quentin's pulse pitched. *Dreams always carried their own kind of certainty, but this one hummed with intent, like the place had been waiting for him specifically.*

"Hello?" he called, though his voice seemed to fall straight down, crushed by the weight of the air.

A figure detached itself from the half-built angles and stepped into the unfinished illumination. Tall. Cloaked. The robe was the color of old plans turned to ash, stitched with lines that might have been cracks or might have been blueprints. The hood was deep enough to make a face impossible, but when Quentin strained he thought he saw planes—cheek, brow, the ghost of a smile that had never learned kindness.

"You've touched what was keyed to me," the figure said, and the words didn't travel through the air so much as vibrated through the plain, Quentin's ribs, and the mark in his right palm.

He clutched his sleeve without thinking. The pressure deepened under the fabric. "I don't know what you mean."

A soft, amused sound. Not a laugh. More like the idea of one, sketched and left unfinished. "Ah. You do know. But you've been taught to call it by a prettier name." The hood tilted toward his hand. "How does it feel, little keeper? Does the pressure between moments scrape at your bones? Do your breaths arrive before the world is ready for them?"

Quentin swallowed. The unfinished edifice loomed taller. Ropes stirred without wind, pulleys creaked without burden. "Who are you?"

"A question asked properly," the figure murmured, as if pleased. "Names are scaffolds. I've had many." The hood turned, considering the tiers of the structure with an artisan's pride and disdain. "Once, when stone obeyed and kings thought themselves eternal, they called me the Architect."

Something in the word rang—older than blueprints, older than chisels. Quentin's mouth went dry. "Are you... with them?" He couldn't bring himself to say Order, not here. "The ones in robes."

"The robes are new," the Architect said, almost bored. "Fashions crumble faster than limestone. But their hunger is old. They keep my memory in a dark jar and call it service." A pause, then a tone like a fingertip across glass. "You call your shard an Echo. Poetic. I prefer mechanism. Component. A piece of machinery that still works when the rest of the clock has rusted."

The plain stretched outward, empty of landmarks. Even the horizon felt rehearsed, a line someone had drawn lazily and then forgotten to ink again. Quentin took a step back. Grit whispered. The monument's shadow did not shift.

"I didn't ask for it," he said, hating the tremor in his voice. "Whatever this is."

"No one of consequence ever does," the Architect replied. "Kings, prophets, chosen children—history prefers accidents." He lifted a hand—long, elegant, the skin eerily smooth—and the ground obeyed. A slab rose from beneath the dust and settled between them: a stone table veined with darkness, its surface etched in fine lines that moved if he didn't look directly—maps of chambers under chambers, ribs under ribs.

On the slab, a single fragment held a trapped gleam. Not gold this time but a vitreous amber—a simulation of time caught in a lens. Quentin felt the tug of it like a hook through his chest.

"You've tasted Endurance," the Architect said, each syllable articulated like a measured cut. "The first of seven. Endurance that refuses to be eroded." His hood turned, and Quentin felt—impossibly—that eyes had settled on him. "I built these places so the world would not lose the pattern. When memory grew noisy, I partitioned eternity into pieces and hid each in a wonder. Clever, yes?"

He said it as if inviting praise. Quentin's hands curled. "If you made them, why… why are they secrets? Why hide them?"

"Hiding is a kind of building." The Architect's head cocked. "Walls are not only around things, boy. They can be around years. The Echo you carry is a brace against collapse. A beam in a storm. It will hold you when the world wants to finish you."

Quentin's traitor heart leapt at hold you, and then recoiled. "I don't want it."

The hood bent closer, the voice softening, coaxing. "Don't lie to yourself. You wanted, once. To be seen. To matter. To not slip like a footprint. The Echo answers small prayers with large tools."

Behind the Architect, the unfinished structural mass exhaled dust like breath. Somewhere, deep in its half-made belly, something struck stone in a steady rhythm: *chip, chip, chip*. Quentin's chest matched it unwillingly.

"You came to me," he said, "just to… gloat?"

"To welcome." The word had edges. "To measure the boy who will carry my old work across a newer age. To see if you will waste your beam shoring up other men's roofs, or whether you will learn to build."

Quentin stared at his sleeve. *Even here, he felt the resonance under his skin.* The void-black sky pressed low, the plain whirred, the scaffolded pyramid watched like a patient beast.

He dragged in a breath. “I won’t help them. The ones who hunt me.”

The Architect’s not-laugh moved again. “No, little keeper. You will help someone. The only question is which edifice you’ll choose to hold.” The hood tipped, almost conspiratorial. “And whether you will ask for payment.”

“Payment?”

“For being the hinge upon which doors swing,” the Architect said gently, as if explaining arithmetic to a child. “The world remembers its hinges. Or it breaks.” He turned toward the edifice, and the shadow of his gesture cut the plain. “Come. Let me show you how a dream can be built into permanence.”

He set his palm against the stone. The unfinished tiers trembled. Somewhere within the geometry, passages unfurled like scrolls, and light ran along seams as if poured.

Quentin hesitated, fear crawling cold under his skin—but curiosity pushes, relentless as tide.

He followed the Architect into the monument that was both half-born and eternal, and the door closed behind them without a sound.

— Δ —

The air inside the dream pyramid was heavy, vibrating with a low hum that seemed to seep from the walls themselves. Sand sifted down in thin veils from the unfinished ceiling, but when it touched the stone floor it vanished like smoke. The passage stretched ahead in impossible symmetry—perfect angles, no cracks, every block stained by its own trapped pallor, as if the stone remembered daylight.

Quentin followed, though his trainers made no sound here. The Architect glided, cloak brushing the floor, and with every step the structural mass seemed to widen, lengthen, complete itself, as though it were building around him in real time.

"Look," the Architect murmured, spreading a long hand.

The walls shivered. A pale current ran through the etched lines, then bloomed outward in panels of shifting vision. Quentin stumbled, blinking at the sudden overexposure.

Before him rose the Lighthouse of Alexandria, towering and pristine, its beacon sweeping a white arc across a glittering sea. Ships bowed their masts toward it in reverence. The scene shifted—the Colossus of Rhodes straddling a harbor, bronze gleaming, crowds gathered like ants at its feet. Then the Hanging Gardens, lush and impossible, water cascading down terraces green with vines.

One by one, each Wonder came alive in glory—the Temple of Artemis, the Statue of Zeus, the Mausoleum, each perfect, intact, untouched by ruin or time. Their stones shone as though freshly quarried; their builders sang praises; their kings smiled from gilded thrones.

Quentin's throat tightened. *All his life, the Wonders had been ruins in textbooks and fragile fragments in museums. But here, they lived—whole, dazzling, eternal.* And something inside him ached to reach for them, as though his hand might close around history itself.

"Magnificent," the Architect whispered, his voice weaving through Quentin's awe. "Once, I shaped the bones of nations. Once, I taught men how to build eternity. They thought themselves lords of earth and sky, but I… I gave them permanence."

The visions expanded, armies marching in ordered lines between the colossal statues, priests bowing before flaming altars, entire cities bending like grass to the shadows of the Wonders.

And in each Wonder, Quentin saw it—*the Echo*. Not a physical object, but a distortion in the very architecture of reality, a pressure-frequency that made the air feel thin and tight. It thrummed with the same sub-zero

load as the density in his right palm. His hand twitched, the sleeve dragging back to reveal the indurated antique-gold of the mark, and the skin around the mark tightened with a cold, axial frequency in recognition.

"Each Echo is a protocol of existence," the Architect said, tone smooth, coaxing. "Seven governing layers carved from the very foundations of the world. With one, you brace what time erodes. With all, you architect the marrow of reality."

Quentin tore his gaze from the wonders to stare at the hooded figure. "Architect it? For what? To… make people bow?"

"Not bow. Endure." The Architect leaned closer, the edges of his voice glinting with steel beneath silk. "You fear vanishing, boy. You fear being no more than a faint trace in other people's lives—forgotten when your bones are dust. These fragments—my fragments—mechanize memory. With them, you need not fade. With them, you could be calibrated into the world's foundation, as integral as the stars."

The load in Quentin's palm answered—cold and absolute. He thought of the jeers back home, the way Raj sneered, the way Sophia sighed with irritation, the way he'd been invisible at school until he tripped or fainted or spoke out of turn. He thought of how the group looked at him now—liability, nuisance, fool.

To matter. To finally matter. The lure ached in his chest.

But even as the temptation pulled at him, unease wormed through. The armies bowed too easily, their eyes blank with devotion. The priests' flames burned like threats, not prayers. The Wonders gleamed—but gleamed like cages, not marvels.

Quentin dragged in a breath. "You want me to… rebuild them? For you?"

"For the world," the Architect said, voice wrapping like velvet over steel. "For memory. For eternity. And for yourself. With me, you could be remembered forever. Not a boy stumbling after brighter stars. A builder. A Hinge. A name carved deeper than kings."

Quentin's stomach twisted. The visions pressed against his eyes, dazzling, overwhelming. But somewhere under the roar of promise he felt the mark settle again—steady, stubborn.

"I don't want forever," Quentin whispered. "I just want… truth."

The Architect stilled. For the first time, the hood dipped as if disappointed.

"Truth," he said softly, almost pitying. "You'll learn. All truth crumbles without a frame to hold it."

The walls trembled faintly, dust whispering from the seams. The glow of the visions flared, too bright, then fractured. The Wonders cracked like glass, their armies dissolving into sand.

The Architect stepped closer, voice dropping to a sharper chord. "But before you learn, you must lose. And loss, boy… loss is the greatest architect of all."

The pyramid groaned, the ceiling splitting wider as torrents of sand spilled like rivers, rushing around Quentin's shoes and swallowing the glowing slabs. The Architect's presence pressed heavier, suffocating, until it filled the entire chamber.

Quentin stumbled back, shielding his face, grit scraping his skin.

The Architect's hood loomed larger, his voice a whisper that cut like stone chisel against marble:

"Shall I show you?"

— Δ —

The tremor grew, running up through Quentin's feet like a living thing. The once-perfect walls cracked, hairline at first, then splitting wide, sand pouring from them in streams. The glowing visions shattered in sequence—Zeus's throne splintering like glass, the Colossus folding soundlessly at the waist, the Hanging Gardens withering into brittle vines before dissolving to dust.

Quentin staggered, arm over his face. "What's happening?"

The Architect did not move, though the structure shuddered around him. His cloak flared slightly in the shifting wind, but his voice remained smooth, steady, unnervingly calm. "Nothing lasts without me. Not kingdoms, not wonders, not lives."

Quentin gasped, forcing his eyes open through the storm of sand. "You said these Echoes were about permanence."

"And permanence is mine to calibrate—or revoke."

The Architect leaned closer, his hood eclipsing the fractured light. His words curled like smoke around Quentin's ear. "But beware, boy. Those who oppose me fall first. Even those you… care for."

The sand swirled faster, reshaping itself into a clinical simulation—clearer, sharper than the visions of the Wonders. A courtyard bloomed in the dust: stone shattered, rubble scattered. Beneath it, a body pinned, still as broken glass. Aisha's braid lay dark against her cheek, her eyes closed, blood pooling at her temple.

"No!" Quentin shouted, the word tearing his throat raw. He lurched forward, but the vision stayed just out of reach, held behind some invisible pane. "That's not real—it's not real!"

"Not yet." The Architect's tone was almost kind, a parody of comfort far crueler than threats. "But all structures must settle into their final form. Even hers."

The rage in Quentin's chest pressed harder than the Echo, drowning out fear. His whole body shook as if his bones could not contain it. "You're lying!" he cried. "You're just trying to—"

The ground split with a thunderous crack. Sand geysered upward, swallowing his words. The image of Aisha flickered, warped, then crumbled like everything else, buried beneath the collapse.

Quentin clawed at the shifting floor, his trainers sinking into dunes that hadn't existed moments ago. His lungs filled with grit, the air sharp as knives. Around him, the monument's interior peeled apart like a fragile model, its perfect geometry unspooling into chaos. His chest heaved, vision swimming.

The Architect stood unbothered, framed in the destruction. His presence grew larger in proportion to the ruin, as if collapse itself revealed his true scale. "Permanence has no mercy," he said, as if imparting a final lesson. "But it rewards obedience."

Quentin's fists clenched, his marked palm loading so hard it felt recast—as if the hinge were being tightened with a wrench inside bone. "I won't believe you!" he shouted, voice cracking. "I won't let that happen to her!"

At that, the Architect's head tilted, the hood dipping low, as though amused—or perhaps intrigued. A ripple of something—approval, hunger, promise—moved through the silence between them. "We'll see."

The walls caved in. Sand roared like the sea, sweeping Quentin off his feet, pulling him under. He fought to breathe, to see, to cling to anything—but the more he struggled, the deeper the grains dragged him. The Architect's silhouette blurred into a spire above him, dark and immovable, until even that dissolved in the storm.

Quentin's last sight was Aisha's braid again, half-buried in rubble, before the sand closed over his eyes.

And then there was nothing but darkness.

— Δ —

Quentin lurched upright with a cry, sweat slicking his hair to his forehead in damp clumps. His chest heaved as if he'd run the length of Cairo, lungs dragging for air that tasted stale and sour. The dormitory came into focus slowly—the slant of dawn light creeping across the ceiling, the soft hum of the fan, Liam's guttural snores.

Ischemic-like pain drove deep—structural—as if the bones in his right palm were carrying a load they weren't built for.

He ripped his sleeve back. The mark in his palm darkened into burnished old-gold, the hinge-geometry sharpening as if clamped from the inside. The skin around it went inelastic, tendon-tight—like cable under load. When he flexed, the sensation wasn't heat; it was sub-zero density, a weight that made his wrist feel bolted to something unseen.

Across the room, someone stirred.

Aisha.

She wasn't lying down. She was sitting upright in her bunk, back against the wall, eyes fixed on him. Watching. Her skin looked almost translucent in the half-light, but her gaze was sharp, too sharp for someone who had just woken. She hadn't been asleep at all. She had been waiting.

Quentin's throat scraped dry. "You… you saw that?"

Her eyes flicked to his exposed palm, then back to his face. She said nothing.

He swallowed hard, words tumbling before he could stop them. "I dreamed—I think I dreamed. A man. The pyramid unfinished. He called himself… the Architect. He—he showed me the Wonders, whole again. And then—" Quentin's voice cracked. "He showed me you. Buried. Bleeding. Said I'd lose you."

The air in the dorm thickened. Sophia shifted in her sleep, murmuring, but didn't wake. Liam snorted and rolled over, muttering something about camels. Nia curled deeper into her blanket. Raj lay still as stone, his back turned, but Quentin felt the weight of his attention—the stillness of someone listening too hard.

Aisha's fingers curled slowly around the blanket on her lap. For a heartbeat, she looked younger, vulnerable—then the mask slipped back into place. Her voice was low, careful. "That voice…"

Quentin leaned forward, desperate. "You know it."

Her eyes closed briefly, lashes trembling. When she opened them, something raw flickered there before it hardened again. Her reply was almost a whisper, as if the words themselves carried chains. "It's the one I was trained to obey. And the one I learned to survive."

The words struck harder than any blow. Quentin stared, the silence between them taut as wire. "Then you're—"

"I said enough." Her tone cut like glass, sudden and sharp, meant to end it. She turned her face to the window, the pale dawn tracing her profile.

Quentin pressed his marked right hand to his chest, the pressure refusing to ease. His head spun with the Architect's words, with Aisha's confession, with the image of her broken beneath rubble. The fear that had chased him through the dream still clung to him—sticky, suffocating—yet tangled now with something colder: the certainty that she carried secrets even darker than his own.

He wanted to ask a hundred questions, to demand the truth she kept smothered under her coldness. *Why obey? Who had trained her? Was she spy, prisoner, or something far worse?*

But Aisha's jaw was set, and her silence a wall higher than any edifice.

The fan creaked. The city stirred awake outside, voices rising faintly through the shutters—the call of a bread seller, the honk of a horn, the first shouts of children. The dormitory breathed steady, oblivious.

And Quentin sat trembling in the new morning, the Architect's echo still lodged in his bones, the weight of his mark refusing to ease, and Aisha's words anchoring him in fresh, unbearable truth.

She was bound to the same automated darkness that hunted him—whether as captive, accomplice, or something in between, he couldn't yet tell.

But the one certainty that settled over him—heavy, immovable—was this: she wasn't free. And neither was he.

Chapter 12
The Cost of Obedience

"A promise made in chains binds the heart more deeply than the iron."
— Axiom of the Shadow Order, Loyalty V.

— Δ —

Dawn slid into the courtyard like a shy guest, painting the tiles from slate to pearl and setting the fountain in motion with glints of scattered coins. Quentin sat on the low wall, hoodie wrapped tight though the morning was already warming. His notebook lay open beside him, pages ruffled by a breeze that smelled faintly of damp stone and baking bread. He'd sketched and crossed out until the lines blurred into one another: the unfinished pyramid, a hooded figure with no face, a braid half-buried in rubble.

His right palm throbbed. Every pulse of the mark sent a thin ache up his wrist—a sub-zero vibration tapped from the inside. "You've touched what was mine." The Architect's voice clung to him, cool as shadow.

And under it, Aisha's—low, almost breaking—"It's the one I was trained to obey."

The gate hinges creaked. Quentin flinched—ridiculous, yet reflexive, and then felt stupid for flinching at morning. A cat slipped through first, pausing to sniff a fallen bougainvillea petal before deciding it wasn't edible. Behind it came Aisha.

She had no makeup of scorn on, not this early. Just a grey hoodie, sleeves pushed to her elbows, hair braided clean and tight. Her expression looked thinner than usual, less armored, as if sleeplessness had softened the sharpness without erasing it. For once, she hesitated at the threshold, eyes flicking to him as if asking permission to enter a room that was not hers.

"You're up," she said. It wasn't much, not even a question, but the edges were softer.

"So are you," Quentin managed. His voice came out rough, scrapes of dream still clinging to it. He closed the notebook on a sketch before she could see. *He was not sure which felt worse—that she might have seen it, or that he wanted her to.*

Aisha stepped into the light. Her gaze took in the fountain, the bench, the tremor in his hand that he tried to still against his knee. She didn't come too near; she didn't keep her distance either. Balanced, as always, on some private line.

"Are you…" She let the word trail, then chose a different one. "All right?"

It was so ordinary—so un-Aisha—that it startled him more than any cut of sarcasm. He swallowed, buying time with breath. "Fine. Sleep was…," he began, and then remembered the image the Architect had spun of her and couldn't finish the sentence. The air scraped his throat going down.

"Liar," she said, without bite. Her tone was matter-of-fact, almost weary. "You look like you swallowed a sandstorm."

He huffed something between a laugh and a cough. The silence that followed wasn't hostile. It was tired, the way silence is when both people have used up their fight for the night and haven't yet found the next supply.

"I dreamt," he said finally, because the words needed somewhere to go that wasn't his rib cage. "About him. The Architect. He built… everything. Or said he did. He called the Echo a component. Like I'm carrying a spare part from his old machine."

Her face changed by degrees—no flinch, but a small tightening around the eyes, as if the sun had grown too bright. "He would," she murmured. "He doesn't love the world. He loves the blueprint."

Quentin stared at her. "You talk like you've sat at his lessons."

Aisha's mouth lifted, not a smile, exactly—more a weary curve. "Not at his feet. At a distance. Through others." She glanced toward the stairwell where the dormitory door sat, closed and sensible. "What did he want from you?"

"To build," Quentin said, the word tasting wrong. "To be… remembered. He showed me the Wonders as they were. I could feel them like—like notes in my bones. It was…" He searched for a word he wouldn't hate himself for. "Beautiful. And horrible. Like a cathedral that breathed."

Aisha looked at his right sleeve. He felt it even before she spoke. "And your hand?"

He watched his own fingers curl, slow and automatic. "Pressure-cold," he said. "Like it's thinking."

Her gaze lifted. The morning made her eyes look lighter, flecks of gold where he'd never seen them. "It is," she said softly. "In its way. The Echo isn't a jewel you wear. It's a verb. It does."

A cat leapt onto the fountain rim, considered the water with profound suspicion, and decided against drinking. The tiny sound of its landing was absurdly loud in the stillness. Quentin found himself watching it as if the right arrangement of whiskers could solve anything.

"He said I'd lose you," he blurted, and then wished for a retractable tongue. "He showed me you—hurt. Crushed."

Aisha's lashes flickered. A single heartbeat, and then the tactical veneer returned—not cruel, but careful. "He would," she repeated, as if that explained everything. "He drafts fear before he lays the first stone."

"I know it was a dream." Quentin pressed his thumb into the edge of his notebook hard enough to leave a crescent. "But it didn't feel like one."

"Not everything unreal is unloaded," Aisha said. The sentence landed between them and sat there, inconvenient as luggage in a doorway. She unwound one sleeve, then rewound it, as if her hands needed something to do before they betrayed her face. "Quentin… I meant what I said. About the voice. About my training." She glanced away. "I won't pretend I'm not… entangled."

"Entangled," he echoed dryly. "That's one word."

"It's the only honest one I have right now." She looked at him again. "You have every reason not to trust me."

He let out a breath he hadn't known he'd been holding. The admission should have made it easier; somehow it didn't. He searched her face for the angles he recognized: the contempt, the sharpened wit, the bureaucratic stillness. They were there, but dulled, like tools clean from use. Beneath them—something else. *Fatigue. Fear's outline.*

"Then why are you here?" he asked, and hated that the question sounded vulnerable.

Aisha considered the fountain, the cat, the first proper beam of sun spilling over the wall. "Because you look like you're about to shatter," she said simply. "And because if you do, you'll cut everyone near you."

He barked a laugh, surprised by it. "Poetic," he said, and immediately regretted teasing, as if that might scare the moment off.

But her mouth tipped again. “Don’t get used to it.” She shifted her weight, and the spell of softness thinned but didn’t break. “Eat something. You’ll think straighter. And try not to be alone today. Even if it’s with Liam.”

“Liam counts as two people,” Quentin said, the joke pulling a small, startled snort out of her. It felt like finding a phantom numbness where a wound should be.

She turned toward the door, then paused, fingers on the latch. “Quentin?” she said without looking back.

“Mm?”

“If the Architect comes again—don’t believe the first thing he offers, even if it shines.”

The latch clicked soft as a held breath. She was gone.

Quentin stared at the space where she’d stood, his chest a mess of load-sick throbs—the mark, the memory, the ridiculous relief of being asked if he was all right. He opened his notebook and found, beneath the gouged sketches, a single line he didn’t remember writing: *Hiding was a kind of building.*

He didn’t know if it was his thought or the Architect’s. He didn’t know if Aisha’s sudden gentleness had been mercy or mortar.

He only knew the morning had crept closer, and though the light spilled wider across the courtyard, he was no less lost inside it.

— Δ —

Evening slid down the buildings in honeyed sheets, and the city shifted keys—from brass-bright day to a lower, thrumming night. The hostel’s common room had been claimed by Liam’s card game and Sophia’s relentless inventory of “what went wrong today.” Quentin lasted five minutes before the noise scraped at his raw edges. He slipped into the stairwell and stood on the landing, breathing paint and dust, counting each heartbeat until the indurated mark in his right palm stopped feeling like it was trying to solder bone to bone.

The door below creaked. Aisha stepped into the narrow space as though she'd been conjured by his need to be alone. She didn't start; she never did. "You're hiding from the crowd again," she said mildly.

"Not people." Quentin pushed a hand through his hair. "Noise."

"Noise is a kind of cover." She tipped her head for him to follow. "Walk with me."

He hesitated. *Daylight Aisha—sharp, scornful, iron-boned—would have been easy to refuse. But this evening Aisha, in a plain black scarf and trainers... she was harder to turn away.* He thought of the courtyard that morning and the way relief had hurt as much as anything. So he nodded, more to himself than to her.

They cut through the lobby and out into the street, where the air tasted of diesel and frying oil, where shop lights blinked awake and the first calls to prayer braided through traffic horns. Aisha didn't take the main road to the market; she slipped into a side street where the cobbles had been patched with newer stone, where walls wore old posters like palimpsests. Laundry lines sagged overhead, a shiver of shirts against the bruised sky.

"I need…" Quentin began, then failed to finish. *Answers. That was what he wanted. But the word sounded greedy and childish both.*

Aisha saved him the attempt. "You need context," she said. "You need language for what's happening, or it will use you without asking your permission."

He almost laughed. "I thought that's what it was already doing."

"Then let's take back a little ground." She glanced at his pocket. "You still have the sketches?"

He faltered mid-step. "Why?"

"Because they'll fade," she said. "Not from the page—from your head. Dreams rot quickly. The Echo won't. But the shapes you saw around it…

they'll distort." She smoothed a curl of peeling poster with her fingertips, her movements oddly reverent, as if even scraps deserved their place. "Show me what you remember from the shaft. All of it. Don't edit."

Quentin's suspicion kicked, slow and late. He tucked his hands deeper into his hoodie. "You could just tell me," he said, aiming for flippant and landing on wary.

"I could," she agreed. "And you'd mistrust it because it came from me." She looked at him then—fully, not with the sidelong glances she tossed like decoys. Her eyes were steady but not hard. "Let's do it the other way round. You give me your version, and I'll tell you where it breaks."

He felt the old ache in his chest—the one that answered to teachers who saw the wrong person in him, to friends who didn't know how to carry his silences. He wanted—disastrously—to be seen correctly for once. "And if I'm not wrong?"

"Then you'll know you've got a map worth keeping."

They turned again, into a narrower alley pinched by leaning walls. A boy kicked a dented can past their feet, called out to a friend, vanished into a doorway that smelled of cumin and damp linen. Aisha led without seeming to lead—never hurrying, never quite falling into step with him, always half a stride ahead.

"You can't carry this alone," she said, softer now. "You know that. Liam will make jokes until the world ends. Sophia will turn problems into lists. Nia will draw and tell you nothing. Raj—" a flicker at her mouth, a grimace that looked more like truth than any of her words—"Raj will not help you."

Quentin's grip on the notebook in his pocket loosened. "And you will?"

"I can read some of it," she said. "Enough to keep you from drowning."

He stopped beneath a lopsided balcony where a geranium drooped like a tired flag. "Why?" The question surfaced harsher than he intended. "Why help me?"

"Because if you break," she said quietly, "you'll bring the rest of us down with you."

A beat.

"And because—" Her voice hitched and then shut itself off, as if even admitting the thought was dangerous. When she spoke again, the words were neat, scrubbed clean. "I know what it feels like to be given a burden without a manual."

The alley breathed. The sky above them deepened from pewter to indigo. A fan hummed behind a grated window.

Quentin took out the notebook.

He flipped to the pages he'd worried since that first day in the shaft—glyphs repeated until the pencil tore the paper, coils, feathers, circles lashed with lines, a constellation of marks that made sense if he didn't stare directly and refused sense when he did. He held the book halfway between them, as if either might snatch.

Aisha didn't. She bent her head close, and he caught the clean smell of soap, the warmth of a day's sun still in her braid. "That's not a hawk," she murmured. "It's a vulture. Mothers and graves. Endings and what remains." A fingertip ghosted a curve. "You keep confusing the rope with the water ripple. That one means binding. That one, temporal pressure registering."

He swallowed. "And this?"

Her breath hitched so slightly he almost missed it. "Echo," she said, and the mark in his palm answered like a plucked string. "And that—" She traced the small, sharp triangle he'd drawn again and again without knowing why "—is a warning. The way scribes mark something that can't be spoken aloud."

"How do you know this?" The question broke out of him sharper than he'd planned. "No more riddles. Say it straight."

She met his gaze. For a moment he thought she might. Then she touched his sleeve instead—lightly, a grounding, the way one steadies a cup someone else is spilling. "Because someone made sure I did." The touch was gone as quickly as it had come. Her tone was final, but her eyes—just for a moment—weren't. "Walk. There's someone who can explain the parts I can't."

They moved again. The alley narrowed, then widened into another without him registering the transitions. Quentin's unease stirred, came fully awake, lay down again under the balm of her low voice naming symbols he hadn't known he remembered. He let himself believe, for a handful of blocks, that they were only two students in a foreign city, comparing notes in twilight. That the world, just for this street, might be simple.

"You're sure about this 'someone'?" he asked.

"I'm sure," she said, and didn't add what she was sure of.

He was tired, and the Architect's words still gnawed at him, and her hand on his sleeve a minute ago had left a phantom numbness in his skin that made suspicion feel like ingratitude. He nodded, and they walked deeper into the city's veins, the hostel falling away behind them like a light closed in a distant room.

— Δ —

The evening had thickened into something close and secretive. The lamps strung above Cairo's main streets burned gold, casting wide nets of safety where families strolled and vendors hawked spices, scarves, and copper trinkets. But Aisha avoided those lights. She threaded Quentin through arteries too narrow for cars, into alleys where the glow fractured in uneven slabs, where the voices of the city dulled to a hush.

Quentin's trainers scuffed against stone slick with yesterday's wash-water. His notebook weighed heavy in his hoodie pocket. He told himself Sophia's relentless lectures would be better than this tightening in his chest—but each time he slowed, Aisha's glance over her shoulder drew him forward, wordless and unrelenting.

They passed a butcher closing his shutters, a boy balancing bread on a tray, a cat slipping from shadow to shadow. Each turn peeled away more noise until only the hum of neon from a broken sign and the faint whistle of wind down the corridor of walls remained. Quentin rubbed his palm against his thigh, trying to ease the constant cold load.

"This someone," he said, his voice too loud against the quiet, "who is he?"

"You'll see." Her answer was clipped, almost gentle in its refusal. Her fingers flexed once at her side—like she was resisting a string someone else had yanked.

"And if I don't want to see?"

Aisha stopped. For a heartbeat, she looked almost humanly conflicted, shoulders rising and falling as though weighing words. Then she touched his arm—light, brief, enough to steady him as he stumbled on a loose stone. The contact sent a jolt through his skin, at once disarming and treacherously reassuring.

"You'll want to," she said, her gaze holding his for one unsettling beat before she turned away, moving again before he could answer.

They went deeper. The air grew cooler, the light thinner, until even the stray voices of Cairo seemed left behind. Graffiti sprawled in flaking paint across the walls—arrows that pointed nowhere, names smudged by time. Quentin's unease mounted with each step. The notebook in his pocket felt suddenly like a beacon, its presence pressing against his ribs like a secret begging to be found.

"Where are we?" he asked, quieter now.

"The old quarter." Aisha's tone was factual, stripped of inflection. "Few tourists. Fewer questions."

The alley bent left, then again, narrowing like a funnel. Ahead, where the shadows gathered thickest, Quentin caught movement—figures standing too still, too deliberate. A prickling raced up his neck. He slowed.

Aisha didn't.

The figures separated from the dark as if they had been carved from it: robed shapes, hoods low, eyes glinting faintly beneath. Their silence was more menacing than any shout. One lifted a hand in greeting—or command. Quentin couldn't tell.

His breath came fast. "Aisha—"

"Keep walking," she said.

His heart tried to claw out of his ribs. "Who are they?"

Her grip tightened briefly on his sleeve, enough to guide him forward. "The ones who claim they can explain the glyphs."

Quentin's pulse stuttered. The echo of the Architect's voice curled up through his memory: *Those who opposed him would fall first. Even those he cared for.* He looked at Aisha's profile—calm, certain, more composed than she had ever seemed—and a chill spread through him.

"Explain," he said, voice almost breaking.

She didn't answer.

The robed figures closed the mouth of the alley. Behind them, the city's noise was gone, sealed away as if this narrow passage had slipped outside Cairo's map entirely.

Quentin felt it too late: suspicion blooming, sharp and bitter—but by then the trap had already closed around him.

— Δ —

The alley widened suddenly into a courtyard hemmed in by crumbling stone. A single lamp buzzed overhead, its glow thin and sickly, casting nervous shadows that clung to the walls like stains. The smell of damp dust thickened the air. Quentin's trainers scraped to a stop.

The robed figures stepped forward in a half-circle, their hoods swallowing their faces. The leader spoke in a voice like gravel ground against steel. "The boy is marked."

Quentin's gut turned to ice. He staggered back a step, notebook half out of his pocket as if paper sketches could shield him. "Aisha?" His voice cracked.

She was already moving. Past him, forward, into the pool of light where the shadows deepened around her. No hesitation, no backward glance. She didn't flinch at the Order's presence; she didn't question it. Her expression had lost its morning softness, its almost-kindness. Her mouth was a straight line, her eyes sharp.

"You wanted answers, Quentin," she said, voice carrying in the still air. "Here they are." Her voice didn't shake. Her hand did—just once—before she curled it into a fist and hid it in her sleeve.

For a second, he didn't understand. He searched her face for irony, for the flicker of a joke badly told. But her expression didn't shift. Only certainty stared back at him.

"No." The word tore out of him, raw. "No, you—you brought me here?"

Her silence was the confirmation.

Rough hands seized his arms before he could move. Iron cuffs bit into his wrists, cold and final. He twisted, tried to wrench free, but the mark in his right palm indurated—a sudden sub-zero density that cabled his tendons tight and buckled his wrist like a joint taking too much mass. The strength bled out of him in waves, leaving only the sting of chains and the throb of betrayal. The figures moved with efficiency, practiced. This was no chance encounter. It had been arranged.

Quentin lifted his head, desperation cutting through his voice. "Why? Aisha, why?"

Her eyes flickered—just once. For a heartbeat, he thought he saw hesitation, guilt. But then her chin lifted, and her words came clipped, rehearsed. "You're not ready for what you carry. Better it's taken from you before it destroys more than yourself."

"You don't get to decide that!" His voice cracked against the stone walls, wild and useless.

The leader of the Order inclined his hooded head toward her, as though she had passed some test. Chains clinked as Quentin was hauled upright, his breath shallow and ragged.

Aisha turned away. The dark pendulum of her hair swayed with the motion, maddeningly ordinary. Too ordinary, when everything else had shattered. She didn't look back—not once.

Something fractured inside him then—not the mark, not the visions, but the small, fragile bridge he had been building between them since the courtyard that morning. A bridge made of hesitant trust, of questions shared in half-light—and now splintered beyond repair.

Her silhouette, caught in the buzzing lamplight, wavered at the edges. For the barest instant, her stride faltered. But she didn't stop.

Quentin's voice dropped to a hoarse whisper only he could hear. "Please… don't do this."

But she was already gone into shadow.

And he was left bound in the Order's grasp, the weight of betrayal pressing harder against his chest than the shackles cutting into his skin. The sound of another pair of cuffs snapping shut on his ankles was almost drowned out by the thud of his own despair.

— Δ —

The courtyard dissolved into movement and restraint. Quentin was half-dragged, half-shoved down a narrow stairwell hidden behind a sagging iron gate. The hinges screamed as the Order forced it open, and the smell that met him was worse than the sound: stale water, rust, and the breath of stone left too long without light.

The steps spiraled, each one stealing a little more air from his lungs. The cuffs clanked with every jolt of his arms. His trainers slipped once on moss-slick stone; a fist in his collar yanked him upright before he could fall. They didn't speak. None of them did. Their silence pressed heavier than the chains, a judgment passed without words.

The passage ended at a door that looked more like a slab pried from the earth than something built by men. A shove between his shoulder blades sent Quentin stumbling into a chamber no larger than the hostel lounge. The walls sweated damp. A torch guttered in an iron bracket, its smoke staining the ceiling black. Beyond it, shadow reigned.

The Order's hands shoved him again, and he crashed against the far wall. The cuffs rang as they struck stone. He bit back a cry, anger knotting with pain until his throat felt scorched.

The leader murmured something in a language Quentin didn't know, and then they left. The slab-door ground shut. The lock turned like the grind of old teeth, sealing him in.

Darkness settled.

Quentin slid down the wall until he was sitting on cold stone. His breath came sharp and fast. He pressed his bound hands against his chest, willing the pressure in his palm to fade. It didn't. The mark pressed denser, as if mocking his helplessness.

From somewhere beyond the walls came sound—low, rhythmic, almost like a heartbeat at first. Then he realized: *chanting.* The syllables rolled in waves, incomprehensible but heavy, like stones tumbling over one another. Each phrase seemed to crawl into his bones, vibrating through marrow.

He squeezed his eyes shut. *Don't listen. Don't give them the ground they want.*

But the words from earlier cut through anyway: "You wanted answers, Quentin. This is the price." Aisha's voice, flint and final. He saw again the way her shoulders had squared, the way she had turned from him. And worse—the flicker in her eyes. That half-second of guilt that made the betrayal sharper.

"She meant it," he whispered, the sound rasping in the cold. "She meant it."

But another part of him refused. *She hesitated. She didn't look back because she couldn't.* That hesitation replayed in him like a splinter, too small to grasp, too sharp to ignore. He hated himself for clinging to it, hated how his chest twisted at the memory of her hand steadying him in the alley.

The torch guttered again, throwing shadows like grasping hands across the walls. Quentin turned his head into his knees, his breath fogging the stone.

"Why, Aisha?" The words slipped out, cracked and fragile. "Why?"

The chant beyond the walls swelled. The mark in his palm packed down, sub-zero and brutal, until his wrist felt like a bolt sunk into bone. He pressed his forehead against his bound wrists, feeling smaller than he ever had, more powerless than when he'd first fainted in the Pyramid, when the world had seemed to tilt away from him.

His heart pounded against the cuffs, the metal biting harder each time he moved. The chanting beyond the walls rose and fell in heavy waves, and the mark answered—not with light, not with heat, but with load. A sub-zero density settled into his palm until his bones felt bolted to something unseen, a hinge tightened by an invisible wrench. It wasn't enough to free him. It wasn't enough to silence the voices. But it was there—awake, insistent, refusing to vanish.

In the dark, Quentin let the question hang unanswered.

And in that silence, the shadows seemed to lean closer, as though listening for his surrender.

Chapter 13

Iron and Afterimages

"The isolation of the vessel ensures the purity of the infusion." **— Fragment of the Architect's Scroll, XIII.**

— Δ —

Stone pressed on him from every direction, a weight he could taste.

Quentin woke with grit in his mouth and iron biting his wrists. For a long second, he didn't know where his body ended and the wall began. Cold leached through the back of his skull into his thoughts. When he tried to move, the movement stopped at the clink of chain and a sharp, starving throb up both arms.

Darkness wasn't total. A slit of light seeped in from somewhere high and mean, catching the damp on the stones so they glistened like the inside of a throat. Dust hung in the air, visible only when it wandered through that thin blade of light and turned to drifting cinders. The rest was shadow, dense and layered, stitched with the soft, steady pulse of sound from far away—voices, low and rhythmic. Chanting. The Order's words crawled like ants along the walls, too muffled to understand, too exact to ignore.

He swallowed. His tongue felt like a dry rag. When he breathed in, the air smelled of cold mineral, old ash, rust, the faint animal tang of sweat. His shoulders shook once—an involuntary shudder as the cold found his core—then settled into a throb that matched the pressure in his right palm.

He flexed his right hand against the stone at his side. Cold packed under the skin where the Echo had marked him, an ache of a bruise pressed too hard. He could almost sense its outline even in the dark, bruise-metal beneath skin. It answered the chanting with its own dim rhythm, as if the sound reached into him and tugged strings.

"No," he whispered, and the word cracked like a twig. The stones swallowed it whole.

He tested the chains. Left wrist: a manacle winter-cold and gritty with sand, the edge chewing his skin raw. Right wrist: the same, the chain links bolted into the wall, unforgiving. Ankles: shackled too, not enough slack to lie flat; the angles forced by the shackles made his lower back complain in a dull, persistent swell. He drew his knees up until the iron bit, then let them fall again. Each shift sent a small chime of sound rippling along the metal into the wall.

He breathed through his nose, measuring. *In. Out.* The chant didn't change. His heart still raced as if he'd been running. He wasn't. He was still.

Now he had nowhere to move, nothing to draw—a slit thin as a paper cut. His knee twitched anyway, and the chain answered with a tiny kiss of metal on metal that sounded loud as a door slam.

Think.

The word arrived without comfort. He obeyed anyway. He pictured the corridor he'd been dragged through—torchlight smeared into gold by tears he refused to admit; the pressure of hands on his shoulders; the slam of a door that didn't echo as long as he'd expected, like the room had been waiting for him. He pictured Aisha's face at the last moment he could see it, hard as the blade of light, turned away.

His jaw locked. The pressure in his palm sharpened.

He lifted his hand as far as the chain allowed and pressed the marked skin flat to the wall. The stone felt slick and indifferent beneath his palm. He let the air fight its way into his lungs and out again, and he concentrated on the mark. On the way it didn't ache like injury but pressed like physics—a constant, sub-zero insistence. He didn't have the words for it, so he found other ones. *Quiet. Hold. Slow.*

For a breath, nothing changed.

For the next breath, the world... tightened. The trickle of dust through the beam of light seemed to stretch; the motes thickened like snow deciding mid-fall to hover. The cold under his palm thinned to something else—vibration, faint as a cat's purr.

Yes. He leaned into that sensation, teeth gritted, chasing the shiver of almost. The chains creaked. He imagined them older than iron, imagined the links remembering a time before they were shaped, remembering ore in earth, heat and hammer. He imagined time around them loosening like a knot.

Pain knifed across the tendons of his wrist. The purr went out. The dust fell like ordinary dust again. The chant snapped back into focus. The mark in his right palm indurated—hardening back into a rigid, sub-zero knot.

Quentin sagged against the wall and let his head thump the stone once, softly. The sound was small and mean and made him flinch as if someone else had struck him.

"Fine," he said to the dark, because if he didn't say something he'd drown in it.

His throat wanted water. His stomach wanted anything. His muscles wanted a bed and an absence of iron. None of those were here. What he had was the weight of the walls and the slow drip—he heard it now, metronomic—from somewhere behind him. What he had was time, and time here felt carnivorous.

He tried again—because stopping felt like surrender dressed in logic. He braced his boots, took what slack there was in the chains, and pulled. Not with the Echo this time—just with his body. The iron held. The bolts ground faintly in the stone; that awful halfway sound of something willing to move but choosing not to. His shoulders burned; his wrists screamed; his breath frayed at the edges. He let go before something in him tore and left him less than chained.

He slumped. Iron bit deeper because that's what iron does when you relax—it takes. He tilted his head until his cheek rested against the wall and closed his eyes because the room looked the same either way.

Silence crept in around the chanting and the drip. Not real silence—silence made of small sounds you stop counting before they drive you mad. His thoughts tried to flood in. He didn't let them. Not the image of Aisha's hand leaving his sleeve. Not the memory of Liam's voice making everything stupidly brighter. Not the shape of Nia's pencil moving in air, lines pulled from the future like threads. Not Sophia's stare—the one that weighed and found him lacking. Not his father—no. Not yet. He held the door against all of them with the fragile barricade of his breath.

The Echo didn't care about his barricades. It pulsed anyway, a heartbeat under skin that didn't belong to the rest of him. When he focused on it, the cell felt narrower; when he ignored it, the cell felt infinite. The paradox made his teeth ache.

He wondered how deep they were. How far from the sky he'd looked at on the rooftop and pretended meant something. He wondered if the

Great Pyramid knew he was under it, if the stones that had watched dynasties go to dust had any opinion about one student chained in a hole. The thought was absurd enough that his throat caught on something like a laugh, but the sound broke jagged halfway out.

The ritual chant grew, or felt like it did. A phrase repeated, climbing and falling, a melody without mercy. It made his skin crawl. He tried to track its pattern and failed; every time he thought he had caught the measure, they slipped like wet rope in his hands. He pressed the back of his head harder into the stone until the pressure overruled the sound for a second.

"Stop," he told the not-quite-voice that sometimes bent the air around him. "Stop. Please."

Nothing stopped. The drip kept time. The chant kept speaking a language he hoped never to know. The dust kept floating in and out of the light like a constellation with nowhere to be. His mark kept time with all of it and with none of it, stubborn and separate.

He let his hands go slack in the iron. Pins and needles flared as blood returned to fingers he hadn't realized were numb.

"Okay," he told the cell, because the cell was listening if nothing else was. "You win this part."

He didn't add *for now*. The stones would hear the lie. He breathed. He decided on a next breath after this one. And then one after that. The Echo throbbed on, mean and constant, a cold insistence that told him he was still here even when every other part of him wanted to leak out between the stones and be gone.

He tilted his head toward the seam of light and tried to imagine the sky. It was easier to picture the way the bazaar lamps had caught in glass than the real sun; easier to remember the blue pendant warm in his fingers than to believe something warm existed above him.

His throat worked again. A single word stirred and curdled there. He didn't let it out. Not yet.

He closed his eyes tighter and listened to the drip and the chant and the clink of his own breath catching on iron, and he counted in a language that belonged to no one but him: *inhale, exhale, endure. Again.*

— Δ —

The dark pressed differently when his eyes closed.

Quentin sagged against the wall, exhaustion a weight heavier than chains. His body was still, but his mind wouldn't stop moving, tumbling back into places he thought he'd outgrown.

It started with a voice. Not Archon Thales, not the Architect, not even Aisha's sharp-edged words. It was his father's, low and flat, replayed so clearly he could almost hear it bouncing off the cell's stone: "You're not like the others, Quentin. You're ordinary."

He winced. That word had followed him like a second shadow his whole life. Ordinary in class, ordinary on the basketball court where his friends vaulted past him, ordinary at family dinners when his cousins traded stories of scholarships and trophies. His father never yelled—he didn't need to. His sentences landed like quiet verdicts, as casual as brushing crumbs from a table: "You're not special, Quentin. Not like them."

He pulled against the chains again, as if effort might overwrite memory. The manacles scraped skin raw, the sound loud in his ears. He let his arms drop. He couldn't fight steel any more than he could fight that voice.

Ordinary.

And yet… here he was, locked beneath the earth because something inside a pyramid had chosen him. He remembered the vision—priests intoning, stone walls alive with light, the shard pulsing with impossible power. The mark tightened into his palm. The bazaar breaking into countable instants—blades too close, dust too sharp, every detail over-resolved as if the world refused to move until he did. It had felt like the world yielding, even though it was only him being forced to endure it.

Was it a mistake?

He'd asked himself that question in a hundred shapes since the Pyramid. *Why him, of all people? He was not the smartest—Sophia outpaced him without trying. He was not the funniest—Liam could make anyone laugh. He was not the strongest, the boldest, the anything. Just the kid who sketched at the edges and hoped not to be seen.*

And yet the Echo had noticed.

He tried to picture it choosing someone else—Raj, maybe. Confident, competitive, someone who demanded attention. Or even Aisha, who carried herself like someone already carved from destiny. They would make sense. They fit the part.

Not me.

His father's voice came again, sharper this time, like it had cut through the layers of stone to find him. *Ordinary. The kind of person the world could misplace and never notice.*

Quentin pressed his forehead to the cold wall, chains clinking as he leaned into the ache. The Echo's pressure in his palm pulsed harder, a counter-beat to the voice, but it didn't silence it. If anything, the pressure only mocked him—because it didn't care what anyone called him. It was there. Constant.

The mark loaded once, abruptly, a sub-zero clamp tightening through tendon and bone. His fingers jerked against the cuffs, not from heat—from the wrongness of weight where weight shouldn't be, like gravity had shifted a half-degree inside his palm.

Maybe his father was right. Maybe the Echo chose wrong.

His throat went tight. He let his breath out slow, ragged, and in the silence that followed he whispered into the dark: "I don't know if I'm enough."

The words didn't echo. They died against the stone like they had been waiting there all along.

For a moment, he thought the chanting outside had answered—that the syllables bent around his confession, sharper, hungrier. His skin prickled. He shut his eyes tighter, burying the thought. But the load in his palm didn't fade. It throbbed once, twice, steady as a drum he couldn't drop, as if disagreeing.

He curled his fingers despite the cuffs, chasing that stubborn rhythm. The cell didn't care. The voice didn't care. But the Echo did—small, insistent, refusing to agree that ordinary meant empty.

Quentin swallowed, tasted dust, and let the counter-beat mark time for him: *not special, maybe; not chosen well, maybe; but still here.*

— Δ —

The dark thinned.

Not by light—by something shifting in Quentin's head. One moment the cell was stone and chain and the drip-drip of water. The next, it blurred, edges bending, as if he'd slipped sideways between breaths into another layer of the world.

He blinked, but his eyelids did nothing. The images came anyway.

Liam first. Always Liam first, like the world expected him to lead with noise. But there was no noise now. His voice should've been there, brash and ridiculous, but it wasn't—his mouth moved soundlessly, wide with panic, before a rough hand slammed him against stone. The absence of laughter hit harder than the violence—like someone had ripped the air out of him first. Quentin's chest knotted.

Then Sophia. Rigid, unyielding Sophia, gagged with rough cloth, arms bound behind her back. She kicked once, twice, spine straight even as shadows dragged her. Her eyes found Quentin through the haze, sharp as broken glass, a language of fury and plea at once, stabbing through him like accusation carved into stone.

Nia followed, seated cross-legged on the ground, her sketchbook open in her lap. But her eyes were closed. Her hand moved anyway, pencil scratching across the page in strokes too quick to follow. Her face was pale, lips murmuring something he couldn't hear. The pages filled with shapes that twisted when he looked too long—glyphs he half-recognized, warnings he didn't want to. Her sketches seemed to deepen faintly, the marks writhing as though alive, searing themselves into Quentin's vision even after he looked away.

And Aisha—Aisha was last. She hung against chains like his own, but her eyes brimmed with tears. She didn't look at him. She looked at the floor, shoulders trembling.

Quentin's throat closed. He lurched forward, chains rattling, but he didn't move in the vision. *He was both inside it and outside, trapped as witness.* The helplessness was worse than pain—it hollowed him out, left him raw and useless in front of the people who trusted him least but still stood beside him.

And then came the voice.

Smooth. Heavy. Sliding through the gaps between his thoughts.

"You cannot protect them."

The words weren't spoken in anger. They were stated, plain, inevitable.

Quentin's skin went clammy. "Stop," he whispered.

"You cannot protect them," the voice said again, almost kind this time. "You cannot even save her."

Her.

Aisha's head lifted. Her eyes finally found his, and they were broken glass—sharp, shattered, impossible to hold. The sight speared him worse than the voice did.

"No," he rasped. His chains dug in, cutting his wrists as he strained forward. "I won't let this happen."

The laughter came soft, curling like smoke around his ears. It didn't rise or echo. It just coiled close, intimate, like it already lived inside him. "Won't let?" The voice didn't need to say more. The words unspoken were worse: "You don't decide."

The images shifted, flashing quick as lightning: Aisha struck down in the collapsing chamber, Sophia's scream strangled, Liam's jokes choked to nothing, Nia's pencil snapping mid-sketch. Over and over, like a cruel gallery hung only for him. The scenes repeated with slight differences each time—different angles, different endings—until Quentin felt trapped in an infinite loop of failure.

Quentin tried to shut his eyes. Tried to shut his ears. But the visions lived under his skin now, behind his eyelids, written in the stutter of the Echo itself.

"You are weak," the voice breathed. "You are ordinary. They will fall, and you will break."

His father's words twisted into it, merged, became indistinguishable. *Ordinary. Not enough.* It was his father's disappointment and the Architect's disdain, fused into one verdict too heavy to outrun.

His breath came ragged, head pressed against the chains until the iron cut deeper.

And still, somewhere beneath the weight of dread, the Echo pulsed. Slow. Stubborn. As if it didn't care about the voice. As if it only cared about the next beat.

Endure.

Quentin clung to that word like a handhold, but the vision didn't break. It thickened, pressing harder, until he felt the stones themselves shudder with it. His own heartbeat synced with the mark, defiant in its rhythm, whispering through the dread: *not finished yet.*

— Δ —

The silence after the visions felt louder than the chant.

Quentin sagged, chains digging into his skin, chest heaving like he'd run miles without moving an inch. His throat burned from words he hadn't said aloud. The images clung—Aisha in chains, Nia's blind sketches, Liam's silence. They lingered like afterimages burned into his sight, impossible to blink away.

He pressed his forehead to the stone and let the cold leech at the panic in him. The wall was rough, jagged in places, damp in others. For a moment he thought it would hold him steady. *He wanted it to—wanted to believe the wall was solid where he was not.* But when he shifted, something different whispered across his skin.

Not stone—air.

He blinked into the dark and dragged his face sideways until his cheek scraped. His fingers, bound but still free enough to reach, groped along the wall. The surface felt solid, unyielding. And then, just near the corner where the chains angled, his nail dipped into a hairline crack.

A line of weakness. And through it, faint as breath, a thread of light touched his skin.

It wasn't torchlight—it was something purer, thinner, like moonlight smuggled through stone.

Hope jolted through him so sudden it hurt.

He wedged his right palm against the crack. The Echo answered instantly—not with heat, not with light, but with a hard, cold axial pulse that numbed his skin and made his teeth ache. The stone didn't glow. It thrummed. A fine vibration traveled up his arm, into the iron, into the wall—like the chamber had become a tuning fork and he'd struck the note by accident.

The damp on the rock shifted. Moisture beaded along invisible lines, gathering where the surface wasn't quite flat. In the thin blade of light from above, those beads gathered and outlined something that had been there all along: etched grooves—old, shallow, patient.

Glyphs. Faint, not shining—simply made visible, as if the wall had decided to stop pretending it was blank. A vulture shape. A circle split by a line. The sharp triangle of warning. They didn't blaze; they clarified, trembling in the condensation like breath on glass.

And in that heartbeat, the chains shifted.

A clink, a fraction of slack.

Quentin's breath caught. He pulled hard, wrists jerking until the manacles bit flesh. For a second, he swore the iron softened, not bending, but… lagging—like it couldn't keep perfect time with his pulse. Outside, the chant seemed to drag, syllables stretching as if someone had dipped the sound in thick water.

Yes.

But then—nothing.

The vibration collapsed. The damp lines broke apart into ordinary wet stone. The glyphs vanished back into invisibility. The chains snapped taut again, sharper, crueler. The world resumed its tempo like a throat clearing after a stumble.

Quentin sagged against the wall, cold all the way through. The crack remained. Just a hairline flaw in the rock. Just enough to prove the wall could lie.

"Aisha…"

The sound carried everything he didn't know how to name—hate, hurt, need, and a fragile hope so thin it felt cruel just to hold.

Her name filled the cell, quiet but sharper than the chanting beyond, a blade he didn't know if he meant for her or himself.

Silence answered.

The drip went on. The low-frequency ritual went on. And Quentin sat, chained and small, the Echo's mark throbbing weakly against his right palm—a structural anchor, refusing to let him come apart.

Chapter 14

The Shadow's New Servant

"A misplaced component must be repurposed, or discarded. There is no middle ground." — **Axiom of the Shadow Order, Efficiency I.**

— Δ —

The stronghold smelled of old smoke and stone that had never seen the sun.

Aisha stood in its heart, a wide chamber where the walls hunched close and torches bled shadows across carved glyphs. The air was heavy with incense, thick and acrid, the kind that clamped her lungs rather than cleansing them. She kept her chin high, though her gut still twisted with Quentin's face in the alley, the disbelief in his eyes when the Order seized him.

She told herself this was victory. That it was proof she had not failed the purpose she'd been raised for. That his betrayal of trust was necessary, not personal.

At the far end of the chamber, Archon Thales waited. His robe was the color of midnight, his hood casting his face into darkness, but his presence filled the room like a weight pressing down on her chest. The robed figures, other leaders of the Order, flanked him, silent, faceless, waiting for her words.

"He's captured," she said. Her voice was steady—she made sure of it. "The boy who carries the mark. He will not trouble us further."

The silence stretched. A flicker of torchlight revealed the faint curve of Thales's mouth, not a smile, not approval—something cooler, emptier.

"You have served your purpose," he said at last, voice low and measured, carrying without effort. "The Echo is contained. The boy is in chains. You will step aside now."

Her throat caught. "Step aside?"

Her voice broke the chamber's hush, too sharp, too human.

One of the figures beside him tilted their head, as if amused by her question. Thales did not look at her when he spoke again. "Do not presume you matter beyond this. The Order has no use for sentiment, no patience for ambition beyond what is assigned."

Aisha's blood went cold. She had expected recognition. At least a nod for her cunning, her precision. She had been groomed since childhood for this work, told that her place within the Order was special, sacred. That obedience would be rewarded with belonging, safety, greatness.

Her entire life had been poured into this moment, and now it was discarded with a sentence. Dismissed with a flick of words.

Expendable.

"I brought him to you," she said, before she could stop herself. Her voice cracked against the stone. "I—"

"You obeyed," Thales cut in, tone clipped and final. "Nothing more."

The torches sputtered. Shadows leapt like jeering faces along the walls.

Even the carved glyphs seemed to mock her, their golden edges catching flame as if whispering: *nothing, nothing, nothing.*

Aisha kept her body rigid, but her insides were collapsing. Memories rose unbidden—endless drills in barren courtyards until her arms shook, blades cutting empty air until her hands blistered. Masked tutors whispering that loyalty was life, that she was chosen, that sacrifice was glory. Ritual nights when her body was painted with ash and she was told she was part of something eternal.

Every scar, every bruise, every sleepless night had been an offering. And now those offerings were dust. As if she were nothing.

Her mouth went dry. She bowed her head to hide the fury rising behind her eyes, the kind of fury that was dangerous if seen too soon. The chains she had imagined binding Quentin felt suddenly like they were on her wrists as well.

"Yes, Archon," she said softly. The words scraped her tongue. Obedience, even now, was all she had left to offer.

Thales turned away. His dismissal was complete. The other robed figures melted into the shadows, their whispers like dry leaves.

Aisha stood alone in the dim chamber, torchlight guttering, smoke curling around her. For the first time in years, the certainty she'd carried like armor cracked. She had given them Quentin, and in return, they had stripped her of everything she thought she was. The victory she'd promised herself tasted of ash.

And in the hollow that betrayal left, something unfamiliar stirred.

Doubt—and beneath it, the dangerous spark of anger she could no longer name as loyalty.

— Δ —

The corridor outside the cells breathed cold.

Aisha moved through it like smoke, silent, her steps swallowing the torchlight puddles one after another. The stone here was different from the chamber—rougher, less sanctified by ritual, its damp honesty closer to a dungeon than a temple. Chains rattled when the air shifted. Somewhere far down, a guard coughed and then tried not to.

She told herself she was here to confirm security. To ensure the mark-bearer was where he needed to be before the ritual moved forward. To keep the Order's work clean.

But her heartbeat refused to steady. Her feet felt heavier with each step, as if walking through water.

She paused at the corner where the hall narrowed and the temperature dropped a degree. The torches along the wall hissed, their flames caged in iron. On the left, a slit window no wider than a hand let in a line of night. It knifed across the floor, cold as water. She remembered standing at a slit like that as a child, pressing her face to the stone to feel the outside world as a stripe on her skin.

A sound drifted from the second cell on the right. Not the clank of iron, not the shuffle of a guard. A voice. Ragged, low, as if dragged over gravel.

"...enough..."

Aisha stopped.

Another murmur, barely shaped. The syllables failed, started again. "...don't... I don't know if..."

His voice. Quentin's.

The Order taught her to hear without listening, to gather information without being gathered by it. She had spent years walking past suffering and cataloguing it for usefulness. But now she stood and let the sound touch her instead of deflecting it. The words weren't for her. That made them more dangerous. And truer.

She stepped closer to the bars.

He was a darker shape in the dark, knees drawn, wrists lifted by iron, head bowed to the stone as if receiving a benediction from a cruel god.

In the thin seam of light from the slit window, dust drifted around him like pale insects. His breath fogged faint and then vanished. The mark beneath his skin tightened, a cold density she could almost feel— a cold lock pretending to be calm.

"Ordinary," Quentin whispered into the stone, as if confessing to it. The word snagged in him, cut him as it came out. She flinched. Not at the word itself—she'd heard worse laid on people—but at the way it sat on him, ill-fitting and heavy, a chain forged elsewhere and locked on him when he was too young to resist.

In her mind, other voices answered. "Obedience is safety. Belonging is earned. You are a blade; a blade has no desire except the wielder's." They were the catechisms she'd been fed in shadowed rooms by teachers who never removed their tactical veneer. She had believed them because belief kept you warm when the world did not. Because the Order promised to lift her out of the smallness of being a girl in a narrow alley of a city that ate girls.

She studied him, that strange boy who had stumbled into a shaft he shouldn't have found and touched a wall he shouldn't have touched, and the Pyramid had answered.

He was not what she would have chosen. Not sharp enough. Not hard. He apologized with his eyes even when his mouth tried to be brave. He fumbled jokes in the wrong places. He drew when he should have hid. When the world bent around him, he looked terrified that it might break.

And yet—even when she warned him—he had kept moving. Even when she delivered him into chains.

She leaned her forehead briefly to the cold iron of the doorframe, so the stone could steal some of the ischemic flush from her face. The torch down the hall hissed; a guard shifted. Aisha straightened and moved on, forcing herself past his cell as if the air there were no thicker than anywhere else.

But the corridor didn't release her. Not the way it usually did when she walked the stronghold and took inventory of the Order's assets and liabilities. Her steps slowed again at the next intersection, and she found herself looking back. The torch behind her guttered; the shadows lengthened to beckon. *Ridiculous.* She was not a recruit anymore to be jerked on a leash by impulse. She had learned control. She had learned to empty herself and be useful.

She closed her eyes. Let the old lessons spool by like prayer beads through her fingers:

They found you in a slum courtyard—thin, angry, hands already quick.

They trained you until bruises turned to muscle and fear sharpened into edges.

They gave you a name worth saying in their halls, a name that never left them.

And in return?

Obey. Don't presume to matter.

The words from the chamber hit her again, a slap that kept echoing. The Archon's voice had always been iron wrapped in velvet. Tonight he'd taken the velvet away. She had delivered the boy. She had performed the work. She had proven her usefulness. And he had shown her, with surgical precision, how easily she could be discarded.

Through the bars behind her, Quentin made a sound—half-breath, half word. It should not have reached her. It did.

"—Aisha." Barely there. Not an accusation in that breath; not yet. A drowning person saying the name of shore.

Her hand tightened on the edge of her cloak until her knuckles ached. The Order had a rule about visiting prisoners without sanction. Another about allowing names to reach you. Names made bridges. Bridges could be crossed in both directions.

She pictured herself at twelve again, sitting on cold tile while a bureaucratic tutor unrolled a cloth full of knives and said, "Choose one."

She had touched the smallest blade because it looked least cruel. The tutor had laughed softly and pressed the heaviest into her palm until her wrist bowed. The world chooses the weight. You learn to carry it.

She turned back toward Quentin's door.

Not in, not yet. Just close enough that the iron cooled the heat riding her cheekbones. Close enough that if she breathed lightly she could hear the uneven rhythm of his, the hitch when a vision snagged him, the forced steadying when he tried to hold himself together. She watched the way his fingers worried at the chain as if he could will it to soften.

This was not yours, she told herself in the silent language the Order had taught for thoughts-that-could-not-be-said. *This was the work. He was the work.*

But another part of her—small, treacherous, the part that had once grabbed his arm in the collapsing shaft—whispered instead: *He was a person.*

She swallowed hard. The word felt foreign in a mouth taught to say asset, lever, threat.

Down the corridor, footsteps approached, slow and bored. A guard on rotation. Aisha stepped away from the bars, cloak settling, expression arranged back into neutrality. The guard nodded at her as he passed, eyes down; she was still a blade here, even if the Archon had tried to shove her back into the sheath.

She let him go by. When his tread faded, she remained where she was another breath and then another, as if time could be stretched here by will alone. It could not.

Aisha turned at last and walked the corridor again, slower. At the far bend she stopped and touched the wall with her fingertips. The stone was cold, impersonal. Beneath it, she imagined the older bones of the Pyramid, the deep places that remembered more than any Order ritual. The Echo pulsed somewhere in those depths, distant as a heartbeat in someone sleeping in another room. When she closed her eyes, she could almost hear two rhythms answering each other—his mark, steady in pain; the stone, patient in time.

Her certainty fissured wider. Light crept in through the crack. She hated that it felt like relief.

By the time she reached the stair that climbed toward the chambers where the Order ate and argued, she had already decided a thing she told herself she hadn't decided. It waited for her at the edge of her thoughts, finished and dangerous: she would go back, later, when the guards changed again and the torches burned lower. She would step across the bridge that his voice had built when it said her name.

She didn't know what she would say.

She only knew she could not keep walking past that cell and pretend she was nothing but a blade.

— Δ —

The night pressed heavy in the stronghold.

Most of the torches had guttered low, their flames twitching in narrow cages of iron. The corridors breathed a quieter rhythm now, guards pacing slower, shadows stretching wider. Somewhere above, the Pyramid's bones shifted with a sound like stone sighing.

Aisha moved like part of the dark. Hood drawn low, steps mapped to the guard rotations she had memorized since childhood. Her body was steady, drilled into silence, but her pulse raced with a cold rush in her throat, a sterile chill she couldn't master.

She stopped at Quentin's cell.

The iron door loomed, black and absolute, but the slit in the wall let a pale band of moonlight cut across the floor. Inside, she could just make out his shape—slumped against the wall, wrists shackled overhead, head bowed. Even asleep, his posture looked like surrender braced for violence.

Her hand hovered over the latch. She told herself she only needed to look, to confirm. But her fingers betrayed her. She moved the latch with the practiced ease of someone raised on these locks—the kind that still yielded to her clearance—until someone remembered to revoke it. The door creaked open.

Quentin stirred instantly. The chains clinked as his head lifted, eyes bleary but snapping sharp the moment they found her. Fury lit them faster than recognition.

"You." The word was raw. He yanked at the chains, as if he could lunge at her. "You sold me out."

Aisha didn't flinch, though the accusation landed heavier than iron. She stepped inside, closing the door behind her, the torchlight from the corridor shrinking to a thin outline.

"Yes," she said quietly. There was no sense denying. "I did."

He always seemed to laugh in the wrong places—half a beat behind, like he was tuned to a different rhythm. Quentin laughed, bitter and short. "At least you're honest about it now." He sagged against the wall, rattling the chain. "Congratulations. You got what you wanted. I hope they give you a nice little throne beside them."

She shook her head, the hood shadowing her eyes. "That's not how it works."

"Of course it is." His voice cracked, jagged with exhaustion. "You hand me over, they pat you on the head, and I rot here while they play with whatever's in me. All because I was stupid enough to think you… to think—" He bit the words off, shaking his head hard, chains scraping like teeth on stone.

Aisha stepped closer. "I didn't know," she said, and hated how thin the defense sounded in her own ears. "I didn't know they would—dismiss me too. That I was only… a tool."

Quentin barked a laugh that was more pain than humor. "So now you feel sorry for yourself? That's what this is?"

She crouched down in front of him. The mark on his palm loaded faintly, outlining the bones of his hand in a cold, wrong pressure. It hollowed his features, carved down to bone and fury. But his eyes, lit by anger, stayed sharp—alive in a way despair alone could never make them.

"I came to correct a mistake," she whispered.

His head snapped toward her. "Help me?" He spat the word like it was poison. "Why should I trust you? You led me straight into their hands. You watched them chain me."

The silence after hung like a blade. She couldn't fill it. She couldn't say anything that would scrub out the truth.

So she didn't. She kept her eyes on him, letting the weight of his fury burn into her.

The only sound was the drip of water in the corner, steady and merciless.

For the first time in years, Aisha had no words, no excuses. Her silence became confession—guilt, defiance, and the ache of something she refused to name.

— Δ —

The silence broke—not from either of them, but from the corridor.

A slow clap, deliberate, echoing between the stones.

Quentin's head jerked up. Aisha spun toward the door, her hand going to the knife she wasn't sure she'd use—or if she even wanted to.

Raj leaned against the iron bars, torchlight painting his smirk in unstable amber. Behind him, two Shadow Order guards loomed, hoods low, hands resting easy on their weapons.

"Well, well," Raj drawled, voice carrying a lazy amusement. "Isn't this cozy? The traitor and the fool, whispering in the dark."

Quentin's stomach dropped. "Raj?" His voice cracked between disbelief and fury.

Raj straightened, dusting imaginary grit from his sleeve. "You really thought the Order found you by accident?" His grin sharpened. "Some of us don't wander into traps. We build them." He tapped his chest once with mock pride. "While you were stumbling around like a lost puppy, I was making sure someone useful would actually benefit."

Quentin stared at him, chains biting as he lurched forward. "You—You sold us out?"

"Sold?" Raj's grin widened, feral. "No, no, my friend. I invested. You're chained to a wall clinging to some cold scar you don't even understand. Me? I chose the winning side."

His words hit harder than the chains. Quentin's chest hollowed, the betrayal sharper because it wasn't from the Order, not from some faceless robed figure—it was Raj. Someone who had stood shoulder to shoulder with him, argued over snacks, teased Liam, rolled his eyes at Sophia's lectures.

Quentin's throat tightened. "We trusted you."

"And that's why it was so easy," Raj said simply, tilting his head as if studying an insect pinned to glass. "Trust makes people blind. You never even asked where I slipped away, what I whispered, who I smiled at when you weren't looking."

Aisha's hand tightened on her knife. "Enough."

Raj's eyes flicked to her, sharp and amused. "Oh, don't start polishing your halo now, Aisha. You led him here. You chained him. Don't pretend your guilt makes you different from me."

Her jaw clenched, but she didn't move. Her silence, for once, wasn't obedience—it was restraint.

Raj leaned closer to the bars, lowering his voice, though the venom still dripped. "Here's the truth, Quentin: you are ordinary. You've always been nothing-special. The Order knows it. Even Aisha knows it. The only mistake they made was wasting chains on you when they should've just left you in the dirt."

Quentin's palm loaded harder than before, the Echo thrumming like a pulse trying to claw free. *His vision blurred with rage, humiliation, and something hungrier—the Echo seeking a structural release.* The chains rattled as he pulled hard enough to slice his skin raw.

Raj only smiled, watching as if Quentin's suffering was proof of his point.

The guards shifted, waiting for his signal.

And in that cramped cell, Quentin realized betrayal had come not once, but twice—first from Aisha's silence, now from Raj's smirk. Both halves of trust collapsing at once, leaving him with nothing but the cold pressure crawling under his skin, begging to be unleashed.

— Δ —

The stone resonated—low and structural—like someone struck the Pyramid's ribs.

At first it was faint—a tremor underfoot, like the pyramid itself exhaled. Dust sifted from the ceiling, sprinkling Quentin's hair and shoulders. Then the stones groaned, a deep animal sound that rolled through the corridor and into the cell.

The guards stiffened, one snapping his head toward the far end of the passage. "What was that?"

Raj scowled, the smirk faltering. "It's nothing. Just the foundations shifting. This place is old—"

The tremor deepened. This time it carried instruction. Thin veins of glyphs clarified through the stone, crawling like cracks made of liquid frost. Their glow pulsed once—burnished from within—matching the sub-zero rhythm in Quentin's right palm. The iron chains thrummed, not with heat, but with a vibratory frequency that made the shackles feel momentarily out of sync with reality.

Quentin's breath caught. He couldn't stop the sound that tore out of him—half gasp, half groan—as the Echo surged beneath his skin, alive and insistent.

The guards exchanged sharp looks. One muttered a prayer and bolted down the corridor, boots pounding. The other hesitated, torn between staying with Raj and obeying the order that seemed to hum through the stone itself.

"Go!" Raj barked, snapping back into command. "Find the Archon. Now."

The second guard fled, robes vanishing into shadow.

In seconds, the corridor was empty save for Raj, the fading echo of his authority, and Aisha still crouched near Quentin, drawn taut as a bowstring.

The light dimmed, leaving silence thick as wool. Quentin slumped against the wall, sweat slicking his temples. His wrists were raw where the chains had bitten deeper, but the brief slack they'd given him still lingered in his memory like a promise.

Raj glared at the ceiling, then back at Quentin. His voice sharpened, forced, as though he needed to hear himself sound certain. "Whatever that was, it changes nothing. You're still in chains." He shot Aisha a sharp look. "And you're still the Order's hound, no matter how guilty you play."

He turned on his heel and stalked after the others, cloak whipping behind him. But his stride lacked its earlier swagger, the tremor's echo gnawing at his certainty. His footsteps faded until only the drip-drip of water returned.

Aisha remained. Her knife hung loose in her hand, her face caught in the flicker between resolve and fear. She turned her head toward Quentin.

“I’ll get you out,” she whispered—not command, not strategy, but raw, fragile promise.

Quentin met her gaze, eyes hard, jaw set. The words scraped at the back of his throat, but none of them made it past his lips.

She lingered one heartbeat longer, then slipped into the corridor’s shadows, swallowed whole.

Quentin was alone again. Alone with the chains, the glyphs’ afterglow fading in the cracks, and the faint memory of her voice vibrating through the stone.

Chapter 15

Resonance and Ruin

"When the power answers two rhythms, the conduit must collapse to contain the surge." — Guardian Teaching, The Cleansing Fire.

— Δ —

The iron clamped tighter around Quentin's wrists as rough hands jerked him forward. His boots scraped as his weight dragged rather than carried. Two guards hauled him down a sloping corridor, torches flickering against walls that seemed to close in with each step. The air grew heavier the deeper they went, thick with dust and the faint tang of ash.

Quentin's shoulders clamped in an ischemic grip, his throat raw from shouting words no one answered. He twisted once, chains biting into his skin. "Let go!" The guards didn't flinch.

Behind them, other footsteps echoed—measured, deliberate. Raj's voice followed, smug and unhurried.

"Careful with him," Raj said, as though offering instruction on handling cargo, not a classmate. "He's not much, but the Echo marked him. That makes him… valuable."

Quentin turned his head, hatred simmering in his eyes. Raj smirked back, his silhouette haloed by the torchlight.

And then there was Aisha.

Two guards flanked her—not chained, but boxed in close enough that her freedom felt like a performance. Her stride was stiff, her face schooled into the expression Quentin had seen so many times before: unreadable, cold. But even through the facade, tension radiated from her shoulders, a rigidity that betrayed the battle inside her.

"This is what you wanted?" His voice rang sharp against the walls. "To watch them drag me like some… animal?"

Aisha didn't answer. She didn't even glance at him, though her fists curled tight at her sides, tendons standing out against the torchlight.

That silence cut deeper than chains.

The corridor twisted downward, its incline steepening. Faint glyphs began to shimmer in the stone, just enough to show through the grime, pale as veins under skin. The guards avoided looking at them, their eyes fixed ahead, but Quentin couldn't tear his gaze away. The markings pulsed faintly, in rhythm with the ache in his palm.

Every step made the pressure stronger.

The passage opened suddenly into a vast chamber, air colder, sharper. Quentin stumbled as they yanked him inside. The ceiling soared into shadow, supported by colossal pillars etched with winding symbols. Along the walls, braziers burned with unnatural fire—blue flames that hissed without smoke.

At the sanctum's center waited an altar of black stone, polished so smooth it reflected the flames in warped fragments. The surface gleamed with faint golden lines, waiting, expectant.

The guards hauled Quentin toward it, forcing him to his knees. His chains clattered against the stone floor.

Aisha was shoved forward too, though less roughly. She caught herself, straightened, and walked the last few steps under her own power. Still, she didn't meet Quentin's gaze.

Raj lingered at the threshold, arms folded, watching with the satisfaction of someone who believed he'd already won. His shadow stretched long across the inner belly's floor, as if the room itself was complicit in his triumph.

Quentin's voice broke the silence, low and raw. "You sold me out. You… and now what? They'll use me until I'm drained, then toss me aside like they did to you."

Her composure faltered, the barest flicker in her eyes. For an instant, her lips parted, as though denial or defense was on her tongue—but nothing came.

The guards forced Quentin's arms against the altar. His antique-gold palm pressed flat against the cold stone, and for the first time, the chamber itself seemed to stir.

A low hum vibrated through the air, rattling the chains, crawling up Quentin's spine. The glyphs along the walls clarified, their etched depths saturating with an internal light that stretched toward him like threads pulled taut. The altar drank in the metallic resonance, feeding on the indurated geometry in his skin.

The sound was not only in the air but inside him—like a chorus of voices too ancient to belong to the living, whispering through his veins.

And through it all, Aisha stood close enough for him to hear her breathing, but far enough to remain unreachable.

Quentin turned his head, eyes blazing. "Say something. Anything."

Aisha's lips parted, but no words came. Only silence, thick as ash, heavy as stone.

— Δ —

The hum thickened into a living thing.

It crawled up from the altar through Quentin's bones, turning each breath fragile as glass. The black stone under his palm drank the kinetic energy of his mark and gave it back as vibration—low at first, then rising until it buzzed in his teeth. Around the sanctum, blue flames went still, held in the air as if listening.

A figure stepped forward from the shadows—one of Thales's lieutenants, hooded, voice carrying the same smooth inevitability as the Archon's. Hands lifted. The chant began.

Not the mutter Quentin heard in the cells—this was precise, each syllable a chisel strike. The sound ran along the carved pillars and woke the glyphs etched there; pale lines brightened, then flared, a constellation scrawled into stone. The resonant frequency converged toward the altar in threads so thin they could have been spider silk.

Quentin's palm pressed hard. He tried to wrench his hand away. The guards forced it down harder, the manacles grinding his skin against stone. The altar pressed back with suffocating intensity, a core stoked by pain.

Across from him, Aisha stood very still.

The flicker of glyph-light washed over her face and, for a heartbeat, revealed something not quite on her skin and not quite under it—lines like fine filigree, a lattice of faint sigils threaded along her forearms, up her throat, across her collarbone where her cloak gaped. Not the raw brand of his mark. *Older. Woven.* A history written in ash and ritual and years.

Quentin stared, the pain in his hand momentarily blanked by astonishment. "You… you're marked too."

"Not an Echo," she rasped. "A leash. A listening grid."

Aisha's eyes cut to his, and in them, for the first time, was naked fear. *Not of him. Of this.*

The chant climbed.

The lines on the altar flashed from gold to white. The reflections of the flames shattered across its surface and reassembled in new shapes—triangles, spirals, maps of places he did not know but which somehow knew him. He felt the recognition like hands turning his face toward a mirror he didn't want to see.

His palm tightened. The chamber answered.

And then Aisha answered it back.

Her filigree—those faint, woven sigils, laid there by ritual—woke as if a breath had passed over coals. They warmed from ghost-pale to ember, circuitry of frost threading through her—ordered, precise, and beyond his ability to follow. Not the same rhythm as his mark, but close enough to harmonize. *Two heartbeats. Two songs, discordant until they weren't.*

The air changed. The threads of light rushing toward the altar split at the last instant—half poured into Quentin through his hand, half veered toward Aisha, flowing into her like water into dry earth. Her jaw clenched; she didn't make a sound. But her shoulders braced as the inner vault's attention landed on her as surely as it had on him.

Quentin's thoughts stuttered like the world had in the market. "It's… reacting to you."

"I know," she breathed, as if admitting a crime.

The lieutenant's voice sharpened. "Hold her."

Hands closed on Aisha's arms—not rough, but firm with the confidence of men who thought they understood the tool in their grip. She didn't fight them. Not yet. Her eyes stayed on the altar, on Quentin's hand fixed there, on the way the stone fractured light around his skin like cracked ice.

Raj drifted closer, drawn by the spectacle. He wasn't just watching—he was waiting for a sign the Pyramid might mistake ambition for eligibility. The smirk he wore for show faltered at the edges, pupils pinning to slivers as the chamber saturated with an antique-gold hue. For the first time, awe cracked his arrogance. "Finally," he murmured, hunger in it. "Do you see, Quentin? This is what real power looks like when someone knows how to aim it."

Quentin barely heard him. The chant had found a second voice—deeper, older, not human. The pillars carried it, the floor hummed with it, the air thickened until each breath felt like wading through dusk. The blue flames trembled, then steadied, bending toward the altar as if the fire itself leaned to listen.

He felt something reach for him.

Not fingers. Not claws. Pressure, like a tide under his skin trying to reverse. The mark in his right palm throbbed in time with lines in the stone; echoes of the vision-chamber flooded his senses—priests' hands, sand in his teeth, the taste of centuries. He fought the urge to pull away even while the guards held him fast. *He didn't know whether tearing free would save or shatter him.*

"Aisha," he said, because her name was the only thing that cut through the sound. "What did they do to you?"

Her lips moved. "They called it binding." The word came out bitter. "A way to… listen for the Echo. To serve it. To serve them."

The light braided tighter between them. Quentin felt it like a rope cinching a knot. The altar's glow pulsed once—a question. His mark answered—unwilling, inevitable. Aisha's filigree aligned in response. The glow from her threads didn't speak capitulation. It spoke fluency, like a language long forgotten suddenly remembered.

The lieutenant's tone rose, exultant. "The conduit responds. The echoing pair stands."

Conduit. Pair.

Quentin's stomach rolled. He looked at Aisha, and in her gaze he saw the same calculation—fear and recognition and something like regret. If they were two parts of the same circuit, the Order intended to close it and let the current run until it burned them both hollow.

The hum climbed to a pitch that hurt. Glyphs burst alight in rings around the altar, each ring spinning in opposite direction. The light wasn't light anymore; it was weight, pressing on Quentin's shoulders, on his chest. The black stone under his palm vibrated like caged thunder. He could feel the inner sanctum searching along him, testing where he ended and the Echo began, prodding at seams he didn't know he had.

His vision narrowed. He clung to the smallest anchor he could find—his breath, the roughness of granite where the altar's polish had chipped, the small nick on Aisha's lip from some battle she never mentioned, the dust clinging stubbornly to her cheek. The world would not stop leaving its mark on her.

"Aisha—" He didn't know what he was asking.

Her answer was a fraction of a nod. Not assent. Not apology. A vow carved in silence: "I'm here."

The first ring of glyphs reached them.

It brushed Quentin's skin like cold wind and plunged through as if he were only a suggestion. Pain lanced his arm, clean and bright, close to unbearable. His mark flared white; the chamber roared without sound. The second ring struck Aisha. She jerked, the filigree flaring along her throat under the strain. Her hands fisted, nails biting her palms. She didn't look away.

The Order pressed them forward those last inches, forcing Quentin's marked hand flush to the altar, forcing Aisha's forearms to the stone until her woven sigils kissed the carved lines. The light met its match. Something locked.

The world tilted.

For a heartbeat, he stood in seven places at once—on sand under a sky so old it didn't have a color; in a hall that smelled of cedar and blood; beneath a colossus that exhaled heat; atop a garden that moved like a living thing; within a temple that echoed with names he didn't know; at the edge of a harbor where a giant's shadow drowned ships; inside the Pyramid, always inside the Pyramid.

He snapped back with a sound like the inside of thunder.

Around them, the pillars shed dust in gentle curtains. The braziers' flames leaned so far toward the altar they almost spilled out. The lieutenant's chant didn't falter, but there was a tremor under it now—triumph shading into awe, awe crawling toward fear.

Quentin coughed a laugh he didn't mean. It came out broken. "It's not just me," he said, voice rough with pain and revelation. "It never was."

Aisha's answer was the breath she let out through clenched teeth. It fogged in the shimmering air and fell, as if even exhalations obeyed the gravity of the Echo now.

The rings spun faster.

The chamber's attention narrowed until it felt like a gaze—vast, impersonal, ancient—and it rested on both of them at once. The altar drank deeper. The floor trembled.

Somewhere beyond the hum, Raj finally took a step back. "Archon?" he called, for the first time sounding as if he wanted someone else to be responsible for the thing he'd wanted so badly to witness.

No answer came. Only the next pulse, heavier, the light crowding out shadow, the stone beginning—impossibly—to breathe.

Quentin's fingers spasmed. Aisha's jaw locked. Their marks—brand and filigree—flared together, found each other, and for an instant, harmonized into a single tone that made the world's edges blur.

The Echo was awake.

And the Pyramid initiated containment.

— Δ —

The altar shuddered beneath Quentin's palm.

This wasn't anger. It was protocol.

A deep crack tore down its center, bleeding molten light in golden rivers. The vibration climbed until it rattled his bones, drowning out the lieutenant's chant, drowning out thought itself.

The sanctum roared awake.

Pillars trembled, dust raining down in choking clouds. Braziers toppled and split, their blue fire slithering across the floor like serpents, hissing as they scorched stone and flesh alike. The Order's rhythm faltered—chants splintering into gasps and panicked cries.

The manacles lagged—just a fraction—failing to keep perfect time with his pulse. A link unseated. Slack. Breath.

The Pyramid had no more use for bonds weaker than its own.

The guards who'd held him stumbled back, shielding their eyes. One tried to seize him again, only to recoil with a scream as the light flared brighter at Quentin's touch. His palm indurated into a sub-zero block, pulsing with the altar's fury.

Beside him, Aisha fell to her knees. The filigree across her skin burned like liquid silver, brighter with every heartbeat. She pressed her hands to the floor to steady herself, and glyphs flared wherever her palms met stone, spreading outward like veins of fire.

The lieutenant shouted above the din, voice cracking with desperation. "Hold them! Seal the conduit! The Echo is ours!"

But his command rang hollow.

Another fissure split the wall, racing upward like lightning frozen in stone. Blocks shuddered and shifted. The ceiling groaned. A massive slab cracked free and plummeted, smashing two chanting robed figures to pulp before anyone could move. The others scattered, their order unraveling into chaos.

Quentin drew in a ragged breath, coughing against the dust. "The Pyramid—" His throat burned, but he forced the words out. "It's not accepting you. It's rejecting you."

Raj's voice cut sharp from the edge of the chamber. His smirk was gone, his face washed pale in the glow. "No. No, this—this is power! It just… it just needs control!"

"Then control it!" Quentin shot back, his voice breaking. He thrust his indurated palm toward Raj, the altar answering in furious arcs of light. "Go ahead. Try."

Raj flinched, eyes darting to the splintering altar, then to Aisha, whose body shook under the strain of light rushing through her. His lips curled, not into confidence this time, but into fear wearing the mask of disdain. "You're both going to burn. And I won't be standing in the ashes with you."

He bolted toward the corridor, shoving past fleeing guards, his figure swallowed by smoke and falling debris.

The chamber groaned again, louder, almost a voice. Quentin's knees buckled. He pressed both hands to the altar now, not by choice but by instinct—as if letting go meant the Pyramid itself would crush him in an instant.

The surge overloaded him, blinding, filling his head with visions he couldn't hold onto: sand and water, fire and stone, shadows of colossal figures bending over the world. It was too much. *His chest clenched, his breath strangled, his body shook apart under the weight of it.*

Then Aisha's hand found his.

Her fingers were ice-cold, but the marks on their skin spiked under contact, the air around them snapping into a violent chord. Her voice cut through the roar, hoarse but steady. "Don't let it take you."

He turned his head toward her. She was pale, trembling, her braid loose and dust-caked, but her eyes—fierce, defiant—held him fast. "Fight it," she said. "With me."

Another fissure cracked the altar, spraying shards of glowing stone. The guards screamed and fled; the lieutenant's chanting crumbled into broken syllables. All around them the chamber collapsed in violent fits, stone and fire pouring down like a storm.

Quentin held her hand tighter. "If I let go—"

"We both die," she finished. She forced a laugh, bitter and soft. "Story of us, isn't it?"

The ceiling buckled. A slab the size of a wagon wheel crashed down and split, dust billowing in a choking wave.

Quentin coughed, eyes stinging. *He wanted to shout, to curse, to demand answers from the Echo itself—but there was no space left for words. Only survival.*

The light inside the chamber didn't relent. It pressed harder, searing through them both, as if measuring, testing, weighing their worth. *It no longer felt like choice. It felt like judgment.*

Another shockwave tore through the floor. The altar heaved, tilting, hurling Quentin and Aisha sideways. He slammed into the stone, his shoulder jolting with pain, but his hand didn't release hers. The pressure between their marks intensified, as though refusing to separate.

Through the chaos, he heard Aisha's voice again, ragged but resolute. "Whatever happens—don't stop enduring. That's what it wants from you."

Quentin blinked against the dust, vision blurring. Her words carved themselves into him like the mark had. *Endurance. Survive. Hold on.*

Around them, the Shadow Order fled screaming into the collapsing halls. The lieutenant shouted once more, but the sound cut off in a crash of falling stone. Only the two of them remained at the heart of the storm—two marks locked in unison as the Pyramid's fury tore its own chamber apart.

And in that chaos, Quentin understood with sick clarity: *the Echo was awake now. And nothing in the world could force it back to sleep.*

— Δ —

The chamber was dying.

Stone screamed as it split overhead, fissures racing like lightning through the vaulted ceiling. The altar's light had become a storm, its molten veins flaring and bursting in violent arcs that hurled stone across the floor. Each collapse shook the ground harder, a heartbeat gone wild.

Quentin stumbled, still clutching Aisha's hand, their marks straining in unison. He tried to drag her toward the edge of the chamber, toward the narrow corridor where the last of the Order had fled. But the ground buckled beneath their feet, throwing them sideways into rubble.

"We have to move!" Quentin shouted, his voice raw from dust and smoke. "We'll be buried alive!"

Aisha coughed, pressing a bloodied hand to her ribs as she staggered upright. The filigree of her mark remained under load across her skin, though the light flickered, weakening with each tremor. She shook her head. "There's no way out—not while the Echo's awake. It's the Pyramid itself that's collapsing, not just the chamber."

"Yes there is!" He pulled at her arm, desperation cutting through exhaustion. "We just have to keep running—"

The ceiling cracked with a deafening snap. Quentin looked up and froze.

A boulder, massive and jagged, tore free from the collapsing dome. It plummeted straight toward him.

He had no time to react. His limbs locked, his lungs emptied in a silent scream. The oppressive mass of the stone filled his vision, blotting out everything.

A weight slammed into him from the side—Aisha's shoulder driving into his chest with brutal force.

She shoved him hard, with all the strength left in her. Quentin tumbled across the floor, chains clattering as he skidded into rubble. The air split with the thunder of impact. Dust exploded upward, choking and thick.

When it cleared, Quentin saw her.

Aisha lay crumpled beneath the boulder, her body pinned in a grotesque angle. Blood spread dark across the stone, hissing faintly as the last of her filigree faded.

"No—no, no." The words tore out of him in a broken litany. Quentin tried to speak, but his vocal cords seized in a vasovagal lock.

He reached her side, pushing at the boulder that weighed tons, his strength breaking uselessly against it. His arms shook, shoulders screaming, but the stone didn't budge.

"Aisha!" His voice cracked, breaking into a sob. "Why would you—why would you do that?"

Her eyes fluttered open. Dust streaked her face, blood staining her lips. Yet she smiled faintly, weak and soft, like someone finally laying down a burden. "Because if it crushed you, they would've won. I couldn't let that happen."

Quentin's throat closed. He slid down beside her, cradling her head with trembling hands. Her skin was cold already, though the residual light along her sigils still pulsed faintly, fading with every beat.

"You don't understand," he whispered fiercely, desperate. "I'm no one. I was never meant for this. You should've let it crush me."

Her gaze found his, steady even as her breath rattled. "You don't get to decide what you're meant for." A cough wracked her body, blood staining her chin. She winced, but her hand lifted with effort, brushing his cheek. "I saw you fight, Quentin. Even chained, even terrified—you kept moving. That's why it chose you."

Tears stung his eyes. He shook his head violently. "It chose us. You—you can't just leave me with this!"

A weak laugh escaped her, broken by pain. "Then carry both of us. Live. Survive. That's the only way my choice means anything."

Her hand slipped from his cheek, falling limp against the stone.

"Aisha—" His voice cracked, panic rising like a tide. He pressed his forehead to hers, whispering in a rush of pleading. "Stay with me. Please. I should've saved you. I should've—"

Her lips moved one last time. He barely heard it through the roar of the collapsing chamber.

"Endure."

The residual light along her filigree flickered once, then drained away. Her chest stilled beneath his hands.

The world around them raged, the chamber tearing itself apart, but he heard only silence.

He pulled her body into his arms, holding her close as if he could will warmth back into her. Dust stung his eyes, tears streaked down his face unchecked. *His heart pounded in time with the Echo, but it felt hollow, like a drum with torn skin.*

The altar cracked apart behind him, spraying shards of light into the air like dying stars. The ground heaved, threatening to bury them both. But Quentin didn't move. Couldn't.

He rocked her gently, whispering the same words over and over, a prayer and a curse.

"I should've saved you..."

And still, she lay silent in his arms, her sacrifice carved into the ruin around them.

— Δ —

The Echo stirred in his palm.

He flinched as pain surged up his arm, compressing his chest. The mark compressed with a sub-zero intensity. For a moment he thought it was punishing him—numbing him for his failure. But then the signal split, sharpening into images not his own.

Not his vision. Hers.

He gasped as the world tilted.

A narrow alley, rain-soaked and cold. Aisha as a child, knees drawn to her chest, hiding from faceless men who prowled with blades. Her stomach growled with hunger. She whispered to herself, "I'll never be weak again."

The scene shifted. A barren courtyard at dawn, ash rubbed into her hands as masked tutors whispered, "Obedience is safety. Belonging is earned." She nodded, even as tears streaked silently down her cheeks.

Another flash—her standing alone in a dormitory of stone, listening to the muffled laughter of others in the halls. She pressed her forehead to the wall, whispering, "If I serve well enough, maybe they'll let me belong."

Quentin sobbed as the visions kept coming, raw and relentless. He saw her sparring until her arms went numb, every strike a plea for recognition. He saw her in the ritual chamber, the filigree burned into her skin in ritual, as she bit her lip until it bled rather than cry out. He saw her standing before Thales, spine straight, face carved into obedience while inside she trembled.

And finally, he saw her moments ago, choosing. Shoving him clear. Taking the crushing blow. Letting the chamber break her so it would not break him.

The visions shattered. Quentin was back in the ruin, dust swirling, the world collapsing. His palm clamped with a systemic finality, the Echo demanding he accept what the Echo showed.

"No!" His cry broke against the stone. Tears streamed down his face, hot and unchecked. He pressed his hand against Aisha's chest, as if the mark could spark her filigree alive again. "Don't show me what I lost—give her back! Please, take me instead!"

But the Echo gave no answer. It pulsed once, hollow, as if mocking his plea.

Quentin bent over her body, clutching her close. "You were supposed to be stronger than me," he whispered, his voice breaking into a laugh that wasn't laughter. "You were supposed to survive this. Not me."

The ceiling shifted again, another boulder smashing into rubble nearby. Dust choked the air. The stronghold groaned as if ready to bury them both.

Quentin didn't care.

He rocked Aisha gently, the way one might soothe a child, his voice raw and low. "I should've saved you." The words became a mantra, a penance. His tears stained her hair, his body shaking with every breath.

The perceptible intensity of the Echo receded in his palm, though its throb remained, steady and cruel. *It did not care for his grief. It did not care for her sacrifice. It only pressed—insistent—as if reminding him the burden was his now.*

Quentin raised his head, eyes red and burning, and screamed into the chamber. The sound tore from him like a wound, echoing off stone and rubble until it seemed to come back a hundredfold. It was not a cry for help. It was despair made sound.

And when the echo died, silence fell.

The chamber gave one final groan, a quake that sent cracks racing across the floor. Dust settled thick, muffling everything. The last flames guttered out.

Quentin was left in stillness, Aisha's lifeless body in his arms, the ruins of the altar smoldering around them. His palm still clamped with a structural finality, but it felt less like power now and more like a brand—a mark of everything he had lost, everything he had failed to save.

He buried his face against her hair and whispered, hoarse and broken, "Endure? Without you?"

But there was no answer.

Only the dead weight in his arms and the hollow throb of the Echo, leaving him utterly, unbearably alone.

Chapter 16
The Price of Survival

"The mark remains after the fire, a scar that cannot be outrun." — **Guardian Teaching, Scarification Rites.**

— Δ —

The silence after the collapse was worse than the chaos.

Dust hung thick in the air, curling through shafts of faint old-gold resonance that still bled from the altar's shattered veins. The once-massive chamber had folded in on itself, its roof splintered into heaps of stone. Fires guttered and died among the rubble, leaving only smoke and the acrid tang of ash. The chants, the screams, the thunder of falling blocks—all gone.

Only Quentin remained.

He stirred with a cough, dragging in air that scraped his throat raw. His body throbbed in a dozen places, bruises blossoming beneath torn clothes, blood running hot and sticky down his arm. He rolled onto his side, wincing as a sharp edge of rock bit into his ribs. Every muscle screamed at him to stay down.

But memory was sharper than pain. Memory pulled him upright.

His eyes darted through the haze until they found her.

Aisha.

She lay a few feet away, half-buried in dust, her body unnaturally still. The boulder that had crushed her had rolled just enough to free her torso—too late to matter. Her face was pale beneath streaks of blood and ash, her braid torn loose and matted with dirt. The filigree that had once marked her skin was dark now, faded into faint scars.

Quentin dragged himself toward her, every movement a jolt of agony. He didn't care. He reached her side, fumbling to clear rubble from around her with trembling hands.

His throat locked. He pressed his palm against her cheek, willing warmth back into her skin.

Nothing.

"No…" His voice cracked. He pulled her against him, cradling her head to his chest.

Her weight in his arms was unbearable—not because she was heavy, but because she wasn't. She felt insubstantial, as if she were already gone, a body more memory than presence.

The mark in his hand throbbed faintly, a cruel reminder he was still alive. He clenched his fist until pain flared through his fingers, as though he could crush the fact of it. The Echo answered anyway—weak, steady, non-sentimental—pure function, its pressure threading through the broken stone like a pulse with nowhere to go.

He pressed his forehead against hers, whispering. "Why did you do it? Why me?"

There was no answer.

In the silence, grief took shape. It was jagged, raw, heavier than the stones that had buried the sanctum. He had thought her betrayal would leave only hatred in him. He had sworn never to forgive the way she'd led him here.

But now, with her slack in his arms, hatred had nowhere to land.

His chest heaved, but no air seemed enough. He wanted to scream, to claw at the stones until his throat bled, but all that came out was a rasping whisper. "I should've protected you. I should've been the one—"

The rubble around him glowed faintly as the last glyphs sputtered, their light dimming into silence. The Pyramid's fury had passed, leaving only ruin. Quentin glanced around, dazed. The inner belly was eerily still now, as if holding its breath.

Everywhere he looked was wreckage—the remains of a ritual gone wrong, the Order scattered, the altar cracked open like a broken heart. But his eyes always came back to her.

He brushed the dust from her brow, streaking it with blood from his own scraped knuckles. His lips trembled. "You mattered," he said softly, his voice breaking. "You always mattered. Even when you thought you didn't."

The words broke him open. His body shook as sobs tore free, raw and unrestrained. He clutched her tighter, burying his face in her shoulder, inhaling the fading scent of sweat and ash and smoke.

The chamber dimmed further as the last glyphs died, leaving only dull reflections along broken stone—light without warmth, meaning without mercy. That dull light pulsed across her features, like a heartbeat that wasn't hers anymore. The sight hollowed him.

Quentin closed his eyes and let the vault's stillness crush him. The glyphs had gone dark, the altar dead. Only the Echo in his palm vibrated with sterile ache, refusing to let him forget.

He held her, numb, grief and rage twisting together until he couldn't tell where one ended and the other began.

And in that blurred edge between love and fury, something inside him shifted—something small, but alive.

Then the mark pulsed again—insistent, impatient with grief.

Quentin slumped against the fractured altar, breath shaking, ash thick on his tongue.

The Echo answered. He winced. "Leave me alone."

Pressure intensified—cold, compressive—sending a tremor through the fractured altar. Faint residual lines along the stone flickered in response, then faded again. *It was as if the Pyramid itself was still awake, watching, waiting.*

Quentin's fist tightened until his knuckles blanched. He expected the Echo to shove another memory into him—another cruel lesson, another proof that her pain could be catalogued like data. But it didn't. It only pressed, cold and steady, as if waiting for what grief would make of him.

He bowed over her once more, jaw locked, letting the grief set into something usable.

— Δ —

The ruin seemed to listen.

Quentin leaned against the fractured altar, residual light clinging faintly to his palm. Aisha's body lay close, wrapped in his hoodie to shield her from the dust. He couldn't bring himself to move farther from her, even as rubble shifted dangerously overhead.

The silence deepened until it pressed on his ears. Then it cracked.

A voice slid into the stillness, smooth and cold. The mark tightened—cold, axial—and the sound didn't enter his ears so much as rise inside his bones.

"She chose poorly."

Quentin jerked upright, his heart hammering. His gaze darted around the ruined chamber—nothing but shadows and settling dust. Yet the voice rang clear, close, curling around him like smoke.

"You would have died in her place," it continued, deep and resonant. "And the world would not have noticed. She spent her life buying a moment that wasn't worth the price. And for what? For you?"

His breath caught. His hand curled into a fist against the altar. "Show yourself."

A low chuckle rippled through the air. "You already know me."

Recognition hit like a blade.

The Architect.

Quentin's pulse quickened, fury surging hot through the cracks of his grief. "Get out of my head."

"Your head?" The chuckle deepened, more cruel now. "Boy, I am in the marrow of you. I am the whisper that kept you moving when you should have stayed down. I am the structural load in that mark, the reason she had to save you at all. And you hate me for it."

Quentin slammed his palm against the stone, golden light flaring in answer. "You don't own me."

The underbelly shook faintly, dust sifting down. The Architect's voice echoed, louder, wrapping around every stone. "She thought she could protect you. She thought endurance was enough. And now her body lies still while yours still moves. Do you see the truth yet? You were chosen not because you endure—but because you break. And breaking is how I enter."

Quentin's throat burned. His grief ignited into rage. "I'll never serve you! Never!"

His shout reverberated off the rubble, so raw it left his chest aching.

For a moment, silence reclaimed the chamber. His shoulders sagged as the weight of despair pressed harder. A poisonous seed took root—*What if the Architect was right? What if he was nothing but fracture waiting to happen?*

Then another sound stirred.

Not mocking. Not cruel. Softer.

It came like a breeze through broken stone, faint but steady. A second voice, older, kinder. Not a person—an imprint. A teaching carried in stone.

Endure.

Quentin froze. His head snapped up, eyes searching the ruin.

The voice lingered, fragile as thread. "Not all power is corruption. Not all breaking is the end. Endurance is not glory, but it is survival. Hold on when all else collapses."

His chest tightened. It wasn't Aisha's voice—too old, too distant. But it carried something of her final breath, her final word. It resonated through the faint glow of his mark, threading between his grief and his rage.

The Architect hissed, cutting across the gentler tone. "Do not listen. That voice is dust. A remnant of dead stone trying to soothe you into weakness. I offer you strength. With me, you will never lose again."

Quentin pressed his hands to his temples, shaking his head violently. "Stop!" The clash of voices rattled inside him, pulling him in two. His chest heaved as if it might split.

The kinder voice whispered again, steady. "Grief is not weakness. Let it shape you. Let it teach you what you will not allow again. Do not burn. Endure."

The Architect thundered over it. "She wasted her life for you. Spit on her sacrifice and rise stronger. Become my vessel. Become more than the ordinary disappointment she died for."

Quentin doubled over, teeth clenched against the pain of voices colliding. He slammed his fist against the altar again, his cry tearing from deep inside. "Enough! Both of you!"

The echo of his shout rattled through the ruined sanctum, louder than either voice for a breath. Silence followed, broken only by his ragged breathing.

He collapsed to his knees beside Aisha's body, trembling. His mark still glowed faintly, its rhythm unstable—pressure surging and receding in uneven waves. He pressed it to his chest, curling around the ache.

"I don't know what's real," he whispered. His tears blurred the rubble, blurred her still form. "I don't know who to believe. I don't even know if I can survive this."

The Architect's laughter rumbled faintly, retreating into shadow. "You will break. And when you do, I will be the one who shapes what's left."

The gentler voice lingered softer, almost fading. "Do not let despair be the end. Endure."

Then both were gone, leaving Quentin trembling in silence, the inner vault heavy again with dust and ruin.

His breath rattled. His chest ached. His grief clamped with an ischemic finality, but under it lay a seed of something else—not hope, not yet. Only a choice not to collapse.

He curled around Aisha's body, clutching her tighter. "Endure," he whispered back into the stillness, not sure if it was to her, to the voice, or to himself.

The Echo in his palm pulsed once, faint but steady.

— Δ —

Silence returned, thinner now, as if the ruin itself were listening for what came next.

In the distance, faint voices echoed down the ruined corridors—muffled, harsh, clipped, urgent.

Quentin stiffened, head jerking toward the sound. *The Order. Survivors—searching the rubble.*

He swallowed hard, his chest heaving. *If they find him there, broken and half-buried, they'll finish what the chamber had not. And if they find Aisha—he couldn't bear it. The thought of their hands on her, reducing her to an asset even in death, made something sharp and dangerous ignite inside him.*

He whispered into her hair, voice raw. "They're coming. I know I need to move. But I can't—" His words broke, caught in a sob. "I can't leave you."

The rubble groaned under shifting weight somewhere beyond the structure. Torchlight flickered faintly at the edge of a collapsed corridor, painting the dust in trembling gold.

Quentin shut his eyes. For a heartbeat, he imagined lying still, letting them come, letting the ruin bury him with her. The temptation was real—an end to the fight, an end to the ache. The thought carried a dangerous sweetness—an end to the ache, a reunion in silence.

But her final word burned in his ears.

Endure.

He shuddered. His tears fell faster as he pressed his lips to her temple, whispering through clenched teeth. "You're gone," he whispered, "but I hear you."

The voices in the distance grew louder, their echoes sharper now. Stones shifted closer.

Quentin dragged in a ragged breath and tightened his cloak around her body, sealing her against him. His limbs screamed as he pushed himself upright, his knees threatening to buckle. He hooked his arms under her and hauled her up against his shoulder—more drag than carry, his legs shaking with every step. Every movement felt like tearing open a wound still bleeding—but he forced himself to move anyway.

He staggered toward the darker corner of the vault, away from the faint glow of the torches, into shadow. Each step was agony, but he kept moving, pressing her close as if she were the only anchor left in a collapsing world.

His mark pulsed faintly, guiding him deeper into shadow, away from the approaching light. The Echo was quiet, but not absent—its presence settling into his bones like a compass made of grief.

He whispered one last vow into the silence, voice hoarse and breaking. "I'll carry you until I can't anymore. And when I fight them, it will be in your name."

The chamber groaned again, dust raining in thin curtains, but he pressed on.

He could not stay shattered forever.

Not if her sacrifice was to mean something.

Not if he wanted the world to remember her the way he did—sharp, brave, and finally, free.

Chapter 17

Vow in the Void

"The greatest defense against chaos is not power, but commitment." — **Guardian Teaching, The Final Anchor.**

— Δ —

The silence broke.

It was faint at first, muffled by stone and dust—the scrape of boots on rubble, torches rasping in damp air.

"Over here!"

"Clear the rubble! The Archon will want the body if nothing else."

"Check the conduit. The boy must not have escaped."

Quentin froze.

He pressed himself deeper into the shadowed corner of the ruined chamber, Aisha's weight sagged against his chest—too loose, too quiet. His arms ached from carrying her, his lungs raw from dust. He clutched her tighter, as though he could shield her from their words. Stone dug into his spine; his legs had long since gone numb. The thought of putting her down hurt worse than any bruise.

His heart hammered. Every instinct screamed at him to move—to run, to hide, to survive. But his body refused. The thought of leaving her here, among them, for their hands to paw at, their eyes to reduce her to nothing more than a failed asset—he couldn't. They had owned her in life; he would not let them catalogue her in death.

The voices drew closer, accompanied by the grind of shifting stone. Torchlight began to flicker faintly at the mouth of the ruined passage.

Quentin's breath caught. He bent low over Aisha's body, whispering into her hair. "They're coming."

Her face was pale in the torch-spill bleeding into the chamber; his right palm was only a dull, bruise-metal geometry under skin, visible because his sleeve had ridden back. She gave no answer.

Quentin clenched his fist. "No," he whispered harshly. "Not like this."

But the Echo loaded again—cold and compressive—like sterile weight settling behind his sternum. A low hum vibrated in the cracked altar nearby, faint glyphs sparking to life as if awakened by his indecision. The ruin answered in small ways—stone thrumming at the altar seam, old cuts in the floor catching light—feedback, not attention.

He staggered to his feet, still holding her, his back pressed to the wall. His knees shook, his body screaming with exhaustion. He looked down at her—so still, so silent—and his chest hollowed with anguish.

The sound of boots grew louder. Stone clattered as the Order pried open a gap in the collapsed passage. Their voices were closer now, words clearer.

"He must be buried in here—find him!"

"Bring the girl's body too. The Archon will want proof."

Rage tore through Quentin at the thought. They would not have her. Not after everything. Not after she'd finally chosen something for herself—and for him—instead of for them.

Quentin pressed his right palm to the stone, trembling. Cold density climbed from wrist to elbow, tendons tightening as if a cable had gone taut—his body bracing around a load it didn't want.

The thought split cleanly in his chest—survive alone, or risk everything for her.

His chest heaved. The choice weighed more than the stones overhead. Each second narrowed the world, until all that remained was his hand, her stillness, and the roaring in his veins.

Quentin lifted her hand to his lips, pressing a trembling kiss against her cold knuckles. "Tell me what to do," he whispered, though she could not answer.

The mark hardened—edges sharpening into that hinge geometry—while the altar seam answered with a faint shimmer that made dust look briefly metallic.

The voices in the corridor stopped. A tense silence followed, as if even the Order felt the pressure building in the air. One of them muttered a hurried prayer; another hissed for quiet.

— Δ —

The world narrowed.

Quentin staggered back against the cracked altar, clutching Aisha's hand hard enough to hurt himself. Torchlight at the far end smeared at the edges of his vision—not because the corridor slowed, but because his body dumped everything nonessential. Sound tunneled. Distance collapsed into vectors: boots, stone scrape, breath.

Cold weight packed into his right arm. The hinge-mark didn't burn—it densified, tendon-deep, as if his joints had been asked to carry something too heavy to name.

His mind did what it always did under pressure: *ran outcomes.*

First: he let the panic win. He turned that braced arm outward, met the breach with blunt violence—bodies down, corridor quiet, his lungs still pulling air. Survival by subtraction.

And in his arms, Aisha stayed slack. Unchanged.

Second: he spent the margin on her. No spectacle—just him pinning his palm to her sternum and refusing to let her slide past the edge. He imagined holding the failing rhythm long enough for her body to remember its own—one breath, then another—while his own vision greyed, knees folding, the world tilting toward blackout.

Two outcomes. Not destiny—triage.

The Order's voices sharpened at the threshold. "Almost through! Brace the stones—he's inside!"

Quentin looked down at Aisha's face—dust, blood, that unbearable stillness—and felt the thought split cleanly again: *keep himself intact, or carry her collapse too.*

His throat closed. "I can't do this without you," he said, and hated how true it sounded.

Cold density tightened. The altar seam hummed. Not a demand—an edge he could feel, waiting.

— Δ —

The chamber trembled, dust cascading from the fractured ceiling. The voices of the Order pressed closer through the rubble—echoes of boots, clatter of stone shifting. Quentin clung to Aisha's body, head bowed, his right hand locked in that hinge-hard density—skin pulled tight, knuckles pale. His tears blurred everything.

There was no room left for outcomes—only the weight of them, pressing in from every direction.

Her voice rose in his memory instead—sharp, angry, alive—layered over the silence.

Not words. *Warnings. Orders.* The way she'd always sounded when there was no time left.

Quentin's throat closed. His tears came harder, his body shaking as he clutched her cold hand to his chest.

"You're not here," he whispered, the words tearing out of him anyway.

Cold density rippled through his palm, a pressure wave that had nowhere to go. The altar seam flickered once, dull and mechanical, then went still.

His thoughts fractured. Memory, fear, exhaustion—everything bled together until he couldn't tell what belonged to the moment and what belonged to loss.

Quentin bowed his head until his forehead pressed to her knuckles. His breath came ragged. Every part of him wanted to scream that it was a trick, another temptation like the Architect's visions.

It wasn't power driving him. It was the memory of her.

He saw flashes behind his eyelids—her sharp eyes when they first met, her smirk that cut and intrigued in the same breath, her blade flashing as she fought beside him, her voice snapping warnings even when she pretended not to care. And then, the last image: her shoving him aside as the boulder fell, her whisper broken with blood—"Because I couldn't let them win. Not with you."

Quentin sobbed, shaking against her still body. "I don't care if it kills me. I can't let that be the end of you."

The glyphs on the altar flared, responding to his vow. The seam-lines in the stone registered overload—brief shimmer, then dull—like a system flickering under strain. The walls thrummed in answer. He felt like the Pyramid itself leaned in—responsive, not commanding, not judging.

A phrase surfaced in his head with the wrong texture—too clean, too structured to be his: *Fool. Do not romanticize load.*

Quentin's jaw clenched. He squeezed her hand tighter, pressing her palm against his cheek, refusing to let go. His chest heaved, and he cried out, "Then take it! Take it all!"

The Echo loaded hard—cold, compressive—pushing his muscles into bracing. His vision pinched at the edges as his body dumped everything but balance and grip. His muscles spasmed, every nerve screaming as though the choice itself would shatter him. The pain felt purposeful now—like a door he was forcing to open with his bare hands.

He bent down, his lips against her ear, his words a vow carried through blood and tears—unspoken, irreversible.

The chamber seemed to pause, a heartbeat's silence where the world itself held its breath. Even the dust hung still, suspended as if waiting for her answer.

Then the altar seam caught—one brief shimmer—like feedback snapping into a closed loop. The hinge-mark tightened until his forearm shook. His body arched, teeth gritted, a sound torn from him as cold pressure climbed his arm and packed behind his ribs until breathing felt optional.

The power threatened to burst outward, to annihilate everything in its path. He forced it down, every ounce of will dragging it inward, pressing his right palm flat to her sternum.

"Aisha," he whispered through the pain. "Breathe."

The walls shook violently. Dust poured in sheets from the ceiling. The Order's shouts echoed nearer, panicked now.

Quentin barely heard them. His entire world narrowed to the girl in his arms and the crushing pressure tearing through him from the inside out. The ruin vanished from his awareness—only the place where her rhythm had been—the place where breath should have been—filled the universe.

His tears struck her cheek. His palm locked tighter, pressure spiking until his forearm shook.

Quentin clung to her, body convulsing as though the choice would kill him. And still, he pressed harder.

"I've made my choice."

— Δ —

The break wasn't light. It was load.

Quentin pressed his right palm harder to Aisha's chest and felt the hinge-mark clamp—skin inelastic, tendons cable-tight—cold pressure drilling down to bone. His breath stuttered. His pulse spiked, then forced itself into something organized, as if his body had decided panic was a luxury.

He didn't push anything into her. He held.

Held her failing rhythm in place the only way he knew how—by letting the collapse route through him. Autonomic cross-talk snapped tight: *a borrowed hitch of breath in his lungs, a lag in his own heartbeat that didn't belong to him.*

The ruin responded with thin feedback—glyph seams catching, then dimming—like a system registering overload. Dust shook loose from the ceiling in soft sheets. The Order shouted somewhere beyond the rubble. Quentin heard it as if through water, not because time changed, but because his bandwidth did.

"Stay," he rasped into her hair. "Just—stay."

His vision greyed at the edges. A warm trickle hit his lip; he tasted iron. His forearm tremored. He kept his palm planted anyway, jaw clenched so hard his teeth hurt.

For a long second, there was nothing—only her weight and that terrible quiet.

Then her throat hitched. Not drama—reflex. A convulsive pull that scraped like it had to tear its way back through dust and pain.

Air came in broken. Real. It rasped, wet with dust, and turned into a cough she couldn't stop.

Quentin sagged with a sound that wasn't a laugh but wanted to be. He didn't let go.

The altar seam flashed once—sterile feedback—then dulled, as if the system had logged the event and moved on.

His right palm stayed dense under skin, burnished-gold and shaking, then slackened as the load eased.

He went hollow in its wake.

But Aisha—Aisha dragged in another breath, ragged and alive.

— Δ —

Sound returned in slivers.

Then her fingers moved.

A twitch, faint as a sigh, but real. Quentin's breath caught, dragging him back from the edge of darkness. His eyes fluttered open, blurred with grit and tears.

Aisha stirred. Her chest rose unevenly, her lips parting as though she were learning how to breathe again. Her eyes opened a fraction, pupils dilated against the glow of the chamber's dying glyphs. Confusion clouded them, but they were alive, filled with something he thought he'd never see again—awareness.

The faint gleam of rekindled filigree pulsed along her throat, soft as embers waking to life.

Quentin choked on a laugh, half sob, half relief. "You're alive," he rasped. The words scraped his throat raw, but he forced them out again, as if repetition would anchor the truth.

Her gaze turned toward him, slow, unfocused. For a moment, she didn't seem to recognize him. Then her brows knit faintly, her lips shaping his name. "Quentin?"

"Yes," he whispered, tears running fresh. He gripped her hand tighter, though his own shook violently from weakness. "It's me. I'm here."

She blinked at him, her expression wavering between disbelief and something softer, fragile. Her eyes drifted downward to his hand—his palm heatless and darkened, pressed to her chest a moment ago. She saw the scorch marks along his skin, the exhaustion carved deep into his face. Realization flickered.

Her gaze softened into something almost reverent—and terrified.

Her breath hitched. "What… what did you do?"

Quentin's throat tightened. He swallowed hard, unable to hold her gaze. "I held you," he whispered. "I kept you from slipping past it. And it nearly took me with you."

Her eyes widened, tears brimming in their dust-lined corners. Her lips trembled, as though she wanted to speak but couldn't find words. A single tear clung to her lashes before falling—slow, disbelieving.

Quentin forced himself to look at her again, even as his vision swam. "Don't—don't be angry. Just… just be alive. That's all I want."

Aisha shook her head weakly, a tear slipping free to streak her cheek. "You fool," she murmured. But there was no malice in it, only a breaking softness. Her trembling hand rose, fingers brushing clumsily against his jaw. "You nearly killed yourself."

Her voice cracked on the last word, as though the truth physically hurt her.

He caught her hand against his cheek, closing his eyes at the touch. "Worth it," he breathed. "Always worth it."

For a moment, silence hung between them—fragile, unspoken, heavier than the ruin around them.

It felt like the eye of a storm, the only stillness they had left.

And then the chamber itself reminded them they weren't alone.

The ground shuddered violently, a fresh cascade of rubble tumbling from above. The glyphs pulsed faintly, then flared one last time as if in warning. Beyond the walls, shouts echoed louder, torches blazing against cracks in the stone.

Aisha's fingers tightened around his face, forcing his gaze back to hers. "We have to move," she whispered, urgency straining her broken voice. Fear flickered in her eyes—not for herself, but for him.

Quentin almost laughed at the absurdity. His body was wrecked, every muscle screaming, his vision threatening to fold again into blackness. "Move?" he croaked. "I can barely… breathe."

"Then lean on me."

Her tone cut through the tremors like a blade—sharp, steady, impossibly familiar.

The same Aisha who had once barked orders, smirked at his stumbles, shoved him out of danger. But this time, her voice trembled—not with authority, but with fear of losing him.

He managed a faint smile, dizzy and raw. "Didn't think… I'd ever hear you say that."

Her lips trembled into something almost like a smile, though tears still tracked her dusty face. "Don't get used to it."

Another crash reverberated down the corridor. The Order's voices grew frantic, calling commands, closing in. Quentin tried to rise, but his legs buckled instantly. Aisha, though barely stronger, shifted to brace him. Their bodies leaned together, two broken figures holding each other upright in the dying glow of the Echo.

They moved like halves of the same wound, incomplete without the other.

Quentin's hand still pulsed faintly against hers, his hinge-mark still visible—dull, dense—while her filigree answered in a faint, emberlike return. Not blazing, not triumphant—just alive.

He whispered, voice cracking, "We're not done yet."

"No," Aisha murmured, her arm steadying his waist as another tremor rattled the chamber. "But we will be, if we stay here." Resolve flickered through her filigree, as if even the Echo agreed.

The words anchored him. With one final glance at the shattered altar, at the ruin that had demanded so much from both of them, Quentin looked forward. His chest burned with exhaustion, but his heart thudded with something sharper than despair—resolve. A resolve born of loss, of love, and of a promise he intended to keep.

The Order was coming. The hunt wasn't over.

But Aisha was beside him, no longer slipping away.

That was enough.

For now.

CHAPTER 18

FRACTURED STEPS

"The geometry of the passage resists the time that is not its own." — **Fragment of the Architect's Scroll, XVIII.**

— Δ —

The tunnels still breathed dust.

Quentin half-staggered, half-dragging himself along the broken corridor, Aisha's arm hooked around his shoulders. Her weight pressed into him, heavier than her frame should have been, every step punctuated by her ragged breaths. She had come back, but life clung fragile and raw to her bones, like a candle flame struggling against the draft. Every time she stumbled, the memory of her lying crushed under stone flashed behind his eyes, sharper than any pain in his own ribs.

Behind them, the Order's torches glowed through the haze. Voices echoed—shouts, curses, the clatter of boots on stone. The pursuit was not blind; it was deliberate, relentless. The Pyramid might have collapsed the ritual chamber, but its enemies had survived the wreckage, and they were closing in. The collapse hadn't buried the worst of them—it had only shaken them loose.

"Faster," Quentin urged, though his own lungs burned with every word.

Aisha's laugh came broken, faint. "That's rich… from you."

Her tone almost made him smile, but the weight of danger crushed it before it could form. He tightened his grip on her waist, guiding her over a pile of fallen masonry. Her steps faltered, knees buckling, and for a moment he thought she would collapse again.

"I've got you," he said, his voice sharp with both fear and determination. "Just keep your feet under you."

Her head dipped against his shoulder, strands of dust-matted hair brushing his cheek. "I don't deserve that."

"Don't." He bit the word out, shoving them both forward. "Not now. Just move."

The hallway narrowed, its ceiling cracked and sagging. Rubble littered the floor, uneven chunks of stone that scraped their boots and threatened to trip them. Above, the groan of shifting earth sent vibrations down the walls, as though the stone itself resisted movement that wasn't its own.

The place felt less like a tomb now.

More like a throat trying to swallow.

Shouts rose behind them.

"There! They're ahead!"

"Close the gap!"

Torchlight flared brighter, shadows dancing along the rough walls. Quentin's stomach turned cold. They wouldn't outrun them—not with Aisha leaning against him, her strength bleeding out more with each step.

"I'm dead weight," she tried, like an order.

The words stabbed him like a blade. "No."

"You can still make it out if you—"

He stopped so abruptly she nearly stumbled. He turned, his eyes burning through dust and exhaustion, pinning her with a glare that cut sharper than any words he could summon. "I did not drag you back from death just to let them take you again. Do you understand me?"

Her lips parted, but whatever retort she had died in her throat. She searched his face, saw the fire there, and lowered her gaze. For once, silence was her answer. Her fingers tightened, almost imperceptibly, in the fabric at his shoulder—as if some part of her believed him despite herself.

The sound of boots grew louder. Stones clattered as agents shoved their way through the rubble, their silhouettes beginning to take shape in the dust-choked gloom. Quentin's grip tightened around Aisha's waist. His body screamed at him to run, to fight, to do something.

"But what can I do?" His strength was spent, his mark dimmer than it had been in hours. Every step felt like walking on broken glass. And yet—the Echo still throbbed faintly in his right palm, a residual vibration refusing to die. Each pulse was a reminder and a temptation.

He thought of unleashing it again, of letting the fire crush the corridor under an absolute load. His chest tightened at the thought; he could almost feel the power clawing to be released.

But then he looked at Aisha, leaning on him, her breath shallow, her pulse weak beneath her skin. If he used the Echo in this narrow passage, she would burn with them. The thought chilled him to the marrow. He hadn't traded his life for hers just to make her collateral damage.

They reached a junction where the passage split. To the left, the tunnel collapsed entirely, sealed in ragged slabs. To the right, the way curved deeper, narrower, toward the heart of the Pyramid's buried passages.

Quentin forced them down the right-hand path, breath rasping.

Aisha's voice came low, broken by her effort to keep moving. "You should've chosen differently."

"What?" His tone was sharp.

"At the chamber. You should've... kept the power. Survived. Now we're both—"

He cut her off, dragging her onward. "I'd make the same choice a thousand times."

For a moment she said nothing. Then he felt the faintest squeeze of her hand at his shoulder. Weak, fleeting, but deliberate. An apology without the word.

The hallway shook violently. Dust fell in curtains, stinging their eyes. Stones cracked overhead, one slab crashing down a few feet behind them. The sound echoed like thunder, mixing with the agents' shouts.

"They're there!"

"Don't let them reach the stair!"

The stair? Quentin's pulse quickened. Somewhere ahead, a way up, a way out. Hope, faint but real, dug its claws into his chest. He shoved them forward with what little strength remained. The idea of open air felt as distant and impossible as another lifetime—yet it pulled at him all the same.

The passage narrowed again until they had to move sideways, scraping shoulders against stone. Torchlight licked at their backs, shadows stretching long before them. Quentin's mark throbbed in time with his racing heart, each beat sharper, louder.

Another shout echoed—closer than ever. "I see them!"

Quentin cursed under his breath, pushing Aisha ahead of him through the gap. Her steps faltered, but she forced herself through, scraping skin raw against the serrated wall. He followed, chest heaving, ribs aching with every breath.

They stumbled into a wider corridor at last, its floor sloping upward. The faint draft of air touched Quentin's face—cool, almost clean compared to the choking dust. The promise of the surface. He sucked it in like someone who'd been drowning for hours, not minutes.

But the Order's torches spilled into the narrow gap behind them, cutting through the dust. Their hunters were too close. Quentin could hear their breath, their weapons clattering against stone.

Aisha sagged against him, her strength draining faster than the distance closed. Quentin tightened his grip, hauling her forward even as his vision swam.

They couldn't outrun them. Not like this. Not both of them.

And yet, he refused to let go. If the Pyramid wanted to take something from him, it would have to pry her out of his hands.

— Δ —

The corridor groaned like a dying beast.

Quentin shoved Aisha forward, their feet scraping over broken stone. The slope pitched upward, promising a stair somewhere ahead, but the rubble narrowed into a choke of jagged debris. Above, the cracked ceiling gave a warning shudder. Dust cascaded in fine curtains. Each breath tasted like chalk and copper.

Then, with a sound like thunder splitting rock, a slab of stone cracked free.

It came down toward them, massive, unstoppable.

Quentin's instincts screamed too late—he couldn't dodge, couldn't push Aisha clear. The boulder filled his vision, darkness swallowing light. His hand shot up in reflex, right palm locking under crushing pressure.

As the mark indurated into burnished gold beneath his skin, it didn't just wrap around him. The load-stutter spilled outward—wide enough to catch Aisha—and suddenly, her world didn't just slow down—the falling mass no longer reached her. The moment stretched just enough for her to clear it—nothing more.

And the world broke.

The stone hit resistance—momentum stretched thin, the fall turning syrup-slow in his perception.

The dust that had been falling in sheets caught in the stutter, glittering in the faint shimmer of his mark like a constellation of tiny stars. The torchlight from behind bent strangely, its flames stretching in thick arcs, as if painted across water.

The sound of boots pounding after them dulled into distant thunder. The agents' shouts stretched into warped echoes, elongated vowels that melted into silence. Even his own heartbeat sounded wrong—slow, deep, like it belonged to someone else.

Quentin's chest heaved. His arm shook, the mark densifying until the fissures in the walls seemed to answer the pressure. "What—what is this?" he rasped, though no one could answer.

The stutter bit deeper.

He staggered sideways, dragging Aisha against him. She blinked, her lashes heavy with dust, eyes widening in slow-motion awe. "Quentin—" Her voice dragged, distorted by the stutter. "The second—it's... loaded."

The realization struck harder than the falling stone. His stomach lurched. He looked around—the debris hung mid-fall, the dust dragging downward in slow threads, the torches bending, the Order agents locked in a strained forward lean, their mouths open but voices stretched past meaning. The corridor looked painted over—motion pressed flat, everything warping like heat-haze.

Not stopped—overloaded.

Quentin alone could move through it. Move—but every step drove more weight into his palm.

Static prickled his skin. Awe flared—then terror cut it off.

His mark densified under a terrible pressure. His veins ached cold, and warmth dripped from his nose—blood. His stomach dropped. The Echo wasn't just bending the moment; it was grinding his body between its teeth to pay for it.

Aisha's weight nearly pulled him down. She was alive, awake, but only barely. Every ounce of his strength screamed to let her go, to collapse beside her in the impossible stillness. But he clenched his teeth and hauled her forward, his voice a growl torn from his chest. "Not letting them have you. Not ever."

The slab of stone that had threatened them hovered inches above his head, ragged edges glinting with suspended dust. He dragged Aisha beneath it, feeling the crushing load of the mark driving down his arm like buried iron.

Each step was torture. His muscles caught and wouldn't release, his vision blurred at the edges. The longer he held the distortion, the heavier the air became, pressing down on him like invisible chains. The silence grew suffocating, as if even sound itself was resisting his defiance. The entire weight of the second rested on his chest, threatening to crush him. The moment resisted, trying to snap back into place and shear him out of it.

He stumbled, nearly falling, but Aisha's faint grip tightened on his sleeve. Even barely conscious, she anchored him. He forced his legs to keep moving, dragging them both beneath the slab, past its stalled shadow-line.

Once they cleared, he released a strangled gasp. His arm buckled. The pressure in his palm stuttered.

The world lurched.

The moment snapped back with a deafening crash. The boulder struck the ground behind them, shattering into a storm of shards. Dust exploded outward, torchlight flared, and the shouts of the Order agents returned in a violent rush of sound. Sound slammed back into him.

Quentin fell to his knees, dragging Aisha with him. His vision whited out, his ears ringing. Blood ran hot from his nose. He panted, chest hitching with each breath.

Aisha slumped beside him, her hand fumbling against his. "You—" She coughed, words hitching. "You stretched it. You bought a second."

He shook his head violently, smearing blood across his cheek. "Not… stopped. Just… dragged." His words came broken, shredded by exhaustion. Even speaking felt like pushing sound uphill.

The passageway trembled again. Stones rattled loose overhead, and behind them the Order's torches burned through the dust, closer now. Quentin glanced back and saw their silhouettes breaking through the haze, their faces twisted with fury and fear.

One agent shouted, "He's wielding it! Don't let them escape!"

Quentin pressed a trembling hand to the wall, his mark flickering faintly in the stone. The temptation roared through him—to unleash it again, to force the moment itself into submission. He felt the possibility clawing at his bones, a tide begging to be set loose. But his body rebelled at the thought; his vision tilted, his pulse stumbled in his veins. He knew he couldn't hold it for long. The last bend had already chewed chunks out of him. Another might finish the job.

Aisha's voice brushed against him, weak but firm. "Quentin… you can't burn yourself out. Not for me."

His jaw clenched. "Already burned. Already given. And I'll keep giving," he rasped, dragging her up to her feet again. "Not stopping now."

Her lips trembled, caught between anger and something softer. She leaned into him, letting him take more of her weight, and whispered, "Then don't let it hollow you. Don't forget you're more than the mark."

The words pierced through the haze in his head, grounding him. He nodded once, sharp, forcing his body forward. He wasn't sure he believed her—but he wanted to.

The corridor sloped higher now, leading toward what he prayed was the stair. Every muscle screamed, every heartbeat felt stolen. But his hand still pressed faintly, a ticking weight in the dark.

And he knew now—it wasn't just force. It was the moment itself, overloaded and unstable, waiting to either settle or tear him apart. And every time he touched it, it left a little less of him behind.

— Δ —

The moment warped again—not violently, but weakly, like a grip slipping under too much weight. The choke-point dulled and stretched around them, the world resisting him with every step. He forced himself forward, dragging Aisha through a thinning distortion that cost him blood, breath, and something deeper than strength. By the time the stair loomed ahead, his body was already coming apart.

The stair rose before them, an irregular spine of stone climbing toward a shaft of dim light. Quentin's body shook violently with every step, his vision narrowing to a tunnel of fractured images. Aisha leaned heavier against him, her breaths shallow, her weight an anchor he refused to let go of. The ground tilted beneath his feet, as if the world itself was trying to shake him off.

The distortion thinned unevenly, slipping in places, snapping back in others. Sound bled through in stutters. Weight returned in pulses. The moment no longer held—it fought him.

His mark burnished deeper, searing him with bone-deep compression. His blood felt molten, forcing its way through veins too fragile to hold it. Each heartbeat slammed against his chest like a hammer blow. He tasted metal, sharp and bitter, as if time itself bled through him.

And then it happened. His legs buckled. The glow in his palm flickered wildly, sputtering like a dying star. He couldn't hold it anymore.

The distortion shattered, and the world came back too fast—sound, heat, motion—like a slap he couldn't dodge.

Quentin collapsed to his knees, dragging Aisha with him. The world tilted, his equilibrium shattered by the sudden return of gravity and momentum. A high-pitched, crystalline whine rang in his skull, deafening and relentless. He reached up to steady his head, and his fingers came away wet. It wasn't just the nosebleed anymore; a warm, thick trail of blood-tinge fluid was leaking from his left ear, staining his jaw. He'd pushed the moment too far. His body was paying the toll.

"Go!" an agent bellowed. "They're at the stair!"

Boots thundered behind them, closing the distance. Quentin tried to rise but his muscles held, trembling uncontrollably. The corridor seemed to tilt beneath him, the stair stretching impossibly far away. *He felt like he was sinking, as though the stone itself were swallowing him.*

"Get up," Aisha whispered hoarsely, her arm trembling around his shoulders. She was weaker than him, barely standing, yet her voice pressed sharp urgency into the haze clouding his mind. "Quentin, you have to move."

He shook his head faintly, unable to form words. The thought of standing again felt like asking his body to lift mountains. His limbs felt carved from sand—ready to collapse at the slightest touch.

"Don't you dare stop now," she hissed, her tone cracking but fierce. Her fingers dug into his arm, anchoring him. "Not after what you did for me. Not after you chose me."

Her words speared through the fog, cutting straight into his chest. A spark of defiance surged—a memory of her gasping back to life in his arms. He forced a breath into his lungs, sharp and ragged, and clawed his way upright. His knees buckled once, twice, but he staggered upright, hauling her with him.

The stair loomed.

They climbed.

Every step was agony. His legs trembled, his chest spasmed, his vision blurred with black spots. But Aisha's hand clutched his sleeve, her presence a constant demand: *keep moving.* She leaned on him, yet somehow it felt like she was the one holding him upright. Her will pushed against his collapse, a fragile lifeline refusing to snap.

Behind them, the Order's pursuit thundered closer. Shouts echoed, weapons clattered, torches blazed.

"Don't let them reach the surface!"

"Cut them down!"

Stone cracked as blades struck the walls in fury. The echoes spurred Quentin forward, each sound a whip at his back. Fear sharpened into adrenaline, a last, desperate fuel.

Halfway up the stair, his strength faltered again. He stumbled, nearly dragging them both down. His hand slapped against the wall to catch them, his palm smearing blood across stone. His vision swam, his breath came in ragged gasps. The stair twisted in his sight, doubling, then tripling.

"I can't—"

"Yes, you can," Aisha cut him off, her voice raw but sharp. She gripped his jaw, forcing his gaze to hers. Her eyes burned with fragile fire, her filigree flickering dim but alive. "You brought me back, Quentin. Don't you dare throw yourself away now."

His throat tightened, tears stinging his dust-caked eyes. He nodded once, unable to speak. The simple gesture cost him nearly everything.

Together, they dragged themselves upward.

At the top of the stair, the corridor widened into a fractured archway. Moonlight spilled faintly through cracks in the stone, painting silver streaks across the rubble. The open air lay just beyond. The promise of night felt like a hand reaching for them.

Hope struck Quentin's chest so hard it nearly broke him.

But the Order was too close. Their torches flared at the base of the stair, their shouts echoing up, weapons raised, fury driving them upward.

Quentin stumbled into the archway, collapsing against the wall. His body shook violently, sweat and blood streaking his face. He couldn't go further, not yet. His legs refused. The outside world felt inches away yet impossibly far.

Aisha sagged beside him, gripping his arm with trembling fingers. She glanced back at the stair, then at him, and for once her voice carried fear not for herself but for him. "They're coming," she whispered, her throat raw. "And you can barely stand."

Quentin clenched his fists, forcing himself to straighten. His chest heaved, his mark pulsed weakly, but he met her gaze. "Then we move anyway. Even if it kills me."

She stared at him, her lips parting as if to argue, but then she caught something in his eyes—something stubborn, unyielding. Slowly, she nodded. Her grip tightened, a silent vow to match his last breath with her own.

Together, they staggered toward the crack of night beyond the archway, the sound of pursuit crashing ever closer.

The Pyramid was collapsing, the Order unrelenting, but for the first time since the chamber, their strength felt shared.

And it was enough to keep them climbing.

Enough to make survival feel possible again.

— Δ —

The stair spat them out into night.

Quentin stumbled through the fractured archway, the weight of Aisha still clinging to his shoulders, and nearly collapsed as the cool air struck his face like a slap. The shift was staggering—gone was the dust-choked heat of the corridors, replaced by the crisp bite of desert wind. The air filled his lungs like water after drought. He doubled over, gasping, coughing until blood speckled the sand at his feet. The taste of iron coated his tongue, sharp as panic.

Aisha slumped against him, her breaths shallow but steady. Her skin was pale beneath streaks of dust, her filigree dim, barely alive with each rise of her chest. *Alive. Still alive.* He didn't trust that she'd stay that way.

They staggered forward a few more steps before Quentin's knees gave out entirely. He sank to the ground, pulling Aisha down with him. The sand was cool beneath his palms, soft compared to the brutal stone below. For a long moment, neither moved—just breathing, just existing under the vast sky. The silence wrapped them like a trembling embrace.

Above them, stars spilled across the darkness, sharp and endless. Cairo's lights shimmered faintly on the horizon, a distant constellation of its own. Between the desert's stillness and the city's glow, the Pyramid loomed behind them, fractured and half-buried, its shadow a jagged wound against the stars. It looked less like a monument now and more like the carcass of something ancient finally exhaling its last breath.

Quentin tipped his head back, chest still heaving. He had never seen the night sky like this—not from within the choking corridors, not through the haze of dust and rubble. It felt like the world had opened, offering them space to breathe. A freedom so vast it hurt.

Then the shouts came.

Behind them, the archway blazed with torchlight. Shadow Order agents spilled from the stair, their weapons catching the glow, their faces masks of fury. They halted at the threshold, eyes narrowing against the desert's openness.

One barked an order: "Hold the line!"

Another spat, voice sharp. "They won't get far."

But none advanced. The open sand stretched before them, unbound by stone walls, watched over by stars. The Order hesitated, wary of chasing prey into ground they couldn't control. Out here, the Echo had room. Their torches guttered in the desert wind, their shadows thinning against the vastness. And their authority shrank—reduced to flickering pinpricks swallowed by the dunes.

Quentin saw it—saw the doubt in their stances, the hesitation they tried to mask as strategy. Relief quaked through him, sharp as laughter. He sagged back into the sand, clutching Aisha's hand. "They're not coming," he whispered, as though saying it louder might shatter the fragile truth.

Aisha turned her head weakly, her gaze drifting past him to the agents clustered at the arch. Her lips curved into the faintest, dust-cracked smile. "Afraid of the dark," she murmured. Out here there were no corridors to choke, no ceilings to seal—and no geometry to pin the Echo against.

Her voice was a thread, but the smirk—small as it was—felt like defiance reborn.

Quentin laughed then, broken and ragged but real. It tore at his ribs, but he let it come, let it scrape his throat raw. The night sky stretched above them, vast and untouchable, and the Order stood shackled by their own fear. After hours—maybe days—he felt something close to freedom. A sliver of victory, scraped raw from exhaustion.

Aisha's hand twitched against his, fingers curling weakly into his palm. Her eyes fluttered shut, exhaustion claiming her. Quentin shifted closer, pulling her against him, his arm around her shoulders.

"You're safe," he whispered into her hair. The words were more prayer than promise, but he needed them spoken. He needed her to hear them—if only to believe them himself.

Her lashes trembled, then lifted. She looked at him through the haze of pain and fatigue, eyes wet with something softer than she'd ever allowed before. "You chose me."

The words struck deeper than any blade. *He couldn't answer—not with words.* His throat closed, his chest ached, his vision blurred with tears. Instead, he tightened his grip on her hand, threading his fingers through hers. The gesture said everything he couldn't voice: *He'd choose her again. Every time.*

A faint residual timing lingered between them—autonomic cross-talk after overload—two systems still sharing a weak signal.

Two faint resonances, still beating in the same rhythm.

They lay there in the sand, side by side, watching the stars. The desert wind carried the faint hum of Cairo's distant life—horns, voices, the pulse of a city unaware of the war in its shadows. To Quentin, the sounds felt impossibly normal, like echoes from a world he no longer belonged to.

The Order lingered at the archway, their torches glowing like angry fireflies. But none dared cross into the open. They watched, seething, before slowly withdrawing back into the stair's shadows. Their retreat felt less like mercy and more like an admission—tonight, the desert had chosen its side.

Quentin closed his eyes, pressing his forehead to Aisha's temple. For now, they had escaped. For now, they had each other. And the world felt survivable.

But even as relief washed over him, he knew this was not the end. The Pyramid still loomed, fractured but not defeated. The Echo still pulsed in his veins, dangerous and unyielding. And the Order would not stop until they reclaimed what had slipped through their grasp.

Yet under the stars, with Aisha's hand warm in his, Quentin allowed himself the smallest luxury.

Since the chamber, he let himself believe they might survive.

Chapter 19

A Bruised Alliance

"The truth of the wound binds those who choose to share the pain." — **Guardian Teaching, The Oath of Scars.**

— Δ —

The trek from the edge of the Plateau had been a fever dream of shifting sand and the distant, rhythmic wail of sirens that never drew closer. Liam and Sophia had appeared out of the dark like ghosts, guided by Dr. Farouk—who had revealed herself not as a mere professor, but as a Guardian operative bound to the same ancient Protocol the dunes had whispered about. She had bundled them into a nondescript van, her parting words a jagged warning: the stronghold was collapsing, and Aisha was a blade for the Order. That much he'd stitched together from Liam's frantic, overlapping account in the van's dark—between counting Aisha's breaths and the blood-hum in his ears.

They had driven in a tense, headlights-off silence until the towering silhouette of the Pyramid was swallowed by Cairo's industrial outskirts.

Farouk had promised them the storage building was "off the grid"—a structural blind spot the Order hadn't yet mapped. She had disappeared into the Cairo night with a sweating, terrified Professor Ellis in tow, claiming she had to "scrub their trail" and intercept the first police questions, leaving the students with nothing but a single lantern and the echoes of her warnings.

The door groaned on its crooked hinge as Quentin shoved it open with his shoulder. The abandoned storage building yawned before them, dark except for a single lantern perched on a crate. Dust motes swirled in the thin beam of light, the smell of rust and old oil clinging to the walls.

Aisha stumbled beside him, her weight dragging at his arm. They were both half-dead with exhaustion—clothes torn, streaked with blood and grime, their steps unsteady on the cracked concrete floor. Quentin barely had the strength to guide her forward, his vision still swimming from the ordeal beneath the Pyramid. Every breath scraped his ribs; every step felt borrowed.

For one fragile heartbeat, silence filled the room. Then—

"Quentin!" Liam shot up from where he'd been sitting cross-legged by the wall. His face split into an incredulous grin as he rushed forward, arms out as if he meant to pull his friend into a crushing embrace. "Holy hell, I thought you were buried alive!"

But he never reached them.

Sophia's arm shot out, barring his path. She stepped in front of him, her boots firm against the floor, her expression carved sharp by the lantern light. "Don't," she said, her tone flat but edged.

Liam blinked, thrown off balance. "What?"

"Look at them," Sophia snapped, her eyes cutting to Quentin and Aisha. "Covered in blood. Gone for who-knows-how-long. And her—" She pointed a hard finger at Aisha. "She's already betrayed us once. You'd run straight into their arms without a question?"

Liam's grin faltered, the words hitting harder than he'd admit. He glanced back at Quentin, then at Aisha, and swallowed. "They made it out alive. Isn't that worth—"

"Not if it costs the rest of us." Sophia's voice carried no softness, only iron.

From the shadowed corner of the room, Raj's laugh curled low and sharp. He leaned against a pillar, arms folded, grin sharpening like a blade being honed. "Listen to her, Liam. Finally someone's saying it. Heroes don't crawl back half-dead with the enemy still clinging to their side." His gaze slid toward Aisha, dripping with false sympathy. "Or maybe she's just here to finish what she started."

Quentin's head throbbed with a dull compression behind his eyes. He looked at Raj, and for a heartbeat the storage room slid away.

Black stone. Metallic dust. Thales's voice swallowed by crushed silence.

His teeth ached with it—pressure where sound should've been.

A figure stood near the altar—half-turned, unchained, face smeared by torchlight and distance. Not close enough to be sure. Not far enough to dismiss.

Quentin reached for the memory and found only static, as if the moment had been sealed under glass. The pressure behind his eyes tightened, warning him off. Every time he tried to force the detail into focus, it felt like pressing on a bruise inside his skull.

Had he really seen Raj there? Or was his mind stitching a familiar face into a gap because the truth was worse?

Raj's smirk in the lantern light made his stomach turn. That, more than the memory, frightened him.

Beside him, Aisha went still. Not a flinch—worse. A trained blankness, like someone had wiped her face clean. Her gaze snagged on Raj for a fraction of a heartbeat, then dropped to the concrete as if it had been burned.

The hand at her side tightened once—controlled, silent—then loosened again. Quentin felt it through her weight on his arm: recognition. Containment. *Don't.*

Quentin's teeth clenched. His fingers tightened reflexively around Aisha's waist, knuckles whitening. He wanted to step forward, to snap back, but his legs trembled under Aisha's weight. Every nerve screamed for rest. He tightened his grip on her waist instead, steadying her, and let silence be his defiance—for now.

At the back of the room, Nia hadn't moved. She sat perched on a crate, sketchbook balanced on her knees, her pencil trembling in her fingers. Her wide eyes darted between the new arrivals and the rest of the group. Slowly, hesitantly, the graphite began to scratch the page again. Quentin caught a glimpse of two figures taking shape—bent, leaning on each other, shadows clinging to their forms like open wounds.

The sound of her pencil cut through the room louder than any voice.

Liam's jaw tightened. He sidestepped Sophia's arm, though slower now, less certain. "Look, I get it," he said, voice pitched to be reasonable. "But we're all we've got. You really want to throw them back to the wolves because it's messy?"

Sophia's eyes didn't leave Quentin. "Messy is one thing. Dangerous is another."

The words sliced through the air. Quentin flinched, not from the bite of them but from the truth they carried—the Echo still pulsed in his veins, dangerous, volatile, and he knew it. He saw it mirrored in Sophia's gaze: not hatred, but calculation, the cold weighing of risk. To her, he wasn't just Quentin anymore; he was a variable she couldn't control.

Aisha's knees buckled. Quentin lowered her gently onto a crate near the wall, his own body sagging beside her.

As she sank, something hard knocked faintly against her ribs beneath the torn jacket—metal on metal. Compact. Concealed. A blade, then. Not student gear. Quentin's stomach tightened. He opened his mouth, but no words came.

Quentin reached up, fingers trembling, and touched the side of his face. His skin felt tight, masked in grit and something darker. He wiped the dried copper from his upper lip and the edge of his ear canal—blood crusted there, brittle proof of the pressure that had nearly split his skull beneath the dunes. His head still throbbed with a hollow, rhythmic ache, but the wetness was gone—for now.

Sophia crossed her arms. "You expect us to welcome you back without question. But the rest of us fought to stay alive and bled doing it, not knowing if you'd ever return. Forgive me if I'm not ready to celebrate."

Raj's mouth curved. "Hear, hear."

Nia's pencil stopped. She looked at the sketch she'd drawn, then down at her trembling hands. She didn't speak—but her silence spoke louder than words. Even on the page, the two figures she'd drawn looked like they were about to fall apart.

Quentin finally found his voice, raw and torn. "We're not here to be celebrated. We're here because we had no choice." He looked at each of them, eyes burning despite the exhaustion dragging at his bones. "Believe me or don't. But we're not your enemies."

His words hung in the air like thin wire, waiting for someone to snap it.

Sophia's jaw tightened. Liam's fists clenched. Raj's expression sharpened. Nia turned another page, her pencil shaking as it touched down again.

— Δ —

The silence that followed Quentin's words was ragged, as if the room itself braced for what would come next. The lantern on the crate hissed softly, throwing long shadows against the rust-streaked walls.

Sophia stepped forward, boots striking concrete with clipped finality. She planted herself in front of Aisha, arms folded, chin raised. "Enough dancing around it. We deal with this now."

Aisha shifted where she sat, her body still weak, her breaths uneven. Quentin leaned slightly forward, instinctively shielding her with his posture, but Sophia's eyes were fixed on Aisha alone.

"You betrayed us once already," Sophia said, voice like steel. "You led Quentin into the Order's hands. You stood with them while the rest of us were hunted. And now you're here, claiming you've changed. Why should we trust anything from you?"

The accusation cut through the stale air like a blade.

Liam flinched, starting to speak—"Sophia, come on—"

She raised a hand, silencing him. Her gaze didn't waver. "I'm not interested in excuses. I want an answer. From her."

All eyes turned to Aisha.

She drew in a slow, shaky breath. Her hands trembled in her lap, her filigree pulsing faintly under skin still pale from her ordeal. The glow looked wrong on her now—less like a badge of rank, more like a scar that refused to fade. For a long moment, she said nothing, her gaze fixed on the floor.

Then she lifted her head.

"I did betray you," she said. The words came flat, unflinching. "I won't twist it. I made choices that led Quentin into chains. I carried out the Order's commands because I believed in them—because they built me."

The admission landed heavy. Even Raj, lounging in the corner, tilted his head slightly, as if savoring it.

Sophia's expression hardened further. "Then why should we believe you now?"

Aisha's lips parted, but her voice faltered. She clenched her hands, her eyes glassing over. "Because..." She swallowed, shaking her head as though the words weighed too much. "Because when it mattered, I turned against them. I saved him. I chose him over everything they drilled into me. And it nearly killed me."

Her voice cracked at the last word, raw and unguarded. She closed her eyes for a heartbeat, letting the silence carry the confession.

Quentin's chest ached. He wanted to speak for her, to cut off the scrutiny, but he held back. This was hers to carry. The Echo thrummed faintly in his palm, as if reacting to her words, but he forced his hand to stay still.

Liam took a step closer, his grin gone, his voice quieter than usual. "She's not lying. Look at her—she wouldn't be here if she hadn't flipped."

Sophia's jaw tightened. "Or maybe this is just another mask. They trained her for deception since she could walk. Tears and trembling don't erase that."

Aisha's eyes snapped open. She met Sophia's stare with sudden fire, though her voice trembled. "You think I don't know that? You think I don't wake up choking on the things they made me do?" Her breath hitched, a tear sliding unbidden down her cheek. She swiped it away furiously. "I'm not asking you to forgive me. I'm telling you I burned the bridge behind me. There's nothing left but him."

Quentin saw her eyes flick—not to Liam, not to Nia—but toward the pillar-shadow where Raj lounged.

Aisha swallowed hard.

And Quentin understood the trap: say a name without proof, and the room would turn on her harder. Raj would smile and call it manipulation. Sophia would believe him. He saw then what she was really doing: not hiding the truth — *holding it in reserve until it could kill cleanly.*

Her gaze flicked to Quentin, brief but sharp, before returning to Sophia. "I chose him."

The words hung in the room, sharp as glass and just as fragile.

Liam's eyes widened, the weight of her admission sinking in. Even Nia's pencil faltered against her sketchbook, the sound of graphite scratching pausing mid-line. On the page, the lines around Aisha's eyes darkened, as if Nia couldn't help but draw the guilt there.

Raj, however, smirked in the shadows. "Adorable," he drawled, his tone dripping with poison. "Almost makes me believe in love stories. Almost."

Sophia ignored him, her attention locked on Aisha. The rigidity in her stance didn't soften, but her eyes flickered with something—doubt, conflict, perhaps the faintest crack in her armor.

Aisha's shoulders slumped, her fire dimming into quiet exhaustion. "Maybe I will," she admitted. "I don't know how to undo what I've been. I don't know if I can. But I know this—" She lifted her chin, steady despite the tears streaking her face. "I won't betray him again. Even if it kills me."

The silence after those words was heavier than any accusation.

Liam scrubbed a hand through his hair, letting out a breath. "Bloody hell, Sophia. If that doesn't count for something—"

"It counts," Sophia cut in, her voice sharp. "But it doesn't erase. She can say all the right things, but until she proves it, I won't gamble the rest of us on her word alone."

Aisha lowered her gaze again, her strength spent. The crack of her vulnerability remained, raw and visible, a truth none of them could unsee. For the first time since they'd met her, her tactical veneer wasn't just slipping—it was gone.

Quentin finally leaned forward, his hand brushing hers in quiet solidarity. She didn't look at him, but her fingers curled faintly into his.

Sophia caught the motion, her mouth a hard line. "Fine. She stays. But this isn't trust. And it sure as hell isn't forgiveness."

Raj's smile glimmered in the shadows, pleased at the fracture deepening in the group.

The lantern hissed. The silence stretched. And the fault lines grew wider. Quentin felt them under his feet—hairline fractures spidering through the only family he had left.

— Δ —

Sophia's gaze dropped once—caught the flash of metal at Aisha's ribs—and her posture hardened like a verdict.

The sight of the weapons—professional, lethal, and so clearly not belonging to a student—only made the air in the room feel thinner.

Something inside him snapped. He surged to his feet so suddenly the crate beneath him scraped against the floor. "That's enough."

His voice rang louder than he intended, sharp in the stillness. The others turned toward him, startled. Even Sophia blinked at his uncharacteristic force.

Quentin's hands curled into fists at his sides, a pressure under his skin tightening like a heartbeat. His chest tightened—not just with anger, but with the weight of everything: the chains, the visions, the betrayal, the sacrifice. His pulse synced with the Echo's throb, the mark responding to his rising emotion like a latch under load.

"She saved me," he said, voice raw. "You can hate her. You can doubt her. But you don't get to erase that. You think I'd be standing here if she hadn't chosen differently?"

Sophia's jaw set. "And if she hadn't betrayed you in the first place, maybe you wouldn't have needed saving at all."

Quentin flinched at the truth of it, but his fury didn't fade. He took a step closer to her, his shadow stretching across the cracked concrete. His voice stayed low, tight—a coil pulled to breaking. "You think I don't know that? You think I don't replay it every time I close my eyes? But I was there when she shoved me out of the way, when the stone came down. I was there when she bled because she couldn't let me die."

His voice cracked, grief clawing at his throat. "She chose me over them. And I'll keep saying it until it gets through that iron wall of yours: she saved me."

His fist tightened—and the air seemed to thicken around it.

Not light. Density.

The lantern didn't dim. Its flame leaned instead, as if the room had gained a new, invisible weight. A few dust motes hung a fraction too long, as if the room couldn't decide how to fall.

Quentin swallowed, forced his fingers open, and showed them his palm. The mark sat under the skin like a locked hinge—lines too precise to be veins, too deliberate to be injury. It didn't shine. It *pressed.* Looking at it made the back of the throat tighten, like standing too close to a drop.

Gasps rippled through the group.

Sophia's eyes widened. "Your right palm—"

Quentin opened it slowly, deliberately. The mark of the Echo tightened across his skin, the geometry re-aligning, as if the skin were a diagram struggling to hold its shape. The room's stillness dragged—sound lagging half a beat behind his breath. Dust hung too long in the air.

"This is what they were after," he said, lifting his hand for all of them to see. "This is why the Order wanted me. This is what nearly killed me. And it's what I used to keep her from slipping away."

The revelation slammed into the group like a physical force.

Liam's eyes went round as saucers. "Mate," he breathed, a crooked grin tugging at his lips despite the gravity of it, "that's… I mean, it's dangerous, sure, but also kind of awesome."

Nia's pencil skidded across her page, her sketch lines suddenly jagged. She lifted her head, gaze flicking between Quentin's marked palm and Aisha, silent but wide-eyed. She clutched her sketchbook to her chest, as if bracing herself against what she was seeing.

Sophia, however, recoiled. Her face hardened, her voice sharp as a knife. "That thing isn't a gift. It's a weapon. And you're wielding it like a child yanking on gravity in a crowded room."

Quentin's temper flared. "I never asked for it!" he shouted. "It chose me. And every time I use it, it tears me apart. You think I want to feel my blood run cold, my head split open, just to make the world drag for a heartbeat? You think I wanted to be marked, hunted, nearly broken?"

He lowered his hand, the pressure easing but not releasing entirely. His voice softened, thick with exhaustion. "But if I didn't, none of us would be standing here. If I hadn't poured everything into it, Aisha wouldn't be here. So call it a weapon. Call me reckless. But don't you dare say she doesn't deserve a chance."

The words hung heavy, raw and unvarnished.

Sophia's lips pressed into a thin line. Her eyes glimmered with fear more than anger, though she masked it well. "And what happens when it consumes you? What happens when you lose control, when the damage doesn't know the difference between enemy and ally?"

Quentin met her gaze unflinching. "Then stop me. But don't stop her."

The challenge reverberated through the room, quiet but seismic. Even the lantern flame seemed to lean toward him, flickering in the tension.

The silence that followed was electric, humming with the unspoken fracture between them.

Liam, trying to ease the edge, cleared his throat. "Well, on the bright side, if we all die horribly, at least we'll die knowing one of us can bully gravity. That's… something, right?"

No one laughed, but his voice loosened the tension just enough to breathe.

Raj, leaning lazily against the wall, smirked. "Oh, stirring speech, Quentin. Power tightening the room at just the right moment. You've got the theatrics down, I'll give you that. Too bad speeches don't kill the Order."

Quentin's head snapped toward him, but Raj only spread his hands innocently.

The lantern flickered, shadows stretching long across the walls. The group remained divided: Liam leaning closer to Quentin, eyes bright with rough loyalty; Nia trembling, her sketch of Quentin's marked hand smudged across the page; Sophia rigid, distrust etched into every line of her face.

And Aisha, silent beside him, tears glistening unshed as she clutched her knees. She didn't speak, but her hand sought his again, curling faintly into his. Her touch was barely there, but it steadied him more than any argument could.

The line was drawn, and everyone in the room knew it. Not between just trust and distrust—but between who Quentin had been, and who he was becoming.

— Δ —

The group drifted apart in uneasy silence after Quentin's outburst. The lantern's glow flickered against cracked plaster, throwing each of them into uneven silhouettes. Liam fussed over a scrape on his elbow, muttering jokes that fell flat. Nia bent over her sketchbook, though her pencil moved without focus, strokes loose and uncertain. Quentin remained close to Aisha, who sat hunched, head bowed, the last traces of tears drying on her cheeks. Her shoulders curled inward, as if bracing for judgment even in the quiet.

Sophia paced near the far wall, arms locked tight across her chest, her jaw working as though chewing through words she refused to release.

And Raj watched it all with quiet delight.

His eyes tracked each person like pieces on a board—seeing where they stood, where they wavered, where they could be nudged.

He waited until the others had scattered into corners of fatigue and mistrust, until the tension hummed without breaking. Then, as if by chance, he drifted toward Sophia. His footsteps were soft, measured.

"You see it too, don't you?" he murmured.

Sophia stiffened but didn't look at him. Her gaze stayed pinned to the floorboards, her face caught in the half-light. "See what?"

Raj leaned against the wall beside her, arms folded casually, though his eyes gleamed sharp. "That pull in the room when his hand goes tight. The way it shifts every time he loses control. You felt it earlier—when he got angry. He's changing, Sophia. And not into something you can trust."

Her lips pressed into a thinner line. "He held us together. You saw what state he came back in—and he still didn't let it break us."

"Oh, of course," Raj said smoothly. "Heroic, wasn't it? But you also saw how close he was to collapsing. The blood crusted under his nose. His whole body shaking as if tearing itself apart. Tell me honestly—does that look like power he can control? Or does it look like a boy dangling on the edge of a cliff, about to drag all of us down with him?"

Sophia's fingers curled against her biceps, gripping tighter. Her head tilted, the thought already seeded. Her silence was answer enough.

Raj allowed a sliver of a smile. He lowered his voice, intimate, conspiratorial. "I know you pride yourself on discipline, order. You crave structure. But look at us now—chaos following a boy marked by something none of us understand. If the Order couldn't contain it, what makes you think he can?"

Sophia finally turned her head, eyes narrowing. "And what would you suggest? Abandon him?"

Raj gave a low chuckle. "For now. But I'm not talking about abandoning him. I'm talking about being prepared. Someone has to be willing to step in if he loses control. Someone who won't hesitate when the moment comes. Someone strong enough to protect the rest of us from him."

The words landed like stones dropped in still water, rippling through her expression. Sophia's brows furrowed, her lips parting as if to argue—but no words came.

Raj pressed the advantage, leaning just enough to invade her space, his voice dropping to a whisper. "You've felt it. That unease in your stomach every time the mark drags the moment. That fear you bury under all your rules. Don't deny it—I see it in your eyes. And if you, Sophia—the most disciplined of us—can't ignore it… what does that say about the danger we're all in?"

Sophia's throat bobbed as she swallowed hard. She looked away, her hands tightening against her arms. The steel in her posture trembled—not breaking, but bending.

"You're twisting it," she said finally, but the conviction in her tone wavered.

Raj smiled again, slow and self-satisfied. "Maybe. Or maybe I'm the only one willing to speak the truth while the rest of you cling to pretty little lies about friendship and redemption. Quentin's not just carrying some shiny relic. He's carrying a fuse. And sooner or later, it's going to burn down."

He let the silence linger, let her sit with the weight of his words.

Sophia shifted, her jaw locked tight. When she finally spoke, her voice was quieter than before. "He's still one of us."

Raj leaned back, smug. "Of course he is. Until he isn't. That's why you have to be ready."

From the other side of the room, Liam snorted, breaking the tension without realizing it. "If you two are plotting world domination over there, at least keep it down. Some of us are trying to nurse our wounds in peace."

Sophia flinched, stepping away from Raj as though caught in something illicit. Her cheeks flushed—not with embarrassment, but with the realization she'd let him get too close. Raj only chuckled, smooth as ever, and gave her a little nod.

He had planted the seed. That was enough.

Doubt was slower than poison, but far more permanent.

As he strolled back to his corner, the smirk never left his face. He had seen the crack form in Sophia's resolve, and he knew exactly how to pry it wider.

And across the room, Quentin sat with Aisha, oblivious to the poison seeping into the group around him.

— Δ —

The air on the rooftop was cooler than below, touched with desert wind and the faint smell of the city beyond. Quentin climbed the creaking ladder slowly, every muscle aching, his chest still raw from the night's ordeal. Aisha followed, quieter, her steps hesitant but steady enough. She paused once halfway up, as though unsure she deserved the space at his side.

When they emerged, the skyline of Cairo stretched before them. The city glimmered with scattered lights, distant and alive, while above, the stars burned sharp against velvet black. The ruined outline of the Pyramid loomed faintly on the horizon, its broken silhouette like a scar against the night.

For a long moment, neither spoke. They just breathed—air untainted by smoke and blood, air that didn't press down like stone walls closing in. Quentin leaned against the low ledge, staring up at the stars until his vision blurred. Aisha lowered herself onto the rooftop beside him, knees pulled close, her arms wrapped around them like armor. Her posture made her look smaller than she ever allowed herself to appear.

“They don’t trust me,” she said at last. Her voice was quiet, not defensive, just… tired. “And maybe they shouldn’t.”

Quentin turned his head, watching the way the wind tugged strands of her hair loose, the lantern glow from below casting faint shadows across her face. “Sophia doesn’t trust anyone she can’t control,” he said softly. “And Raj—Raj doesn’t trust anyone because he’s too busy trying to twist them into pieces he can use.”

Aisha’s breath hitched. For a long moment she stared at the city lights like they were something she could decode.

“Raj was at the altar,” she said. No theater. Just fact.

Quentin’s spine went cold.

“I know,” she added. “I saw him. I… heard him say he built the trap. That he invested in you.” Her jaw flexed, anger and shame crossing too fast to name. “But in that room, I’m the blade. I’m the one they already want to call a liar.”

She turned her face toward him, eyes bright and exhausted. “If I accuse him without proof, he wins. He calls it discord. And the Order taught me exactly how fast a room turns on the wrong voice. Sophia believes him. And you end up alone.”

Her fingers curled around her knees. “So I kept him close. Where I could watch his rhythm. Where he can’t vanish.”

A weak laugh escaped her, dry but genuine. “And Liam?”

“He trusts too easily,” Quentin said with a faint smile. “He thinks people are worth the risk. Which makes him the bravest of us, I think.”

Her eyes softened, but she shook her head. “It doesn’t change what I did. I was their enemy before I was anything else. And even if I wanted to… I can’t erase that.” She tightened her arms around her knees, her gaze fixed on the city lights. “Every instinct I have… they built it. Hardwired it. You saw what I became down there.” A breath shivered out of her.

"The Order raised me to betray, Quentin. It's in my blood. Maybe it's all I'll ever be."

Quentin leaned closer, resting his elbows on his knees. "Then don't erase it. Outlive it. Prove them wrong."

She glanced at him, searching his face. "And if I can't?"

He hesitated, then reached for her hand. His palm was still marked, the hinge-lines faint under the skin—warm, real, and heavier than they looked. The pulse steadied—subtle, rhythmic, as if the mark listened to her touch instead of his fear. "Then let's give them a reason to believe in you anyway. Even if it takes time. Even if it's just me at first."

Her fingers trembled in his grasp, but she didn't pull away. The silence stretched between them, filled with the distant hum of Cairo, the whisper of the wind.

Aisha exhaled, her shoulders sagging. "You shouldn't have paid that price," she said softly. "You could've let me go. You could've kept all that power, maybe even used it to crush them. But you gave it up for me."

Quentin's throat tightened. "I didn't choose weakness," he murmured. "I chose you."

Not as an apology. As a decision.

His throat worked. "I didn't weigh it out, Aisha. I just knew I couldn't lose you."

She blinked rapidly, her eyes shining in the starlight. "You're a fool."

"Probably," he admitted with a small, tired smile. "But I've never regretted it."

For a long moment, they sat in quiet, side by side, the rooftop their fragile sanctuary. Aisha leaned against him at last, her head brushing his shoulder. He felt the weight of her there—not the burden she believed herself to be, but the choice he had made, the tether he refused to let go of. Her breath steadied slightly, matching his.

"They may never forgive me," she whispered.

Quentin tilted his head, resting his cheek against her hair. "Then let's make sure they can't ignore what we do next."

Her lips curved faintly at the edge, the ghost of a smile. "That sounds like trouble."

"Good," he said, a spark of steel in his tone. "Trouble means we're still alive."

Above them, the stars burned steady, eternal witnesses to the fragile bond forming in the shadow of betrayal. Below, the murmurs of their fractured group still carried through the building, sharp with suspicion, heavy with fault lines.

But here, on the rooftop, Quentin and Aisha sat together—two survivors, two souls tethered by choice. The Order hadn't stopped hunting. The Echo still pulsed dangerously in his veins. The group still eyed them with distrust.

And yet, for this one breath, they weren't enemies.

They were something closer to hope.

Chapter 20

The Bridge to Nothing

"If the plan fails, it is not the strategy that is wrong, but the loyalty of the executor." — **Axiom of the Shadow Order, Failure I.**

— Δ —

The sky outside the cracked windows was the color of bruises, predawn pressing toward light. In the storage building, the lantern had burned down to a nub, throwing a coin of dull gold onto the circle of crates they'd pushed together as a makeshift table. The place smelled of tin and old rope and a sweetness that might have been spilled fuel. Everyone looked carved out of shadow.

Sophia stood instead of sitting. That single choice told Quentin everything about how this would go. Her spine was straight as a drawn line, hands braced on the crate as if she could force the world into order by posture alone.

"We need to contact the program," she said, each word clipped, precise. "Dr. Farouk, Professor Ellis—someone who can get us onto a plane and out of this country before sunrise. We go to authorities, we go official, we go now."

Liam lifted two fingers as if in class. "Hey, quick thought—do we tell them about the cult, or save that for the in-flight entertainment?"

Sophia didn't look at him. "We tell them there's been an incident. We don't elaborate."

Quentin sat hunched on a crate, Aisha on one side of him, her shoulder brushing his, Nia at the other end of the table with her sketchbook open like a secret she was trying to smother under her hands. *The fatigue in his bones felt like slow poison, seeping into every thought.* Still, he managed, "The Order has feelers everywhere—tourist police, airport security, maybe even the program itself. You think they haven't planned for frightened students running to authority? We step into a terminal, we disappear."

Sophia pivoted to him, the movement clean as a blade turn. "We do nothing, we disappear slower."

"We move them, not us," Quentin said. "We change locations now, disappear in the city before the Order reshuffles. There's an old service tunnel Liam noticed near the tram—"

"Excuse me, I noticed a snack cart," Liam said. "The service tunnel noticed me."

"—and we work our way to the outskirts, find transport with no questions."

Sophia's eyes narrowed. "Your plan relies on luck, improvisation, and a lot of not being seen by people who excel at seeing."

Quentin met her gaze. "My plan relies on us staying alive long enough to have any plan at all."

The lantern hissed softly. From the far corner, Raj sat on a stack of pallets, elbows on knees, gaze flicking between speakers like a spectator at a tennis match he'd bet on both sides of. He hadn't spoken yet, but the attention was its own kind of calculation.

Nia's pencil began to move, barely audible, a moth-wing whisper on paper. Quentin glanced. A bridge took shape beneath her hand—two spans drawn in quick, sure strokes. The center cracked, graphite crumbling into the white space like falling dust. She paused, then darkened the break until it was a wound.

Liam noticed too. His voice gentled. "Hey, Ni. What is it?"

She didn't look up. "I don't know until it's done." She said it apologetically, like she was sorry for the truth. The pencil kept going, sketching tiny figures on the bridge, scattered—some running forward, some turning back. One, near the break, was half-erased.

Aisha's eyes flicked to the page and then to Sophia. Her voice was sanded raw, but steady. "We don't go to the program. They'll hand us over without knowing it."

Sophia's chin lifted. "And we trust you to know who's safe?"

"I know who isn't," Aisha replied, not rising to the barbed edge. "I grew up inside that net."

Liam leaned his forearms on the crate, trying on a grin that couldn't quite hold. "Soph, I vote Team Don't-Get-Arrested-By-Cult-At-Check-In. Not because I don't love paperwork. I adore paperwork. Paperwork is my love language. But I would also like to continue breathing."

Sophia inhaled slowly through her nose. "We are not a democracy, Liam."

"Ah," he said. "The old benevolent dictatorship. How's that working out for dictators this century?"

Quentin cut across before she could snap back. "Sophia. Please. Listen." He kept his voice low, the anger flattened into something calmer that felt truer. "We barely got out alive. If we walk into a bureaucracy we don't control, we hand the Order time. And time is what they win with. We run now. We keep our circle small. We find shelter without ink on a ledger."

"And then what?" Sophia asked quietly. "We hide forever? We play at being ghosts until someone kinder than the Order finds us? We are students. Not soldiers. We need adults."

"We are what the Echo made us," Quentin said. The words surprised him, landing between them with a weight he didn't intend. He forced a breath. "We didn't ask for this, but we're the ones standing here. No one's coming to fix it for us."

Sophia stared at him. For a moment, the mask slipped—he saw the fear behind the iron. "Say we follow you into the dark. Say we avoid every checkpoint, every camera. You can guarantee their safety?" She pointed—not at him, but past him: to Nia's bowed head, to Liam's tired eyes, to the faint filigree threaded under Aisha's skin. "You can look me in the face and swear that your… power won't slip and bring them down with you?"

The mark slept there, dull and latent. He swallowed. "No. I can't swear that. But I can swear I'll keep fighting to make it shield them instead of crushing them. That's all I have."

Sophia's laugh was paper-thin. "That's not a plan. That's a prayer."

"Prayers have gotten us this far," Liam said. "Plus a lot of sprinting."

Raj finally spoke, voice smooth as oiled rope. "Sophia is right about one thing—we are out of our depth. But Quentin is right about another—the Order has hands in pockets we can't see. The airport will be a sieve." He lifted one shoulder in a languid half-shrug. "Walk into their gates, and you might as well hand them your boarding pass and your neck."

Sophia turned on him, surprised. "You agree with him?"

Raj spread his hands. "I agree with prudence. Call the program if you like. But not from here. And not as ourselves." He offered a half-smile that showed nothing. "We move. We be difficult to catch."

Quentin felt Aisha shift beside him, her shoulder touching his with intention. It steadied him more than any argument. Her filigree pulsed faintly under the grime, a weak reminder of what he'd already spent to keep her here.

Sophia rubbed her temple, exhaustion fraying the edges of her posture. "Fine," she said at last, like conceding a point in a debate she planned to win later. "We move at first light. We find transport off the grid. But we keep options open. If we see a safe window to call, we take it."

"First light is now," Liam said, peering at the slit of window where grey was turning less grey. "We could beat the breakfast rush and the cult rush. Two birds. One stone. One terrified flock."

"Pack," Sophia said. "Water. Anything that can be carried without slowing us."

Nia closed her sketchbook gently, as if the paper could feel pain. "The bridge… it breaks," she murmured, cheeks pale. "We have to stay together or we fall."

Sophia's gaze softened by a fraction. "Then we stay together."

Quentin stood, legs complaining. The room tilted once and righted when Aisha's hand found his wrist. He glanced at her. "You ready?"

Her mouth curved in a shard of a smile. "For running? Always."

Liam slung a threadbare backpack over his shoulder. "For the record, if anyone asks, I'm only here for the snacks."

"Then you're in luck," Raj said lightly, rolling his shoulders as if warming up for a jog. "We're about to be chased. Adrenaline is very slimming."

Sophia moved to the door, checked the alley through a crack, and froze the team with an upraised palm. The room stilled around her.

"Clear?" Quentin whispered.

"For now," she said. "Five minutes. We leave in pairs. Liam with Nia. Raj with me. Quentin…" A pause. "…with Aisha."

Aisha's fingers tightened on Quentin's wrist, a brief pulse. He nodded once. The choices fell like tossed coins—light in the moment, heavy later.

Sophia looked over them, the leader she refused not to be. "No heroics. No detours. If you lose sight, you shout. We hold the bridge."

Nia's breath hitched.

"Bad metaphor," Liam muttered.

Sophia opened the door. The sky had lightened another shade toward morning. Wind hissed low along the alley. Somewhere, a call to prayer climbed into the air and hung there, clear as a thread.

They filed toward the threshold, packs small, eyes larger. Quentin squeezed Aisha's hand once, quick, before letting go.

"Together," he said.

"Together," she echoed.

It wasn't agreement so much as a promise they didn't know how to keep. But it was enough to step into the waking city and try.

— Δ —

The Cairo streets were still more shadow than light, alleys webbed with trash bins and broken shutters, air thick with the smell of diesel and spices lingering from markets long since closed. The call to prayer drifted faintly over the rooftops, haunting in the pre-dawn quiet.

Sophia led the group in a staggered line—paired but spaced, each duo separated by a few paces—her stride clipped and efficient, eyes cutting at every corner. Raj lingered just off her shoulder, hands shoved in his pockets, posture loose but gaze sharp. Liam trudged with his backpack bouncing against his spine, muttering jokes under his breath that only Nia heard. She clutched her sketchbook to her chest like a lifeline, her gaze darting nervously at shadows that stretched too long.

Quentin stayed close to Aisha, his hand brushing her arm whenever she stumbled. Her skin was clammy, her steps uneven, but she held her head high, blades hidden beneath her torn jacket, eyes restless and watchful.

Every now and then, her filigree fluttered weakly at her throat, a tired ember that made him want to slow down—even as Sophia pushed them faster.

Suddenly, Nia stopped. She didn't just hesitate; she slammed her back against the damp brick wall, her sketchbook falling open to a page that was already filled with jagged, overlapping lines.

"No," she gasped, her voice thin but sharp enough to stop Sophia in her tracks. "Don't go past that lamp. The shadows... they have teeth."

Sophia frowned. "Nia, we have to keep moving. We're almost to the transit line."

Sophia glanced past her—down the branching alleys, each one either shuttered, gated, or dead-ended into stacked scrap. "Then tell me which way doesn't," she said, and it wasn't a challenge so much as a plea sharpened by time.

"The line is broken!" Nia shrieked, her eyes wide and fixed on the empty air ten feet ahead. "I see the light snapping. If we step under that lamp, the trap closes!" There wasn't time to debate—only to choose the least-wrong corridor and keep moving.

Quentin didn't know if she saw the future or felt the moment choose itself—but his gut agreed.

The alley they turned into was narrow, walls rising high on either side. A single lamp flickered overhead, painting the passage in sickly yellow.

Something in Quentin's gut twisted. *Too quiet. Too contained.* The kind of silence that waited for a signal.

He opened his mouth to warn the others—

Torches flared at both ends.

Raj was already two paces behind Sophia—then three—then he slipped behind a jut of shadow and didn't come out the other side.

Figures stepped into view, cloaked in black, glyphs glaring faintly across their forearms. Order agents. Dozens.

Sophia's curse sliced the silence. "Trap."

The agents moved as one, their boots echoing against stone, weapons drawn—short blades etched with glowing runes, chains coiled like snakes in their fists. The runes pulsed in time with the torches, hungry and precise.

Liam let out a sharp, disbelieving laugh, the sound bouncing harsh off the alley walls. "Well. Guess this is the part where I make a heroic last stand, right?"

He lunged forward, but before he could do anything reckless, an agent slammed into him, knocking him flat. He grunted, the air leaving his lungs, his quip cut short.

"Liam!" Nia cried, clutching her sketchbook tighter, frozen in place as agents closed around them. Her knuckles whitened on the worn cardboard cover, as if she could draw herself out of this if she just held on hard enough.

But the fear didn't paralyze her this time; it ignited her. Panic didn't freeze her—it focused her. Lines came first, then meaning. Angles. Outcomes. A heartbeat ahead. She ripped a page from the book, her eyes darting between the drawing and the chaos.

"Liam, duck!" she screamed.

Liam didn't ask why. He dropped flat to the stones just as a weighted chain whistled through the space where his head had been a second before.

"Sophia, two o'clock!" Nia called out next, her voice gaining a strange, rhythmic authority. "Behind the crates—he's lunging low!"

Sophia spun as the agent lunged. She wrenched the Order blade free from his grasp as he overextended—metal slick in her hand—and drove it low in the same motion, catching his ankle exactly where Nia had predicted.

For a heartbeat, the group wasn't just fighting; they were moving to a tempo Nia was setting. She was decoding the ambush before it could crush them.

Sophia surged into motion, her movements a blur of discipline. She kicked the first agent in the chest, spun, and smashed her elbow into another's jaw. The Order blade flashed, clean and efficient, drawing a quick red line through the chaos.

"Nia, move!" she barked.

But her body couldn't. Her hands trembled, her pencil sliding from her grasp, rolling across the stone. Her lips moved soundlessly, as though praying to the page she could no longer draw.

Quentin's mark pressed hard beneath his skin, numbness bleeding through his sleeve. He grabbed Aisha's wrist. "We need to run. Together."

Her blades sang free of their sheaths, gleaming under the lamplight. She planted herself at his side, expression cold, deadly. "Then we carve the way."

The first agent rushed them, chain snapping through the air. Quentin ducked low, Aisha striking high—the blade cut clean through the man's shoulder, dropping him before his chain could coil.

Quentin's heart slammed against his ribs, the numb pressure in his palm pulsing harder, louder. The urge to unleash the Echo clawed at him. But Aisha's voice cut through the panic: "Not yet. Don't crack yourself open—we fight first."

Liam groaned from the ground, pushing an agent off him with sheer stubbornness. "Little… help?"

Sophia yanked him upright by his collar, slicing another attacker across the thigh. "On your feet!"

Nia looked at her sketchbook one last time. The drawing of the bridge was crumbling, the graphite smearing under her trembling thumbs. "The center—don't hesitate!" she yelled to Quentin. "If we commit to the lamp, the trap closes. We jump now—that gap still breathes!"

Nia pointed toward a side passage that looked like a dead end—unless you knew what to look for. "There! The light is still holding there!"

Aisha spun, blade cutting a circle around them. "Pick a way!"

He looked—one end of the alley thick with advancing agents, the other just as blocked. His pulse roared in his ears, his palm pressing hard enough to numb. He clenched his teeth.

"Through them," he said.

Aisha bared her teeth in a grim smile. "Good answer."

They surged forward together, blades cutting as the air thickened around them. But the alley was a maw closing fast, Order torches and glyphs hemming them in from all sides.

And he knew—if he didn't risk more than steel, if he didn't unleash what drags inside him, they would all fall here, one by one, swallowed by the Order's chains. The Echo pulsed at his bones, waiting for him to say yes.

— Δ —

The alley was chaos—steel striking stone, boots pounding, the sharp tang of blood mixing with the sour reek of spent glyphwork. Quentin's chest heaved, his muscles screaming, his vision splintered by torchlight. All around him the group was already scattered—Liam stumbling after Sophia, Nia vanishing into a side passage.

The Order pressed in, wolf-fast. Chains cracked, blades slashed, their formation a tide of black and fire. Every rune on their weapons pulsed with the same predatory rhythm, the same frequency the Echo inside him answered to.

Quentin's palm went phantom-cold, the kind that didn't touch skin so much as sink into bone. Without thought, he raised it—his mark pressing like geometry bruising the world.

Fatigue didn't vanish so much as get compressed, every ounce of effort forced into brutal clarity.

Sophia didn't *think* faster—she felt the air announce each strike a fraction of a second before it arrived, vibrations telegraphing intent through bone and breath. Beside her, Liam's panic narrowed into something hard and survivable, his motions stripped clean because there was no time.

They weren't empowered. They were aligned—caught inside the Echo's pull, their bodies obeying the same warped second. And as long as Quentin held the moment open, those caught inside it moved as one thing, not stronger—just temporarily impossible to break.

And the world buckled.

The air *weighted*—not slower, not stopped, just dragged into alignment, like the alley had become a deep current. Torch flames leaned. Footsteps landed half a beat late. The Order's rush turned clumsy, their momentum suddenly too heavy to steer.

Quentin staggered under the strain, veins bulging against his skin, blood streaming hot from his nose. His chest convulsed, but he forced the power outward, spreading it through the alley like a net.

"Move!" he gasped, his voice reverberating strangely in the slowed air—warped, doubled, as though spoken by two versions of him out of sync.

Aisha blinked at the frozen storm around them, alarm flashing through her features. Then she grabbed his arm, hauling him forward. "Quentin, stop—"

"Not yet," he croaked, pushing harder.

He shoved his marked hand outward, and the suspended debris—loose bricks, shattered bottles, even a fallen torch—jerked violently like pieces on invisible strings, scattering the Order agents like puppets. Their movements stuttered, each displacement leaving the agents caught mid-motion, as if the alley couldn't decide which second to live in.

Quentin half-dragged, half-carried Aisha through the slowed chaos, their feet splashing in puddles that moved like syrup. Dust hung above them like stars, each mote a spark suspended in the drag.

But every step cost him. His vision blurred with double images, the edges of his sight blackening. His ears rang with a high whine, piercing and relentless. His heartbeat no longer felt like his own—too slow, too loud, out of rhythm with the world.

He could hear Aisha's voice, distorted but urgent: "You'll kill yourself—stop!"

He shook his head violently, forcing his legs to keep moving. "Not… until they're clear."

Through the haze he glimpsed Sophia dragging Liam toward the far end of the alley, their movements jagged in the frozen stutter. Nia was a shadow vanishing into a side gap, sketchbook clutched like a shield.

Quentin tried to spread the net further, to hold them all, to keep every single one safe. His mark pulsed; numbness deepened as its geometry bit into cracked stone.

And his body gave out.

The distortion snapped like glass.

The world roared back into motion.

Debris crashed to the ground, torches flared violently, shouts thundered as the Order agents surged forward. The alley snapped alive again, every sound too sharp, every light too bright.

Quentin collapsed to his knees, his hands clawing at the ground. His chest seized, blood spilling from his nose, copper sharp against his lips. His ears rang with a hollow thud—his own pulse struggling to catch up with reality. The mark on his palm faltered, its pressure loosening into a dull, dead weight beneath his skin.

"Quentin!" Aisha dropped beside him, one arm slashing outward to hold off an advancing agent, her other hand gripping his shoulder. "Stop it—you'll tear yourself apart!"

"I can't—" His voice cracked, a whisper shredded by pain. "I couldn't save them all."

Aisha's blade cut a clean arc, forcing space around them, her movements sharp despite her exhaustion. She crouched low, eyes burning. "You don't have to save them all alone. Do you hear me? You're not alone."

But he couldn't answer. His body convulsed, his breath hitching, his vision fading in and out like a broken film reel. The strain of the Echo had hollowed him out. He felt weak, as though every bone was ash inside his skin.

The Order saw it.

They surged toward him with renewed fury, chains whipping forward. One wrapped around his arm, the glyph etched into the links searing cold as it clamped shut. He cried out, the pressure in his palm stuttering weaker. The chain's runes hissed on contact—designed to choke the Echo out of him.

"No!" Aisha lunged, slicing the chain apart with a desperate strike. Sparks flew as metal screamed, and the severed links clattered to the stone. But more chains followed, more agents pressing in, their weapons glowing with the same runes that smothered the Echo's pull.

Quentin tried to rise but collapsed again, his limbs trembling, useless. He was spent, emptied, his power stuttering like a failing pulse.

Aisha dropped to her knees beside him, blades raised, her body between him and the encroaching tide. She trembled violently, but her stance didn't waver. Her voice shook but rang out steady: "You'll have to go through me."

And the Order, grinning beneath their hoods, seemed ready to do exactly that.

— Δ —

The alley was a choke of noise and motion again—chains snapping, torches flaring, Sophia's blade striking sparks against stone as she fought to keep Liam on his feet. Nia's shadow had vanished deeper into the warren of alleys. Quentin lay half-collapsed, the pressure in his palm guttering, sensation collapsing in on itself, the last pulses of the Echo flickering helplessly against the glyph-forged chains closing in.

And Raj chose his moment.

He stepped out from the shadows, untouched, unbothered, his smirk carved like a knife across his face. His eyes swept the chaos, lingered on Quentin's collapsed form, and then gleamed with cruel calculation—a spark of triumph that made Quentin's stomach twist.

"The Echo-bearer," Raj called, voice calm enough to be command—too practiced to be spontaneous. "Spent. Now."

Quentin's head jerked up, not in surprise—only in that sick confirmation he'd been trying not to earn. "Raj."

The betrayal tasted metallic in his mouth, sharper than blood.

The Order agents faltered for a heartbeat, then surged toward Quentin with renewed purpose. Chains whipped forward, glowing glyphs biting at the air.

Aisha spun, fury burning through her exhaustion. "You bastard!" Her blade met the first chain, sparks flying as she slashed it aside. She pressed herself tighter against Quentin's side, her body a shield. "You sell him out, you sell us all!"

Raj only shrugged, backing toward the Order's rear line, palms up as though to show his innocence. "Better him than the rest of us. Someone has to survive." His grin widened, all teeth. "Might as well be me."

Sophia's head snapped around at his words. For a moment, her ferocity faltered, horror slicing through her discipline. "Raj!" she screamed, voice cracking. "What are you doing?"

But she had no time to stop him—two agents lunged at her, forcing her back into the fight. She blocked high, ducked low, and Liam stumbled against her, his weight dragging at her balance.

Raj's betrayal was complete. There was no hesitation in him. No regret. Only self-preserving clarity.

Order agents swarmed Quentin and Aisha. One chain coiled around Quentin's arm, the glyphs searing cold into his skin. He cried out, the mark in his right palm stuttering weaker under the glyph-forged iron. Another wrapped his chest, crushing his ribs, pinning him to the ground.

Aisha fought like a cornered wolf, blades flashing in desperate arcs, her strikes fueled by rage more than strength. She cut through one set of chains, then another, but they kept coming, relentless, endless. Her breath hitched with each blow, her movements staggering, but she did not fall back.

Quentin's breath hitched, blood spilling down his chin as the glyph-etched iron tightened. "Aisha—go," he rasped. "They want me—"

She snarled, slashing another attacker across the thigh. "Shut up. I'm not leaving you."

Two agents crashed into her, knocking one blade from her hand. She jammed her shoulder into the first, twisting to stab the second, but a third slammed a chain across her back, driving her to her knees.

Quentin thrashed weakly, fury clawing at his chest. He tried to call the Echo, tried to summon even a flicker of its strength—but the chains smothered it, their glyphs drinking the pull like poison. He felt hollow, powerless, rage boiling useless in his veins. The Echo sparked once, a dying pulse, then sank into painful silence.

"Aisha!"

She fought, but more chains coiled around her wrists, her waist, dragging her down beside him. Her eyes burned into his, fierce even as her body gave out. "Together," she whispered through clenched teeth.

Order agents hauled them upright, binding them with frost-cold links, dragging them toward the alley's edge. Quentin's vision blurred, the world smearing with smoke and fire. He saw Sophia still fighting desperately, Liam clinging to her side, both shouting but too far, too outnumbered.

And through it all, Raj stood untouched, a spectator to the ruin he had orchestrated.

Sophia's voice broke across the chaos. "Raj, you coward! You traitor!"

He only bowed mockingly, his smirk venomous. "Survival, Sophia. You should try it sometime."

His silhouette looked wrong beside the Order—too easy, too practiced—like he'd been waiting to stand there all along.

Quentin's knees buckled as the agents yanked him forward, the chains biting deeper. His last sight before the alley blurred into haze was Raj walking free alongside the Order, his shadow lengthening in the torchlight.

And Quentin knew, in the hollow of his chest, that the betrayal was no longer suspicion. It was fact.

Raj had chosen his side.

And he'd chosen it long before tonight.

— Δ —

The night swallowed them.

Quentin and Aisha were shoved forward, chains biting into their wrists and chests, glyphs etched into the links burning cold as frostbite. The Order agents marched in grim silence, their torches flickering like watchful eyes. Behind them, the sounds of the skirmish faded—Sophia's shouts, Liam's frantic curses, the clash of steel against stone—all muffled by distance and dust.

The agents dragged their captives through twisting alleys until they reached a waiting transport: a covered wagon, old wood reinforced with black iron, its wheels etched with runes that glowed faintly in the torchlight. The horses stamped and snorted, their eyes covered with dark cloth, guided only by the handlers' sharp clicks.

"Inside," one of the agents barked, yanking Quentin by the chain. He stumbled, his knees scraping the cobblestones, blood smearing into the cracks. Aisha tried to resist, jerking back against her captor, but another chain coiled around her neck and tightened until she choked. Her blades—usually so fast they sang—lay useless at her sides, her body drained from the fight. She was shoved hard into the wagon, the boards groaning under the impact.

Quentin followed, half-thrown, half-falling. The doors slammed shut behind them with a metallic snap, and the inside plunged into suffocating darkness.

The wagon jolted into motion, wheels grinding against uneven stone. The chains scraped with every rattle, digging deeper into their skin. Quentin tried to move closer to Aisha, but the restraints pulled tight, forcing him back against the wall. The pressure in his right palm stuttered once—weak, strangled by the glyph-forged iron—then sank into nothing.

For a long moment, only the sound of their breathing filled the space—ragged, exhausted, broken.

Then Aisha shifted, straining against her chains until her shoulder brushed his. Her voice was hoarse but steady. "Quentin."

He turned his head toward her, though he could barely make out her outline in the gloom. "I'm here."

Her breath caught, and when she spoke again, the words were edged with despair. "I should have seen this coming. Raj. The Order. All of it. They conditioned me to predict traps. I should've known. I should've stopped this. I dragged you into this—"

"No," Quentin cut her off, sharper than he meant. He swallowed, forcing his tone softer. "You didn't drag me anywhere. I walked in. I chose this. I chose you."

The words hung between them, heavier than the chains.

She closed her eyes, her lips trembling. "And now look where that choice has brought us."

Quentin leaned his head back against the wall, staring into the dark as the wagon rattled on. "Together," he whispered. "That's what you said. If we fall, it's together."

Her chains shifted as she tried to reach for him. Their hands couldn't meet, but their shoulders pressed closer in defiance of the iron that bound them. The faint pulse of her filigree brushed the cold, latent pressure beneath his skin—not a glow, not a surge, but a remembered alignment, a trace of what had held when everything else failed.

Outside, muffled voices drifted through the slats of the wagon. Orders exchanged, boots crunching on gravel. And then—a voice Quentin knew too well. Smooth, mocking, unhurried.

Raj.

"Careful with him," he told the agents. "The relic doesn't work without its vessel. Break the vessel, and you waste what we've all been fighting for."

A bitter laugh from one of the guards. "You speak as if you're not disposable yourself."

Raj's smirk was audible. "I'm still standing free, aren't I? That's more than your prisoners can say."

His voice held no triumph—only calculation, cold and practiced, as if switching sides had required no effort at all.

Quentin's fists clenched, the chains rattling violently. Rage surged through him, sharp and useless, scraping at his throat. "Coward!" he shouted, his voice muffled by the boards. "Traitor!"

The wagon didn't slow. If Raj heard, he didn't answer.

Quentin flexed his hands; the links bit and scraped, useless. The phantom-cold under his right palm lay muted beneath the iron, but the rage didn't.

"We knew," he said quietly. "On the roof."

Aisha's breath hitched once. "We knew," she agreed. "And it still wasn't enough."

The wagon jolted. The links bit deeper.

"I thought keeping him close bought us time," she went on, voice thin but steady. "I thought I could see the turn coming."

Quentin swallowed. "He waited until I was empty."

"Yes," she said. No denial. Just truth. "That's what hurts."

Silence pressed in, broken only by the grind of wheels.

"We don't redo that choice," Aisha said at last. "We live with it."

Quentin closed his eyes. "Then next time—"

"There *is* a next time," she cut in softly.

Her shoulder pressed against his, firm despite the chains.

"Together," he said.

"Together."

Aisha turned her face toward Quentin, the dim light catching the shimmer of unshed tears in her eyes. "We lost," she whispered, the words heavy as stone. "This time… we really lost."

Quentin pressed his forehead against the rough wood of the wall, his chest heaving. "We lost." The truth of it hollowed him in a way even the Echo's collapse had not.

For the first time since the chamber collapsed—since the Echo chose him—he felt truly powerless. The pressure in his palm lay muted and unreachable, his strength hollowed out, his friends taken elsewhere and beyond reach, and his enemy walking free beside the captors who held him.

The wagon rattled onward beneath a sky scrubbed pale by early morning. The sun hung low and distant, its light thin and angled, casting long, merciless shadows across the road. Torches still burned along the route, their flames diminished and unnecessary now, guttering weakly against the encroaching day.

The world had shifted into exposure rather than safety—too bright to hide in, too cold to promise relief.

Quentin leaned into the faint, grounding pressure of Aisha's shoulder against his. Their chains bound them; betrayal still pressed close. The light revealed everything—but it loosened nothing.

But he wasn't alone. Not while she still breathed beside him. Not while his mark—dim but alive—and her filigree pressed in quiet defiance against the dark.

Chapter 21

The Seam

"A fracture is an opportunity, provided one is willing to step through the break." — **Guardian Teaching, The Broken Map.**

— Δ —

The cell was a rectangle carved out of night and old breath. Torchlight guttered in iron brackets, painting the stones the color of old honey and making every shadow look like a watching thing. The air tasted of damp and rust; somewhere water dripped, patient as a clock.

They'd chained Quentin and Aisha side by side but not quite touching, a cruelty measured to deny even comfort. *Close enough to taunt. Far enough to hurt.* The chains were etched with tiny glyphs that bit cold into skin, the links slick with some oil that smelled faintly of ash and fennel—ritual-clean, like they'd dressed the metal for a purpose. Every time Quentin tested the slack, the glyphs crawled along the links, and the chains tightened, making his mark shrink back like a joint yanked out of alignment. The sub-zero pressure that used to brace him was gone—like a brace bar removed mid-step.

He hated the quiet most. After the wagon, after the crash of wheels and muted orders and Raj's voice like a knife's smile, the cell's hush made room for the other sounds: his heartbeat stumbling; Aisha's breath halting around a bruise; his own thoughts, which had never been kind.

"I failed them all," he whispered, and the walls gave the words back to him smaller, meaner. "Liam. Nia. Sophia—"

"Stop." Aisha's voice was raw sand, but familiar enough to steady him. She let her head rest against rough stone and closed her eyes, lashes leaving tiny shadows like glyph-strokes on her cheeks. "You're still breathing." A breath. "I'm still breathing. That means we're not finished."

He huffed a humorless sound that aimed for a laugh and missed. "That's a low bar."

"Bars are appropriate," she said dryly, cracking a corner of a smile that hurt to look at and helped anyway. She rolled her shoulder against the wall and winced. "They etched these chains to smother the mark. Clever. Nasty."

"Effective," he said, and immediately hated himself for how small that sounded.

Silence stretched, sticky with torch smoke. The corridor outside scraped occasionally with passing feet—leather, stone, the hiss of a robe. Somewhere deeper, someone chanted, a low droning hum that wormed under the skin. Quentin tried not to hear words in it. He tried not to hear the Architect in the lower notes—that same pressure behind the chant. And worst of all, he tried not to picture Raj walking freely past those torches, nodding like he belonged.

He swallowed. "Sophia told me once that leadership is protecting people, even from you." He let his head thump softly back against the wall, as if the stone could decide the argument for him. "I couldn't even protect you."

"You brought me back," Aisha said simply.

He flinched. The images came in a rush: her body lax and wrong in his arms, the chamber's light like broken glass, the way his mark had emptied into her like a torn vein. He'd been reliving it every time he blinked since. "I shouldn't have had to."

"No," she agreed. "But you did. That matters." She tipped her face toward him, eyes catching the torchlight. "Listen to me. The Order loves despair. It's their favorite room temperature. You sit in it long enough and you become furniture."

He snorted despite himself. "Poetic."

"I'm delirious," she said, and for a heartbeat the old smirk ghosted across her mouth. Then it faded, and she watched him like someone measuring broken bones. "Say the words if you need to. Get them out. But don't live there."

He looked down at his hands. The mark under his skin was faint, a bruise made of old gold. He flexed his fingers; the glyphs in the chain crawled again, and pain shot up his forearm like ice. The Echo recoiled. *The cell, the chains, the torch-smoke—everything felt calibrated to make him small enough to fit the Order's version of him: a container, a problem, a prize.* And the worst part was that he recognized the shape—they'd only carved him into what he'd already been trying to be most of his life: *invisible, quiet, small.*

"That's what Raj saw," he whispered, the words soft enough the torch couldn't catch them. "The truth. I'm just an ordinary disappointment, and the only thing special about me is the mark I didn't earn." The lie cut deeper than the truth. He slammed his head back into the wall, a hollow thud. He would not let Raj's vision of him be the last one.

The chant in the deep halls lifted, a phrase swelling before thinning again. He imagined it like a tide: patient, insistent. Somewhere in that undertow sat Thales with his calm eyes and arithmetic cruelty, tallying wins. Somewhere behind him, the Architect smiled with teeth like marble.

"Do you ever… feel it listening?" Quentin asked, ashamed the second the question existed. "The Echo. Even like this. Like it's… waiting."

Aisha's eyes flicked to his hand, to the old-gold bruise of the mark under his skin. "Yes," she said. "It doesn't belong to them. Or to you." A pause. "But it answers you. That makes them afraid."

"I'm afraid," he admitted.

"Good," she said. "Fear isn't failure. It's a handrail."

The corridor hushed; the drip counted a few more seconds alive. Quentin tasted grit and old iron and the ghost of cumin someone had tracked in on a boot. It was stupid, the things the brain saved when everything else fell apart.

He let himself breathe with the rhythm of the drip. *In, out. Slow.* He thought of the rooftop—stars like nails punched through black cloth, Aisha's weight light against his shoulder, the word *together* like a rope they both gripped. He thought of Nia's sketch of a bridge broken at the center and the tiny figures split like spilled seeds. He thought of Sophia's face when she'd said we keep our options open, as if options were things you could hold under your tongue and not swallow accidentally.

The despair was still there. It would sit with him as long as the torch did. But breath by breath, it made room for something else. Not optimism—he wasn't that flexible—but a small, hard refusal. A stub of iron under the bruise.

"Say it again," he murmured, because he wanted her words in the air to fight the chant in the stone.

"You didn't fail," Aisha said, and this time there was no sand in it, only certainty worn thin but stubborn. "You're still breathing. I am too. We're still fighting."

He nodded, then realized she couldn't see the gesture and said, "Okay."

"Okay," she echoed.

Quentin had been worrying the shackle seam for an hour, millimeter by millimeter. It wasn't loosening—just... learning him. Like metal memorizing pressure. Another fraction of slack gave and their hands found each other, fingers cold, grip careful around the crawling glyphs. Their marks tightened in sync—not bright, not visible, just undeniable—edges sharpening into that hinge geometry for a breath, pressure recognizing pressure.

Footsteps passed the cell. A bar scraped; a key clinked against other keys and moved on. Quentin and Aisha didn't release their hands.

In the humming dark, beside the wet stone and the smoking torches, the first click didn't feel like triumph at all. It felt like not-moving. Like refusing to be furniture. Like naming a cliff and deciding not to jump.

Breath in. Breath out.

Still here. Still theirs.

— Δ —

The cell had settled into its rhythm again—the drip, the chant, the rasp of chains when either of them shifted too far. Quentin leaned against the wall, half-asleep but too knotted inside to rest. Aisha's head lolled near his shoulder, her breathing shallow but even, each rise and fall a small reassurance against the gnaw of silence.

Then—soft as breath, sharp as a cut—came a whisper.

"Oi. Lovebirds."

Quentin jolted upright, chains clattering. Aisha's eyes snapped open, knives of alertness where exhaustion had been.

The voice chuckled low. "Shh. You'll bring the whole choir down on us."

Quentin blinked, scanning the shadows. "Liam?"

A hand appeared through the bars, waving as if they were meeting at a café instead of a dungeon. Then Liam's face emerged in the faint torchlight, battered but unmistakable, a grin stretched across a split lip. His hair was a mess, his left eye swollen nearly shut, but his spark still held stubborn in the wreckage of his face. He wasn't in the corridor—he was in the opposite cell, pressed to the bars. Across the narrow corridor—close enough to whisper, too far to touch. He'd slipped there through the vents.

"Told you I'd stick around," he whispered, dragging himself closer to the bars. His movements were stiff, every inch of him aching, but his grin didn't falter. "You two just can't stay out of trouble, can you?"

Relief hit Quentin so hard it almost hurt. His chest ached with it, like an old bruise pressed suddenly tender. "You—how did you—?"

"Escape?" Liam supplied, lowering himself to a crouch. "Sheer charm. And one idiot who can't tie an ankle chain." He tapped the side of his nose, then winced at the pain.

Aisha gave him a look that might have been incredulity, might have been admiration—it was hard to tell with her bruises darkening both eyes. "You crawled back here? Into the belly of the beast?"

Liam shrugged, pulling a lump of bread from under his shirt and shoving it between the bars and sliding it across. It dropped to the flagstones, skidded across the corridor, and Quentin hooked it with his fingertips through the bars. "What can I say? I missed your sunny dispositions."

Quentin stared at the bread as if it were treasure. His hands shook as he broke it, giving half to Aisha before shoving the rest into his mouth. It was dry, stale, but it scraped down like salvation.

Aisha chewed slowly, her eyes never leaving Liam. "This is suicide."

"Maybe," Liam said cheerfully, though his eyes darted nervously toward the corridor beyond. "But you looked worse off than me. Thought I'd lend a hand—or at least half a loaf. Don't say I never give you anything."

"Why aren't you running for the surface?" Quentin whispered, his fingers curling around the bars. "You could find Farouk. You could get help."

Liam's grin twitched, turning into something flatter, more sober. "I tried, mate. I found a service vent, but the gates are sealed with a glowing blue lock that doesn't care about picks or brawn. And outside? The Order's got the whole perimeter pinned down. If I run, I'm just a target in the sand. But if I stay here, moving through the ventilation gaps, I'm a ghost. I can keep you lot fed and watch the guard rotations. I'm staying because when you're ready to blow this place apart, you're going to need someone on the outside of the door to catch you."

Quentin swallowed, forcing the bread past the lump in his throat. "You shouldn't have risked it."

"Would've been rude not to," Liam shot back. His grin softened for a moment, genuine under the bruises. "Besides, what else was I gonna do? Sit out there and wait for them to come back? Nah. I'm rubbish at waiting."

Aisha leaned back, shaking her head faintly. "You're going to get caught. And when you do, they'll chain you worse."

Liam spread his arms, wincing as his shoulder popped. "Probably. But until then, I've got a talent for slipping through cracks. Don't worry, I won't play hero. Just... sidekick. Less glamorous, more practical."

Quentin pressed his forehead against the bars, fighting the sting in his eyes. The glyphs in his chains crawled, cold, as if offended by the hope creeping in. "You don't understand. I nearly killed myself trying to hold them back. And you still—"

"Still here," Liam interrupted. His tone was softer now, stripped of the jokes. "That's the only headline that matters, mate. Still here. You. Me. Even her." He jerked his chin at Aisha, who gave him a glare sharp enough to cut. He only grinned wider. "Look at us, the world's worst band, somehow still on tour."

The sound that escaped Quentin was half laugh, half sob. His chest loosened a fraction, the weight on him shifting from crushing to merely heavy.

Aisha exhaled, long and slow. She closed her eyes, leaning her head back against the stone. "You're insane."

"Thank you," Liam said brightly. Then, after a pause, his grin faded. "Don't tell Sophia I'm this close. Not yet. She'll scold me worse than the Order."

Quentin frowned. "She's alive?"

Liam nodded once, quick. "Last I saw, still swinging. She doesn't go down easy. Neither does Nia. They're out there. Somewhere."

Hope, thin but real, pierced Quentin's exhaustion. He clutched the chain tighter, the glyphs stinging his skin, and whispered, "Then we're not done."

"No," Liam agreed, his bruised grin crooked and fierce. "Not by a long shot."

The corridor groaned with the sound of boots approaching. Liam's head snapped up, eyes widening. "Gotta vanish." He winked, already backing into the shadows. "Eat slow. Don't choke. I'd hate to rescue you twice in the same night."

Then he was gone, swallowed by dark, leaving only the taste of bread and the echo of his reckless courage.

Aisha murmured into the silence, her tone unreadable. "He's going to get himself killed."

Quentin stared at the empty corridor, that small, hard refusal from earlier flaring a little brighter. "Not if we get out first."

— Δ —

The bread sat like a stone in Quentin's stomach, heavy but anchoring. Its warmth didn't last, but its reminder did: *someone out there still cared whether they survived.* He leaned back against the wall, letting the brief taste of warmth linger. Across from him, Aisha's head rested against the stone again, eyes half-closed, her breathing slow but alert. The silence pressed in, broken only by the drip from somewhere unseen.

Then, faintly—so faint he thought at first it was memory—came a voice.

"Quentin?"

He stiffened. Aisha's eyes snapped open.

The voice was muffled, blurred by stone, but it was familiar. Gentle, hesitant.

"Nia?" Quentin whispered.

"Yes," came the answer, soft as dust shifting. "There's a crack. Between the cells."

"My fingers won't stop buzzing," Nia whispered. "Like the stone's humming through my bones." Her words thinned, as if she were speaking through cloth. "I can hear you. Can you hear me?"

Quentin pressed his palm against the wall, ignoring the sting from the glyphs in his chains. "Yes. I hear you."

Aisha leaned closer too, her expression unreadable in the half-light.

For a moment, silence stretched, and Quentin thought maybe she'd drifted away. Then Nia's voice returned, steadier, threaded with something almost urgent.

"I drew again."

Quentin's chest tightened. Her sketches—the ones she never fully explained, the ones that sometimes felt like riddles, sometimes warnings. "What did you draw?"

Her breath caught audibly, then steadied. "You. With chains around you. But… breaking them. Light spilling everywhere. So much light it filled the page. I didn't want to stop drawing, but my pencil broke—or my hand did."

A shiver went through him. The glyphs etched into his chains crawled as though mocking the thought, as though laughing at the impossibility. "That hasn't happened," he said quietly.

"No," she agreed. "It hasn't. Not yet—because the load hasn't shifted. The Order thinks they've got you pinned. But pins fail when the weight moves."

That small pause—those two words—slid under Quentin's ribs like a key turning.

The way she said it made the torchlight feel brighter, like it bent closer to listen.

Aisha tilted her head, eyes narrowing. "Nia," she called softly, "are you saying what I think you're saying?"

The girl's voice quavered but didn't falter. "Sometimes the drawings… aren't just pictures. Sometimes they're warnings. When the pressure spikes, my hand starts mapping where things want to fail—like the bridge, and the lamp."

Quentin felt the cell tighten around him, as if even the stone leaned in to hear the admission.

A pattern. The word landed heavy, though none of them spoke it aloud.

Quentin let out a harsh laugh, too sharp to be amused. "We're chained in the Order's dungeon. Raj sold us out. Whatever this is—it's blocked. And you're telling me you drew me breaking free?"

"Yes," Nia said, and though her voice shook, there was iron in it. "Because you will."

The air seemed to shift, the silence humming louder, as if the stones themselves were caught by her certainty.

Another voice broke in—sharper, controlled. Sophia. Her tone carried from the next cell down the corridor, strained but unmistakable. "What are you whispering about?"

Nia hesitated. Quentin pictured her biting her lip, sketchbook clutched tight to her chest. Then she said, louder, "I saw Quentin free. I drew it. He hasn't yet. But he will."

Sophia snorted, but the sound cracked, too brittle to hide the tremor. "You're clinging to fantasies. Drawings aren't strategy. Hope isn't a plan."

"Neither is despair," Nia whispered back, and even through stone her words carried like a blade.

That line hit Quentin harder than any chain. Despair had been winning. Now it wasn't.

Quentin closed his eyes. For the first time since the wagon, since the alley, he felt something click faintly in his chest. It wasn't strength, not yet. But it was a thread. A lifeline.

Aisha leaned back, her lips curling faintly. "Smart girl."

Quentin exhaled, slow and uneven. "Nia… thank you."

He didn't know if she heard the gratitude in it, or the fear, or both.

Sophia's silence lingered, heavier than her words had been. When she spoke again, it was quieter, almost grudging. "If there's even a chance she's right, then we'd better be ready. Because the Order won't give us long."

Nia's reply was barely audible. "We'll be ready."

Quentin let his head rest against the wall, the stone cool through his tangled hair. His chains still cold, the glyphs still crawled, but the words sat in him like weight on a lever—not movement, not yet, but force waiting.

He whispered to Aisha, so soft only she could hear. "Breaking chains. Light spilling everywhere."

Her eyes caught the torchlight. "I like that picture."

And Quentin realized, with a sharp ache, that he did too. For the first time in hours, Quentin let himself believe in it. Even just a little.

— Δ —

Another dawn pressed faint fingers against the prison's narrow slit-windows, streaks of pale light seeping into the gloom. The torches burned lower now, smoke curling sluggishly toward the ceiling as if even fire grew weary in these walls.

Quentin sat slumped against the stone, Aisha beside him, their chains binding them in place but not keeping their shoulders from brushing. He could feel her breath, warm and uneven, a small reminder that they were still here—still alive.

The others had quieted after Sophia's admission. Even Liam, usually irrepressible, had gone silent in the corridor beyond, conserving what little strength he had. Only Nia's occasional scratch of pencil against paper broke the hush.

Quentin looked around the dim cell and felt the press of despair again, threatening to coil back around his ribs. He could taste the defeat still—Raj's betrayal, the crash of the wagon doors, the sound of his friends scattered into shadows. Part of him wanted to sink into it, to let the chains weigh him down until he was just another body the Order left to rot.

But then he thought of Nia's voice—*Not yet. You will.* Of Sophia whispering together at last. Of Liam slipping bread through the bars, a grin on his bloodied face. Of Aisha's hand clutching his even as glyph-etched chains stung cold.

Something warm and stubborn pressed upward inside him, like pressure finding its seam.

A guard's laugh drifted down the corridor, casual as a yawn.

"We're not done."

The sound startled even him. It was hoarse, almost breaking. But the silence snapped open around it, and all at once, the others were listening.

Quentin raised his head. "Not until the Echo is safe—out of the Order's reach. Not until the Order falls. They want these chains to end us. They think because we're in the dark, we've already lost. But we're still breathing—and that means the story isn't theirs yet."

Beside him, Aisha's eyes shone faintly in the torchlight. She squeezed his hand, her grip weak but steady.

From the corridor, Liam let out a ragged chuckle. "Damn right. You think I crawled back here just for stale bread and better scenery?" His voice cracked, but the humor still carried.

Sophia shifted, the clink of her chains echoing. When she spoke, her voice was steady, almost formal. "You're right. Despair is what they want. Order built on silence. They want us to stop speaking because silence is surrender. But if we still speak, if we still plan, we aren't theirs."

Nia's voice was soft, almost dreamlike, but certain. "I drew this. I drew us together, light breaking through the stones. It hasn't happened yet. But it will."

The faint scratch of her pencil resumed, as if she were sketching even now—adding to a future she refused to abandon.

For a long moment, Quentin couldn't speak. His chest tightened, his throat raw. He wasn't sure if it was belief or desperation driving him, but it didn't matter. Both could be force.

He turned toward Aisha, voice lowered to a thread. "Then let's give them a reason. You said it before—they haven't won."

Her lips curved faintly. "Not while we're breathing."

He looked back at the others, at shadows of friends fractured by stone and bars. He kept it low, tight, urgent—more hiss than speech.

"Together," Sophia said, and the word didn't sound like strategy so much as a stake driven into the dark.

"I'm in," Liam rasped.

"I promise," Nia whispered.

Aisha's fingers brushed Quentin's—barely a touch, but deliberate. "So do I."

Quentin swallowed hard. "Then we wait for the seam. When it opens—we move."

The words settled, heavy and alive.

Beyond the cells, a new sound rose—the low murmur of chanting, faint at first but swelling like a tide. It rolled through the stones, a reminder of the Order's grip, of the Architect's shadow waiting.

For once, the chant didn't shrink him.

It only made the pressure inside him set harder.

Quentin lifted his eyes to the small strip of dawn above. "They think we're broken," he whispered. "Let them."

And for the first time since their capture, he didn't feel like prey waiting to be devoured. He felt like a fault-line waiting to slip.

Chapter 22

The Golden Defiance

"The counter-resonance will tear the containment. It requires pure, focused will." — **Fragment of the Architect's Scroll, XXII.**

— Δ —

The shouts in the corridor grew louder—boots finding their rhythm, voices sharpening into orders. Torchlight flickered and flared, shadows stretching like clawed hands along the bars.

He didn't decide. Only the moment the pressure inside him finally found its seam—and the cuffs answering with a sharp, ugly snap that turned silence into alarm.

Quentin's broken cuffs lay where they'd fallen, iron suddenly ordinary. His wrists still ached with the after-pressure of forcing a locked thing to yield, and the corridor beyond was waking fast—distant voices converging, steps multiplying.

Quentin's hands still trembled, his body screaming from the Echo's surge, but he pressed his palm to Aisha's chains anyway. The glyphs hissed in defiance, sparking red against gold, but she held her breath, bracing against the pain. And the links cracked with sharp snaps that echoed through the cell block.

Her chains clattered to the ground, the suppression glyphs dead and dull. Aisha staggered free, catching Quentin as he nearly collapsed again.

"You'll kill yourself if you keep burning like this," she warned, her tone sharp but her grip gentle.

He nodded like he agreed—then moved anyway, riding the Echo the way he rode a crumbling stair: fast and without looking down.

"Not an option," Quentin panted. He glanced toward the others. "Liam and Nia—next."

They hurried to Liam's cell. He was already on his feet, grinning through the bars, bruised but unmistakably himself.

"Took you long enough," Liam said. "I was beginning to think this was a trust exercise."

Aisha slipped her hand through the bars, and Quentin pressed his palm beside hers. The mark didn't blaze—it set, lines tightening beneath his skin as a cold, crushing pressure surged outward, bracing against the suppression glyphs until, with a sharp metallic shriek, the cell lock buckled and tore free.

The door sagged inward.

Liam stepped out, rolling his shoulders with theatrical relief. "Ah. Freedom. Again. Honestly, I should start charging for the encore."

"Quiet," Sophia snapped. "They're coming."

"Exactly!" Liam grinned. "Which is why it's time for me to do what I do best."

Quentin frowned. "Which is?"

Liam winked. "Cause chaos."

Before anyone could stop him, he darted into the corridor, bare feet slapping against the stone. He grabbed an empty bucket from a corner and banged it against the wall with a deafening clang.

"Oi! Over here, you robed rejects! Your prisoners are having a party—and shocker—you weren't invited!"

The noise echoed like thunder. Guards shouted in confusion, their footsteps converging toward Liam's racket.

Aisha cursed under her breath. "He's going to get himself killed."

But Quentin saw it—the way the guards funneled toward the noise, leaving the other cells suddenly thin of guards.

"No," he whispered, almost in awe. "He's buying us time."

"Or a swift execution," Sophia muttered, though a grudging flicker of respect crossed her face.

Quentin staggered toward Nia's cell. She sat huddled on the floor, sketchbook clutched against her chest as if it were armor. Her wide eyes glowed with terror and something else—something fierce—as Quentin knelt by the bars.

"Nia," he said softly, pressing his palm against the chain binding her wrists. "It's going to hurt. But we're getting you out."

She nodded quickly and pushed her hands forward. The Echo surged—dense, overwhelming, razor-sharp—through both of them, a cold load snapping tight along his nerves as he placed his hands. The glyphs cracked and hissed before bursting apart, golden sparks scattering like fireflies across the stone.

Nia gasped as the chains fell away. She stared at her wrists, then at Quentin, awe widening her eyes. "It's just like I drew," she whispered. "The chains breaking. Light everywhere."

"Good," Quentin breathed, catching himself against the bars. "Then draw the next part—us alive."

Nia's fingers tightened around her sketchbook. Her pencil was already moving in frantic strokes.

Liam's chaos roared louder. He had found a stack of metal bowls and was hurling them down the corridor—each one clattering like a gong. His voice carried above the uproar.

"What's wrong, boys? Can't catch one unarmed prisoner? Maybe try both hands instead of chanting at the ceiling!"

A guard snarled, metal shrieking against stone.

Sophia muttered, "Reckless idiot..." Then, after a breath: "But useful."

Quentin's knees buckled. Sweat blinded him. The Echo inside him pulsed like a wounded thing, desperate and tightening. But he forced himself upright.

"Sophia's next—end of the run," he rasped. "We need everyone free."

Aisha gripped his arm. "You're burning out, Quentin. Look at you—you can barely stand."

He met her gaze, pulse thundering. The memory of her hand over his was still warm. "Not alone."

"Then not alone," she said, steady as bedrock.

Together, they moved toward Sophia's cell as Liam's thunderous chaos bought them the seconds they desperately needed—seconds they would not waste.

— Δ —

The corridor was alive with sound—metal clashing, guards shouting, Liam's taunts bouncing off stone like drunken fireworks.

Quentin pressed his marked palm against Sophia's chains. The glyphs resisted, flaring bright red as if fighting harder for her. Sweat stung Quentin's eyes, his muscles locking under the strain. Aisha's voice cut through, steady and sharp: "Push, Quentin. Don't fight it alone. I've got you. Together."

The chains cracked, sparks bursting outward. With a final wrench, they split, crashing to the floor in a dying hiss.

Sophia stepped free, rubbing raw wrists. Her gaze swept the hall—the oncoming guards, the still-dizzy Quentin, Nia clutching her sketchbook like a shield, and Liam down the corridor hurling stones in sloppy arcs like a street juggler on fire.

"Idiots," she muttered, though her eyes burned with something fiercer than contempt. But when she looked again, the heat in her stare held something else—determination, sharp and steady.

Sophia's gaze flicked over him—blood, tremor, the mark still set under his skin. "Stay on your feet," she said. "Use the Echo in bursts. If you drop, we drag you."

Then her attention snapped outward. "Positions. Now."

Quentin nodded once—breath ragged, resolve set—and turned with her.

The guards poured into the corridor, armored boots striking stone in unison. Their torches flared, casting jagged shadows. Blades flashed as they raised them high, chanting fragments of the Order's language that made the air itself hum.

Sophia planted herself at the front, her stance solid, every movement sharp with training. "Now!" she shouted.

Quentin raised his palm instinctively. The Echo set, the mark tightening into familiar, braced lines beneath his skin. Time seemed to thicken around the nearest guards—their blades slowed, their feet dragging as though they moved through water. Their chants slurred into deep, distorted growls.

"Go!" Quentin gritted, his vision swimming.

Aisha was already moving. She drove forward into the slowed chaos, wrenching a short blade from a guard mid-lunge as she passed. The weapon felt wrong in her hand—lighter than her usual, humming faintly with glyph residue—but she didn't hesitate. She turned it into motion.

The blade cut clean arcs, striking where the dragged guards were most vulnerable. She moved like a shadow given form, precise and merciless, every step borrowed from instinct and survival rather than training.

Sophia stepped in beside her, wielding the short blade she had ripped from another fallen guard, intercepting an oncoming strike with a sharp parry and counter. Her movements were efficient and unflinching. She pivoted to shield Nia, placing herself between the girl and the press of bodies, each strike calculated not to win—but to hold the line.

Sophia's voice stitched the corridor together—short, clean calls that turned panic into motion.

Quentin braced the Echo in quick, brutal pulses. Aisha slipped into the openings. Liam made noise where they needed space.

It worked. That was enough.

Quentin hit the wall, swallowing nausea. He set the Echo again—short, brutal—buying them another breath.

Sophia cut down the last guard in their path, her blade slicing clean across his spear shaft. She kicked him aside, then turned, chest heaving, eyes scanning.

When she spoke again, her voice wasn't just commanding. It was resolute. United.

"Forward!" Sophia barked.

He fell into step beside her, Aisha flanking, Liam dragging debris behind them, Nia clutching her drawings close.

The prison shuddered with shouts and pounding boots, reinforcements on the way. But as they surged together toward the exit, the group felt less like broken prisoners and more like an army in miniature—united, defiant, alive.

— Δ —

The corridor spilled them into a final chamber, narrower than the cell block but taller, the ceiling lost in shadow. At the far end loomed the prison's last gate—an enormous slab of stone covered in glyphs that shimmered faintly with suppressed light. Thick iron braces locked it in place, pulsing with the same cruel magic as their chains.

Quentin staggered to a halt, every nerve in his body frayed. His vision swam, his mark still locked in a dull, crushing pressure beneath the bite of suppression. "That's it," he rasped. "The door."

Liam groaned, leaning on a broken spear like a walking stick. "Lovely. A door carved by nightmares. Sure it doesn't open into a bigger dungeon?"

Sophia shot him a glare but said nothing. Her eyes were fixed on the glyphs. "Steel won't touch that."

"No," Aisha said, steady but firm, "but he can." Her gaze slid to Quentin, sharp with both faith and worry.

Quentin felt the weight of their stares, the expectation pressing heavier than the chains had. He stepped closer, the glyphs in the stone answering with a low, grinding pressure that seemed to lean into him. His mark locked tight beneath his skin—braced, resisting the pull.

But when he lifted his hand, his knees buckled. The Echo inside him flared in protest, searing through his veins until he thought he might split apart. He dropped to one knee, clutching his chest, gasping.

"Quentin!" Aisha dropped beside him, her arm around his shoulders. "Stop. You'll burn yourself out."

"I have to," he wheezed. "We don't have time—"

Sophia crouched in front of him, her voice sharp but steady. "You're no use to us dead. We'll find another way—"

"No," Nia interrupted. Her small voice carried from the shadows, trembling but unyielding. She held up her sketchbook, a fresh drawing scrawled across the page. Her hands shook, but the lines were bold, frantic with urgency.

The picture showed the massive stone door—splitting open down the middle, light pouring through in golden streams. Around it, she had drawn their figures: Quentin in front, the others behind him, all bathed in light.

"It's this door," she whispered.

The chamber stilled. Even the distant shouts of guards seemed muffled, held at bay by the gravity of her words.

Quentin stared at the sketch, his chest heaving. Something in him shifted. He thought of her earlier promise: "Not yet. You will."

A quiet steadiness settled into him—not strength, not certainty, but resolve. A shape he recognized, one he had carried since the chamber earlier. He let his hand drop from his chest and pressed his palm against the stone.

The glyphs shrieked as the pressure met them—containment lines warping under a force they had not been built to bear. Pressure-cold tore through him, deep and crushing, but he did not fight it. He locked against it and endured—forcing his will into the fracture, steady and unforgiving. He remembered Aisha's hand steady at his back. He remembered Sophia's vow, Liam's reckless laughter, Nia's trembling certainty.

"I am not alone. I endure," he whispered, voice trembling. "We endure."

The Echo answered. The pressure under his skin deepened, flooding through the glyphs.

The door shuddered, cracks splitting down its center as contained light poured from within, blinding and fierce. The chamber shook, dust cascading from the ceiling.

As the stone split, a high-pitched whine shattered his focus, and he felt the familiar crawl of blood from his nose and ears. His equilibrium tilted, the world turning into a blurred mess of gold and red.

The others shielded their eyes, but they did not retreat. They stepped closer instead, their presence anchoring him, their breaths ragged but unified.

Aisha's hand hovered close to his back, ready to catch him. Sophia planted herself between Quentin and the guards' approach, blade raised. Liam braced the fallen bench deeper into the archway, cursing creatively. Nia stood with the sketchbook clutched to her chest, staring at the unfolding scene with wide, shining eyes. *All of them—holding him upright without touching him.*

The braces snapped one by one, metal screeching as if torn apart by unseen hands. The glyphs dimmed, fading into nothing.

With a deafening boom, the stone split down the middle. Golden light flooded the chamber, brilliant and expansive, spilling onto their faces like sunrise.

For a heartbeat, none of them moved.

Then Liam whooped, voice echoing. "Knew you had it in you, mate! Official title: Door-Opener Supreme—tell history!"

Sophia barked, "Move!" Already she was pulling Nia forward, scanning the shadows for more guards.

Aisha helped Quentin to his feet, her arm firm around him. His body shook, his vision still hazy, but when he stepped into the light, the shaking eased just enough for him to stand.

The light seemed to answer him—soft, not overwhelming, like it aligned with him. Like it had been waiting.

They burst through the opening together, stumbling out into the night. Cool air hit them—crisp, real. Above, stars scattered across the sky, endless and free. In the distance, Cairo's lights glimmered faintly.

Behind them, the shouts of guards grew louder as the prison erupted into chaos. Torches flared, orders barked, boots thundered closer.

They were free—for now. But the chase had only just begun.

Quentin clutched Aisha's hand, his mark still set beneath the skin, and whispered into the night, "We endure."

The light stayed where it was—but something inside him finally moved. The phantom-cold under his skin loosened just enough to let the night in.

CHAPTER 23

DUST AND DOMINION

"Conquest is not in the striking, but in the certainty that the enemy will fall." **— Axiom of the Shadow Order, Dominion IV.**

— Δ —

The desert met them with a silence so wide it felt like the world had pulled apart.

After stone corridors and the stink of torches, the open air seemed wrong—too empty, too clean. Sand rolled away in every direction, dunes smoothed by night wind into pale, sleeping waves. Overhead, the stars were fading, their hard brilliance softening as the horizon bled from black to bruised violet.

And there, where the world seemed to end, the Pyramid of Giza rose out of the sand.

From a distance, it looked almost whole again—an illusion the haze was kind enough to give. As the first threads of light slid across its face, the upper stones caught and held them, turning to faint, cold gold. To anyone else, it should've looked majestic. From here, it only looked… inevitable.

Quentin couldn't see majesty. He saw a sentence he hadn't finished writing.

The Echo in his palm stirred the moment the Pyramid came into view. A slow, insistent thrum started up under his skin, out of step with his own pulse, tugging him forward—a hook behind his ribs. Every few heartbeats, the mark drew tight—load threading under the skin.

They trudged over the sand in a rough line. No one had the energy for formation.

Liam walked slightly ahead, limping—subtle unless you knew what to watch for. He had slung a half-broken spear over his shoulder like it was a hiking stick, muttering under his breath about sand in places sand should never be. Nia stayed close to Sophia, sketchbook hugged flat against her chest as if it were the only thing keeping her ribs from caving in. Sophia herself moved with a rigid economy of motion, not wasting a single step, the cut above her eye gone crusted but ugly against her skin.

Aisha walked at Quentin's side, their shadows long and frayed across the sand. She kept one hand near the knife at her hip, the other sometimes brushing his as they climbed and dipped with the dunes. Her breathing was shallow, controlled. The bruises blooming along her throat and arms looked almost black in the thinning starlight.

Nobody spoke for a long time. The silence between them wasn't the cell's heavy, suffocating kind. This was different—strung tight, humming, like a bow pulled back and waiting for the arrow to let go.

The Pyramid grew with every step, stone swallowing sky, its shadow stretching like a dark tide across the sand.

At last, Aisha broke the quiet.

"If the Order takes it," she said, her voice low but cutting through the dawn air, "the world won't survive—not as itself."

She didn't say it dramatically. It wasn't a threat. Just a fact laid bare.

Quentin turned to look at her. The sun had not yet cleared the horizon, but there was enough light to catch the edges of her face—the set jaw, the hollowed cheeks, the eyes that had seen too much and refused to look away. He searched for a crack—fear, doubt, anything.

All he found was certainty, hard and cold and familiar.

She noticed his gaze and, after a beat, added more quietly, "That's why I came back. Not for them." Her chin tipped almost imperceptibly at the memory of the others. "Not even for me. Because some things are bigger than us."

Before Quentin could answer, Liam gave a rough cough, like his throat objected to the seriousness.

"Great, love that," he said. "Nothing like existential doom to start the morning. For the record, though, if I've gotta go, I'd rather die dramatically at the base of an ancient wonder than in some damp hallway getting lectured by robed creeps."

Sophia sent him a look sharp enough to cut cloth, but the corner of her mouth twitched, betraying her for half a heartbeat. She shifted her gaze to Quentin instead.

"You feel it, don't you?" she asked. There was no accusation in it this time. Just a straightforward question.

Quentin lowered his eyes to his hand. Even in the weak dawn light, the mark shimmered faintly under his skin, as if his mark were catching a stronger signal. The closer they got, the harder it was to ignore—a cold crawl in his bones.

"It's pulling me," he said. "Like it knows this is where it ends. Or… changes."

Sophia's jaw tightened. The old Sophia would've jumped in there—lectured, warned, tried to wrest the steering wheel out of his hands. Instead, she exhaled slowly, fingers flexing once on the hilt of her blade.

"Then we follow your lead this time," she said. "All of us." She met his eyes, steady. "But understand this—if you falter, I won't hesitate to do what must be done—to protect the rest of us."

A few days ago, he would've heard that as a threat. Now it landed differently. Not a promise to control him, but a promise to protect everyone—even from him—if it comes to that.

He nodded, throat tight. "Fair."

Behind her, Nia's pencil was already moving. The faint rasp of graphite on paper somehow carried over the whisper of wind. She walked and drew without looking up, feet finding their way by memory and trust.

After several minutes, she slowed. "I… finished," she murmured.

Sophia glanced back. "Let us see."

Nia turned the sketch so they all could glimpse it as they walked. The Pyramid towered on the page, lines sharp and anxious, drawn with a speed that showed in every stroke. At its base, tiny dark figures clustered—too many to count, hooded shapes massed like a shadow that had grown teeth. At the pinnacle, instead of a smooth, broken point, there was a burst of wild light, shading so dark it nearly tore the paper, radiating outward.

"It was just my hand moving," Nia whispered. "But it feels like… what's coming."

Liam squinted at it. "So. Big scary crowd, blinding explosion on top, probably death in between. Very on brand for us."

No one laughed. The quiet held—full of what none of them wanted to name.

Quentin reached out and steadied the edge of the notebook with two fingers when the next gust of wind threatened to snap it closed. His knuckles brushed Nia's. Her fingers were cold, shaking.

"Then we face it," he said. "Not because we're ready. Not because we're good at this." He tried to smile. It didn't quite land. "Because there's no one else."

The wind shifted, blowing from the direction of the Pyramid. It carried the faintest scent of smoke—torches, incense, something harsher beneath. Gooseflesh prickled along Quentin's arms.

Sophia drew her blade with a soft rasp. Dawn finally broke over the horizon, washing the steel bright.

"Then to Giza," she said.

"To Giza," Aisha echoed, her fingers brushing the knife at her hip.

"To death or glory," Liam added. "And if we're lucky, snacks."

Nia said nothing, but her pencil moved again, a tiny flare of white where she was rubbing out some earlier line, rewriting the future one stroke at a time.

Quentin looked back up at the Pyramid. Its shadow stretched out to meet them, a long, dark reach sliding over the sand. The Echo thrummed in his palm—too loud, too fast—but beneath the fear there was something else, small and iron-hard.

On the prison floor, Aisha had given him a word.

He whispered it now, tasting dust and dawn. "Endure."

Aisha heard him. Without looking away from the Pyramid, she slipped her hand into his and squeezed once.

Together, they stepped into the Pyramid's shadow.

— Δ —

The sun had barely crested the horizon when they reached the base of the Pyramid. The first rays of morning struck its limestone sides, gilding the ancient stones in fire. What should have been awe-inspiring was instead suffocating—because the Shadow Order was already there.

Torches ringed the ritual platform at the Pyramid's base, their flames still visible even in daylight. Robed figures stood in perfect rows, hoods pulled low, the desert wind tugging at the edges of their garments. A hum filled the air—low, steady, and unnatural, the cadence of their collective chant. The sound crawled under Quentin's skin, vibrating in his teeth, as if the desert itself had learned to whisper in their language.

At the center stood Archon Thales. His robes were darker than the others, stitched with silver glyphs that shimmered faintly with every breath. His face was gaunt yet sharp, eyes like pits of black glass that seemed to swallow the light around them. He didn't move when the group emerged from the desert, but the air itself leaned toward him, pulled by a gravity of menace. Even the torch flames seemed to tilt his way, bending as if afraid to burn without his permission.

And beside him, smiling as if he'd been waiting all along, was Raj.

His posture was easy, arrogant, hands clasped behind his back like he was the one welcoming them. His eyes flicked over the group, landing on Quentin last. He smirked, lips curling in a sneer. "Well. Look who crawled out of their cage."

Liam muttered under his breath, loud enough for only them to hear. "I'll give him this—he's got a talent for surviving punches that should've killed him." His fingers tightened around the stone he still carried, like he was reminding himself there were always more punches.

Quentin's stomach knotted. The Echo in his right palm tightened, reacting to the place—its buried current, the weight of what slept in the stone. The antique-gold saturation deepened beneath his skin, denser with each heartbeat. The mark set, pressure stacking toward release, to answer the rising current threaded through the stones of Giza—but he held it back with sheer, shaking will.

Thales raised one skeletal hand, and the chant behind him ceased instantly. Silence dropped heavy as stone. His voice carried across the sand with unnatural resonance, neither loud nor soft, yet impossible to ignore.

"The Echo chose you, boy." His gaze fixed on Quentin, sharp and unyielding. "But all power bends eventually. To will. To wisdom. To inevitability."

Quentin clenched his fists, the chains of memory rattling as vividly as the ones he'd only just broken. "It doesn't bend to you."

A faint smile ghosted across Thales's lips, colder than any sneer. "You think you defy me. But already you carry it poorly. Each use erodes your biological frame. Your anatomy wasn't built for this load. You are a failing brace, Quentin. And when you break, it will return to us—reclaimed by what preceded you."

The Echo surged at his words, compression seeping up his arm. He hissed softly, clutching his hand. Aisha touched his arm, grounding him. Her fingers were cool and steady, the only thing in him that wasn't shaking.

Raj chuckled, stepping forward, his grin infuriatingly casual. "You know, Quentin, I almost admire it. The way you stumble into being everyone's hero. It's almost funny—how many people you'll get killed along the way." His gaze slid deliberately to Aisha, his smile twisting. "Especially her."

Aisha stiffened, her hand tightening on the hilt of her blade. For a heartbeat, Quentin saw the younger version of her—the girl trained to stand at Raj's shoulder, not opposite his blade—and then it was gone, burned away by resolve.

Quentin's teeth ground together, fury boiling beneath his skin. "You sold us out. You'd stand with them after everything?"

Raj's smirk widened. "Stand with them? I am them. Unlike you, I chose the winning side."

Sophia stepped forward, her voice cutting like steel. "You chose cowardice. Betrayal. You're nothing more than their pawn."

Raj's grin faltered for only a breath before snapping back into place. "Better a pawn on the board than a fool under it." His eyes flashed, just for an instant, with something rawer—hurt, jealousy, something he buried as quickly as it surfaced.

Thales lifted his hand again, and the Order's ranks straightened. "Enough talk. Bring them forward. Let them see what inevitability looks like."

The robed figures stepped as one, moving with unnerving precision, spears and blades catching the new sun. Sand stirred in eddies around their feet, as if the Pyramid itself exhaled in anticipation. Each step they took pressed a new pattern into the sand, concentric marks that looked disturbingly like ritual circles closing in.

Quentin swallowed hard, his heart hammering, his hand burning hotter with every step the Order took toward them. He could feel the pull of the Echo—not just inside him, but in the Pyramid itself, glyphs faintly glowing along the stones as if the ancient structure answered the disturbance he carried. The whole plateau felt wired to him, like he had stepped into the center of a circuit he didn't understand.

He looked up, past the robed agents and the swirling sand. High above, near the jagged, flat top of the Pyramid where the capstone was missing, the air was glowing with a sickly violet light, too precise to be natural. The energy Thales was driving through the base was being pulled upward, funneling toward the summit.

Quentin could feel the Echo in his chest shivering under load; the Pyramid was acting as a lens, and if that energy hit the peak, it would broadcast the Order's will. He felt it with sick certainty—once the current peaked, Thales wouldn't need to stand here at all.

"We have to reach the summit!" Aisha shouted over the rising wind, parrying a spear thrust. "If we don't break the resonance at the apex, Thales won't need to climb—he'll already be everywhere!"

He met Thales's gaze and forced the words out, low but defiant. "We're not bending. Not now. Not ever."

The air thickened, the silence charged like a storm about to break.

Aisha drew her blades. Sophia leveled her stance. Liam picked up a stone and twirled it like it was a sword. Nia clutched her sketchbook tighter, her pencil already scratching frantic lines across the page. Her hand shook, but the lines came anyway—shadows, light, the curve of raised blades—like she was trying to catch the first frame of a disaster before it happened.

The desert seemed to hold its breath. Even the wind went thin and high, a single, keening note around the Pyramid's edges.

And then, with a voice like a hammer striking iron, Thales gave the command.

"Take them."

— Δ —

The Order surged forward, but Quentin noticed a strange omission in their charge. There were no rifles, no modern firearms. A discarded sidearm lay near one of the ritual stones, its metal filmed with crystalline frost—dead weight. Out here, at the heart of Giza, ignitions just... failed. Only the old ways held: steel, bone, and the Echo itself. Even the robed agents moved with a synchronized, metronomic stiffness, their pulses dragged into the Pyramid's tempo.

Sand exploded beneath their boots as a line of robed figures charged, blades flashing, voices raised in a guttural chant that made the ground tremble. The torches flickered madly though the sun was climbing higher, as if the light itself recoiled from what was coming. Even the air felt wrong—thick, vibrating, tuned to the rhythm of the Order's spellwork.

Quentin's heart hammered. The Echo inside him flared, cryogenic pressure climbing up his arm, begging to be unleashed. *But he forced himself to hold—wait for the moment.*

"Go!" Sophia shouted, her voice sharp as steel against the desert wind.

Liam was the first to move. He bent down, scooped up a fist-sized rock, and hurled it with all the force his wiry arm could muster. It smacked against a guard's mask with a hollow clonk. "Oi! I'm over here, you bed-sheet rejects! Come get me!"

Several guards broke rank, peeling off toward him. Liam darted sideways, weaving between fallen stones, his laughter echoing across the sand. He flung another rock and shouted, "Careful! They say a pebble once killed a giant!"

Sophia seized the distraction. "Form up!" she barked. Her blade was already drawn, gleaming in the new sun. She positioned herself in front of Nia, shielding her with practiced precision. "Stay close. Don't wander."

Nia nodded quickly, sketchbook clutched tight against her chest. Her pencil scratched across the page even as fear widened her eyes—tracing the geometric failure points she couldn't yet explain. Her hand shook, but the lines she drew came fast, frantic, as if she could outrun fate by putting it on paper first.

Aisha moved like a shadow, twin blades in her hands, eyes fixed on the nearest agent. She darted forward, her strikes fluid and merciless. One guard lunged at her; she parried, spun, and drove her elbow into his ribs before slicing clean across his arm. He dropped with a strangled cry. Another came at her from behind, but she twisted low, her blade flashing back to catch his leg. Her movements were a dance—deadly, precise, unstoppable. Where Aisha moved, guards fell; where she paused, sand darkened.

Quentin took a shaky step forward. The Order's chant rolled over him, pulling at his mind, at his blood. He raised his marked hand, breath catching. The Echo surged, antique-gold veins hardening beneath his skin.

The second loaded—only for him.

The Echo packed cold into his bones, widening the moment until it felt padded, survivable. The guard's blade didn't "slow" so much as Quentin finally had time inside it—time to read the arc, to move his own body before it finished. He pivoted, hauling Aisha clear by the wrist, his tendons cabled tight under the load.

"Now!" he gasped.

She didn't hesitate. Her sword lashed upward, carving through the slowed guard before he could finish the strike.

Quentin released the load, and his senses snapped back with a painful jolt. The chant roared louder, his head swimming. Blood trickled hot from his nose. His knees buckled, and for a heartbeat the world pitched sideways—but he forced himself upright before anyone could reach him.

"Don't overdo it!" Sophia barked, parrying a strike that would have gutted a distracted Liam. "You'll burn out before we reach the top!"

Quentin staggered, breath ragged, but lifted his hand again. "I'll use it when it matters," he croaked.

The Order pressed harder, their coordination chilling. Every strike fell in rhythm, their movements drilled and precise. They fought like one body, their chant binding them together. Every footstep, every breath seemed choreographed, as if they were puppets moving to strings Quentin couldn't see.

Sophia countered with discipline of her own, her voice a sharp parry against the noise. "Nia, left! Liam, behind the stones—draw their aim!" She shoved a guard backward over the edge of a five-foot stone riser, her eyes scanning the climbing ranks. "Use the blocks! The incline is our only shield! Don't let them flank us—force them to climb over their own dead!"

The sheer scale of the Pyramid's masonry became their greatest ally. The Pyramid forced the Order into a bottleneck—only a few blades could reach them at once.

Nia wasn't just drawing; she was screaming directions. Her eyes were fixed on the page, her pencil flying in a frantic blur of graphite, but she wasn't looking at what *was*—she was looking at what was *coming*.

Nia didn't feel the Echo—not directly. She felt pressure: weight, angle, motion lining up before it broke. Her sketches sharpened not into futures, but fault-lines. Quentin didn't power her—he narrowed the chaos until only the next failure point showed.

"Left!" she shrieked, her voice cracking over the roar of the wind. "Aisha, the pillar is falling—move left!"

Aisha didn't hesitate. She threw herself sideways just as a massive limestone shard, loosened by Thales's signal, shattered exactly where she'd been standing a second before. Nia didn't look up; she just tore the page away and started another. "Liam, stay down! The next wave is coming from the shadow of the second riser—three of them, wait for the flare!"

Liam ducked, pressing his back into the stone. "I don't see them, Nia!"

"Wait for it," she whispered, her pencil snapping under the pressure of the line she was drawing. A heartbeat later, the violet light from the summit flared, illuminating three robed figures crouching in the dark of the blocks exactly where she had predicted.

Liam ducked behind a broken pillar, pelting guards with a rain of stones. "You lot couldn't hit a barn if it was chanting your hymns back!" he yelled. One guard stumbled into Sophia's reach, and she dispatched him with a clean thrust.

Aisha fought back-to-back with Quentin, blades flashing as she carved a circle of space around them. "Focus on breathing," she told him, even as sweat streaked her face. "Not the fight. Just one breath at a time."

He nodded, grounding himself in her words, in the rhythm of her movements beside him. Every inhale steadied the Echo; every exhale kept it from consuming him.

The clash stretched across the Pyramid's steps—steel on steel, sand kicked high, chants against shouts. The rising sun painted the battlefield gold, but the heat did nothing to warm the cold certainty pressing on them: they were outnumbered, pressed against the base of something older and darker than all of them combined. The Pyramid seemed to watch, ancient and silent, as if waiting to see who would bleed first.

Still, they held.

Quentin raised his hand again, the Echo pulsing faintly. "Endure," he whispered. And the mark went pressure-bright under his skin—burnished gold like old metal under stress—buying them a widened heartbeat just long enough for Aisha's blades and Sophia's strikes to carve them down.

Together, bruised and bloodied, they pushed forward—step by step—up the Pyramid. Each step felt like defying gravity itself, but none of them stopped. Not while breath remained. Not while the Echo still answered.

— Δ —

The clash rolled higher up the Pyramid steps. Sand sprayed with every strike, the chants of the Order swelling like a storm tide. Quentin's breaths came ragged, his arm trembling from the Echo's pull, but still they fought upward. Every step felt heavier than the last, as if the Pyramid itself resisted their ascent.

Then a familiar voice cut through the chaos.

"Quentin!"

He spun—and there was Raj.

He stood several steps above, framed against the rising sun, a blade in his hand gleaming crimson with etched glyphs. His robe was torn at the shoulder, his hair plastered to his forehead with sweat, but his smirk was untouched. He looked almost triumphant, as if he'd been waiting for this exact moment.

"You think you've won her heart," Raj called, his voice carrying over the din. His eyes flicked toward Aisha, sharp as daggers. "But she'll betray you again. Like she betrayed me."

Quentin froze, the words hitting harder than any blade. For a heartbeat, the battlefield vanished—only Raj's voice remained.

Aisha stiffened beside him, her jaw clenching. "Raj," she said, her voice low and dangerous. "You know why I left. You know what they turned us into."

Raj laughed, a jagged sound. "I know you chose him." His smirk twisted cruelly. "And now I'll show you how well your choice holds up."

Before Quentin could move, Raj lunged—not at him, but at Aisha.

Their blades clashed with a scream of metal on metal, sparks flying. Raj's grin widened with every strike, his blows wild but fueled by rage. He fought like a man trying to carve the past out of existence.

Aisha met him strike for strike, her movements sharp and precise, but he pressed harder, fueled by fury and betrayal. He slashed across her arm, drawing blood. She hissed but did not falter, spinning low and cutting across his leg.

Quentin felt the Echo rising, dense and frantic, begging to intervene. He raised his hand, antique-gold saturation cabled along his veins. "Aisha!"

She blocked another blow, her blade ringing against Raj's. "Don't—!" she shouted.

Raj shoved her back, eyes gleaming. "See?" he spat. "She doesn't even trust you!"

Quentin's vision blurred as time began to slow—the chant of the Order dipping into a deep, distorted hum, Raj's blade dragging through the air toward Aisha's chest. The power surged, turning his arm into a cold brace under overload. He felt the Echo clawing at him, hungry, desperate to be released.

His Echo surged—ready to seize control—and he realized that was exactly what Raj wanted.

"Trust me!" Aisha screamed. Her voice was sharp, desperate, cutting through the haze.

Quentin's heart stuttered. The Echo surged again, but he forced it down, clenching his fist, refusing to unleash it. The Echo shrieked inside him, furious, but he let it vibrate rather than collapse. *For the first time, he chose restraint—not instinct. Not fear. Choice.*

Aisha seized the opening. As Raj overextended, her blade twisted under his guard, slicing across his ribs. His smirk faltered, eyes wide with shock. She pivoted, drove her hilt into his jaw, and with a final reversal, she cut across his thigh.

Raj staggered, choking on a laugh that sounded more like a sob. "You... chose him," he gasped, blood spilling hot across the stone. His blade clattered down the steps. The sound echoed like a verdict.

Aisha's chest heaved. Her eyes were steady, cold. "I chose me," she said, and with a final shove, she sent him sprawling. They weren't high—only a few tiers up—but the steps were brutal enough.

He tumbled down the steps, his body impacting the tiers with a rhythmic, sickening thud—the sound of a structure finally meeting its failure point—before crumpling at the base of the Pyramid. The chant faltered for an instant as nearby robed agents saw one of their own fall. Even the storm of voices hesitated—as if shocked by the fall of a loyal blade.

Quentin's breath tore from him, his knees nearly buckling. Relief and grief and fury tangled inside him until he couldn't breathe. Raj's face—once friend, then traitor—flashed behind his eyes, twisted with rage and regret.

Aisha stood over where Raj had fallen, blood streaking her arm, her blades trembling in her hands. Her face was pale, but her eyes—her eyes were iron. Unbroken. Unapologetic. Herself.

She turned back to Quentin, her voice ragged but certain. "I told you to trust me."

Quentin swallowed hard, his throat tight. He nodded once, silently. The gesture carried more weight than any vow he had ever spoken.

Sophia's voice cut through, sharp and urgent. "We can't stop! They're regrouping!"

Indeed, the Order was rallying, their chant surging louder, more furious. Thales had not moved, but his eyes gleamed, and the ground beneath the Pyramid thrummed with something ancient and terrible. It felt like the entire structure was waking up—angry.

Quentin forced his legs to move, climbing the steps again, Aisha at his side. Their hands brushed briefly as they climbed, and though neither spoke, the touch said what words could not. *Together.*

Raj was down.

His betrayal ended not with triumph, but with his own downfall. And Aisha's loyalty—sealed in blood and fire—was no longer in question.

— Δ —

The Pyramid groaned.

As Raj's broken body lay crumpled below, the chant of the Shadow Order swelled again—louder, harsher, their voices colliding into a single resonance that made the ancient stones vibrate. Dust rained from the higher steps, and the air grew heavy, as though the desert itself was holding its breath. The entire structure seemed to wake in anger, stone grinding like teeth beneath their feet.

At the top of the stairs, Archon Thales finally moved. He raised both arms, and the Order answered with a thunderous roar. Glyphs carved into the blocks ignited one by one, lines of crimson current racing upward like veins of blood across the Pyramid's face. Each glyph pulsed with increasing speed, like a heartbeat nearing collapse.

The sand around them whipped into spirals, stinging skin and eyes. The torches sputtered and flared high, their flames bending inward toward Thales as though drawn to his gravity. Wind twisted unnaturally, circling him as if he were the center of a gathering storm.

Quentin froze halfway up the steps. The Echo in his palm pulsed violently, no longer in rhythm with his heart but discordant, fighting against Thales's pull. His knees nearly buckled under the weight of it. It felt like invisible hooks were dragging the Echo toward Thales, threatening to rip it straight out of him.

"What's happening?" Liam shouted, ducking as a burst of sand lashed across his face.

Sophia shielded Nia with her body, blade raised though it was useless against wind and glyphs. Her voice was grim, taut. "He's channeling. Drawing on more than the Echo—he's binding fragments."

Aisha's head snapped toward her. "Fragments?" Another tremor rolled through the steps, nearly knocking them off their feet.

Sophia nodded sharply, her eyes never leaving the crimson glow spreading across the Pyramid. "I saw redacted site reports—Alexandria, Halicarnassus. Energy readings that didn't match erosion or quakes."

She watched a bolt of violet lightning crackle in Thales's palm, her face paling as the pieces finally clicked together. "They weren't just visiting those ruins, Aisha. They were scavenging them. Thales has been collecting the dying embers of the other Wonders for decades, waiting for a vessel strong enough to bind them all."

She broke off, eyes narrowing against the gale. "He'll be more than a man." The fear in her voice was rare, sharp enough to chill the air despite the heat.

Thales lowered his hands slowly, deliberately. Condensed force coiled in his palms, alive with tendrils of fractured violet frequency that hissed and cracked like living chains. When he spoke, the words reverberated like stone splitting.

"You carry one Echo, boy," he said, his gaze spearing Quentin. "I carry many. The weight of centuries. The will of inevitability itself."

The Pyramid shuddered. The steps glowed with red glyphs, pulsing like a heartbeat that wasn't theirs. The stones beneath Quentin's feet vibrated, as though warning him to turn back.

Quentin clenched his fist, forcing himself upright. Every instinct screamed to run, but the Echo inside him burned brighter at Thales's presence. It was terrified, yes—but it was alive. And it was his. For the first time, he felt it wasn't just a burden but something choosing him back.

"We've beaten you before," Quentin rasped, his voice barely carrying over the storm.

Thales's lips curved faintly, colder than mockery. "You delayed me. Nothing more."

The wind howled louder, sand lifting into a cyclone around the Pyramid. Liam pressed himself against the stone, shouting, "We're about to be flayed alive by the weather! Someone please tell me the plan doesn't end with our bones on display!"

Quentin stumbled forward another step, the Echo hardening with a sub-zero pressure that made his lungs feel brittle. His gaze caught on the glowing chamber near the Pyramid's crest—glyphs there pulsing like an open wound. He didn't know how, but he knew it was the center. The source. The chamber drew him, the Echo vibrating in recognition like a tuning fork struck against stone.

He turned to the others, his voice cracking with strain. "We have to reach that chamber. If we don't stop him there, everything ends."

Sophia's jaw was set, her eyes narrowed but steady. "Then we fight our way up. Together."

No hesitation. No doubt. Command and devotion bound into one.

Aisha moved to Quentin's side, gripping his hand in hers. His mark flared. Aisha held on anyway, steel and breath and refusal. Her voice was low, for him alone. "Together. No matter what he throws at us."

Her fingers tightened—a silent vow, fiercer than the wind.

Nia clutched her sketchbook, her face pale but her eyes shining with eerie certainty. She whispered, "I drew this too. Us, standing in the light… just before the storm swallowed everything."

Quentin's throat tightened. It sounded more like a warning than hope, but even so, it steadied him. Her visions had never been wrong. And she was still here. Still fighting.

The storm howled. Glyphs pulsed. The Echo inside Quentin compacted toward release.

It clawed at his ribs, begging to discharge, begging to meet Thales's power with its own.

And yet, amid the terror, he felt their hands, their breaths, their presence. He was not alone.

Not anymore. Not ever again.

He looked up at Thales, at the storm writhing around him, and whispered the word that had become his anchor.

"Endure."

Then he tightened his grip on Aisha's hand, steadied his steps, and pushed forward into the heart of the storm.

Together, they moved—not as fugitives, not as victims, but as a force rising to meet the storm.

Chapter 24
The Hinge of Eternity

"The point of decision is the moment the structure is most vulnerable to re-design." — **Fragment of the Architect's Scroll, XXIV.**

— Δ —

The chamber at the Pyramid's summit blazed like a wound in the world.

Glyphs carved into walls, ceiling, and floor pulsed in jagged rhythm, their lines shifting like molten rivers—crimson to violet to gold, never settling, never still. Light crawled over the stone as if the Pyramid itself were breathing, inhaling power, exhaling heat. Every step forward felt like walking into the heart of a thunderhead.

At the center of it all stood Archon Thales.

He loomed behind a towering altar of obsidian, its surface carved in spiraling glyphs that seemed to twist if Quentin looked too long, like they were un-writing his thoughts. The Echo's energy swirled around Thales in tendrils of dark flame that bent the air, whipping his robes in winds that didn't touch anyone else. Fragments of other Echoes spun in his aura—shards of sapphire, emerald, and silver light orbiting him like chained stars, their radiance warped and dragged into his gravity.

The sight made Quentin's stomach twist. *As if Thales had reached into ruins and memory and stolen pieces of eternity, forcing them to kneel.*

"You finally arrived," Thales intoned. His voice was calm and cavernous at once, the chamber itself seeming to speak through him. "The boy who thought endurance meant surviving pain. How quaint."

Quentin's breath came rough and uneven. The mark in his right palm throbbed under his skin, each pulse a cold punch of pressure. The pressure surged toward the surface, as if trying to answer the storm—only to collapse inward again, smothered by the altar's counterfield. Every fiber of his body wanted to stop—just drop, let the stone catch him, let everything end. He forced his boots forward anyway. The floor shuddered with each step as if objecting.

"You think endurance means resisting?" Thales descended the altar steps with a slow, terrible grace. "Resistance is brittle. Resistance breaks."

He lifted one thin hand.

A coil of violet lightning snapped from a fragment circling him, lashing into the floor. Stone split open with a deafening crack, a jagged scar gouged across the chamber. Dust burst upward, suspended in the glare before raining down.

"True endurance," Thales murmured, "is bending the world until it cannot break you."

The words slid under Quentin's skin like cold glass—*wrong*, but familiar, echoing too closely to another voice. Marble and smoke and promises.

The Architect. Not Thales—older. Colder.

For a moment, the chamber blurred. He tasted the cell, the chains, the whisper in the dark that had offered him everything.

He clenched his jaw until it hurt. "Endurance isn't control," he rasped, the words scraped from somewhere raw. "It's surviving when control is gone. It's getting back up when you've already lost."

Thales's thin smile was colder than any sneer. "And yet here you are, clinging to scraps of philosophy while eternity stands within your reach. Tell me, boy—how many times will you bleed before you admit what the Echo demands?"

Quentin's knees threatened to buckle. Before they could, Aisha stepped into the space beside him, a blade in each hand. The unnatural light turned the blood along her arm almost black, but her eyes—dark, steady—didn't waver.

"You talk about endurance," she said, voice cutting clean through the hum of power, "but you built everything on fear. You hollow people out and wear what's left. That isn't strength. That's cowardice with better robes."

Thales's gaze turned on her, predator-sharp. "Ah. The prodigal traitor." He tilted his head, studying her like a specimen. "You knelt before me once. You whispered oaths with that tongue, swore your life to the Order. And now you cling to the boy's hand, as if redemption could rewrite what you were."

Aisha's grip tightened until her knuckles blanched. For a second, Quentin felt the tremor in her arm—but when she spoke, her voice was iron.

"I swore once," she said. "Every time I stand against you, I break that vow again. That's my endurance. That's my redemption."

Something fierce surged in Quentin's chest. *Pride. Terror. Both.*

He lifted his braced right palm to his heart and shifted closer until their shoulders almost touched. "She's with me," he said, louder than he felt. "And we're not yielding."

The chamber reacted.

Glyphs along the ceiling flared, the light strobing hard enough to sting. The floor vibrated, a low growl rumbling through the stone. For a heartbeat, Quentin could've sworn the Pyramid itself had registered them.

Thales's expression shed the last of its amused mask. What remained was older—raw, offended, almost… personal.

"So be it," he said softly.

The words were barely more than breath, but they slammed into the chamber like thunder. The fragments orbiting him flared blindingly bright. The altar trembled, glyphs cracking at the edges as power surged through it. Lines of light shattered into sparks that rained from the air like burning snow.

From behind the entrance, Liam's voice floated in, thin but stubborn. "No pressure, mate, but if you're planning to save the world, maybe speed it up before he turns us into decorative ash."

Quentin huffed out something like a laugh that turned into a hard, brittle cough. The Echo writhed, pressing against bone, begging to be used. To be unleashed. His body was failing; he could feel it in the tremble of his fingers, the hollow ache in his ribs, the way breath kept catching shallow and sharp.

But Aisha was beside him, blades lifted, gaze steadier than any anchor. Somewhere behind them, Sophia stood with blade ready, Liam with his easy jokes and raw loyalty, Nia with her trembling pencil and impossible visions. They'd chosen him, again and again, even when he hadn't chosen himself.

The weight of that settled on his shoulders—and then slid lower, into his spine, his stance. *He straightened.*

Quentin raised his braced right palm; a thin gold seep showed through the pressure.

"This ends here," he said.

The Echo shivered in answer, brightening, not wild this time, but focused—as if, for once, it locked into place.

— Δ —

The instant Quentin spoke, Thales struck.

The Archon's hand swept outward, and the fragments around him blazed in response.

The chamber stuttered. The floor rippled under Quentin's boots—not water, stone under stress—glyphs flashing out of sequence.

A chunk of ceiling tore loose and fell, and for one sick beat the world felt out of step with itself—force misrouted, weight lagging through the structure—then it hit, absolute and final, stone exploding into dust and shards that rang off the glyphs.

Quentin staggered. His stomach lurched, bile rising as his senses tried to reconcile what his eyes told him.

"He's splicing the moment," Quentin rasped. "Turning stone into a weapon."

Thales advanced, calm amid the storm. "Experience, boy. You stumble through borrowed strength. I've spent decades learning where structure gives way—where joints fracture under load. I've mastered it."

He thrust his hand, and a drag-wave rolled off the fragments—load distortion shearing the air—ears popping, breath thickening. Quentin's limbs felt suddenly overweighted, as if mass had abruptly reweighted through the chamber.

Quentin barely reacted, the chamber dragging—air thick, breath expensive. The Archon's blade swept toward his chest.

Quentin gritted his teeth, forcing the Echo to answer. Golden light surged from his palm and the arc stopped inches from his skin—caught, braced. He twisted sideways, wrenching the blade past him. Pressure spiked through the chamber—sparks scattering erratically, Aisha's hair torn sideways by the surge, Sophia's shout swallowed by a grinding thunder that wasn't sound so much as pressure.

He shoved with all his strength, breaking the hold. Structural tension released all at once, sound and movement slamming into him like a tidal wave. Quentin staggered, dropping the brace as blood dripped from his nose. His knees buckled, and for a heartbeat the world pitched sideways—but he forced himself upright before anyone could reach him.

"You can't keep that up!" Sophia shouted from the chamber's edge, holding her blade ready against oncoming elites.

Thales smiled coldly. "She is right."

He snapped his fingers, and the chamber flickered—not history returning, but impressions scraped into the stone. Shadows of old violence stuttered across the glyph-light: a swing that wasn't there, a scream without a throat, the afterimage of a battle the Pyramid remembered like a scar.

The ground beneath him destabilized. One moment, he was standing. The next, he was stumbling as an image of sand poured upward to the ceiling. He barely caught himself on one knee. Blood trickled from his nose, warm against his lips.

"You see it, don't you?" Thales murmured, voice carrying over the distortion. "Structure is a river, boy. And I've learned where it cuts the bank. You're a child trying to hold weight with bare hands."

Quentin forced himself upright, swaying. The mark in his right palm tightened. "Maybe," Quentin rasped, "but even stone fails when you load it wrong."

He flung his hand forward, and the Echo surged. Golden light burst outward, pressure flaring through the chamber—debris scattering erratically as load vectors collapsed. Quentin shoved into the opening, dragging Aisha clear through grinding stone and choking dust, stealing a single breath before the weight slammed back into place.

One elite toppled to the ground, his blade embedding uselessly into stone.

Aisha shot Quentin a quick look, half awe, half warning. "You're tearing yourself apart with every moment you brace!"

"I know," he rasped, chest heaving. His vision swam, edges darkening. Every bend gouged another piece of him, but he couldn't stop—not now, not here.

Thales swept his hand in a wide arc. This time, the fragments around him glowed in unison. The chamber lurched—load order collapsing, mass surging, then rebounding violently. One instant Quentin moved freely, the next he was hauling himself through crushing resistance, his body wrenched through forces that didn't belong to him. His feet struck stone as it buckled beneath him; his hands reached for holds that shifted under stress. He crashed to the ground, his bones rattling.

The Archon loomed over him, blade raised high. "Endure this, boy."

Quentin raised his palm desperately, golden light flaring. The strike halted inches from his throat—not frozen, but arrested by overwhelming counterforce. The suspended blade pressed down with unbearable weight, as if the entire structure were bearing through it. His body screamed as blood poured from his nose, his ears ringing. It felt less like blocking a sword and more like bracing a failing support with bare hands.

Aisha's voice cut across it, steady. "You can't keep that up!"

Quentin rolled to his knees, gasping. His entire body trembled as though it might shatter. But the Echo pulsed still, weak yet insistent—a heartbeat refusing to stop.

He looked up at Thales—towering, practiced, invincible—and forced the words through his cracked lips. "I'm not fighting you to win," Quentin rasped. "I'm fighting you to endure."

Thales's eyes narrowed, his sneer sharpening into fury. "Then you have already lost. Endurance without victory is just a slower death."

The chamber shook harder, glyphs sparking dangerously, the fragments orbiting him in tightening, unstable paths. Around the Archon, the air smeared—past impressions and afterimages flickering and collapsing with every breath he took.

The storm of misfires deepened—overlapping impressions, sensory overload stacking faster than his body could sort it. The chamber fed him conflicting impressions of collapse and recovery, weight shifting, footing failing and reforming. Quentin's vision doubled, then tripled, and he forced his shaking legs to commit to the one position that still held.

He dragged in a breath that tasted of dust and lightning and blood.

The duel of load and will had only just begun.

— Δ —

The chamber was chaos.

While Quentin and Thales tore at the moment's seam, the Shadow Order's elites pressed in. Their blades gleamed with etched glyphs, their movements unnervingly precise, synchronized with the Archon's storm. They came in waves, silent but for the hum of breath timed to chant.

Aisha stepped forward—into the storm, into her penance.

Her twin blades flashed, steel catching the unnatural glow of the glyphs. She moved with the fluidity of water and the force of fire, striking low, spinning high, cutting through the disciplined rhythm of the Order. Each strike she landed was sharp with purpose, each parry driven by something deeper than survival.

One agent lunged. She caught his wrist, twisted hard, and drove her blade through his guard. Another tried to flank her; she ducked, pivoted, and cut him across the knee before finishing with a slash across the chest. Her movements were relentless, unyielding.

This wasn't just battle. It was penance with an edge—steel writing over her old oaths in red. Every swing was a vow rewritten. Every parry was a severed tie to the girl she had once been.

Still, they came.

Sophia's voice rang from across the chamber: "Hold the line! Keep them from Quentin!"

Nia crouched behind a pillar, sketching furiously, the scratching of her pencil almost drowned by the clash of steel. Liam darted in and out like a phantom, throwing debris and jeering, "Oi! Over here, parchment-wavers!" before vanishing into shadows again.

But the elites focused on Aisha. They knew her name, her face, her past. They remembered her betrayal.

One guard hissed as he swung at her, "Traitor."

She parried hard, sparks spraying, and shoved him back. Her voice was sharp as steel. "Better a traitor than your slave."

Blood streaked her arm, but she pressed on. Another wave surged toward Quentin, who was locked against Thales, the faint gold at his palm fracturing under the Archon's storm of fragments. Aisha cut them off, blades flashing like twin arcs of defiance.

Her lungs burned, her muscles screamed, but she didn't stop. She wouldn't stop.

Then she saw it—Thales raising his hand, gathering the fragments' energy. Quentin was staggered, barely on his knees, blood trickling from his nose and ears. The Archon's blade angled downward, a killing blow glowing with violet light.

Quentin's awareness tunneled to a single point.

Not his doing—Thales's. The Archon forced a brutal clarity into the moment, compressing Quentin's perception until nothing existed beyond the incoming strike.

Quentin's head lifted weakly, his eyes wide. He raised his palm, but the faint gold at his skin fractured and dimmed.

Aisha moved without thought.

She lunged, throwing herself between them. The blade meant for Quentin slashed across her arm, searing pain detonating through her body like fire. She cried out but didn't fall. She planted her feet, blades crossed, holding the strike back with every ounce of strength left in her battered frame.

"You'll have to go through me," she snarled, blood running hot down her arm.

Thales's eyes flicked to her, cold and sharp. "So be it." He pressed harder, lightning crackling against her blades. Her knees buckled, but she forced herself upright again, teeth bared.

Her arms trembled violently. The lightning danced across her blades, crawling up the steel toward her fingers, threatening to tear them open—but she did not let go.

Thales watched as Sophia and Aisha carved through his elites with unnatural coordination, their movements holding longer than they should have under the pressure. "A load bleed," the Archon hissed, eyes narrowing. "You aren't containing the Echo—you're failing to isolate it. The strain is leaking outward. They're standing because you are breaking first. A noble waste, boy."

Quentin's vision cleared through the haze of blood and pain. He saw her—saw the woman who had betrayed him, yes, but who had chosen to bleed for him now, who had taken a strike meant for his life. Something inside him shattered and reforged in that instant, harder, brighter.

"Aisha!" he shouted, voice raw. He surged forward, the residual gold at his palm flaring under the strain, forcing the Archon to give ground, just enough to break the pressure against her. She staggered, clutching her bleeding arm, but her eyes burned with steel.

"Don't you dare stop," she hissed at him, breathless but fierce. "Not now."

Quentin nodded once, his jaw set.

Around them, the elites hesitated for just a heartbeat, unnerved by her defiance. Aisha used that heartbeat like a blade.

She spun, blade slicing through one, elbow slamming into another, moving like the wound was nothing but fuel.

Pain drove her, sharpened her, honed her into something the Order had never meant her to become.

She was no longer fighting just to redeem herself. She was fighting to prove that loyalty—real loyalty—wasn't forged by chains, but by choice.

And she chose him—again.

— Δ —

The chamber was unraveling.

Glyphs shattered across the walls, sparks raining in showers of crimson and gold. The altar pulsed like a living heart, its surface splitting as streams of energy bled upward into the storm above. The air burned with shattered stone and ozone, suffocating in its density.

Quentin staggered toward the altar, every step dragging his body closer to collapse. The Echo within him packed like cold weight, pressure cabled up his arm and spreading into his chest. He could feel it tearing at him, demanding discharge, demanding failure.

Thales loomed ahead, fragments spinning around him in furious orbit, their glow throwing the chamber's structural rhythms out of sequence with every flicker. His smile was cruel. "You see it now, don't you? The Echo isn't mercy. It isn't sacrifice. It's conquest. And it will devour you unless you embrace it."

The words scraped against him, wrong in every way.

Quentin's knees buckled. He caught himself on the altar, his hand leaving a smear of blood across glowing glyphs. His vision fractured, the world splitting into double images—one of the present, one misfiring under overload.

A voice whispered through the chaos.

The Architect.

"You cannot endure as you are," it murmured, silken and sharp. "But you could endure as I am. Accept it. Let structure yield. Let resistance vanish. Never feel the weight again. No more weakness. No more failure. No more loss."

Quentin's head spun. His eyes unfocused as visions poured through him.

He saw himself standing atop the Pyramid, arms raised, golden and violet light wrapping him in a rigid halo of control. Before him knelt the Shadow Order, not in defiance but in worship. The world bent around him like clay. Rivers froze mid-flow, cities bowed, the stars themselves shifted in the sky.

And at his feet—Aisha.

Her body was lifeless, her blades scattered. Her hand hung limp in his.

"No..." Quentin whispered, shaking his head, but the vision clung to him, burning like an invasive mark, forced into him against his will.

The Architect's voice curled around him like smoke. "This is the cost of resistance. But embrace me—embrace what you were chosen to be—and she will never fall again. None of them will."

His palm went pressure-bright, pain lancing up his arm as the load tried to burst free. He screamed. His body convulsed, blood gushing from his nose.

Behind him, Aisha fought with one arm against a wave of elites. "Quentin!" she cried, her voice raw. "Stay with me!"

He looked at her through the haze of the vision. In one image, she was fighting desperately, alive and burning with defiance. In the other, she was broken at his feet, sacrificed to the crown he wore.

His hand shook violently over the altar, the golden glow twisting with violet streaks.

The Architect pressed harder, the voice booming now: "Conquer, boy! Endure by ruling, or die a martyr no one will remember!"

Quentin's breath fractured into ragged sobs. The promise of invincibility pulled at him with terrifying tenderness—whispering safety, certainty, a world without loss. It felt almost merciful. *Almost holy.*

Quentin's heart cracked under the weight of it.

He thought of his father's disappointed words, of nights spent believing he was ordinary, replaceable. He thought of Aisha's betrayal, her sacrifice, her whispered *trust me*. He thought of Liam's reckless loyalty, of Nia's trembling sketches, of Sophia's hard-won respect.

He thought of every moment he endured—not because he was strong, but because they stood with him. Because he was loved.

Loved.

He thought of what endurance really meant.

And he screamed, the sound cutting through the chamber:

"I am not you!"

The visions splintered. The crown dissolved, the kneeling Order gone. Aisha's lifeless body blinked out, replaced by her real self—bleeding, battered, alive.

Quentin slammed his hand against the altar. Residual gold bled across the glyphs as the Echo convulsed under the strain, rejecting the violet corruption. Glyphs cracked and burst, shards of light raining down.

Thales recoiled, fury twisting his features. "Fool! You waste it! You waste eternity!"

Quentin's body shook with the force of it, blood dripping down his chin, but his eyes locked on the Archon with iron defiance.

"I'd rather die myself," he rasped, "than live as you."

The chamber quaked violently, the altar fracturing under the pressure of clashing wills. The Architect's whisper faded into a scream of rage as Quentin tore himself free from its grip.

And for the first time, the Echo answered not with demand—but with silence, as though it had heard and accepted his choice. A silence that felt like agreement. A silence that felt like respect.

— Δ —

The altar shook violently, its glyphs splintering in jagged bursts of light. The air was thick with dust and residual discharge, the storm within the chamber reaching a breaking point.

Quentin staggered upright, swaying on his feet. His right palm burned with cold pressure, gold only visible where the skin strained. His vision blurred, his body screaming in agony—but the Echo pulsed with steadiness now, no longer resisting, no longer demanding. It waited.

Thales stood at the far end of the altar, fury carved into every line of his face. The fragments orbiting him spun faster, streaks of violet and silver light twisting together into a cyclone. "You dare refuse me?" he thundered. "You waste eternity itself on weakness?"

Quentin shook his head, his voice hoarse but clear. "I don't waste it. I choose it."

The Archon roared, sweeping his arm. The fragments shot forward like blades of lightning, tearing through the chamber. Glyphs shattered, stone split, the ceiling cracked as if the Pyramid itself groaned under his will.

Quentin raised his palm. The fragments slammed into the space around him, their force dumping into the altar and floor as the Echo caught and redistributed the load. Stone cracked outward in spiderweb fractures, sparks bursting as the structure failed before he did. The impact drove him to his knees, his arm shaking violently under the weight—but he held.

Behind him, Aisha stumbled forward, her wounded arm pressed to her side, her blade still in her other hand. "Quentin!" she cried, her voice sharp with both fear and faith. "Don't give it all to him. Don't let him win!"

Her voice steadied him.

Something inside him latched onto her words—not strength, but purpose. A tether. A reason to stay upright.

He lowered his gaze to the altar, to the cracks running through its surface. The chamber itself was the conduit—the Order's anchor, their tether to the fragments. Destroying Thales wouldn't be enough. He had to end the source.

The Echo pulsed in his chest, resonating with his vow.

Not conquest. Preservation.

Not domination. Endurance.

Quentin staggered forward, pressing his palm flat against the altar. The glyphs flared in protest, screaming with light as violet and crimson clashed against gold. His body convulsed as the structural load slammed into him, stress shearing through muscle and bone. His teeth ground as he refused release—letting the Echo collapse the altar's power back into itself, like a brace buckling under too much weight.

"No!" Thales bellowed, his voice cracking with fury. He hurled more fragments, but they shattered as the altar began to fail beneath them. The storm twisted erratically, shards tearing loose from his control and dragging toward the collapsing structure. His robes whipped violently, his eyes wide with disbelief.

"This is not endurance!" he howled. "This is surrender!"

Quentin screamed, every fiber of him braced to failure, blood pouring from his nose and mouth. "This is sacrifice!"

The altar gave way.

Glyphs ruptured in cascading fractures, light tearing itself apart as the chamber's load collapsed inward. The fragments around Thales shrieked as their anchors failed, imploding into sparks and dead metal. Elites were thrown backward as the floor buckled beneath them, some fleeing, others crushed by the structure they had trusted.

The failure ripped upward through the Pyramid, stone splitting, ancient supports shearing loose. For a brief, terrible moment, fractured glyph-light leaked through every crack—then the foundations broke, and the monument began to eat itself alive.

The Pyramid roared as if alive, stone cracking, sand pouring in from ruptured seams. The storm collapsed inward, light tearing itself apart as Thales's scream was swallowed and cut short.

When the last fractures stilled, silence fell.

Quentin slumped to his knees, the altar now nothing but rubble beneath his palm. His chest heaved, every breath shallow, his body barely holding together. A faint pressure still pulsed beneath his palm—dim, exhausted, nearly gone.

A hand caught him before he fell face-first onto the stone.

Aisha.

Her face was streaked with blood and ash, her eyes wide and wet. She pulled him into her arms, clutching him tight despite the blood soaking his tunic. "Quentin," she whispered, voice breaking, "you're alive."

He let out a ragged laugh that dissolved into a cough. "Barely."

He lifted a trembling hand to her cheek, leaving a smear of gold-dusted blood.

"But so are you. So are they."

Sophia stumbled forward, blade still in her hand, her expression stunned as she surveyed the wreckage. Liam leaned against a broken pillar, face smeared with soot but grinning shakily. Nia peeked from behind him, her sketchbook clutched to her chest, eyes wide as though she had just seen her drawing come to life.

The chamber was ruined. The Order scattered. And Thales was gone.

Quentin collapsed further into Aisha's arms, his body utterly drained. His golden mark dimmed to the faintest flicker, but he held onto one thought as his vision blurred.

Not victory through domination. Victory through survival. Through endurance.

And as darkness took him, the last thing he felt was Aisha's hand gripping his—steady, warm, alive—anchoring him to a world he had nearly burned himself to save.

Chapter 25

Leaving the Anchor

"The first stone holds the weight of all those that follow. When it falls, the design is forfeit." — **Guardian Teaching, The Weight of Stone.**

— Δ —

The chamber was falling apart.

Cracks split the ancient stone, dust pluming in curtains that turned dawn's first light into shattered bars across the floor. Each groan of the Pyramid's walls echoed like a load-bearing rib giving way, the sound deep enough to rattle the bones. The once-thundering chants of the Shadow Order were gone. Only scattered moans and the scrape of rubble shifting remained, the echoes of a broken army.

Quentin lay sprawled on the shattered floor, his chest hitching in shallow, uneven pulls, each inhale catching like the air didn't want to come. The mark in his right palm had collapsed into a dull, bruise-metal geometry beneath the skin—matte, compressed, no radiance. A faint pulse still lived there, not heat, not light.

For the first time in days—maybe for the first time since he had touched the relic—he felt almost ordinary.

Almost.

Until his nerves replayed the cold load—compression climbing his arm like cabling that refused to let go.

"Quentin," Aisha's voice broke through the haze, raw and urgent.

Her hands were on him, pulling him upright with a strength that belied her wounded arm. Dust streaked her face, blood caked the torn sleeve where Thales's strike had cut through skin and left it blister-stiff, but her eyes were steady, alive. She hooked his arm over her shoulder and heaved, dragging him up from the fractured stone.

He winced, his body screaming, but forced a rasp of a laugh. "I'm… still here."

She shot him a look, fierce and trembling all at once. "Barely. Don't you dare vanish on me now." The words wobbled at the edges, but the grip she had on him didn't.

Around them, the chamber was a graveyard. Order agents lay strewn across the floor—some dead, others crawling away in terror. A few dropped their weapons outright and bolted into the collapsing halls, their robes trailing like shadows dissolving with the dawn. The symbols stitched into their hems, once so precise and menacing, were now just frayed thread and ash.

Nearby, Sophia and Liam held the line in the wreckage—standing, shaking, still here.

Quentin's gaze swept over them, blurry but insistent. They were alive. Against all odds, against the storm and the fragments and Thales himself, they were alive. Each of them looked carved from what was left—bone-tired, blood-smeared, still standing.

But the weight of it crushed him. His body trembled, and the Echo sat quiet—no brace, no surge—only a mute pressure-memory under the mark. The battlefield was eerily quiet now, but it was not the quiet of peace—it was the silence of exhaustion, of a victory too fragile to trust. Silence that felt like a held breath, waiting for someone to say it had all been a mistake.

Aisha shifted, adjusting his weight against her. "We have to move," she murmured, eyes darting to the cracks spiderwebbing the ceiling. "This place won't hold much longer."

He nodded, though even that small motion nearly toppled him. His throat burned with dust, every word scraping like sandpaper. "It's… over."

He hated how much it sounded like a question.

Her jaw tightened. "No. It's finished—for now. But the Order will crawl back from this. They always do." Her gaze flicked over the fallen robed figures, as if she could already see the gaps where others would step in.

The thought made his stomach turn. He looked down at his palm, half expecting the Echo to flare again, to remind him of what was left. But there was no answer. Only the faint warmth of blood and skin—no different than any other boy's hand.

But the current was gone—no cold surge, no load-routing, no tell before collapse. That absence arrived slowly, heavier than rubble. If the Echo wasn't running, he was just Quentin: bruised, breakable, and awake inside his own limits.

"What if it's not answering?" he whispered, barely audible even to himself. "What if I can't call it when it matters?"

Aisha heard him. She squeezed his shoulder, her voice sharp enough to cut through his despair. "Then we fight without it. Together. You don't need a mark shouting under your skin." Her words landed like a handhold on a cliff, something solid to grab when the rest of him wanted to fall.

Her words steadied him, though doubt still clawed at the edges of his mind. He wanted to believe her. He wanted to believe endurance wasn't tied to a mark or a power—but to the choice he had made. To sacrifice instead of conquest. To stepping forward even when every part of him wanted to lie down and stay.

Another tremor shook the chamber, raining more dust across them. Liam groaned loudly from across the floor. "If this is what winning feels like, I'd hate to see losing."

Despite himself, Quentin let out a ragged laugh. It hurt, but it was real. The sound cracked in his chest, half-choke, half-laugh, and somehow that made it feel more honest.

The dawn light widened as more cracks split the stone, spilling across the chamber floor. It caught Aisha's face in a hard dawn wash, turning dust to pale glitter and blood to rust. She looked at him not with pity, not with blame, but with something steadier: *defiance.* A promise in her eyes that said, clearly, that losing the Echo didn't mean losing him.

And for the first time since the fight, Quentin let himself breathe.

The storm was over.

But the silence it left behind was terrifying in its own way. It left a question the Echo had never allowed him to ask: *who are you now, when the mark is quiet?*

— Δ —

The group stumbled down the fractured steps of the Pyramid, battered silhouettes against the pale sweep of dawn. The storm of power had passed, leaving only silence and ruin in its wake. Sand had drifted through wide cracks in the stone, pooling like blood at the base, and the scattered remnants of the Shadow Order fled into the desert's expanse. Behind them, the Pyramid exhaled in slow, shuddering groans, as if even the stone was too tired to hold itself together.

Quentin looked out across the vast, empty plateau. It was eerie—the Great Pyramid was usually swarming with tour buses and shouting vendors by this hour, but the sands were unnervingly still. He remembered the news snippets he'd seen on the hostel television: *Giza closed for structural survey.* The Order had cleared the board before they ever moved their pieces. Even the stray dogs were gone, driven away by the same bone-deep vibration that had nearly shattered Quentin's skull.

Quentin leaned heavily against Aisha, each step a battle in itself. His legs felt carved from lead, his chest tight with exhaustion. The Echo, once a roar inside him, was now no more than a residual thrum he couldn't raise on command. Every breath reminded him how breakable he truly was—how human. Every jolt of his foot against the next worn stone sent a fresh flare of pain through his chest, a reminder that victory hadn't made him invincible—just injured and still moving.

Liam emerged from a tumble of rubble, his tunic torn and his hair caked with dust, but his grin was intact. He raised a hand in mock salute. "Well, if this was a field trip, I'd like a refund. Five stars for near-death thrills, zero for catering."

Quentin almost laughed, the sound catching in his raw throat. "You're… impossible."

"Exactly," Liam said, limping closer. "That's why you keep me around." He bumped his shoulder lightly against a broken pillar as he passed, as if even now he couldn't resist turning wreckage into a stage.

Nia followed a step behind him, moving carefully, her ankle wrapped in a strip of cloth torn from her sleeve. She held her sketchbook against her chest like a shield. Her eyes, wide and shimmering, darted from Quentin to Aisha, then to the Pyramid crumbling behind them. She whispered, "I drew this. The light breaking it apart. It was always going to end this way."

Aisha touched her shoulder briefly, steadying her. "Then keep drawing, Nia. The rest of us need to know where we're going before the world caves in on us again." Her fingers lingered a second longer than necessary, a wordless promise that someone saw how much it cost Nia to keep seeing.

Sophia appeared last, bloodied but upright, her blade still in her grip. She walked with a soldier's discipline, every line of her posture strained but unbroken. Her eyes fixed on Quentin. Dust streaked her face in harsh lines, like war paint smeared by sweat and time.

He braced himself for the sharpness of her judgment, for the familiar note of doubt. But instead, she came to a halt in front of him, wiped the blood from her brow, and raised her hand in salute.

"You led," she said simply. Her voice carried none of its usual frost, only a quiet steadiness. "I doubted you. I was wrong."

Quentin blinked, caught off guard. His first instinct was to deflect, to shrink into the comfort of ordinariness. But the weight of her words settled into him, undeniable. For once, he didn't push it away. *It sat in his chest like a stone—heavy, unfamiliar, but not unwelcome.*

He nodded slowly, his voice rough but firm. "Then let's make sure it wasn't for nothing."

For a moment, the group stood together at the Pyramid's base, dawn spilling over them, the desert wind brushing past. They were bruised, cut, and shaken, but they were alive. For the first time since they had been dragged into this nightmare, Quentin felt something fragile but real threading between them—something more than survival. Unity. Not the brittle unity of the Order's chants, but something messy and voluntary—held together by choice, not fear.

Even Liam seemed to feel it, though he masked it with his usual grin. "Alright," he said, flopping onto a chunk of stone with a groan, "next time someone says, 'Hey, let's explore the ancient death-pyramid,' I vote no."

"Noted," Sophia muttered, though the faintest flicker of a smile tugged at the corner of her mouth. The expression was gone in a heartbeat, but Quentin saw it, and it felt like another crack in the armor she'd worn since Cairo.

Nia settled beside Liam, carefully opening her sketchbook. She began a new page, her pencil trembling in her fingers but steadying with each stroke. She didn't look up as she murmured, "We're not finished. I can feel it. There's more coming."

Quentin glanced down at her, then at his hand. The Echo's light was gone, the skin pale and ordinary, but he felt a faint thrum deep in his chest. Nia was right. The war hadn't ended—it had only shifted. *The battlefield wasn't only stone and sand anymore; it was cities, water, distance—Wonders that hadn't woken yet.*

Aisha's grip on his arm tightened as if she'd read the thought. Her voice was quiet, meant for him alone. "One fight at a time."

He nodded, exhaling shakily. *One fight at a time. Not the whole war. Not the Architect's garden or Rhodes or whatever waits beyond—just the next step, the next breath, the choice not to fall apart right now.*

For now, they had survived. And for the first time, survival felt less like an accident and more like something they had claimed together, hands bloody and hearts still pounding.

— Δ —

The sun had fully breached the horizon by the time they reached the edge of the battlefield. Its light spilled over broken stone and scattered sand, gilding ruin in a deceptively peaceful glow. But the ground was littered with remnants—splintered glyphs, shattered weapons, bodies of Shadow Order agents who had fallen to the storm. The silence pressed heavy, reminding them that victory always demanded blood. Even the wind seemed reluctant to move across the carnage, as though afraid to disturb what had been lost.

Sophia walked ahead, her blade lowered but still at the ready. Liam trailed behind, his limp more pronounced now that the adrenaline had faded. Nia moved carefully between them, eyes fixed on her sketchbook as though it kept her anchored. Quentin leaned heavily on Aisha, every step dragging his battered body forward. His breaths came ragged, his ribs aching with each inhale, the world tilting at the edges like a horizon still shaking from the quake.

Then Liam stopped abruptly, his expression hardening. "Uh… you're going to want to see this."

Quentin forced himself upright, peering past the haze of exhaustion. At first, he thought it was just another body sprawled among the rubble. But then it shifted, a hand clawing weakly at the sand.

Raj.

His once-pristine robe was shredded, his leg bent at an unnatural angle. Blood streaked his face, his smirk twisted but still somehow intact. He coughed, a harsh, rattling sound, and looked up at them with eyes that still glimmered with defiance. Even broken, he radiated that same poisonous arrogance, the kind that made Quentin's stomach twist.

"Well, well," he rasped, his voice raw but mocking. "The golden boy and his… merry little band. Still playing heroes?"

Aisha stiffened beside Quentin, her hand moving instinctively toward her blade. Quentin caught the motion and placed his hand over hers, stopping her. His own stomach churned. Some part of him wanted to let her strike. Another part—the louder, more exhausted part—whispered that crossing that line would change him forever.

Raj coughed again, blood flecking his lips, but his grin didn't falter. "You think you've won. But the Order isn't finished. You'll see. Thales was just the beginning. There are others… stronger, smarter.

They'll come for you." His gaze shifted deliberately to Quentin's hand. "Especially for that."

Quentin's right palm ached, though it no longer glowed. He curled it into a fist. The ache wasn't power now—it was fear, memory, and something dangerously close to guilt.

Sophia's jaw tightened. She stepped forward, her blade gleaming in the morning light. "He doesn't deserve to live. Not after what he's done."

Raj's eyes flicked to her, amused even as blood dripped from his chin. "Ah, Sophia. Always so righteous. Always so sure your sword swings in the name of justice. But here you are—debating whether to kill a man who can't even stand." He spread his arms weakly, as if offering himself. "Do it. Or admit you're too soft."

The group froze. Silence tightened around them. The air itself seemed to hold its breath, waiting for someone to break.

Quentin's chest tightened. He wanted to end it—to silence Raj, to make sure his betrayal never cost them again. The thought of leaving him alive twisted in his gut, dangerous as a wound left untreated. He imagined Raj rising again someday, imagined another ambush, another friend bleeding out on ancient stone. It would be so easy to ensure that never happened. Easy—too easy.

But he also saw something else. Raj's broken body, his defiant grin that covered fear. He saw a boy who had chosen wrong, yes—but still a boy, still human, still breathing.

Mercy clawed at Quentin even as necessity demanded otherwise.

His voice was hoarse when he spoke. "We can't take him with us. He'll slow us down. He'll betray us again." He swallowed hard, forcing the words. "We leave him."

Raj's smirk widened faintly, though his voice cracked. "You had the power to end me, and you wasted it on a prayer. You think that's mercy, golden boy? I call it weakness. The weakness that will get your friends killed when I come back."

The words hit him like a blade—not because they were true, but because a piece of him feared they might be.

Aisha's eyes narrowed, but she said nothing. Sophia looked at Quentin, her expression sharp. "Are you certain?"

He hesitated, then nodded. The choice burned in his chest. "Yes."

Sophia gave a curt nod and lowered her blade. Liam shifted uncomfortably, muttering under his breath, "Not gonna lie, leaving a smug snake in the sand feels worse than killing him."

Nia hugged her sketchbook tighter, whispering, "I drew him, too. Lying here. Left behind." Her voice shook. "It was always going to end this way." Her words felt like prophecy, not commentary, and Quentin hated how right they sounded.

Raj let out a low laugh, broken and bitter. "Then go. Run off to your next miracle. I'll still be here—when the Order comes to collect what's theirs."

Quentin stared at him for a long moment, every muscle screaming for one clean strike. Leaving him alive sat in Quentin's gut like an undressed risk.

A noise cut through the quiet—an engine, low and approaching the plateau.

Headlights raked the dawn through lingering dust, distant but bright.

Sophia's head snapped up. "The Order," she hissed. "Retrieval. Now that they know he's here—"

"We move," Aisha cut in, raw and decisive. "If they find him and us, we're dead."

Quentin turned away. His voice came quiet, almost lost to the wind. "This is the cost. We can't save everyone."

He knew he would hear that line in his dreams. He knew it would hurt.

Aisha's grip on his arm tightened. Sophia sheathed her blade. Liam sighed. Nia scribbled furiously, her pencil scratching like a heartbeat. None of them spoke the truth out loud: *that choices like this didn't end wars—they started echoes.*

They left Raj among the ruins, his laughter following them until the desert wind finally carried it away. And even as it faded, Quentin felt the sound settle into his bones like a curse he'd chosen himself.

— Δ —

The desert stretched endlessly beyond the Pyramid, its sands glowing amber beneath the rising sun. The chaos of the chamber felt distant now, like a half-remembered nightmare—though Quentin's aching body reminded him with every breath that it had been real. Every bruise, every scrape, every tremor in his muscles echoed the battle he'd barely survived.

They stopped on a quiet dune just beyond the ruins, far enough from the collapsing stones that the air was clear of dust. The group settled nearby—Liam sprawled flat in the sand, muttering about naps; Sophia sharpening her blade with mechanical precision, her movements steady despite exhaustion; and Nia sketching in silence, her face half-hidden behind shadow. But Quentin and Aisha drifted a few steps away, apart from the others.

Quentin sank heavily onto the dune, his legs trembling, his chest burning with each breath. Aisha lowered herself beside him, careful with her injured arm. For a long time, they said nothing. They simply stared at the Pyramid's fractured silhouette against the morning sky—broken, scarred, but still standing.

Quentin felt eerily mirrored in it: damaged, not defeated.

Finally, Aisha spoke, her voice low and rough. "The Order raised me to betray."

Quentin turned, studying her profile. The wind tugged at loose strands of her hair, carrying away the sharp smell of blood and stone dust. Her eyes stayed fixed on the horizon, as though she couldn't bear to meet his yet. Her jaw was tight, her posture rigid—holding herself together by force of will alone.

"They took me when I was a child," she continued, her tone flat, stripped of pretense. "They told me loyalty was obedience. That strength was silence. That trust was a weapon. I believed them. For years, I believed them." She glanced down at her trembling hand, still streaked with blood from Thales's strike. "That girl didn't know how to choose anything. She only knew how to follow."

"And when they told me to turn on you… I did. Because that's what I was made to do."

Quentin's throat tightened. He wanted to tell her she hadn't been made, that she still had a choice. But interrupting felt wrong—like stepping into a wound that still bled. So he waited. He let her speak.

Her shoulders slumped. "But I didn't expect you to survive. I didn't expect you to fight for me after I had already given you up." Her voice cracked, and she pressed her good hand against her face, muffling the tremor. "You weren't supposed to matter. Nobody was."

"And yet… when it came down to it, I couldn't let them take you. Not like they took me."

Silence stretched between them, broken only by the hiss of desert wind over the sand.

It wasn't awkward. It was heavy—like the truth finally had room to breathe.

Quentin reached out slowly, his fingers brushing the back of her uninjured hand. She stiffened at the touch but didn't pull away.

"You chose me," he said softly, his voice frayed at the edges.

She turned toward him, her face only inches from his. In the harsh clarity of the morning sun, he could see the gold dust trapped in her eyelashes and the way her pulse jumped in the hollow of her throat. For a long second, the world narrowed to the space between them—the heat of her skin, the shared rhythm of their ragged breathing. Quentin felt a magnetic gravity wanting to close that final inch, a pull stronger than the Echo itself.

He didn't move. Couldn't. He held still and let her see him—no mask, no armor—just what was left.

She leaned in, not to kiss him, but to rest her forehead against his. It was a surrender. They stayed like that, two broken pillars leaning on each other for support, while the sun turned the desert into a white-gold glare off sand and stone.

She nodded once, eyes wet. "I chose you."

The words sounded like an oath said for the first time—not because someone demanded it, but because she wanted it.

The words lingered in the space between them, fragile yet powerful.

Quentin swallowed hard, his chest aching not only from exhaustion but from the weight of what they had endured. He turned to face her fully, his expression raw. "Then… choose me again. Not because you owe me anything."

"Then choose us. For what comes next."

Her eyes widened, startled. He wasn't asking for blind loyalty. He wasn't demanding forgiveness for her betrayal. He was asking for partnership—for a choice made freely, not forced.

He was giving her the one thing the Order never had: *her own voice.*

Her lips parted, then curved into the faintest, trembling smile. "You really are impossible."

He let out a ragged laugh, shaking his head. "So I've been told."

For the first time since the Pyramid had collapsed, the heaviness in Aisha's eyes eased. She squeezed his hand, her grip firm despite her injury. The strength in her touch wasn't physical—it was conviction.

"Then yes. I'll choose you again. And again after that. Until it means something more than survival."

Quentin's chest loosened, the knot of fear and doubt inside him easing with her words. He didn't know what waited beyond this moment, didn't know what shadows of the Order still lingered—but for now, it was enough.

They sat together in silence, watching the sunrise spread across the desert, their hands clasped tightly. The Pyramid loomed behind them, a broken reminder of what they had endured, but the light ahead stretched farther than either could see.

The future didn't look safe. But it looked shared. And that was enough.

They had survived the storm. And for the first time, Quentin allowed himself to believe they could survive what came next—because they wouldn't be facing it alone.

— Δ —

The sun climbed higher, washing the desert in pale gold. The Pyramid loomed behind them—fractured, scarred, but still standing. Its broken stones jutted skyward like the ribs of a buried giant, half-swallowed by the sand that would soon erase it. Quentin felt the sight carve itself into memory: the monument they'd destroyed, the monument that had tried to destroy them.

Quentin stood on the ridge of a dune, Aisha beside him, the others gathered close. For a long moment, none of them spoke. The silence wasn't empty anymore—it was full. Full of everything they had endured, everything they had lost, and everything waiting beyond the horizon. *It felt like standing between the end of one life and the beginning of another.*

Liam broke it first, stretching his arms above his head with a dramatic groan. "Well," he rasped, his voice hoarse but still irreverent, "if I die tomorrow, at least I can say I got to punch a cultist on the steps of a Pyramid. That's bucket-list material."

Sophia shot him a look—sharp, but softened by fatigue. "Try not to make a habit of almost dying. It's becoming tedious."

"Noted," Liam replied with a crooked grin, then winced as he clutched his bruised ribs. Even his jokes sagged under the weight of exhaustion, but he offered them anyway—because that was how Liam endured.

Nia sat cross-legged in the sand, sketchbook open on her lap. Her pencil moved slowly, deliberately, the lines careful despite the tremor in her hands. She glanced up at Quentin, then down again, shading the curve of something monumental. The furrow between her brows hinted she was drawing more than an image—she was drawing inevitability.

Quentin watched her pencil move—too sure, too inevitable. His stomach tightened. "Not again," he breathed.

Nia turned the book.

The drawing showed a giant statue striding across a harbor, one hand raised high to hold a hard-lit flame. The details were rough, but unmistakable—the Colossus of Rhodes. Even unfinished, the statue radiated a presence that made Quentin's skin prickle.

"The next one," Nia whispered, her voice trembling with certainty. "That's where we're going."

Sophia frowned, her brow furrowing. "You're sure?"

Nia hugged the sketchbook to her chest. "I don't know how I know. I just… see it. Like I saw this. Like I saw us walking away from the Pyramid." Her voice cracked. "There's more. There will always be more."

Quentin's hand curled into a fist. He looked down at his right palm, half expecting the Echo to flare again. But the skin was pale, ordinary. And yet beneath it, he felt a throb—faint, stubborn, alive. As the sun struck the mark, he felt the faintest pulse beneath the surface—a ghost of the compression that had nearly folded him.

It wasn't active. Not entirely gone, either—just dormant, withdrawn into bruised metal geometry beneath the skin.

His gaze lifted to the horizon, where Cairo shimmered faintly in the distance, its sprawl of buildings like a jagged seam against the shimmer. Civilization was there—safety, maybe even answers. But farther still stretched seas and coasts and wonders that waited to rise. A road he'd never chosen—one that had chosen him.

The war wasn't finished. It had barely begun.

Aisha touched his arm gently, drawing his attention back. Her expression was tired but steady. "One step at a time."

He nodded slowly. One step at a time.

He clung to her voice like a lifeline—a reminder that he didn't have to face what came next alone.

Behind them, Sophia sheathed her blade with deliberate care, her gaze fixed on the horizon as though measuring the distance already. Liam sprawled backward in the sand, groaning, "If this next place doesn't have beds, I swear I'm defecting to the enemy."

That earned a weak laugh from everyone—even Sophia.

Nia flipped her sketchbook open again, adding small figures beneath the towering statue. Six of them, standing together, tiny against its immensity but present all the same.

Their silhouettes looked fragile on the page—but unbroken.

Quentin counted the marks. Six. He looked back toward the ruins of the Pyramid where they had left Raj broken in the sand. A cold knot formed in his stomach. Nia's drawings didn't account for who deserved to be there; they only showed who *would* be.

Quentin stepped closer, peering over her shoulder. His chest tightened at the sight. "That's us."

Nia nodded. "It always has been."

Her certainty sent a ripple through him—fear and hope intertwined.

The desert wind swept over them, carrying the scent of dust and stone. Behind them, the Pyramid groaned one last time as a section of its wall collapsed inward, sending up a plume of smoke and sand. None of them looked back.

Looking back felt like giving the ruins power they no longer deserved.

Instead, they looked forward—to Cairo, to Rhodes, to whatever waited beyond.

Quentin drew in a slow breath, his chest aching but his voice firm when he spoke. “We endured this. We’ll endure what comes next.”

Aisha’s hand found his, her grip warm despite her injury. Sophia’s posture straightened, Liam’s grin flickered back into place, and Nia’s pencil stilled on the page as if committing the line to fact.

The sun rose higher, blazing across the desert.

The first battle was over. The war of the Wonders had only just begun.

Quentin didn’t feel fearless. He felt braced—and that was enough.

Chapter 26
THE COLOSSUS CALLS

"The component of Endurance is insufficient alone. The design requires completion." — **Fragment of the Architect's Scroll (Disputed)**

— Δ —

The airport smelled of coffee and disinfectant, a strange blend of routine normalcy after the weeks of sand, blood, and stone. Cairo International bustled with tourists dragging suitcases, families herding children, business travelers tapping at phones. Life flowed on here as if nothing had cracked open beneath the desert, as if no Pyramid had groaned with ancient voices or erupted in glyphs and glare. The contrast was jarring—too clean, too bright, too ordinary.

For Quentin, it was suffocating—pressing against him like a lie everyone else believed.

He stood with his bag slung over one shoulder, the weight dragging against sore muscles. His hoodie sleeve covered the bandages on his arm, though the ache beneath them hadn't faded. The Echo's mark had dulled, just another faint scar to anyone who looked. Only he felt its hidden pulse in quiet moments—a reminder the fight wasn't finished, and neither was he.

The official line was already circulating: *Giza Plateau Closed After Unrest. Officials cite tremors. Tourists evacuated.*

Nothing about the Order. Nothing about altered perception or physiological collapse. Nothing about sacrifice.

Truth had been buried as neatly as the ruins themselves.

Sophia handed over her final documents at the counter, posture stiff and precise. Even in jeans and a jacket, she carried herself like a soldier giving a debrief. When she returned, she caught Quentin's glance and gave a curt nod—not warmth, but respect that hadn't been there weeks ago. It steadied him more than he expected.

Quentin still didn't know how Sophia had pulled it off. He'd only seen the last forty-eight hours: her satellite phone pressed to her ear, her voice clipped and absolute, the printer at the hostel spitting out stamps and seals like absolution. Now she slid a thick envelope into her carry-on and didn't look back.

Liam slouched on a nearby bench, one leg stretched stiffly in front of him, wrapped in a brace from the tumble he'd taken during their escape. He waved a granola bar like a baton. "Well, that's that. Exchange trip over. Five stars for excitement, zero for hospitality. Honestly, I think I'll stick to beaches next summer."

Quentin almost laughed, the sound catching in his raw throat. "You're… impossible."

"Exactly," Liam said, grinning through his bruises. "That's why you keep me around."

Even half-broken, he was a spark against the heaviness trying to swallow them.

Nia sat beside him, quiet as ever, sketchbook balanced on her knees. She wasn't drawing landscapes this time. Her pencil traced their silhouettes in the terminal light: Liam's lazy sprawl, Sophia's rigid frame, Quentin leaning against the window, Aisha with her hood pulled low. She captured them not as students or tourists, but as they had become—survivors.

The lines on the page were shaky, but the truth they carried was not.

Quentin pressed his forehead against the glass, staring out at the faint line of desert on the horizon. The dunes shimmered in the heat haze, timeless and unyielding. Part of him longed to run back into them, to prove the nightmare was real. But the scars across his body, the ache in his palm, the shadows in his friends' eyes—those were proof enough.

He didn't need sand under his feet to know what he'd endured.

Aisha stood close, her hood drawn low. The Shadow Order might have been broken here, but their networks reached far. Recognition could mean danger. Her hand brushed Quentin's briefly as she adjusted her sleeve, a fleeting contact hidden from the crowd but grounding for them both. He leaned into the touch without meaning to.

"They'll forget," she murmured, her eyes scanning the bustle. "The officials. The students who weren't caught up in it. The rest of the world. They'll forget what happened in Giza."

Quentin's chest tightened. "But we won't."

"No," she said softly. "We can't."

Her voice carried the weight of everything they had lost and everything they still feared.

Their flight number flashed across the screen above the gate. The line shuffled forward with the weary cadence of travelers eager for home. For most, this was return to classrooms, to families, to stories crafted from reports and half-truths. For Quentin, there was no returning—only moving forward from what he had become at the Pyramid's heart.

Home wasn't behind him anymore. It was wherever they went next.

Sophia shouldered her pack, scanning the group. "We board soon. Stay close."

Liam groaned, levering himself upright with exaggerated effort. "Finally. If I sleep in one more chair that smells like camel leather and instant coffee, I'm filing a complaint."

Nia tore the page from her sketchbook, folding it carefully before slipping it into her bag. She glanced at Quentin as though she wanted to speak, but only gave him a small, hesitant smile.

It was the kind of smile someone gives when they've seen too much to pretend everything is fine.

He returned it, though his heart felt heavy.

As they moved toward the gate, Quentin glanced back one last time. Through the wide airport window, the desert shimmered under the rising sun, endless and unforgiving. Somewhere beneath those sands, the ruins of the chamber still smoldered. Somewhere in its silence, echoes lingered.

Echoes of power. Echoes of warning. Echoes of what waited beyond Egypt's borders.

He turned away, following the others into the narrow steel corridor of the jet bridge, the taste of dust still clinging to his tongue.

They were leaving Egypt.

But Egypt wasn't leaving them. Not now. Not ever.

— Δ —

The cabin lights dimmed to a muted glow, casting the rows of passengers in hushed shadow. The steady hum of the engines filled the silence—soothing, relentless. Quentin sat pressed against the window, his faint reflection staring back at him, the desert long since replaced by clouds and night. His muscles ached with exhaustion, but his mind refused to settle. Normalcy pressed in on him, thin and artificial, like air that didn't quite reach his lungs.

The flight path on the seatback screen showed a tiny glowing icon of a plane inching its way across the Mediterranean toward the English Channel. London lay hours away—a city of rain and stone that felt impossibly distant from the fire and ruin of Giza.

Sleep came in fragments. Each time his eyes drifted shut, memory snapped him awake—glyphs burning into stone, Thales's sneer, the Pyramid collapsing with the groan of a dying titan. The images clung like dust beneath his skin. Eventually, exhaustion dragged him under.

He opened his eyes to a garden.

It might once have been beautiful: marble arches choked with ivy, fountains dry and cracked, statues shattered and half-buried in weeds. Flowers sagged where they grew, petals bruised, stems blackened with rot. The air hung heavy and damp, thick with the scent of soil left untended too long.

Even in the dream, his stomach twisted. Ruined beauty always did that to him.

At the center of the decay stood the Architect.

He seemed farther away this time—indistinct, as though Quentin were looking through smoke—but his presence pressed down all the same, heavy as stone. When he spoke, his voice rolled through the garden like thunder swallowed by rain.

"You may have delayed me, boy. But every seed grows. And you cannot uproot what is eternal."

Quentin staggered back, his gaze snapping to his right palm. The mark surfaced beneath his skin—pressure made visible, stripped of warmth, its bruise-metal geometry stark against his flesh. It didn't feel like his anymore. It felt borrowed. Temporary.

A cold spread through him.

"What do you want from me?" he shouted. His voice sounded thin, swallowed by the air. "You're gone. It's over."

The Architect laughed—low, terrible. "You think cutting a branch fells the tree? The roots run deep. The Pyramid was only the first component—the foundation of Endurance. The next waits already. A beacon of Dominion. From those roots will rise a forest that will choke the world."

The certainty in his voice was absolute—and that certainty was the weapon.

The garden shuddered. Vines tore free from the earth, slithering across the stone toward Quentin's feet. Statues cracked, their hollow eyes tracking him as he stumbled back. He raised his marked hand, but the vines climbed higher, wrapping, tightening.

Panic surged—cold and sharp, even here.

"You cannot endure forever," the Architect whispered. "But I can. I will. And when you break, the Echo will return to me. As it was always meant to."

The vines snapped upward, seizing his wrist.

Quentin cried out as a hard glare ripped through the ruin—white, source-less, without heat. For a heartbeat, the garden restored itself: arches whole, fountains flowing, statues unbroken.

Then the light collapsed.

He woke gasping.

The drone of the engines rushed back, the cabin solid around him. Sweat slicked his hairline. His right palm throbbed faintly, pressure lingering beneath the skin—not power, but memory. The lack of control terrified him more than strength ever had. He clenched his fist and shoved it beneath the blanket, heart hammering.

Disputed or not, the Architect spoke like the world agreed with him.

"Quentin?"

He turned sharply. Aisha was watching him from the seat beside his, her hood down now, dark hair loose around her shoulders. Her eyes searched his face, sharp but not unkind. She looked as tired as he felt, but steadier—a tether he hadn't known he needed until it held.

"You were dreaming," she said softly.

Quentin swallowed, his throat dry. He nodded. "The Architect. He's not gone. Not finished."

Aisha's jaw tightened. She reached across the armrest, her hand finding his beneath the blanket. Her grip was firm, grounding. "Then we'll face him," she said. "Together."

The certainty in her voice soothed something frantic in him, something coiled tight beneath his ribs that finally loosened.

The word *together* echoed louder in him than the Architect's whisper had. He closed his eyes briefly, breathing in her steadiness, letting it anchor him. The pressure-memory in his right palm eased slowly, until it was just a hand again.

Just his hand—no echo, no demand.

He leaned back against the seat, staring at the faint aisle lights. The plane was quiet—Sophia asleep with arms crossed, Liam snoring softly against the window, Nia curled small in her seat with her sketchbook clutched to her chest. Strangers with ordinary lives.

But Quentin knew better. None of them were ordinary anymore.

They had been chosen. Marked by a shared fight and bound to a destiny that would not let them return to their old lives. There was no going back.

And somewhere far away, in a ruined garden that might have been dream or memory, the Architect was waiting—not watching, not hunting, but certain. Waiting for Quentin's next failure. Waiting for the loss that would finally break him.

— Δ —

Dawn seeped slowly through the cabin windows, turning the clouds outside into drifting islands of gold and rose. Passengers stirred with the light—seatbelts clicked, stewards moved down the aisles, sleepy voices murmured requests for coffee. For a moment, the world seemed ordinary again. Too normal, Quentin thought—unnervingly so.

Quentin sat upright, his head heavy but his eyes unwilling to close. The nightmare still lingered, the Architect's words etched like acid in his chest. Yet beside him, Aisha hadn't let go of his hand since the dream. That small, steady touch anchored him more than the Echo ever had. Her fingers were warm, real, a fragile promise in a world that kept shifting beneath him.

A rustle came from the row across. Nia sat curled in her seat, sketchbook open on her knees. Her pencil moved swiftly, her gaze flicking between the page and the horizon. She hesitated once, chewing the end of the pencil, then pressed on. Her movements were sharper than usual, almost urgent.

Liam, half-awake, leaned over with a grin. "Another caricature of me? Please say yes. The one with the lopsided nose was art."

Nia shook her head, offering only the smallest smile. "Not this time."

Her voice was thin, stretched like she was somewhere else entirely.

Sophia, adjusting her bandaged arm, leaned closer. "Then what are you working on?"

Nia paused, as though speaking might break whatever unseen pull guided her hand. Finally, she closed the sketchbook and held it across the aisle. Her eyes found Quentin. "This one… feels like it belongs to you."

Quentin exchanged a glance with Aisha before reaching for the book. Pencil lines sprawled across the page—bold, sharp, shaded with care. What he saw made his breath catch.

A colossal statue rose from the sea, its legs straddling a harbor. One arm was broken at the elbow, jagged stone suggesting a great fall long ago. But in the other hand, the figure held aloft a shard of sunlit brilliance.

Ships crowded below, their sails blazing in reflection. Even the water looked sharpened by reflection.

But the light in its hand wasn't just light. It was structured—banded, geometric, like a signal carved into radiance. And beneath the harbor, Nia had shaded something else: a second shadow under the waterline, too large to be a ship.

The detail was breathtaking—far more confident than Nia's earlier sketches, as if the image had poured through her rather than from her.

"Rhodes," Sophia murmured. Her voice went tight. "So it's not changing."

Quentin's stomach dropped anyway. The mark gave a faint, involuntary tug—memory more than power. "What's different?" he asked.

"I don't know," Nia whispered. Her voice trembled, but her eyes were steady. "I just… saw it. Like the others. It felt like it was waiting for me to draw. I wonder if I'm sketching the future… or if it's sketching me."

The confession hung in the air, fragile and terrifying.

The plane tilted gently, sunlight spilling across the cabin. As sunlight struck the page, his palm gave a faint, involuntary throb—more memory than response.

A soft ache spread through his palm—not painful, but insistent.

Aisha leaned closer, her face pale but resolute. "Another Wonder," she said. "Another Echo."

Sophia's jaw tightened. "So it doesn't end here."

Liam let out a low whistle, rubbing his temples. "Great. We just survived cultists, collapsing pyramids, and a maniac with a god complex… and now we're off to Greece? Brilliant. Somebody pack trail mix this time."

Even beneath the joke, Liam's voice carried an edge—like he already sensed the shift beneath their feet.

Despite the tightness in his chest, Quentin laughed faintly. But his gaze stayed on the sketch. The broken yet radiant giant seemed to stare back, daring him forward. He thought of the Architect's garden, the rotting vines, the whisper that roots ran deep. Egypt wasn't the end—it was only the first chapter.

Whatever waited at Rhodes already had a place in their path.

He closed the sketchbook carefully, handing it back to Nia. "Thank you. For showing us."

Her eyes widened as though she hadn't expected him to treat the vision as truth. She hugged the book to her chest, shoulders trembling just a little.

Aisha reached over and steadied Nia's hand—a gesture so small Quentin almost missed it.

The cabin lights brightened as the captain announced their descent. Passengers shuffled for bags, fastened belts, rubbed sleep from their eyes. To anyone else, they were just students on their way home. No one could guess what they carried—the memory of the Pyramid, the shadow of Thales, the whisper of the Architect, and now, the image of Rhodes.

A map of dangers only they could see.

Quentin leaned back against his seat, eyes fixed on the blazing horizon. His voice was soft, meant only for himself. "The journey's just begun."

Aisha turned her head, watching him with quiet understanding. She didn't speak, but her hand slipped into his once more. This time, she intertwined their fingers deliberately, not cautiously.

The plane cut through the clouds, dawn breaking wide and golden. Ahead lay new lands, new battles, and the towering shadow of a colossal figure holding light above the sea.

The war for the Wonders was far from over. And for the first time, he didn't fear that truth—he felt braced for it.

Not because he was unafraid—but because he knew he wouldn't face it alone.

THE TRIAL IS NOT OVER

You survived **The Endurance Trial**.

But survival was never the point.

Quentin didn't walk out of the Great Pyramid empowered—he walked out **identified**.

Something ancient has recalibrated.

What once tested quietly is now **watching openly**.

And the next trial does not ask whether he can endure—

It asks **what he will allow**.

In **Book Two:** ***The Dominion Trial***, power is no longer resisted.

It is offered.

The Shadow Order evolves.

Force gives way to surveillance.

Control becomes efficient, invisible—and persuasive.

And Quentin must face the truth the system was always building toward:

Endurance was not the victory.

It was the **qualification**.

The trial continues.

⊡ **Begin *Book Two: The Dominion Trial* at** linktr.ee/ramrengelauthor or scan to the QR code below.

If you finished Book One, the system already knows you.

Stopping now won't protect you.

A NOTE FROM THE AUTHOR

This series is written for readers who love

dark academia, ancient systems, and intelligent speculative thrillers—

stories where power isn't flashy,

and the real danger begins *after* you survive.

Quentin was never chosen to rule.

He was chosen to **hold**—and every system eventually asks what it can take from the one who can endure.

Book Two goes deeper:

into consequence, surveillance, and the quiet violence of "necessary" control.

Thank you for stepping into the Echo.

— Ram Rengel

ABOUT THE AUTHOR

RAM RENGEL has spent his career at the intersection of science and survival. As a Doctor of Nursing Practice (DNP), he understands the resilience of the human spirit better than most. By day, he operates within the high-stakes world of modern healthcare; by night, he channels that same intensity into crafting the architecture of the Seven Wonders and the survival of characters like Quentin and Aisha.

Ram represents a bridge between two worlds: the structured, evidence-based reality of a clinician and the limitless, imaginative landscape of an epic fantasist. ***The Endurance Trial*** is his debut novel, born from a desire to explore human endurance beyond the limits of a hospital ward. He lives in Riverside County, California, where he is currently developing the next chapters of *The Wonders Echo* saga.

Connect with Ram:

- **Order Book 2 Now:** linktr.ee/ramrengelauthor
- **Amazon Author Page:** amazon.com/author/ramrengel
- **Instagram/Facebook:** @ramrengelauthor

Creative Process Disclosure

In the spirit of innovation and clinical precision, the author utilizes cutting-edge Artificial Intelligence (AI) tools to assist in the technical and structural refinement of the storytelling process. However, the creative direction, thematic core, character arcs, and world-building—including the original lore of the Echoes and the Seven Wonders—remain the sole intellectual property and 100% original creation of the author.

www.ingramcontent.com/pod-product-compliance
Lightning Source LLC
LaVergne TN
LVHW010631110826
845149LV00014B/2825

* 9 7 9 8 9 9 4 8 8 5 6 0 4 *